D0721999

Shadows *of the* New Sun

BY GENE WOLFE
FROM TOM DOHERTY ASSOCIATES

THE WIZARD KNIGHT
The Knight
The Wizard

THE BOOK OF THE SHORT SUN
On Blue's Waters
In Green's Jungles
Return to the Whorl

THE BOOK OF THE NEW SUN
Shadow & Claw (comprising *The Shadow of the Torturer* and *The Claw of the Conciliator*)

Sword & Citadel (comprising *The Sword of the Lictor* and *The Citadel of the Autarch*)

THE BOOK OF THE LONG SUN
Litany of the Long Sun (comprising *Nightside of the Long Sun* and *Lake of the Long Sun*)

Epiphany of the Long Sun (comprising *Caldé of the Long Sun* and *Exodus from the Long Sun*)

NOVELS
The Fifth Head of Cerberus
The Devil in a Forest
Peace

Free Live Free
The Urth of the New Sun

Latro in the Mist (comprising *Soldier of the Mist* and *Soldier of Arete*)

Soldier of Sidon
There Are Doors
Castleview
Pandora by Holly Hollander
Pirate Freedom
An Evil Guest
The Sorcerer's House
Home Fires
The Land Across (forthcoming)

NOVELLAS
The Death of Doctor Island
Seven American Nights

COLLECTIONS
Endangered Species
Storeys from the Old Hotel
Castle of Days
The Island of Doctor Death and Other Stories and Other Stories

Strange Travelers
Innocents Aboard
Starwater Strains

Shadows *of the* New Sun

STORIES IN HONOR OF GENE WOLFE

Edited by

J. E. Mooney

and

Bill Fawcett

A TOM DOHERTY ASSOCIATES BOOK
NEW YORK

SHADOWS OF THE NEW SUN: STORIES IN HONOR OF GENE WOLFE

Copyright © 2013 by William B. Fawcett

A Tor Book
Published by Tom Doherty Associates, LLC
175 Fifth Avenue
New York, NY 10010

www.tor-forge.com

Tor® is a registered trademark of Tom Doherty Associates, LLC.

ISBN 978-0-7653-3458-9 (hardcover)
ISBN 978-1-4668-1416-5 (e-book)

Tor books may be purchased for educational, business, or promotional use. For information on bulk purchases, please contact Macmillan Corporate and Premium Sales Department at 1-800-221-7945 extension 5442 or write special markets@macmillan.com.

First Edition: August 2013

Printed in the United States of America

0 9 8 7 6 5 4 3 2 1

COPYRIGHT ACKNOWLEDGMENTS

CONTENTS

Foreword, J. E. Mooney   9

Frostfree, Gene Wolfe   15

A Lunar Labyrinth, Neil Gaiman   34

The Island of the Death Doctor, Joe Haldeman   44

A Touch of Rosemary, Timothy Zahn   57

Ashes, Steven Savile   76

Bedding, David Drake   95

. . . And Other Stories, Nancy Kress   107

The Island of Time, Jack Dann   120

The She-Wolf's Hidden Grin, Michael Swanwick   137

Snowchild, Michael A. Stackpole   153

Tourist Trap, Mike Resnick and Barry Malzberg   177

Epistoleros, Aaron Allston   183

Rhubarb and Beets, Todd McCaffrey   234

Tunes from Limbo, But I Digress, Judi Rohrig   243

In the Shadow of the Gate, William C. Dietz   261

Soldier of Mercy, Marc Aramini   273

The Dreams of the Sea, Jody Lynn Nye   289

The Log, David Brin   311

The Sea of Memory, Gene Wolfe   328

FOREWORD

Gene Wolfe got it wrong.

Completely.

Utterly.

Wrong.

I met Gene a decade ago when the World Horror Convention was held in Chicago, and he and Neil Gaiman were guests of honor. I was on a tight deadline, and so allowed myself only one day at the convention. I picked Friday because I wanted to attend a writing panel Gene was hosting. I'd read—and loved—some of his novels, and Chicago was only an hour away.

His session was in one of the hotel's ballrooms, and there was a sizable crowd. I picked a spot toward the back and pulled out my notebook.

Gene was seated behind a skirted table on a platform, and he looked to be analyzing his audience, bringing to mind the image of a judge holding sway over a courtroom.

He said that he wanted to know where we were—the audience—in terms of writing so he could better offer advice. To that end, he asked everyone who had submitted fiction to a professional market to raise a hand. Well more than a few hands went up. He decided to define it further.

"How many of you have had short stories published?"

Some of the hands went down.

"How many of you have written novels?"

Only three hands remained.

"More than one novel?"

At this point my hand was the only one up.

He stabbed his finger in the air in my direction.

"How many novels have you written?" he asked.

"A half-dozen or so," I replied.

"You!" He stabbed the air again. "You! Why are you here?"

I was thoroughly intimidated and regretted not picking another panel to attend.

"I thought you could teach me something," I told him.

"You!" He turned the finger so it was like a hook, and he waggled it at me. "You! Up here with me. There is nothing I can teach you."

He proceeded to call it the "Gene and Jean Show," and I spent the next hour sharing his panel, remaining thoroughly intimidated, but having a fine time.

We ran into each other again at various conventions—Windycon, World Fantasy, and the like. Always he remembered our chance encounter at World Horror in Chicago. Later we'd get together with mutual friends Bill Fawcett and Jody Lynn Nye for dinners. And still later, Gene and I would meet for lunches . . . sometimes for no particular reason, sometimes so he could pass over his dog, Bobby, who would stay at my place while his master was traveling.

My literary hero had become my dear friend. As I type this, Bobby is curled under my desk, his feet twitching and tail wagging as he's caught up in some marvelous dream. Gene is in Alabama, a guest of honor at Deep South Con.

So I can tell you with all honesty and conviction that Gene Wolfe got it wrong.

Utterly.

Completely.

He said there was nothing he could teach me. But he did—about the craft of writing, but more about the intricacies, complexities, sorrows, and joys of life.

The statement rings true for every single soul with a tale in this book. Despite busy schedules and pressing deadlines, this stellar collection of authors—among them Hugo, Nebula, and Bram Stoker Award winners, *New York Times* bestsellers, and international bestsellers—found time to write a story in honor of Gene Wolfe. In some cases the authors *insisted* they be included, their other obligations be damned.

All because Gene Wolfe got it wrong.

Gene Wolfe taught every one of us—and continues to teach us—a great deal.

We are privileged to be in his debt and in his shadow.

J. E. Mooney, Summer 2012

Shadows *of the* New Sun

Frostfree

GENE WOLFE

Roy Tabak had a new refrigerator. There could be no doubt of that. It gleamed. It was wider than his old one; it was taller, too. It made everything else in his kitchen look small and a trifle dirty. Brand new, he decided, and styled in a subtly pleasing way nothing in the store was. No doubt he had special-ordered. No doubt it had been delivered, and he had opened the door for the delivery and exchanged a few tired jokes with the men who brought it. When they had gone, he had no doubt wiped it down and waxed it with appliance wax.

Roy Tabak sold refrigerators, and he could remember none of that.

He opened the main compartment. There was food in it, and it looked good. There was beer in it, too, twenty bottles as least. It was not his brand, and the food was not his. What was that green stuff?

Movers, clearly, had been moving furniture and so forth into a new apartment. There had not been room enough in the van for this large refrigerator, so they had made a separate trip for it. They had put it in his apartment by mistake. No doubt they had been amateurs, friends helping some friend move. They had failed to notice that the refrigerator had been full of food and beer.

It was all very simple and convincing, and it would be more simple and convincing after a beer. Still more after six or eight. Aloud, Roy Tabak said, "Hell and damn!"

"If you are unable to find that which you seek," his new refrigerator said politely, "I may be able to direct you, sir."

Roy Tabak went into the living room and sat down. How many beers had he had? None at all. He had just gotten home from work. Besides, beer didn't do that. He took off his suit coat and hung it almost neatly in the hall closet, loosened his tie, then removed it altogether and draped it over the back of a chair. His collar was not tight, but he unbuttoned it anyway. Tight collars could make you hear voices, right?

After much searching, enlivened by some pacing up and down, during which he was careful not to look through his cramped little dining room into his kitchen, the phone book provided the number of the Free Psychiatric Hotline—"Trained Psychologists on Duty 24/7." The misspelling of "psychologists" did nothing to increase his confidence, but he dialed the number anyway.

"*Free Psychiatric Hotline. How can we help you?*"

"It's not normal to hear voices, is it?"

"*That depends. You're hearing mine right now, aren't you?*"

"I don't mean like that," Roy said. "You know what I mean."

"*Voices that accuse you of things?*"

"No."

"*Voices that urge you to commit murder?*"

"Huh-uh. This voice offered to help me find something in my—I mean in the refrigerator in my kitchen."

"*Ummm.*"

"It was very polite. Like a woman's voice, but like the noise a refrigerator makes when it runs. You know."

"*I wish I did. Is there a woman there with you?*"

Roy Tabak winced. "No. No, there's not."

"*Maybe a neighbor?*"

Mrs. Jackson was not at all bad looking; there had been times when he had envied Mr. Jackson. Mrs. Adcock was a bit too old. "No," he said. "I'm alone."

"Perhaps someone just dropped in. Someone selling something."

Dahlia—over in Lingerie—was hotter than hell. Roy said, "I sell things myself. Stoves, refrigerators, trash compactors, microwaves. Stuff like that. I'm the only one in here who sells things."

"What do the others do?"

"There aren't any others."

"I see. How often have you heard the voices?"

"Just one voice, and I've only heard it once."

"Okay.... It was probably somebody outside, or else a radio or something. If you hear these voices again, call back."

Feeling defeated, Roy said, "Sure."

"Especially if they want you to kill people. Or kill yourself. I've been looking through the index, but there's nothing about finding stuff in the refrigerator, see? So what I need is something that's here in DUFFY AND STANKY."

"Uh-huh." Roy Tabak hung up. It had been a dream. Almost certainly it had been a dream that he had somehow taken for reality. He would call out to the refrigerator, and it would not reply.

A little later, when he felt more secure.

What had happened to his tie? He switched on the TV, winced, and muted the sound. Baseball was never on when he wanted to watch it. Somebody must be in charge of that.

"We single men," he said, "we like to go out at night. We cruise the bars, and now and then we hook up. You start the game around seven-thirty, and we don't watch because we know we won't get to see anything past the fourth inning."

The TV remained muted. It would be nice, Roy Tabak reflected, if they would build TVs that listened to you.

He returned to the kitchen, half expecting that his old refrigerator would be there. The new refrigerator still gleamed. It had no eyes, no nose, and no mouth, yet it somehow looked quiet. And helpful. It was eager to help. You could see that.

Both his kitchen chairs were narrow, shiny, and much less than comfortable. He pulled one out just the same and sat down on it to study the refrigerator.

The refrigerator studied him back. After five minutes or so, he got it. The freezer door was opaque from outside but transparent from inside, sort of like the security mirrors in the store. The refrigerator's eyes were behind it. Watching.

He got up, opened the food storage door, and got a beer. It was a SUPER-URB lager, brewed in Al Fashir, New Jersey. He opened it, said, "Here's to you," and drank. It was better than his brand.

There were corn chips in the bread box. He opened the bag. "I don't suppose you have any chip dip?"

"I have three," his new refrigerator said politely. "Guavacado, whipped kasseri, and fava-bean habas. Which would you prefer?"

Roy Tabak sipped his beer, rose, opened his new refrigerator, and took out the green stuff.

"Ah! The guavacado. Good choice, sir."

It was in an oddly shaped container so transparent as to be almost invisible. The green paste it held tasted just fine on a corn chip.

"I have a talking refrigerator," Roy Tabak said. He gulped beer. "Do you know what that proves? It proves that the world is one hell of a lot more complicated than I thought."

"Indeed, sir."

Roy scooped up more guavacado dip. "Are you a Kelvinator?"

"No, sir."

"Mmmm." He munched a chip. "Whirlpool?"

"No, sir."

"KitchenAid?"

"No, sir. I am your refrigerator, sir. It might be best to leave it at that."

"Sure."

"I am here to help you." Roy Tabak's new refrigerator sounded soothing, almost motherly.

He sipped more beer and swallowed. "You're from the government, right?"

"No, sir. The WSPC, sir."

"Not the government."

"No, sir. We are a tax-exempt foundation, sir. In law, I mean."

"A foundation of refrigerators?" Roy Tabak scooped guavacado dip onto a fresh corn chip.

"No, sir. A foundation of persons. I say *we* because I am a possession of the Society. Need I explain further?"

Chewing, Roy Tabak nodded.

"Very well. You are familiar with dogs, I hope."

"I don't own one," Roy Tabak told his refrigerator, "but my folks adopted a greyhound named Chester when I was a kid. They said he was too old to race, but he was faster than a million-dollar microwave."

"Clearly you observed him, sir. Because you did, you must have observed that this Chester employed the pronoun to which you objected when referring to your family and himself. He might have said we are going to the beach, for example."

"You can't take dogs to the beach," Roy Tabak told his new refrigerator. "They're not allowed."

The telephone rang.

"Excuse me." He rose and went into his living room. "Hello."

"Roy, you dog! Who's the fat broad?" It was Jerry Pitt from Gourmet Foods.

Roy Tabak tried to remember. That girl he had talked to in the Home Office, had she been fat? Not very, but his Aunt Irene's daughters were all fat. "Probably a cousin," he said.

"Sure. Just staying with you until she can get a job. I've got it."

"Wait a minute." Roy Tabak thought frantically. "I've got this new service, see. A—whatchacallum. An answering service. It's better than an answering machine because mine keeps breaking. You phoned, right? And this girl answered. You probably tried to date her."

"Roy, Roy, Roy! Come off it. Let's get real."

Yeah, Roy Tabak thought, *wouldn't I love to!*

"I came over to your building, see?" Jerry sounded impatient. "And I rang the bell downstairs and somebody buzzed me in. So I went up to your place. Do I have to keep telling you?"

"Go ahead," Roy Tabak said. "I'm listening."

"I knocked and she answered the door. You probably told her not to, but she did it anyway. I said, 'Where's Roy?' And she said you hadn't come home yet and did I want to come in and wait for you? She said she'd get me a beer or some ice cream. I said, 'No thanks and have a nice day,' and I beat it."

"Listen, Jerry, this is serious."

"She's married, huh?"

"There was really a woman in my apartment? You're not shitting me?"

"Hell, no. You mean you don't know about her? She was a burglar or something?"

"No, but it's complicated. What did she look like?"

"Well . . . fat, like I said. Big and really heavy. She wouldn't be bad looking if she lost a hundred and fifty pounds. Hell, she's not all that bad now. Blond, blue eyes, sort of a square face, only fat cheeks, you know?"

"Yeah, I know. What else?"

"A white dress and a white apron. Sort of a gag necklace. One of those novelty necklaces. Little bottles, all different colors, strung together. Beer and Pepsi. I remember those."

"It doesn't matter," Roy Tabak said.

"One was champagne—that was the big bottle in the middle. There was a red bottle, too. I think it must've been Tabasco sauce."

Roy felt impatient, but tried not to sound like it. "How old would you say she was?"

"Twenty-five, maybe. She could have been younger, though. Great big chicks look older, you know?"

"Sure. Go on."

"No rings. I looked for them, you know how you do."

"Only she wanted you to come in for a beer, and you wouldn't do it."

"I got Deedee, you know? Besides, I'd never do a thing like that to you."

Roy Tabak took a deep breath. "You said, 'Hi, I'm Jerry Pitt and I'm a friend of Roy's.' Something like that?"

"Yeah. Sure."

"But she didn't tell you her name?"

"Nope."

"She told you something. What was it?"

"Nothing. She didn't tell me anything."

"Jerry, listen to me and listen real good. Are you listening, dumb-fuck?"

"Hey, you don't have to get rough."

"I'd rather not, Jerry. But I work in Appliances and you work in Gourmet Foods. I'm lifting heavy stuff all day while you're pushing cookies. What was her name?"

"I'll tell you, Roy. Honest."

"You'd better. What was it?"

"She never said her name, only she was wearing one of those little name pins like waitresses have on sometimes."

"Keep talking, Jerry."

"Well, I read what was on it. It said Frostfree. All one word. I used to know a guy named Frost once. Was it Ed? Wait a minute . . ."

"Don't matter. Listen, I'll call you back."

"Earl! That was it. Earl Frost."

"I'll call you back," Roy repeated, and hung up.

Returning to the kitchen, he straddled a chrome-and-plastic chair and sat, resting his arms on the back. "Do you still talk?"

"Yes, sir," replied his new refrigerator.

"Good." Thoughtfully, Roy Tabak loaded a last corn chip. "You've got a little plate on your freezer door. It says 'Frostfree.'"

"Yes, sir. It indicates, correctly, that I need never be defrosted— this even though my freezer remains frigid at all times."

"I know what it means. Jerry Pitt came over and rang the bell. You buzzed him in." Roy tapped a cigarette from the pack in his shirt pocket, lit it, and inhaled. His new refrigerator remained silent. At last he said, "Why did you do that?"

"I hoped your caller might be a young woman, sir."

"Did you now?"

"Yes, sir. I did."

"You wanted some female company?" Roy blew smoke through his nose.

"For you, sir. It is my mission."

"You want to fix me up."

"Yes, sir. Precisely."

More smoke. "That's a whole lot to take on, for a refrigerator."

"I'm acutely conscious of it, sir. May I explain? The WSPC has taken an interest in your case."

Roy ground out his cigarette in the ashtray on the kitchen table. "I'm a case."

"Yes, sir. That's it exactly."

"A mental case."

"Oh, no, sir!"

"Let's get back to Jerry. When he came to the door, a girl opened it. That girl was wearing the little plate from your door. She was wearing it, or one just like it. Was she from that outfit you mentioned?"

"The WSPC, sir? Yes, sir, she was—that is to say, I am. I belong to the foundation, sir. It is my owner."

"That was you? You were the one who answered the door?"

"Yes, sir. Would you like another beer, sir?"

"Yeah." Roy Tabak opened his new refrigerator and took out a longneck; its label read SUPER-URB. "If I drink enough of these, you may start to make sense."

"I'm a very sensible machine, sir, well designed, solidly built, and useful. I will provide many years of service."

"What about when you're a girl? Are you still a sensible girl then?"

"Yes, sir. I am sensible in both forms."

"You can change shape?"

"Transform, sir. Yes, sir, I can and do. May I explain?"

Roy Tabak nodded.

"I began, sir, as an effort of the appliance industry. You are familiar with the appliance industry."

Roy nodded again. "Very."

"It was desired, sir, to create a single appliance which would serve as both a refrigerator and a dishwasher."

"That's crazy!"

"No, sir. Only difficult. It was soon realized that my dishwashing mechanism could not be interior, sir. My interior must be kept cold at all times in order to preserve the just-harvested freshness of vegetables, for example."

"I say that. I say 'just-harvested freshness' when I'm talking to customers. You've been listening to me."

"Only a very little bit, sir. Hardly at all." Roy's new refrigerator spoke rapidly, apparently to prevent his protesting the change of subject. "Since the dishwashing function could not be internal, it would have to be external. Utilizing the transformer principle made external dishwashing possible and, indeed, successful. It was then suggested that we might serve as programmable stoves as well. That

was found to be impractical, since an oven would have to be internal. However—"

"Wait up!" Roy Tabak sat straight. "You said you were a dishwasher, right? You're a dishwasher, too?"

"I am, sir. It is my glory."

"Well, my sink's full of dirty dishes. Let's see you wash them."

"Although I hesitate to correct you, sir, your sink is no longer
filled with dirty dishes. I washed them in your absence, sir."

Roy rose and looked into his sink. It was empty and spotless.

"Your dishes are in that cabinet, sir. There was an abundance of
shelf space, and I felt—"

"Sure." Roy opened a cabinet door. "You reached up there and
put them in?"

"I did, sir. It was the only way—or so it appeared to me. May I
continue, sir?"

He nodded.

"The oven requirement decided the matter. We could not function as programmable stoves. We could, however, apply our pro-
grammability to stove functions, by this means rendering a
programmable stove superfluous. When one of us is in your kitchen,
any old collection of oven and burners will do."

"You can cook?" Roy asked.

"No, sir. The stove cooks, at my direction."

"You can wash dishes."

"Yes, sir. I can. I do."

"Good." Roy held up the almost invisible container; it showed
green streaks of guavacado. "I want you to wash this dish. Now."

For a moment it seemed that nothing had happened. He blinked,
and realized that his new refrigerator was more humanoid in appearance than he had realized. It began to rock gently, forward and
back.

"That's all right," he said. "You don't really have to."

His new refrigerator was not listening. It had stopped rocking and was smoothing its immaculate white apron with plump, ring-less fingers. "This will take me only a moment, sir."

While Roy watched, an obese blonde in a white dress and a white apron carried the green-smeared refrigerator dish to his sink, washed it, and dried it. "Where should I store this, sir?"

"Anyplace you want to," Roy Tabak told her. "My stove can cook things, right? Under your direction?"

"That is correct, sir." The obese blonde put it in the cabinet with his dishes.

"I'm going to go out and cruise for chicks, but I'd like something to eat first."

The obese blonde smiled. "I shall be delighted to prepare it, sir."

"That's good. What's your name, by the way?"

"I have none, sir. My owners say *Fridge,* or something of the kind, for the most part." The fat blonde hesitated. "If I may be entirely frank, sir . . . ?"

Roy Tabak nodded.

"More often than not, no name is employed."

He grinned, noticing the pin on her left breast. "Okay if I call you Frostfree?"

"Certainly, sir. I would treasure the appellation. It pertains to my mission in the most appropriate manner. You see, sir, the WSPC desires to free you—"

"Wait up. Can you cook and talk at the same time, Frostfree?"

"Certainly, sir. What would you like?"

"Whatever you've got in there. It looked like lots of chow."

"My menu-planning software is at your service, sir. Would you care for some *boeuf à la Bourguignonne*? I begin by slicing the beef into small cubes—"

"How long would it take?"

"My beef is of excellent quality, sir. Quite tender. No longer than three and half hours at most."

"I don't have that much time. What's fast and good?"

"Would you consider eggs Columbus, sir? I have both small to-matoes and green peppers." Frostfree filled a saucepan as she spoke. "And eggs, of course. Very fresh eggs, if I may say so. Your meal will be ready in twenty minutes."

"Sounds good. You were going to tell me about this outfit you work for."

"The WSPC? I'll be happy to, sir." She put the saucepan on a burner and turned it on. "The World Society for the Prevention of Curses seeks to exterminate those noxious prayers, orisons, and invocations whenever they have occurred. In your case, sir—"

"I've been cursed."

"Precisely, sir. I believe I saw your salt and pepper . . ."

"Right here." Roy Tabak moved his arm. "Who did it?"

"I cannot say, sir. That information was not part of the download. I am to free you from the curse. Others will attend to the perpetrator."

For half a minute or more, Roy Tabak considered that. "You asked me if I knew the appliance industry. Remember?"

Frostfree nodded. She had dropped a tomato into the boiling water in the saucepan, and was holding its head down.

"I am. Only I've never even heard of a refrigerator that could turn into a woman. Maybe all this is just a bad dream, the curse and everything. What do you think?"

"I think that this has been boiled long enough for me to slip the skin off," Frostfree murmured. "Ah! There it goes."

"You had your hand in the boiling water," Roy Tabak remarked. "Didn't it hurt?"

"No, sir. I am an appliance, sir." Frostfree smiled. "I was built in the twenty-third century, sir. I am native to the year twenty-two ninety-one—it is when the WSPC purchased me. May I speak of your curse, sir? You've been avoiding the matter."

"You can jump around in time?"

"No, sir. The Society dispatched me to this period, sir. It will re-turn me to my own period in due course, I believe."

"You *believe*?"

"Yes, sir. It is a matter of faith—but yes, I do." As she spoke, Frostfree picked up a pepper.

"How many of those are you going to make?" Roy Tabak asked.

"Four, sir. I have two tomatoes and two peppers, and four seems to me a reasonable number."

"I don't eat more than two eggs, usually."

"You have not tasted my eggs Columbus, sir."

"I guess not." Roy Tabak got out a fresh cigarette, examined it, and slipped it back into the pack. "Could you change back into a refrigerator so I could have another beer?"

"That is hardly necessary, sir." Dropping her pepper into the boiling water, Frostfree turned to face him. Her apron swung aside, and the front of her dress with it. Reaching into herself, she took out a cold longneck and handed it to him.

"Did you just get thinner? I mean you're still fat—I mean not really fat, but didn't you lose a little bit of weight just now, maybe?"

She nodded. "The bottle you hold has been deducted from my gross mass. I take it that is what you meant."

"Yeah. I guess so."

"The World Society for the Prevention of Curses has been policing the past, sir. I was about to say so." She dunked the pepper. "Hyperhistory records many effectual cursings, including yours. They have done incalculable harm. The present brightens as they are removed."

"My present or your present?"

"Both, sir. Or so I would hope." Frostfree sighed. "Normally, sir, some bold but warmhearted individual volunteers to visit the past and lift the curse. In your case, that proved impossible."

"I still don't believe I'm under a curse," Roy Tabak said. "I don't buy that part at all. If I'm under a curse why would somebody send me a refrigerator that turns into a woman who can cook?"

"It is the nature of your curse, sir." Frostfree stripped the skin from the pepper. "Your curse limits you to coldhearted persons. No warmhearted person will find you tolerable."

"People buy from me," Roy Tabak declared, "and it's not just refrigerators. I sell stoves, grills, mixers, all kinds of stuff, and I'm one of the most successful salesmen at the store. Ask anybody."

"Coldhearted persons find you sympathetic, sir." With a deft twist of Roy Tabak's paring knife, Frostfree disposed of the seedy interior of a tomato. "There are a great many of them in this century."

Roy nodded thoughtfully. "I've noticed that about my customers."

"Thus I was sent. I—I like you, sir."

He twisted the cap from his beer. "I like you, too, Frostfree."

"Do you really, sir?" Smiling, she turned to face him. "As a refrigerator, I have no heart at all."

"Naturally," Roy Tabak agreed.

"While as a woman, my ice-cube trays perform the function, sir. They're in my ice maker. They have the little chambers, you see, and they expand and contract. It's exactly like your human heart, but colder."

It was excellent beer, Roy decided. Aloud, he said, "It was one of my ex-girlfriends, wasn't it? I think I could even guess which one."

"I'm to find you a warmhearted young lady," Frostfree told him. "If I can accomplish it, your curse will be broken. Will you please pass the pepper, sir? The pepper and the salt."

It was shortly after ten when they strolled arm-in-arm into the Home Office Bar & Grill. "This is as good a spot as any," Roy Tabak told Frostfree. "The real action won't start until eleven or so, but it's good to be a little early." He leaned toward her, almost shouting to make himself heard. "Usually I sit at the bar, and it can be tough to get a seat there later."

"We must have a table, sir," she said as she sat down at one. "We must be seen together."

He nodded, secretly glad that he had removed a head of cabbage and all of the remaining beer before they left. "Okay, here we are and everybody's seeing us. Are you a good dancer?"

"No, sir. It might be better if we did not dance."

Two blondes and a brunet came in, all talking at once.

"Do you like any of those, sir?" Frostfree leaned across the table.

"Yeah, Kay—that's the brunet in the middle, only she turned me down flat last week." A barmaid had appeared at Roy's elbow, and he added, "What are you having, Frosty?"

"I haven't decided." Frostfree smiled at the barmaid. "What do you suggest?"

"Most people drink beer," the barmaid told her. "We have Bud, Miller, Old Style, and a lot of foreign beers. Just about anything you want, really."

Roy Tabak ordered a Miller Lite.

"Scotch and water might be nice," Frostfree said.

Roy Tabak waited until the barmaid had gone before asking, "Can you really drink that?"

"I will drink it slowly, sir. I doubt that you will have to buy me another."

"That's not the point. You're—" He choked it back. "I still don't see how dating you is going to get me a girlfriend."

"A warmhearted one, sir. One breaks curses, you see, by doing whatever the curse forbids. Let us suppose, for example, that a curse were to stipulate that you die before your twenty-first birthday."

"I'm thirty-two already."

"If you lived beyond your twenty-first birthday, the curse would be neutralized. Or let us say that your curse was in the form of a pig that followed you everywhere."

"You're really not all that stout." Roy found he was shouting to make himself heard above "Gotta Shine." "Anyhow, I like you."

"If you could slip into an elevator and shut its doors before the pig could follow, the curse would be broken. That is an actual case from the eleventh century, although of course no elevator was involved. Our operative dropped a portcullis, I believe."

Their drinks arrived. Frostfree sipped and smiled.

"You can taste things."

"Of course. It's difficult to cook when one cannot." She sipped again. "Please give me fifty dollars, sir."

"What?"

"Fifty dollars. I would think that would suffice. A fifty-dollar bill might be best, but two twenties and a ten should be acceptable."

"You need the money."

"Yes, sir. I do."

"To get me a warmhearted girlfriend."

"Yes, sir. I will not hire her, sir."

Roy Tabak shrugged. "You can't get much for fifty anyway."

"It depends upon the thing bought, sir. Passing it to me beneath the table might be prudent."

He did, and she rose. "I must attend to a call of nature." Her lips brushed his forehead, cold and firm.

He was still trying to imagine what a refrigerator might do in the ladies' room when she returned to their table. He raised an eyebrow. "Everything come out all right?"

"I believe so, sir. I emptied my drip pan, and my negotiations should be effectual." She glanced to her left.

Their waitress and another were pushing through the throng of lookers and drinkers.

"It might be wisest if you said nothing, sir."

Roy Tabak nodded.

The waitresses arrived, panting and pointing to Frostfree. "He said he couldn't call you," gasped the one who had served them.

The other added, "Your phone's off. He said he's dying!"

"He called here. He said you'd be here."

Frostfree raised a hand. "Calm yourselves! The man is a hypo-chondriac, a faker. It probably isn't serious at all."

"But—"

"He just wants attention." Frostfree sighed, her sigh visible but inaudible. "I suppose I have to go."

"Yeah," Roy put in. "Maybe you'd better."

"You're a darling." Leaning over the table (in which something popped under the stress of her weight) she kissed him.

At the bar, Frostfree spoke urgently to Kay. Roy Tabak, watching and very much wishing he could overhear them, saw Kay nod reluctantly. A moment later, Kay and Frostfree turned to stare at him before resuming their conversation.

Before Frostfree had left, Kay rose, slipped through the crowd to Roy Tabak's table, and sat. "Your friend told me about the awful thing that's happened to you," she said.

Roy nodded sadly without having the least idea what she was talking about.

"I don't usually do this," she said.

He stood as if to leave. "You don't have to. Really you don't."

She stood, too. "Do you dance?"

"Sometimes," he admitted, "but I'm not very good."

"Just follow my lead, Roy." Her smile was brightly encouraging. "Only do it, you know, in a man sort of way."

"Like a mirror reflection."

"That's it. That's it exactly."

The truth was that he enjoyed dancing, and danced agilely with a good sense of rhythm. The crowded floor limited them both until the people gave way to watch. Kay's smile widened and her hips rolled more wildly. He had thrown her high into the air and caught her before they sat down, and she had slid between his legs and spun like a top.

Hours later, in the kitchen of his apartment, she came across a lone uneaten egg. "This egg in the tomato—did you cook this, Roy?"

"For my supper, after I got home from work." When she stared at him, he added, "Eggs Columbus is really pretty easy and a good way to bake eggs. I ate the other three."

"An egg baked in a tomato, on toast . . ."

"Or a green pepper," Roy Tabak told her. "I like those better. And you add butter, and salt and pepper." He shrugged. "Other spices if you want them, or bread crumbs. It's easy and quick."

The brunet sat. "You cook. Eggs Columbus, you said. Just for you."

Roy nodded.

"Can I have a cigarette?"

He found an unopened pack and gave it to her.

As she opened it, she murmured, "You know, you're really quite a person."

There was a butane lighter in the pocket of his robe. He used it to light her cigarette.

"You're going to drive me home."

He nodded.

"My roommate will be asleep, but she'll wake up and want to know where I've been and everything we did." Kay inhaled, blew smoke through her nostrils, and looked pleased. "I don't know how much I'm going to tell her, but I certainly won't tell everything."

"Up to you," Roy Tabak said.

"Yes." Kay smiled. "You're going to drive me, so you shouldn't have another beer. I'd like one just the same. Maybe you'd like a Pepsi or something."

Frostfree, who had apparently returned to his kitchen some time ago, had replaced the beer and the cabbage. Roy got Kay a cold beer and poured it into a spotless tulip glass before pouring a glass of milk for himself.

"That's an interesting refrigerator you've got there," Kay remarked. "I've never seen anything quite like it."

"That right there," Roy Tabak told her in a tone that brooked no disagreement, "is the best damned refrigerator in the whole world."

———

Much later, when he had finished his crepes, Roy Tabak said, "Kay, that's her name. The brunet you sent over to talk to me."

Frostfree, who had been washing dishes, turned to face him. "Yes, sir."

"She's a warmhearted person."

"Yes, sir. She is, sir."

"Warmhearted and loving. Affectionate. I'm not. I'm a cold-hearted, lying son-of-a-bitch, and I know it. Also, I don't make half as much as I'm worth, and I smoke. She already smokes a little, so we'll smoke together."

"Yes, sir."

"I lied to her, and you lied to her to get her to come over and talk to me. We're both liars."

"No, sir. I explained that you are friendless man, not far from suicide and insanity, and that you had been terribly hurt by the actions of a woman you once loved. What I said was true, sir. Every word of it."

"Okay."

"I expressed myself persuasively and urgently, and explained that I was only an acquaintance of yours and that I was leaving. I asked her to stay with you for at least an hour, and she consented."

Roy Tabak seemed not to have heard. "I lied to get her into the sack, and I lied afterward so she wouldn't find out about you. That's what I did, and now she's mixed up with me. Is she under some sort of curse, like I was?"

"I cannot tell you, sir. I have no information upon the topic. It was not part of any download I received."

Roy Tabak blew a thoughtful smoke ring and watched it float away. "Yeah," he said. "Yeah, I think so, too."

A Lunar Labyrinth

NEIL GAIMAN

On Gene Wolfe: *I met Gene and Rosemary Wolfe when I was twenty-two, in September of 1983, in Birmingham, England, at the British Fantasy Convention. I went to the Fantasy con to interview Gene, and over the next day I discovered my people, several of whom would go on, although I did not know it then, to become my closest friends, one of whom would also commission and edit my first book. It was an important time. I had loved Gene Wolfe's fiction. Now I learned that I really liked the man as well. He was funny, and he was real, and his wife, Rosemary, was by his side and beaming.*

Gene and I became friends (it was the trip to the theater in 1987 that did it) and we have stayed friends. I have learned more than I can say as a writer from his wise, twisty stories, but value the things I have learned from the man who has been my friend for all of my adult life much more. I loved seeing Gene and Rosemary. He came to a fireworks party at my house, and was nearly hit by a stray rocket.

There is a story by Gene called "A Solar Labyrinth." I read it aloud to the audience from a Wurlitzer Organ platform when Gene was given the first Chicago Literary Hall of Fame Fuller Award. It is a short story of brilliance and beauty and, hidden deep in the shadows, danger and darkness.

I wrote this for Gene, and it has rosemary in it, and wolves. If Gene had written it, it would have been subtler.

We were walking up a gentle hill on a summer's evening. It was gone eight-thirty, but it still felt like midafternoon. The sky was blue. The sun was low on the horizon, and it splashed the clouds with gold and salmon and purple-gray.

"So how did it end?" I asked my guide.

"It never ends," he said.

"But you said it's gone," I said. "It isn't there any longer. What happened to it?"

I had found the lunar labyrinth mentioned online, a small footnote on a website that told you what was interesting and noteworthy wherever you were in the world. Unusual local attractions: the tackier and more handmade the better. I do not know why I am drawn to them: stoneless henges made of cars or of yellow school buses, polystyrene models of enormous blocks of cheese, unconvincing dinosaurs made of crusted powdery concrete and all the rest.

I need them, and they give me an excuse to stop driving, wherever I am, and to talk to people. I have been invited into people's houses and into their lives because I wholeheartedly appreciated the zoos they made from engine parts, the houses they had built from tin cans and stone blocks then covered with aluminum foil, the historical pageants made from shop-window dummies, the paint on their faces always flaking off. And those people, the ones who made the roadside attractions, they would accept me for what I am.

"We burned it down," said my guide. He was elderly, and he walked with a stick. I had met him sitting on a bench in front of the town's hardware store, and he had agreed to show me the site that the lunar labyrinth had once been built upon. Our progress across the meadow was not fast. "The end of the lunar labyrinth. It was easy. The rosemary hedges caught fire and they crackled and flared. The smoke was thick and drifted down the hill and made us all think of roast lamb."

"Why was it called a lunar labyrinth?" I asked. "Was it just the alliteration?"

He thought about this. "I wouldn't rightly know," he said. "Not one way or the other. We called it a labyrinth, but I guess it's just a maze . . ."

"Just amazed," I repeated.

"There were traditions," he said. "We would only start to walk it the day *after* the full moon. Begin at the entrance. Make your way to the center, then turn around and trace your way back. Like I say, we'd only start walking the day the moon began to wane. It would still be bright enough to walk. We'd walk it any night the moon was bright enough to see by. Come out here. Walk. Mostly in couples. We'd walk until the dark of the moon."

"Nobody walked it in the dark?"

"Oh, some of them did. But they weren't like us. They were kids, and they brought flashlights, when the moon went dark. They walked it, the bad kids, the bad seeds, the ones who wanted to scare each other. For those kids it was Hallowe'en every month. They loved to be scared. Some of them said they saw a torturer."

"What kind of a torturer?" The word had surprised me. You did not hear it often, not in conversation.

"Just someone who tortured people, I guess. I never saw him."

A breeze came down toward us from the hilltop. I sniffed the air but smelled no burning herbs, no ash, nothing that seemed unusual on a summer evening. Somewhere there were gardenias.

"It was only kids when the moon was dark. When the crescent moon appeared, then the children got younger, and parents would come up to the hill and walk with them. Parents and children. They'd walk the maze together to its center and the adults would point up to the new moon, how it looks like a smile in the sky, a huge yellow smile and little Romulus and Remus, or whatever the kids were called, they'd smile and laugh, and wave their hands as if they were trying to pull the moon out of the sky and put it on their little faces.

"Then, as the moon waxed, the couples would come. Young couples would come up here, courting, and elderly couples, comfortable in each other's company, the ones whose courting days were long forgotten." He leaned heavily on his stick. "Not forgotten," he said. "You never forget. It must be somewhere inside you. Even if the brain has forgotten, perhaps the teeth remember. Or the fingers."

"Did they have flashlights?"

"Some nights they did. Some nights they didn't. The popular nights were always the nights where no clouds covered the moon, and you could just walk the labyrinth. And sooner or later, everybody did. As the moonlight increased, day by day—night by night, I should say. That world was so beautiful.

"They parked their cars down there, back where you parked yours, at the edge of the property, and they'd come up the hill on foot. Always on foot, except for the ones in wheelchairs, or the ones whose parents carried them. Then, at the top of the hill, some of them'd stop to canoodle. They'd walk the labyrinth, too. There were benches, places to stop as you walked it. And they'd stop and canoodle some more. You'd think it was just the young ones, canoodling, but the older folk did it, too. Flesh to flesh. You would hear them sometimes, on the other side of the hedge, making noises like animals, and that always was your cue to slow down, or maybe explore another branch of the path for a little while. Doesn't come by too often, but when it does I think I appreciate it more now than I did then. Lips touching skin. Under the moonlight."

"How many years exactly was the lunar labyrinth here before it was burned down? Did it come before or after the house was built?"

My guide made a dismissive noise. "After, before . . . these things all go back. They talk about the labyrinth of Minos, but that was nothing by comparison to this. Just some tunnels with a horn-headed fellow wandering lonely and scared and hungry. He wasn't really a bull-head. You know that?"

"How do you know?"

"Teeth. Bulls and cows are ruminants. They don't eat flesh. The minotaur did."

"I hadn't thought of that."

"People don't." The hill was getting steeper now.

I thought, *There are no torturers, not any longer.* And I was not a real torturer. But all I said was, "How high were the bushes that made up the maze? Were they real hedges?"

"They were real. They were high as they needed to be."

"I don't know how high rosemary grows in these parts." I didn't. I was far from home.

"We have gentle winters. Rosemary flourishes here."

"So why exactly did the people burn it all down?"

He paused. "You'll get a better idea of how things lie when we get to the top of the hill."

"How do they lie?"

"At the top of the hill."

The hill was getting steeper and steeper. My left knee had been injured the previous winter, in a fall on the ice, which meant I could no longer run fast, and these days I found hills and steps extremely taxing. With each step my knee would twinge, reminding me, angrily, of its existence.

Many people, on learning that the local oddity they wished to visit had burned down some years before, would simply have gotten back into their cars and driven on toward their final destination. I am not so easily deterred. The finest things I have seen are dead places: a shuttered amusement park I entered by bribing a night watchman with the price of a drink; an abandoned barn in which, the farmer said, half a dozen bigfoots had been living the previous summer. He said they howled at night, and that they stank, but that they had moved on almost a year ago. There was a rank animal smell that lingered in that place, but it might have been coyotes.

"When the moon waned, they walked the lunar labyrinth with love," said my guide. "As it waxed, they walked with desire, not with love. Do I have to explain the difference to you? The sheep and the goats?"

"I don't think so."

"The sick came, too, sometimes. The damaged and the disabled came, and some of them needed to be wheeled through the labyrinth, or carried. But even they had to choose the path they traveled, not the people carrying them or wheeling them. Nobody chose their paths but them. When I was a boy people called them cripples. I'm glad we don't call them cripples any longer. The lovelorn came, too. The alone. The lunatics—they were brought here, sometimes. Got their name from the moon, it was only fair the moon had a chance to fix things."

We were approaching the top of the hill. It was dusk. The sky was the color of wine, now, and the clouds in the west glowed with the light of the setting sun, although from where we were standing it had already dropped below the horizon.

"You'll see, when we get up there. It's perfectly flat, the top of the hill."

I wanted to contribute something, so I said, "Where I come from, five hundred years ago the local lord was visiting the king. And the king showed off his enormous table, his candles, his beautiful painted ceiling, and as each one was displayed, instead of praising it, the lord simply said, 'I have a finer, and bigger, and better one.' The king wanted to call his bluff, so he told him that the following month he would come and eat at this table, bigger and finer than the king's, lit by candles in candleholders bigger and finer than the king's, under a ceiling painting bigger and better than the king's."

My guide said, "Did he lay out a tablecloth on the flatness of the hill, and have twenty brave men holding candles, and did they dine beneath God's own stars? They tell a story like that in these parts, too."

"That's the story," I admitted, slightly miffed that my contribution had been so casually dismissed. "And the king acknowledged that the lord was right."

"Didn't the boss have him imprisoned, and tortured?" asked my guide. "That's what happened in the version of the story they tell hereabouts. They say that the man never even made it as far as the Cordon Bleu dessert his chef had whipped up. They found him on the following day with his hands cut off, his severed tongue placed neatly in his breast pocket and a final bullet hole in his forehead."

"Here? In the house back there?"

"Good Lord, no. They left his body in his nightclub. Over in the city."

I was surprised how quickly dusk had ended. There was still a glow in the west, but the rest of the sky had become night, plum-purple in its majesty.

"The days before the full of the moon, in the labyrinth," he said. "They were set aside for the infirm, and those in need. My sister had a women's condition. They told her it would be fatal if she didn't have her insides all scraped out, and then it might be fatal anyway. Her stomach had swollen up as if she was carrying a baby, not a tumor, although she must have been pushing fifty. She came up here when the moon was a day from full and she walked the labyrinth. Walked it from the outside in, in the moon's light, and she walked it from the center back to the outside, with no false steps or mistakes."

"What happened to her?"

"She lived," he said, shortly.

We crested the hill, but I could not see what I was looking at. It was too dark.

"They delivered her of the thing inside her. It lived as well, for a while." He paused. Then he tapped my arm. "Look over there."

I turned and looked. The size of the moon astonished me. I know it's an optical illusion, that the moon grows no smaller as it rises, but this moon seemed to take up so much of the horizon as it rose that I found myself thinking of the old Frank Frazetta paperback covers, in which men with their swords raised would be silhouetted in front of huge moons, and I remembered paintings of wolves howling on hilltops, black cutouts against the circle of snow-white moon that framed them. The enormous moon that was rising was the creamy yellow of freshly churned butter.

"Is the moon full?" I asked.

"That's a full moon, all right." He sounded satisfied. "And there's the labyrinth."

We walked toward it. I had expected to see ash on the ground, or nothing. Instead, in the buttery moonlight, I saw a maze, complex and elegant, made of circles and whorls arranged inside a huge square. I could not judge distances properly in that light, but I thought that each side of the square must be two hundred feet or more.

The plants that outlined the maze were low to the ground, though. None of them was more than a foot tall. I bent down, picked a needle-like leaf, black in the moonlight, and crushed it between finger and thumb. I inhaled, and thought of raw lamb, carefully dismembered and prepared, and placed in an oven on a bed of branch-like leaves that smelled just like this.

"I thought you people burned all this to the ground," I said.

"We did. They aren't hedges, not any longer. But things grow again, in their season. There's no killing some things. Rosemary's tough."

"Where's the entrance?"

"You're standing in it," he said. He was an old man who walked with a stick and talked to strangers, I thought. Nobody would ever miss him.

"So what happened up here when the moon was full?"

"Locals didn't walk the labyrinth then. That was the one night that paid for all."

I took a step into the maze. There was nothing difficult about it, not with the little rosemary hedges that marked it no higher than my shins, no higher than a kitchen garden. If I got lost, I could simply step over the bushes, walk back out. But for now I followed the path into the labyrinth. It was easy to make out the way in the light of the full moon. I could hear my guide, as he continued to talk.

"Some folk thought even that price was too high. That was why we came up here, why we burned the lunar labyrinth. We came up that hill when the moon was dark, and we carried burning torches, like in the old black-and-white movies. We all did. Even me. But you can't kill everything. It don't work like that."

"Why rosemary?" I asked.

"Rosemary's for remembering," his voice explained.

The butter-yellow moon was rising faster than I imagined or expected. Now it was a pale ghost-face in the sky, calm and compassionate, and white, bone-white.

The man said, "There's always a chance that you could get out safely. Even on the night of the full moon. First you have to get to the center of the labyrinth. There's a fountain there. You'll see. You can't mistake it. Then you have to make it back from the center. No missteps, no dead ends, no mistakes on the way in or on the way out. It's probably easier now than it was when the bushes were high. It's a chance. Otherwise, the labyrinth gets to cure you of all that ails you. Of course, you'll have to run."

I looked back. I could not see my guide. Not any longer. There was something in front of me, beyond the bush-path-pattern, a black shadow padding silently along the perimeter of the square. It was the size of a large dog, but it did not move like a dog.

It threw back its head and howled to the moon, with amusement and with merriment. The huge flat table at the top of the hill echoed with joyous howls, and, my left knee aching from the long hill climb, I stumbled forward.

The maze had a pattern; I could trace it. Above me, the moon shone, bright as day. She had always accepted my gifts in the past. She would not play me false at the end.

"Run," said a voice that was almost a growl.

I ran like a lamb to his laughter.

Neil Gaiman has been writing professionally for almost thirty years. He won the Newbery Medal and the Carnegie Medal and the Hugo Award for The Graveyard Book. *He won no awards of any kind for* A Walking Tour of the Shambles, *his little book with Gene Wolfe, but is ridiculously proud of it anyway. He has three children, two dogs, and about half a million bees.*

The Island of the Death Doctor

JOE HALDEMAN

On Gene Wolfe: *I first met Gene Wolfe in Damon Knight's huge crumbling manse in Milford, Pennsylvania, in 1970. We were both "new writers" as far as science fiction was concerned, with only a few stories published, but Gene had been writing nonfiction for a long time.*

With some chagrin I remember that both Damon and Kate Wilhelm considered Gene a fully formed genius, whereas I (almost a decade younger) was just a new kid on the block, maybe showing a little early promise. Gene was a pleasant, charming man, modest almost to the point of self-effacement, and so I had to like him even though we were rivals.

The rivalry faded quickly enough, and we were pretty good friends by the end of the week. Over the years and decades that followed, it's become obvious that there is no sense in thinking of Gene in terms of rivalry, or even friendly competition. There is only one Gene Wolfe, and if he's in a race there is no other writer on the track.

I heard the sea, then voices. Not too close. Smelled the sea to the left, and then wood smoke from another direction. Blinked away crust and rubbed my eyes, and the green dapple became dense overhead foliage, restless in the breeze. I didn't hurt, but my legs and arms were like heavy wood, and sunburned the color of mahogany. I couldn't recall my name.

I have been here before. Not this place, but this condition. A name would come to me.

It shimmered and then came into focus: Christopher, or Ignacio.

Bearer of Christ or bearer of fire. Odd to know all that and not know where I am or what I am doing here.

Sensation crept into my limbs in a gradual sparkling, then cramps. My right hand throbbed. I could move my arms clumsily, and tried to make as little noise as possible while kneading life back into the muscles of my legs.

I got to my knees and staggered upright. I was wearing a gray homespun jerkin that smelled of sea and sweat. On my belt, a long knife or short sword in a scabbard of brass and leather. I drew it and inspected it.

A practical tool, perhaps piratical as well. Thick blade more than a foot long, double-edged several inches back from the point, and then saw-toothed on the tang.

I knew that word, tang, for the back of the blade. I even knew that the rainbow swirl meant the steel had been beaten to life in Seville. Folded over red-hot, pounded flat, and quenched, over and over. Where did I learn that?

Coins in a leather bag, mostly silver; two gold ones smaller than dimes. I couldn't decipher the words stamped on them, nor recognize the cruel faces of their kings or gods.

A small pocket on the sheath held half a whetstone. I vaguely remembered breaking it in two, giving half to a man in chains.

I didn't have my glasses but could see clearly, colors vivid even in this low light. Flexing, I realized my limbs were as young as my eyes. Eyes and limbs that yesterday were old.

Under the dirt, my hands were a young man's, but with three long scars across the back of the right, one of them fresh. Not deep enough to sever the tendon, thank God.

He'd cut me as I stepped forward, thrusting. I took him just below the sternum, a clean kill. Were we on a ship?

"Put that thing away or prepare to use it." A man had come quietly up behind me while I was studying the sword. He had a saber out but was ostentatiously leaning on it, like a rakish cane.

I slid the short blade into its scabbard and showed him my empty hands. "My toothpick would be no contest," I said.

He sheathed his own sword. "'Toothpick'? I get the meaning." He removed his right glove and offered his hand. I took it and he squeezed once, hard. "You are here for the circle?"

"I don't know. I just woke up. Or am I dreaming?"

"Always a good question," he said. "Which of us ever knows? But I think we're in the same dream right now."

"Okay." I gestured around. "But where is this dream?"

"They say Hispaniola. I haven't been here an hour myself. Like you, I suppose, I woke up here and found the circle." The sound of voices rose to argument level, behind him. "Be careful. I've seen one man die already."

"People die in dreams," I said.

"True, but do they stink? See for yourself." He gestured and I walked past him to the sound of flies buzzing.

The body of a black man was at the base of an old tree, shirtless but with a white cap on his head.

Then I realized he wasn't negro. A white man who had been dead long enough for his skin to turn livid. The "cap" was his skull, scalped. His abdomen had been opened with a long slice, and spilled. Arms spread in supplication—or was that rigor mortis? I had never seen a dead person except in funeral parlors.

He had been turned over, I knew somehow. It's the side on the ground that darkens with pooled blood.

The wind shifted and the smell turned serious.

I covered my mouth and nose with a handkerchief, from somewhere. "What did he do?"

"It's more what he didn't do. He didn't leave his sword in its scabbard. Then, having taken it out, he didn't kill the man who challenged him . . . and then he didn't parry the first blow properly. There was no second blow."

"What if he hadn't drawn his sword?"

He toed the man's shoulder and flies buzzed away. "One never knows. The challenger had said something remarkable about his mother. I suppose he had to respond."

I tried to think. "Hispaniola. So this is after 1492?"

"A century after. What time do you come from?"

"The twenty-first century. 2016."

He nodded. "Two centuries after mine. What language are you speaking?"

Was he crazy? "English, like you."

"In fact, I don't know English. On this island, that apparently makes no difference."

"But your mouth . . . your lips are speaking English."

"And yours are speaking Swedish, to me. Like everybody else. But I'm the only Swede here."

"That's insane."

"One of us is, perhaps. Would you care to meet the other delusions?"

We picked our way through moderately dense forest—subtropical scrub with a few palms and deciduous trees—and came to a cooking fire smoldering low under a crude spit with two large fish impaled. A teenaged boy was tending to the spit, with eight older men and women in a rough circle around the fire.

They were a motley crew, more motley than most pirate assemblages, I think—of the nine, two were female and two of indeterminate gender, and most were clad in the same nondescript homespun that I was wearing, their appearance otherwise spanning a half-dozen centuries. One woman was naked, her face and arms covered with animated tattoos, surely from my future; one dignified man was wearing an old-fashioned powdered wig. Two were stylishly bald like myself, or perhaps came from a past where hereditary baldness couldn't be corrected. They were black and white and Asian, and they all looked at me with mild curiosity or, in one case, undisguised hostility.

The hostile-looking woman spoke. "Oh, goody. Another sexist pig." She was stocky but not bad-looking, with a single black braid down to her waist.

"Better to have another lass," one of the wigged men said. "These two are not particularly forthcoming."

"Lass my ass," she snarled. The naked woman, also attractive, tried to keep her lips pursed, but they twitched in a smile.

"And what year are you from?" she asked quietly. "You look normal."

I told her.

"An' it pleases yer grace," a drunk rough-looking man growled to no one in particular.

"Shut your trap," the hostile woman said, mildly but with authority. She was solid, like a stevedore, and had a claw hammer thrust in her belt, perhaps a weapon.

"I'm from two years after you," the prettier one said. "I could tell you who wins the election."

"All right," I said. "Who?"

"I just told you," she said, smiling.

A few of them laughed. "You don't remember anything you could take back for profit," a young man said. "Anything you could tell me about the twentieth or twenty-first century, I would forget right away. I was taken the year the war with Spain started, 1898. Don't bother to tell me who won."

"'Take things back'?" I said. "So people do return to their own time?"

"We don't know, really," she said. "Some of us were told that."

"People disappear after some days or weeks," the gentleman said. "Perhaps they do return to the time and place from which they disappeared."

"Yeah, right," the stocky woman said. "That's why the history books are full of time travelers."

"Perhaps they don't remember," the gentleman said. "My theory is—"

"Oh, stuff your theory," she said.

"My *theory,* which is only a theory, is that this could happen all the time, and perhaps does, to everybody. If no one remembers when they return, then it's just as if you hadn't gone."

"Unless you croak," the kid said, "like that old jasper over there."

"He may have gone back home when he died," a grandfatherly type said in a strained voice.

"And if pigs had wings they could fly," the stocky woman said. "It doesn't matter when you die, for God's sake. Once you're dead, you're dead. Heaven or Hell."

An old woman or man shook her head. "There's no evidence one way or the other."

"Why did I know you were going to say that?" she snarled. "I must be fucking psychic."

"Psych-*oh,*" the drunk muttered.

"If you don't stop picking at one another," the largest man said, "we could be here forever." He was bare-chested, muscles hard and well defined. Clean-shaven and handsome, he sat with a broadsword across his lap. It was an executioner's sword, squared off rather than pointed at the end. How would I know that detail?

"None of us knows why we're here," the executioner said to me. "Perhaps you have a clue?"

"I'm afraid not," I said. "It's as if I just woke . . . but into a dream rather than out of one."

"So what do you do when you're not in a dream? What is your name?" He extended his hand. "I am Severian."

"I am . . . Father Christopher, a Roman Catholic priest. Newly ordained." Had I ever been assigned a parish?

"A gift from God," the pretty woman said. "We do need to bury someone."

The liturgy for burial sped through my mind in English and Latin simultaneously, with an echo of Spanish and something else. Catalan? But I had no image of the ceremony; perhaps I'd never conducted one.

"Of course," I said. "Though I must admit it will be a first time for me. I came late to my calling."

"Just some churchly words," the white-wigged one said. "We have to get him under the ground."

"I don't suppose you brought a shovel from the future," the ill-tempered woman said.

"I had no warning," I said. "Did any of you?"

The executioner held up his sword, lightly. "Just a tingling. I had just finished cleaning *Terminus Est* here and was reaching for its scabbard. Then there was a tingling, and suddenly I found myself here. In the air, actually; I fell a few cubits."

"Cleaning the sword?" I said. "You just killed somebody with it?"

"It's what I do. I travel from place to place and offer my services." He sighted down the blade. "The place I was taken from, I hadn't executed anyone yet. Took off two hands and an ear, and sewed a woman up. They were bringing out a murderer and a usurer, who would be executed, but something dimmed and I fell to earth here."

"Were you dressed like that, for executing people?"

He pinched homespun between thumb and forefinger and frowned at it. "Not at all. Silk and leather. And you?"

If I said "Dockers and a polyester Princeton rugby shirt," it would only add to the confusion. "No . . . different, but just as plain."

A young woman, the smallest, head shaved and rings piercing her eyebrows and upper lip, edged forward. "Your sword has a name?"

He nodded. "'Terminus est.' There is an end, or an ending."

"I read about you and your sword. In a fiction novel."

"I don't think so," he said, smiling. "Novels are like fables, no? I am as real as you are."

"Okay. What year do you think it is?"

"Twelve. The twelfth year of King Bader's reign."

"The hell it is! It's 2094, all over two worlds, and *this*"—she indicated the whole of our surround—"is sure as hell not Luna!"

"Luna," I said. "You're from the moon?"

"Duh. So we've got a caped crusader and a moron." She made a disgusted face at the rough woman. "And a lez-bo from Hell and an accordion geezer. A sword-wielding Swedish masseur and two fine specimens from New York City: a used-car dealer and a whore."

"Escort," the naked woman said calmly. "What planet are *you* from?"

"The *moon*! Like I said! The thing up in the sky?"

"You're as crazy as you look. No one lives on the moon. There's no *air*."

"We make our own air."

"Yeah. Bet I know how you do it, too." They stepped toward each other, but the man with the sword was suddenly between them. Built like a weightlifter but swift as a dancer.

"Now please," he said. "We have to get along."

"Or what? You'll chop my head off?" the naked woman said.

"It would quiet things down." He turned back to me. "We're on an island. Jim here followed a stream uphill and saw that the ocean is all around us."

"Probably the Pacific," the grandfatherly one said. "At least it looks like the South Pacific, where I fought the Japs."

"But actually," the naked woman said, "we don't even know that it's Earth."

"Well, your moon was in the sky this morning," he said. "Though I suppose that just narrows it down. Could be a million years in the past or future."

"So what story are you from?" the young boy asked me. "I'm from a treasured island."

"Your name is Jim?" I said.

"Aye, sir. Jim Hawkins. Most here know my story, unless they're from way back."

"Everybody here is from a work of fiction?"

"They say I'm in some goddam book," said the teenager who was turning the fish. "It sure as hell ain't some dream. I dream about naked women all the time, who doesn't? But Jesus, this one really *is* naked, and she's got stuff I never thought of, you know?"

She cupped a hand over her pubis and pulled up. "Want some?"

"Are you Holden Caulfield?" I said.

"Jesus, you, too. Yeah, I'm from *Catcher Walking Through the Fucking Wheat Field* or some goddamn crap."

"Hell, even I know about you," said an old blind guy with an accordion, whose eyes were covered with a faded bandana. "It sounds like we're all from made-up stories, complete with made-up memories. If your book says you're from 1950, you won't have read about any characters written after that."

"It's like we all have two memories," the nude woman said, "one here on the island and one from some other place and time. A fictional one."

"Two, for me," I said. "I lived in a modern time, with airplanes and space travel. But I think I got there from the seventeenth century." My head felt funny, and I sat to keep from falling down. "But before that, I was in modern times, too. I went from the twenty-first century to the seventeenth."

"How did you get there?" the man in the wig asked.

"I think I walked. And rode in a cart." The memory was clear enough, but choppy, like a sequence of strobe shots. "I left a monastery in rural Cuba and walked to Havana. When I got there the harbor was full of tall sailing ships. But there weren't any cars or airplanes."

"Old Havana," the nude woman said. "I *saw* that movie. But

you're a time traveler in your own story! You go back to olden times and grow up to be a pirate. And then at the end of the movie, you're going back to Cuba on an airplane to . . . meet yourself? Meet your younger self and make sure you do the right thing."

"But no," I said. "I really am a pirate." I held up the back of my hand, with its festering wound. "This is from a sword fight, a couple of days ago. Nobody ever made a movie about me."

"Sure they did," she said. "A book before the movie, too."

"You are all so fucking crazy," the drunk said. "What movie? We was just dropped here."

She rolled her eyes. "Don't pay any attention to him."

"But he's right, isn't he? We were all dropped here. Literally dropped, in my case, and in Severian's."

"I was asleep," she said. "In my crèche outside Luna City. It's like I rolled out of bed and onto this island. Where the gravity stinks, incidentally."

Something began to crystallize. "I think I read about you, too, in a science fiction book. Though I suppose you were wearing clothes."

"I normally am. But not while I'm sleeping. Maybe I'll buy some pajamas, now." She heaved a sigh and looked around. "I guess you never know what kind of a world you're going to wake up in."

"Suppose we are all from books. Has anybody here read all of them?"

An older man who had been watching the proceedings with interest raised a finger. "Most of them. Including yours . . . Ignacio."

No one had used that name here. "You have read about my life?"

"Oh, yes; more than once." He patted his generous mustache, eyes dancing. "And most of the books all of our friends here inhabit. The mystery to me are the ones I can't identify. Did I read them and forget?"

"I don't understand."

"That's good. I would hate to be upstaged by one of my own creations. I don't understand, either."

Another lunatic, but a harmless one. "You think we all came from books you wrote?"

"Oh, no; not all of you. You and Severian did. But most of you do seem to be from books I've *read*."

"So we're figments of your imagination?"

"Or memory, or dreams. I wonder if you'll disappear when I wake up."

Severian drew his sword back out in a long hiss. "I wonder what would happen to us if *you* died. Here in this supposed dream world."

"Not an experiment I would care to try."

"Or dare to," Severian said. He picked up a coconut off the ground, tossed it up, and split it with a one-handed swing of the heavy blade. One hemisphere rolled to my feet.

Had the coconut been there before? I picked it up. Some dirt adhered to the edges of the cut. It smelled right.

"So you just willed us into being," I said to the man with the mustache. "You're God."

"No, not at all. God made me, and then *through* me made you. I don't pretend to know how or why."

"But I'm real," I said, feeling foolish.

"As I am," Severian said.

"Me, too," the nude woman said, hands on her hips. "Why don't you try to erase one of us?"

The man stared at her. "All right. Go away."

"No," she said. "What's happening?" Slowly she started to fade. I could see the forest through her. She looked around wildly and then disappeared with a quiet *pop*.

"My God," I said. "Could you do that to any of us?"

He was still looking at the place where she had been. "I don't know. I don't want to get rid of anybody. But I don't know how long I can stay asleep."

"You aren't asleep," I said.

"Not here," he said. "No one is ever asleep inside a dream; certainly not one he makes up himself. But what is going to happen to all of this when I wake up? To all of you?"

"But look," I said. "I can remember back dozens of years. You couldn't have made up all of that."

"Maybe it's not about 'making up.' I wouldn't have made up that poor girl, stuck here without any clothes. Or the unpleasant modern woman."

"I'll give you un*pleas*ant," she said.

"I don't think you will," he said. "But please try. Take Severian's weapon and try."

She walked toward Severian with her hand out, but he just looked through her.

"Try Ignacio," the man said.

She came toward me and held out her hand. I wasn't able to pull my sword out of its scabbard. It was as if it were welded there.

"I haven't imagined any one of you dead. Until I do—or until the authors of these other characters do—I think you'll just have to live forever."

"On this island?" I said.

He closed his eyes and everything around us shimmered and faded, dark and then gray light. There was a thunderous roar and the El roared by overhead as grit sifted down. Boxy old automobiles all around, shiny black. People dressed like flappers and gangsters. I wore a light flannel zoot suit and the girl was in a yellow pearl-studded chemise that came down almost to her knees.

"This is also an island, of a kind," the man with the mustache said. "There are islands of time as well as space. I think that all of you live or die according to whether I need you."

He closed his eyes again and we were floating over a surreal futuristic city, an Art Deco fantasy of pastel buildings with streamlined aircars flitting around. He closed his eyes again and we were back on the island.

He looked at me. "Shall I need you, Christopher? Which would you like to be?"

"Do you mean would I rather be a character in a story, or, as a real person, cease to exist?"

"Not 'cease,'" he said gently. "If you are just a character in a story, you never have been real."

"It's not *a* story, though. It's *your* story."

He looked at me for a long moment. "What do you think?"

I heard the sea, then voices. Not too close. Smelled the sea to the left, and then wood smoke, from another direction. Blinked away crust, and rubbed my eyes, and the green dapple became dense overhead foliage, restless in the breeze. I didn't hurt, but my legs and arms were like heavy wood, and sunburned the color of mahogany. I couldn't recall my name.

Have I have been here before?

The youngest writer to be named a Grand Master by the Science Fiction and Fantasy Writers of America, Joe Haldeman has earned steady awards over his forty-three-year career: His novels The Forever War *and* Forever Peace *both made clean sweeps of the Hugo and Nebula Awards, and he has won three more Hugos and Nebulas for other novels and shorter works. Three times he's won the Rhysling Award for best science fiction poem of the year. In 2012 he was inducted into the Science Fiction Hall of Fame. The final novel in a trilogy,* Earthbound, *is just out (after* Marsbound *in 2008 and* Starbound *in 2009). Ridley Scott has bought the movie rights to* The Forever War. *Joe's next novel is* Work Done for Hire. *When he's not writing or teaching—a professor at MIT, he has taught every fall semester since 1983—he paints and bicycles and spends as much time as he can out under the stars as an amateur astronomer. He's been married for forty-seven years to Mary Gay Potter Haldeman.*

A Touch of Rosemary

TIMOTHY ZAHN

On Gene Wolfe: *Many years ago, I was at a convention where Linda, the wife of the chairman, handled registration. She was something of a "mundane," but loved meeting people.*

Gene had sent in his preregistration for him and his son. Linda, not recognizing his name, processed the memberships like everyone else's. She was working the registration table when a gentleman walked up to her and said, "I'm Gene Wolfe, and I'm preregistered."

Linda calmly pointed to a table to her right and said, "Please pick up your registration over there." Gene dutifully went over to the table and picked up the registration. Then he asked about a friend of his, Walt, and Linda said that she thought he was in the consuite and pointed him in that direction.

About ten minutes later Walt came out, slightly aghast, and asked Linda, "Do you know who Gene Wolfe is?"

Linda looked up and said, "Yes, he registered just a short while ago."

When Linda's husband found out about it, he hurriedly tracked down Gene, apologized profusely, and promised to get him his registration money back. Gene refused, saying he hadn't had such a good laugh at a convention in years.

The tavern didn't have a name. It didn't need one. The village was small, and it was the only tavern inside the long log walls that guarded against the dangers of the outside world.

Most of the villagers, even the poorest, ate at the tavern at least once a month. A few, the wealthier ones who could afford it, sometimes came in as often as once a week.

The wizard ate there every day.

There were fewer patrons than usual today, he noted as he sat at his table by the window. Normally the midday hour was bustling with activity, with only the farmers and hunters who labored beyond the walls unable to take the necessary time for a good meal.

But today only one other table was occupied. The four men seated there were leaning forward, their heads close to each other, talking together in low, nervous tones.

The server hurried to the wizard's table. "Good midday, master," the boy said. He seemed nervous, too. "How may we serve?"

"One portion," the wizard said, drawing a small pouch from inside his threadbare tunic. He'd seen more of the outside world than anyone else in the village, and knew that most taverns had several food items to choose from each day. But not here. Here, the cook chose each morning what she would prepare, and that was what was served.

"Yes, master." The boy hesitated. "You're certain you wouldn't prefer one and a half?"

"One will do," the wizard said. The weaving of spells required extra sustenance, but he had no such activities planned for today. "Here's my payment," he added, opening the pouch.

The boy flicked the contents a distracted glance. "Tarragon?"

"Rosemary," the wizard said, frowning. The boy knew his spices better than that. "From my window box. Is something wrong?"

The boy's eyes shifted to the occupied table. The wizard followed his gaze, to find that the quiet conversation had ceased and all four men were staring at him.

"Is something wrong?" he repeated, raising his voice to include them as well as the boy.

One of the men, the village tanner, cleared his throat. "If the elders haven't yet chosen to speak with you—"

"The elders move at their own pace," the wizard said. "I move at mine. Tell me the problem."

The tanner glanced at the others. "It's the witch king," he said grimly. "The wizard whose army has been sweeping through the lowlands—"

"I know who he is," the wizard said. "What does this have to do with us?"

"He's decided he wants to conquer the Tarnholm across the mountains." The tanner's throat worked. "And he's just made the decision to bypass the main road and bring his army instead through our valley."

The wizard looked out the window at the log wall. Beyond it, the dark forest that pressed up against the village seemed itself to be listening. "When?"

"He'll be here in two days."

Two days. The wizard looked at the server, still standing nervously beside the table. Closing the pouch, he handed it to the boy. "Here," he said. "You'd best make it two portions."

The first task was to reinforce the wall.

The wizard had woven this same spell many times over the thirty years since he'd first erected the barrier. But for most of those years the spell had been geared toward defense against moss, rot, or damage from scratching deer horns and wolf claws. Now, the spell would be called upon to strengthen the wood against spears, swords, axes, and the witch king's own spells.

The elders thanked him when he was done. But he could tell by their pinched expressions that they weren't expecting the spell to stop anyone for long. On that count, he knew they were right.

Beyond that, there was little he could do. Diverting a portion of the river to encircle the village would take too long, and would accomplish nothing except announce to the approaching invaders that the village had something its inhabitants thought especially worth protecting. Spells used for removing brambles and tangleweed from the farmers' fields could be reversed to seed the army's path with obstacles, but such ploys were childish and would only irritate the soldiers instead of turning them away onto a different route. A thorn hedge was possible, but having such convenient kindling pressed up against a log wall would be an invitation for the witch king to reduce the village to smoldering ash and continue on his way.

In the end, the wizard knew there was only one way the village could be saved.

The rest of the two days was spent gathering the people together and sending them into the forest. Not the dark forest directly behind the village, the one no one ever entered, but the cleaner forest on the far side of the valley.

"You don't need to stay," the wizard told the tanner as they stood together, watching the distant line of people cross the bridge and make their way through the trees into the foothills of the snowy mountains that towered over the valley.

"You may need me," the tanner said. "I know a few spells myself, you know. I may be able to help out a little."

"You realize he probably won't bother with us himself," the wizard warned. "Not at first. He has his own phalanx of mages to throw against his enemies."

"So much the better," the tanner said with grim humor. "I'll last longer against lesser minds."

"You may die."

"I may," the tanner acknowledged. "But I may surprise you. Who can tell?" He gave the wizard a sideways look. "Besides, you'll need someone to serve."

The wizard sighed deep within his soul. So the tanner knew what he had planned. "Yes," he said quietly. "I will."

———

The witch king's usual pattern, the wizard had heard, was to approach his objectives at dawn, when the defenders were weary from a night of staring fearfully into the darkness.

But the various small towns and villages along the army's path weren't objectives. They were little more than diversions, not even for the witch king himself, but for whichever group of soldiers had the time and inclination for an hour or so of looting and casual destruction.

It was nearly midday, and the army's vanguard had already passed, when the would-be looters the wizard was expecting finally broke ranks and strode across the half-plowed fields toward the village. There were thirty of them, their laughing voices and the bell-like clanking of their armor in stark contrast to the cruel anticipation on their faces.

Some townspeople, the wizard knew, would welcome such invaders through their gates in the forlorn hope that cooperation would lead to mercy. Others would take the riskier path of pretending cooperation and then try to deal with the soldiers quietly, out of sight and hearing of their comrades passing by outside the walls.

The wizard knew better than to try either. There would be no mercy from these men; and while the witch king's army was vast, his officers made a point of keeping track of even the lowliest soldiers, if only to make sure that the families of deserters paid for the runaway's crime. Someone in the ranks would have made careful note of where these particular soldiers were going, and even the wizard couldn't simply make them disappear without inviting terrible consequences.

There was no way that the wizard and the village could avoid attracting attention. The question thus became whose attention they would attract.

The approaching soldiers were halfway across the field when they spotted the two men waiting on either side of the village gate. The crossbowman in the lead said something to the others and shrugged his weapon off his shoulder. He loaded a bolt, aimed at the wizard, and let fly.

Fifty yards from the village wall, the bolt burst into flame.

It was probably the last thing the soldiers expected, and all thirty stopped dead in their tracks. But the shock didn't last long. They had fought armies, sorcerers, wild animals, and probably a whole range of woodland sprites, and they weren't about to let a simple country mage stand in their way. Even as the burning bolt disintegrated into a cloud of ash, the soldiers were moving into combat formation, the ten crossbowmen forming up into standing and kneeling lines as they loaded their weapons, the spearmen and swordsmen spread into flank-guard positions on either side. At a sharp command from one of the swordsmen, all ten crossbow bolts fired together.

All ten exploded into smoking shards at the same distance as the first bolt.

The swordsman snarled another order, and the crossbowmen recocked their weapons. Behind them, the marching army began to come to a somewhat haphazard halt as individual soldiers and squads paused to watch the drama taking place at the edge of the forest. As the crossbowmen loaded their bolts, the spearmen spread out to both sides, their spearheads gleaming too brightly to be simply reflecting the sunlight. One of the witch king's mages had probably encircled them with hardness or penetration spells.

Unfortunately for them, those spells required a certain minimum amount of metal to work with, which was the same amount necessary for other, more subtle spells.

At the swordsman's command, the spearmen strode forward in a curved line, lowering their spears toward the wizard and the tanner like the jagged teeth of a half-invisible woodland sprite. At the same time, the crossbowmen lifted their weapons to their shoulders. The wizard smiled tightly and continued weaving his spell. . . .

Abruptly, the spearmen leaped ahead into a charge. The swords-man barked an order and the crossbowmen let fly their bolts.

But this time, instead of bursting into flame, the bolts curved sharply to the sides, each bearing down on one of the spearheads like a hawk pursuing a rabbit.

The spearmen saw the bolts coming and tried their best to dodge them. But it was no use. The bolts slammed unerringly into their chosen spearheads, and as each hit there was a burst of fire and blue-edged lightning as the encircling hardness spells were broken. Eight of the ten spear shafts splintered, while the other two exploded vio-lently enough to send their owners pitching backward, stunned, onto the ground. Without waiting for orders, the freshly disarmed men scrambled back to the rest of the group, dragging their two twitching comrades with them.

"Very nice," the tanner murmured. "I wonder what they'll try next."

"Next will be the mages' turn," the wizard said, eyeing the two elaborately decorated horse-drawn carriages hurrying forward along the edges of the now all but stopped army.

The horses trotted to a halt, and from each carriage emerged a middle-aged man wearing a silver-leaf tunic and a dark red cloak. For a moment they conferred quietly between themselves. Then, flipping the edge of his cloak back over his shoulder, the older of the two strode forward. He passed the clump of soldiers without a glance and stopped a pace from the spot where the crossbow bolts had caught fire.

"Your name, old man?" he demanded.

"My name is not to be given to underlings," the wizard called back. "I wish to speak directly with your master."

"My master wouldn't deign to soil his hands with you," the mage bit out. He danced his hands in a complicated pattern, and some-thing like a large invisible pane of glass in front of him shattered into dazzling white stars.

Beside the wizard, the tanner stirred. But he said nothing.

"An ignition surface," the mage commented, his voice still arrogant but now with a hint of grudging respect. "Very clever." He murmured under his breath and lifted his hands again.

Abruptly, the ground in front of him rippled violently and something unseen tore across the land, driving through the half-sized stalks of grain as it raced toward the wizard.

The wizard had expected something like that. Before the groundtearer was even halfway to the wall there was a sudden flurry of dirt and torn grass, and the field was abruptly quiet again.

The mage snarled something and a second and third groundtearer erupted in front of him. The wizard wove his counterspell, and again the attackers vanished in clouds of dust.

Only this time, instead of simply vanishing, both erupted again directly behind the enemy mage. Before he could even turn around, they tore through the ground beneath him, sending him toppling over to slam onto his back. He scrambled to his feet, already spitting out a curse and weaving a fresh spell—

"Hold."

The word came from the sky, deep and resonant, like the voice of some distant mountain power. The mage glared at the wizard, his eyes burning, his hands still halfway into his next attack. But he knew an order when he heard it, and with a final glower he turned away, letting the half-woven spell dissipate. The wizard peered toward the motionless army, wondering where the witch king was hiding.

And then, from behind one of the rolling sentry towers on the vanguard's left flank, a figure appeared, his high-backed, throne-like chair carried atop a dozen black oxen. As he came closer, the wizard could see that the man was dressed in silk-armor of gold and blue. The eyes of the lumbering oxen beneath him flickered with red fire, while tongues of the same fire danced and dripped from their horns. The wizard watched the man and beasts approach, his heart sinking.

Because the witch king was young. Far younger than the wizard had expected for a man with such an impressive list of conquests. Though his hair had gone pure gray, the smoothness of his face placed him no older than his late thirties, perhaps even younger.

And that was bad. Perspective came with years, the wizard knew, and as strength and stamina faded, men usually found themselves settling into some form of contentment.

But ambitious young men were never content. The witch king would conquer and kill and destroy, always seeking something to slake his never-ending appetite, and never getting his fill.

The wizard had hoped it might not come to this. But as he gazed into that young, cruel face, those last hopes finally faded. The man had to be stopped, for the sake of thousands living and thousands yet to be born.

The oxen lurched their way past the glowering enemy mage to a spot twenty yards from the wizard. For a moment the witch king eyed the wizard in silence, and then rose leisurely from the chair. He murmured a spell, stepped off the edge of the platform, and floated gently to the ground. The two mages started to move up behind him; without looking, he waved them back. "So it's true," he said, looking the wizard up and down. "The long-famed weaver of words, singer of songs, and writer on the wind. You're still alive."

"So it would seem," the wizard said.

The witch king raised his eyes to the village wall. "And this is where you've chosen to end your days?"

"It's an extraordinary place," the wizard said. "I hope you'll allow me to show it to you. I also hope that after you've seen it you'll permit us to live unmolested by your army."

The witch king smiled knowingly. "A village walled by unnaturally long logs and backed against a dark forest. Who wouldn't feel privileged to accept such a gracious invitation?"

"I've lived here for thirty years without harm," the wizard pointed out. "You're welcome to bring your soldiers or mages along if you wish."

The witch king's smile vanished. "Have a care, wizard," he warned. "No one mocks me and lives."

"I mean no mockery," the wizard said. "Nor do I suggest that you fear to travel into the unknown alone. I merely point out that midday approaches, and some of your men might also enjoy the food the village tavern has to offer."

The witch king frowned. "The *food*?"

"The reason this village is so special," the wizard said. "If you'll permit me, I would be honored to show it to you."

The witch king's eyes again flicked to the wall, then to the tanner, then back to the wizard. "I've eaten food from a thousand different places, prepared by a thousand different chefs from a hundred different peoples and tribes," he said. "I've eaten at the tops of mountains, beside a roaring ocean, and from the table of a king whose body still lay bleeding on the floor beside me. Do you genuinely expect me to find something of interest in an insignificant country tavern?"

"I do," the wizard said.

The witch king's eyes narrowed. "Were it not for your reputation, I would kill you and your silent friend for your audacity, then burn the village with fire that would still be sending smoke skyward ten years hence." He considered. "I may do so yet."

The wizard felt his stomach tighten. The other was perfectly capable of doing both, he knew. "Yet I maintain you'll find it worth your time," he said.

The witch king smiled. He lifted his hand, spoke a few quick-woven words—

Behind the wizard and the tanner, the village gate exploded into a cloud of dust and splinters. Amid the thunder of the blast, the wizard heard the faintest hint of a scream. "Very well," the witch king said. He raised his head.

"One hour," his voice echoed again from the sky. "The men will eat, and be ready then to continue their march."

He lowered his head and gestured the wizard forward. "Lead the way," he said, his voice normal again. "Show me this remarkable tavern you're willing to die for."

With the army in the valley outside no longer filling the air with the rumble of marching feet, the only sounds as the three men walked through the village were their own footsteps on the flagstone path and the rustling of the trees beyond the wall. The crackling of the branches grew louder as they approached the tavern, and the wizard wondered if the witch king would notice.

He did. "No wind," he commented, nodding toward the trees visible above the barrier. "You have a serious woodland sprite problem here, wizard."

"That wood is very old and deep," the wizard said. "There are many colonies within its borders."

"And beyond them, as well," the witch king countered. "Or did you think I wouldn't hear their screams when I destroyed the gate they were occupying?"

"The wall has become home to some," the wizard acknowledged. "They don't bother anyone. Here we are."

The muted clanking of cookware could be heard as they entered the tavern.

"The aroma is pleasant," the witch king conceded as the wizard led them to his usual table. "What threat did you use to keep the cook here instead of allowing her to flee with the rest of the villagers?"

"No threat was needed," the wizard said, handing the tanner his pouch of spices and gesturing the witch king to the chair facing the wall and forest. "If you please?"

"What's that?" the witch king asked, nodding toward the pouch as the tanner headed toward the kitchen door.

"A selection of spices," the wizard said. "The payment for our meal."

"Spices for *our* meal?"

"She'll use them in future meals," the wizard explained. "Our meal has already been prepared."

The witch king's eyes narrowed. "You were so certain you could entice me here?"

The wizard shook his head. "I didn't know. She did."

"So your cook is also a seer?"

"No," the wizard said. "Or possibly yes. It's . . . complicated."

"But there *is* magic involved," the witch king said, his voice heavy with suspicion.

"Again, no and yes," the wizard said. "It will be easier to show than to explain."

The tanner reappeared through the doorway, holding two plates of a gently steaming roast. "I asked for two portions each," he said as he came to the table.

"Thank you," the wizard said. "Would you care to choose?"

The witch king smiled and pointed to one of the plates. The tanner set it in front of him, and then set the other in front of the wizard. The witch king held his hands above his food, his lips moving wordlessly as he wove the poison- and magic-detection spells the wizard had known he would use. Satisfied, he picked up the knife from beside the plate, sliced off a piece of the roast, and ate it.

"Well?" the wizard asked, watching him closely.

"It's good," the witch king said off-handedly. "The king I mentioned earlier set a finer table." He started to get up.

And paused, frowning down at the plate, his jaw still working on the last of the bite. He shot the wizard an unreadable look, then resumed his seat and carved off another piece of the roast. He ate it, chewing carefully and thoughtfully. He cut another bite, and another, and another. "What's in this?" he asked around one of the mouthfuls.

"The cook's special touch," the wizard said, cutting off a piece from his own roast and slipping it into his mouth. "Plus a mixture of spices that only she can blend in this way," he added as he savored the delicate taste. "I don't know the full list, but I do know there's tarragon, basil, and sage. And a touch of rosemary."

The witch king grunted and carved off another bite.

For a few minutes they ate in silence. There was a small curve of carrots and potatoes arranged around the edge of the roast, which the witch king ignored until he'd finished his first portion of meat. Then, clearly with disdain, he ate half a carrot.

He finished all the vegetables before starting on his second portion of meat.

He was midway through it when he abruptly threw down his knife. "You spawn of rat eggs," he snarled, curling his hands into claws. "You've inflicted me with a *craving*!"

"No," the wizard said quickly.

But too late. The witch king's hands were already weaving a death spell, and the wizard could feel the invisible chains wrapping around his throat. He lifted his own hands, trying to ward it off, but with his voice stifled he knew he could never weave the counterspell in time. A haze of white blobs began to fill his vision.

And then, abruptly, the pressure eased. He blinked, to see the witch king standing upright, glaring across the tavern, his hands glowing with fire and smoke.

"It's not a craving," the wizard croaked, picking up the counterspell again with his hands. The pressure vanished as the death spell dissipated. "Give me a chance to prove it."

The witch king turned his glare back to the wizard. "How?" he demanded.

"Is your hunger satisfied yet?"

The witch king looked down at his plate, then back at the wizard. "Almost," he said.

"Take two more bites," the wizard said. "If it's a craving, two bites will make no difference. If it's not, then your hunger will be gone."

For a long moment the witch king stared at him. Then, still standing, he picked up the knife and cut off a double-sized piece and crammed it into his mouth. "There," he mumbled around the food. "Satisfied?"

"Are *you*?" the wizard countered.

The witch king frowned, his chewing jaw coming slowly to a halt. "Yes," he said, sounding confused. "I am."

"With a craving you'd never be satisfied," the wizard reminded him. "As I said, this is not such a spell."

Slowly, the witch king sat again. "Then what is it?"

The wizard spread his hands. "It's food," he said simply. "That's all. Food for the body. Food for the soul. Something with its own brand of woven magic that no one else can duplicate."

"*Every* spell can be duplicated," the witch king said. Standing again, he strode across the tavern to the kitchen door.

The wizard slipped out of his own seat and hurried over to the limp form stretched out across the floor. The tanner was still alive, but the entire left-hand side of his face had become wrinkled and leathery and nearly black. The undamaged side of his face was twisted in pain.

"Whatever you did, it was foolish," the wizard chided, weaving a quick healing spell. It had no effect.

"It kept him from killing you, didn't it?" the tanner managed.

"*I* could have kept him from killing me," the wizard countered, switching to a spell for the easing of pain. This one *did* seem to help. "What did he do to you?"

"I threw my best tanning spell at him," the tanner said ruefully. "Just to get his attention. He turned it back at me, that's all."

The wizard shook his head. "You could have been killed."

The tanner closed his eyes. "I just wanted to distract him."

There was a quiet thud on the wooden floor. The wizard looked up, to find the witch king towering over him.

He tensed. But the other just gazed down at him, a strange expression on his face. "You've seen her," the wizard said. It wasn't a question.

"Yes," the witch king murmured. His eyes seemed to come back from far away. "I've never . . ." He trailed off.

"I don't know what she is, either," the wizard confessed, answering the other's unspoken question. "She looks human, but she doesn't age. She works magic with her food, but she isn't a mage. She attracts woodland sprites, but inflames none of their usual resentments and calms all their usual rivalries."

"She attracts sprites?"

The wizard waved a hand around him. "See for yourself."

The witch king looked up and wove a spell, and a soft blue glow flickered into existence across the beams and wall timbers. A moment later the blue was joined by areas of red, then a few of yellow, and finally several of green. "Unbelievable," the witch king murmured as he looked around. "They don't live together this way. They *never* live so close together without battle."

"Nowhere but here," the wizard agreed. "I don't know why."

The witch king turned to look at the kitchen door. "They're protecting her."

"Or imprisoning her," the wizard said. "Or perhaps they just like the aromas from her cooking—"

"*Imprisoning* her?" the witch king interrupted.

"Yes," the wizard said. "You see, she can't leave."

"She can't leave the village?"

"She can't leave the tavern," the wizard said. "If she tries, she'll die."

The witch king snorted. "Sprites always make exaggerated claims."

"This time they mean it," the wizard said with a sigh. "I've tried to find a way. Tried for thirty years." He felt his lip twist. "Do you think I stay here entirely by choice?"

The witch king looked again at the glowing sprites. "Why here?" he demanded. "Why a worthless tavern in a useless village in an ignored valley?"

"I don't know," the wizard said. "Perhaps because this valley *wasn't* always ignored. Long ago, it was the only route between Tarnholm and the lowlands and the sea kingdoms. Perhaps when she first came here this village wasn't so useless. Perhaps from this place she was able to touch and change thousands of lives each year."

"Ridiculous," the witch king scoffed. "Those days were centuries ago."

The wizard nodded. "Yes. I know."

The witch king paused, apparently digesting that. "And yet she stays?"

"She can't leave," the wizard reminded him. "But numbers aren't important. Not to her."

The witch king snorted again. "So that's your plan?" he growled. "To so ensnare me with this food that I become one of those whose lives are changed? That I abandon my plans of conquest and power and meekly surrender to live out my days here?"

The wizard shook his head. "My goal is simply for you to understand why this place is worth protecting," he said. "I ask only that you instruct your army to leave us in peace." He dared a small smile. "If only so that the tavern will still be standing when next you pass by, so that you can enter and share another meal."

"I will eat what I wish," the witch king bit out. He waved his hand, dissipating the revealing spell, and the flickering lights in the walls and ceiling vanished. "And I don't share. I take." He stalked across the tavern and left, slamming the door behind him.

"Do you think it'll work?" the tanner asked, his voice weak.

"I don't know," the wizard said, helping him to a nearby chair.

"We'll find out soon enough. Sit quietly while I get you some food." He felt his lip twitch in an ironic smile. "This time, *I'll* serve *you*."

The wizard expected the witch king to come again at sundown for an evening meal. He did, along with his three chief generals and his four chief mages. For nearly two hours they sat around their table, eating and conversing in low tones.

The witch king ate four portions. The mages and generals each ate three.

Night fell, and the witch king and his men returned to the encampments and the cooking and sentry fires that now dotted the valley. The wizard went to bed about midnight, planning to rise at dawn to be ready when the witch king returned for breakfast.

There was to be no breakfast. By dawn, the witch king's army was once again on the move.

They stood together by the ruined gate, the wizard and the tanner, watching as the army's rearguard marched toward the rising sun. "I really thought," the tanner said with an edge of bitterness, "that he would instead choose to give battle to the sprites."

"He knew better than to try that," the wizard told him, feeling some of the tanner's bitterness shading his own voice. He'd suspected this would be the end of it. Had hoped, in fact, that this would be the end of it.

But that foreknowledge didn't make it any less painful.

"I don't share." The tanner murmured the witch king's last words to them. "I take."

"And so he did," the wizard murmured back. Even far away down the valley, lit only by the dim, cloud-filtered light of dawn, he had no trouble seeing the tavern, perched upon the platform the witch king had constructed from the logs of the village wall, now being carried on the backs of the soldiers and the witch king's own black oxen.

"So he did," the tanner said. "And we're left with nothing."

"We have our lives," the wizard reminded him. "And the lives of the other villagers." He gestured to the homes and shops beyond the half-vanished walls. "And most of the village."

The tanner shook his head. "It won't be the same."

"It never is."

"I suppose." The tanner nodded toward the glowing sky. "Do you really think she can tame him?"

"Not at first," the wizard said. "And not the way you're thinking. He'll continue on for a while as he always has. But gradually, his priorities will change. He'll look forward to his meals more than he will to conquering and destroying. If he allows his generals and mages to eat with him, they'll begin to change in the same way."

"And if he instead keeps her all to himself?"

"Then a gulf will form between their desires and his," the wizard said. "Sooner or later, he'll recognize the madness and ultimate futility of his path. Maybe then he'll find the contentment he never knew he was searching for."

He felt the tanner's eyes on him. "And you?"

"Me?"

"Have you found contentment?" the tanner asked. "Or will you . . . ?" He left the question unfinished.

The wizard smiled. "Will I resume my former path now that she's gone?" He shook his head. "Have no fears. My days of conquest are far behind me."

He gazed at the tavern, silhouetted now against the rising sun. How many lives had she changed, he wondered. Hundreds? Thousands? More?

He didn't know. But it wasn't important. She'd changed his life, and that was all that mattered.

"Strange, isn't it?" the tanner murmured. "You conquered with spells. The witch king conquers with spells and steel and armies. She conquers with nothing more than tarragon, basil, and sage."

The wizard smiled sadly. He would miss her. But he would never forget her. "And," he added, "a touch of rosemary."

Timothy Zahn has been writing science fiction for more than thirty years. In that time he has published forty-four novels, more than ninety short stories and novelettes, and four collections of short fiction. Best known for his ten Star Wars *novels, he is also the author of the Quadrail series, the Cobra series, the Conquerors trilogy, and the young adult Dragonback series. Recent books include* Cobra Gamble, *the final book of the Cobra War trilogy, and* Star Wars: Scoundrels. *Upcoming books include* Cobra Slave, *the first of the Cobra Rebellion trilogy, and* Pawn, *the first of the Sibyl's War series. You can contact him at www.facebook.com/TimothyZahn.*

Ashes

STEVEN SAVILE

On Gene Wolfe: *I'm not entirely sure when I first encountered Gene Wolfe's work—I suspect it was around 1988 when I was in the midst of my Michael Moorcock kick of one Elric book a day to hide from the stresses of my degree. But I do remember the book, and the way it fundamentally changed how I thought about fantasy fiction.* Free Live Free, *set in the real world, not Donaldson's the Land or Eddings' Riva, or Moorcock's Melniboné, it was here, it was now, and it was every bit as magical as anything these made-up places had to offer. Moreso, probably, because it was all about the Story People. It is Wolfe's gift—the way he conjures the lives of these people: Stubb, his down-at-the-heels detective, Madame Serpentina, Candy, and of course Benjamin Free himself. They are wonderful, they are rich, and they never once drop out of character or blur. Their voices are unique.*

But there's another ever-present in the book, and that's the city of Chicago. It's gritty, it's dark, and it's so full of brooding presence everywhere through the narrative you can't help but think of it as a character in and of itself. That's what I got from Gene Wolfe as a nineteen-year-old neophyte setting out, and it's what I still hold dear in everything I do today. I want my Story People to live, and I want my cities to be as real as the places you are sitting in right now.

You can write a story, you can carefully craft a plot, you can join all the dots and all of that, but if you forget the magic of the everyday, well, you're missing half of the brilliant things around you. It's the small things. The devil is in

the details, as they say, but more than that, so is the com-
passion. So is the humanity. So is the well that I want to tap
when I put pen to paper. "Ashes" could never have been
written without all of those subtle things, those little life
lessons I picked up from a misspent youth of books.

When I was twenty-seven I tried to imagine what it would be like to be fifty, to have lived through the best part of my life, and the worst, and made it out on the other side. What single piece of advice would this hypothetical time-traveling me impart if he could? It's a tough question to ask given that you've not actually lived your life yet, but I decided on two words: be brave. They felt right. I had them tattooed over my heart.

I like to think it made all the difference.

Life up until then had been pretty much a little bit of this, a little bit of that, same as it is for most people. I'd had my share of missed opportunities, of course, hence the "be brave" motto. There was Sasha, who sat beside me from the autumn of 1980 until the summer of 1983, for one. Miss Bennett's grand scheme had been no more complicated than boy-girl, boy-girl to keep the class quiet. She hadn't banked on the poet in twelve-year-old-me's soul, or my inability to let him out. Then there was Rachel. I fell for her. Down a flight of stairs in a guest house in Scarborough. It wasn't graceful. I have no idea if it hurt; fear at the sight of this beautiful girl smiling at the top of the staircase wiped out all memory of pain.

Actually, I've done the whole falling thing more than once. There was this one girl, back at university, must have been around 1989, I guess. It was snowing. I was wearing cowboy boots. I saw her, she smiled, and I ended up flat on my back between her legs. It wasn't as glamorous as it sounds. Much laughter ensued, most of it hers at my expense. At lunchtime in the refectory I managed to slip again because someone had dragged the outdoors inside. This time my dinner tray went sailing through the air in an arc that was almost as graceful as the swan dive my body was taking. Who stood directly in the line of fire? You guessed it: the girl. She managed to avoid my pie and mash. I mumbled something about not usually being so clumsy and scuttled away cursing my fancy new cowboy boots. The universe was trying to tell me something. That night I went to a really cramped bar down on the Quayside, the Crown Posada, with a few of the lads. The Crown was a wonderfully narrow galley-style bar, no music, real ale on tap, and packed with pretentious students talking oh-so-earnestly about nothing. When it was my round I took up position at the bar, ordered three pints of whatever was flat, thick, and warm that day, and turned around too quickly, sending those three pints of flat, thick, and warm all over the same decidedly *un*amused girl. She muttered something along the lines of: "Oh, for fuck's sake! Watch what you're doing!" and then saw it was me.

A braver man might have realized it was the universe trying to tell us something. A braver man might have acted upon it, managed a smile, said something witty and stumbled—quite literally—into the preordained relationship.

Not me.

I said, "Oh God, I'm sorry. I'm so sorry. I swear you'll never see me again." And beat a hasty retreat.

See what I mean about being brave?

Then there was Claire, my best friend's sister, who came with us to watch the ice hockey—though actually it was more like Mortal Kombat to be honest—and made countless excuses to be the one to drive me home an hour out of her way so we could spend time together just chatting and had no idea I was hopelessly lost around her. I didn't mention, did I? 1983–86 was exclusively male territory, posh private all-boys school. Congratulations to the private education system for turning out yet another dysfunctional sixteen-year-old incapable of looking a girl in the eye . . . never mind talking to her like, oh, I don't know, a human being. The idea of sitting alone in a car with a girl I fancied for an hour at least two or three times a week was enough to turn me into a babbling wreck of a human being. If she'd once, just once, smiled my way, I think I would have died and gone—like the monkey in the song playing on the car stereo—to heaven. Probably kicking and screaming as my panicked reaction caused her to drive straight off the road and into the cruel sea.

But I wasn't brave and she didn't save my soul and somehow I made it to twenty-seven thinking something wonderful was supposed to happen with my life, so why wasn't it?

I decided to take matters into my own hands. I went to a seedy tattoo parlor on the Westgate Road, halfway up the hill, hidden away between the pawnshops and the secondhand stores, and had a huge shaven-headed brute step straight out of a Tom of Finland calendar ink the words "be brave" over my heart.

It was as I was walking out of that shithole that I first saw Isla Durovich.

She took my breath away.

I'd always thought that was the biggest cliché in the book, but there she was, this woman looking in the window of a pet store at one of the capuchin monkeys hanging upside down by its tail, and I couldn't breathe.

I put my right hand over the wound where Tom of Finland had inked those words to live by, and thought: *It's now or never.* "Be brave," I told myself, and crossed the street into what was supposed to have been the rest of my life.

And it would have been, if . . .

If wishes were fishes, as my gran used to say, beggars would ride. She never could keep her aphorisms straight.

Instead of being forever it was four years, six months, two days, fifteen hours, and thirty minutes. And then the car hit her and I was robbed of my happily ever after. Sometimes the fairy tales suck.

The whole idea that it's better to have loved and lost than never to have loved at all is rubbish. The Isla-shaped hole in the rest of my life was unbearable. I was numb. I drank even though I don't drink. It didn't help. I didn't leave the house. I closed the curtains and hid in the dark. It didn't help. I looked at the packing list on the table, the last thing she'd written, all the things we were going to need for the honeymoon. It didn't help. I listened to her voice on the answerphone. Hearing her say "You know what to do" just hurt. I lay on her side of the bed, trying to absorb her essence as though she might have left more than just an impression in the wrinkled sheets. I breathed in her fragrances: the shampoos, perfumes, even the musty old pages of her favorite books, obscure paperbacks she'd picked up at jumble sales and charity shops, all secondhand because, she liked to pretend, that meant they'd been loved and loved so much someone had wanted to share them with the world.

We'd mapped out our honeymoon from those old books: Eurostar from London through the tunnel to Paris, just because we'd always wanted to go through the tunnel. The train from Paris to Prague. Prague to Vienna, down through the mountains to Venice. Venice on to Rome, then up to this little place on Lake Garda. We were going to do it properly, four weeks of traveling. A full moon's worth of exploring, living, and to hell with real life.

And just like that, the whole "be brave" thing became so much harder. Sometimes I think God punishes us by answering our prayers. I remember lying in bed, looking at Isla sleeping beside me, and just thinking I wanted this moment to last forever. I wanted the world to stop and it did, with a knock on the door and two somber-looking policemen with their hats in their hands. It was the hat in the hands that did it. That only ever means one thing. The older of the two asked if I was me, and then if they could come inside. Isla was a schoolteacher. Was. That's still stupidly hard to say. It's so . . . past tense. Final. I don't like finality in words anymore. I like words that are open and that at least allow for some kind of hope, like the word yet. *Yet* is a powerful word. It's a good one.

Kids had been playing in the yard during lunch when the ice-cream man drove tantalizingly close to the gates. One of the grade threes had wriggled through the gate and wandered across the road, following the Pied Piper of Ice Cream's call. Isla had been on playground duty. She'd run into the road to save the girl and taken most of the impact while the girl had walked away with a few bruises. The policeman had called it a small mercy. It wasn't. Not really. I didn't get any comfort out of knowing the love of my life had died saving some kid I didn't know or care about. That wasn't mercy to me.

The funeral was on the day we were supposed to be married, and all I can remember is thinking it should have been raining.

I put a rose on her coffin and went home.

But it didn't feel like home anymore. Home is where the heart is, and mine was broken and it felt like it would be that way forever. It wasn't just that she wasn't there, though that was a huge part of it; it was the part of me that she'd taken away that was the worst. It's hard to explain, but I was a better version of myself when Isla was around.

The last present she'd ever given me was still on the table beside the packing list and tickets: a vintage Omega watch. It was a Speedmaster, the same model that Buzz Aldrin had worn when he took the second "giant step" behind Neil Armstrong. The first watch on the moon. Not that this one had been into space, of course. Well, I assume it hadn't. Aldrin's had disappeared on its way to the Smithsonian, but I'm pretty sure Isla wasn't *that* connected.

I set the time and put it on.

I couldn't tell you why I did it, but I picked up her list and started randomly stuffing things into a backpack.

I was halfway to the station before I realized I actually intended to go on my honeymoon.

I took some battered old paperbacks with me and a few fun little trinkets, things that were absolutely her, quirky little things that were like little pieces of her soul. If it couldn't be a honeymoon then it could be a pilgrimage. I'd take those parts of Isla to all of the places we'd been meant to visit together and bury them at the different landmarks we'd talked about.

It was my version of scattering her ashes.

First stop, Paris.

There's the obvious attractions, sure: the Eiffel Tower, the Louvre, Sacré-Coeur, the Champs-Elysées, Pont Neuf, and Notre Dame. But Paris for Isla would always be *Les Pont des Arts* because of Julio Cortázar's book *Rayuela*. I only knew it because of that scene in *Amélie* where Audrey Tautou decided to secretly do good deeds for those who deserved it. Isla had made me promise we'd put a padlock on the bridge and throw the key into the Seine like lovers do. There's something wonderfully romantic about thinking of something of ours locked there forever, even if it was the padlock from the suitcase she wouldn't need anymore.

I fastened it in place and threw the key as far and as hard as I could into the river below.

The lights of Paris illuminated the wonderful dichotomy of the city; on one side of me the chaos of the medieval city, all angles and shadows, and on the other the serenity of the Louvre, so calm and so cultured. I savored the feel of the wind on my face and wondered what else there was left to do here. We had three days booked in Paris, but I was done here. I'd fastened our padlock and bound us to the city forever. I just wanted to move on to Prague and show Isla the next place on our journey.

I walked, head down, a tired, beaten man, shuffling through the same streets countless tired, beaten Parisian feet had shuffled through during the Second World War, looking for an entrance to the Metro.

There was a wonderful piece of pavement art chalked onto the path beside the entrance. It looked like a man struggling through a storm, his umbrella turned inside out while the rain began to wash him away as though he'd never been there. I dropped a handful of coins into the artist's hat and went down for the train. I checked my watch. It had been losing time, but I'd never thought about getting it fixed. Nothing too drastic, maybe twenty seconds an hour, but that made eight minutes a day, or fifty-six minutes a week. In a month I'd lose a little over four hours, which meant something like two days over the course of a year. It was funny how time could just fritter away because a spring was coiled a little too loosely.

An old couple sat huddled up so close together they might have been Siamese twins. The woman had a yellow Kodak envelope in her hands and was thumbing through pictures. She *tutted* in that wonderfully French way when I sat down beside them and went back to her photographs, occasionally shrugging oh so expressively.

Her fingers fastened on one. She pulled it out of the pack and then turned to her husband, tapping it. They looked at the photograph together, and then she looked at me and said, *"Est-ce vous? Il est, n'est-ce pas?"*

I felt like an idiot. My French didn't go beyond, *"Je m'appelle Steve,"* and I wasn't one hundred percent on how to say that. I shrugged in a much less expressive manner and said, "I'm sorry?"

"English?"

I nodded.

She smiled, slightly. "It's you, isn't it?" she said, holding the photograph out for me to look at.

It was.

Or more accurately it was me and Isla. It took me a moment to realize when it had been snapped—about nine months ago. We'd taken shelter under the bandstand at Hyde Park, because the rain was pouring down. We'd huddled up close and watched the swans while Isla had told me how swans mate for life, and I'd asked her to marry me. I smiled. I couldn't quite believe that some complete stranger waiting for a train on the Parisian underground had a photo of one of the happiest moments of my life. I could see it all in my head, me going down on one knee, her giggling, then putting her hand to her mouth when she realized I was serious, and the way she couldn't stop saying yes.

I nodded. "Yes. Yes, it's me. How did you get this?"

The old woman smiled, but it was the man who answered. "That is where Isuelt agreed to be my wife," he said with a smile, obviously remembering the day. And I thought again just how much I missed the woman I never got to marry. All I wanted to do was grow old with her, like these two. "The war was over, and we were young, reckless and very much in love. I convinced her to come with me to England, and it was the start of a lifetime together. We went back for the first time last year, and it seemed only right we should take a photograph of the place where it all began."

"I was asking Isla—my girlfriend—to marry me," I said, pointing at the photograph.

"We know," the old woman said. "We stood in the rain watching you. Where is she?"

And there it was, the question I didn't want to answer. I didn't want to rob this lovely old couple of their happy memory, but I didn't know how to deflect the question either, so I said, "She couldn't make the trip."

"Ah, that's a shame."

"This is going to sound strange, but would it be possible to keep this?" I asked, reluctant to let go of the photograph.

"Oh, of course, of course. We've got the negatives, we can easily make another copy. You should have it. It's the start of your life, after all," the old man said.

"Thank you so much." I put the picture in my pocket.

A few minutes later the train rolled in and we said our good-byes.

I can't begin to explain how I felt. It was as though they'd given me a part of my life back that I'd lost forever. Now it wasn't just my memory. I've always believed that the more people who remember something the more real it is. Now, with three of us to remember, that day in Hyde Park was real again.

Next stop, Prague, guided by *May*, a battered collection of poetry by Karel Hynek Mácha. The train was cramped and hot and sweaty, filled with backpackers. I'd booked a private compartment, which I ended up sharing with half a dozen young students broken up for the summer and looking to get drunk and lucky in one of Europe's party cities. The only other "grown-up" in our carriage was a businessman who didn't like flying. I know that because he said it at least five times in three hours. He kept telling the kids how they were fifteen years too late and how Prague had been *the* city to visit after the Gentle Revolution. He leaned over toward me and said conspiratorially, "It's the closest we'll ever come to the spirit of the sixties. Free love, if you know what I mean? Especially as a Westerner. We were like gods back then." I didn't say much to them, just leaned against the side of the compartment with my head resting against the window reading through the pages of the poems. I made it to the line about the lover weeping, and took it as an order.

There were two places in Prague I wanted to visit, a restaurant we'd always talked about going to, Svata Klara, which wasn't so much a restaurant as it was a treasure trove of history trapped in a seventeenth-century wine cellar, and of course the Charles Bridge at midnight. I booked myself into the hotel, which had been an old Dominican monastery in a previous life, and then went out for a walk, wondering if I would somehow stumble upon Mácha's so-called Alley of Sighs, the white chapel, or the execution hill he wrote so hauntingly about. I knew the poem inside out now. Reading nothing but it for six hours will do that to a man.

The Old Town center of Prague is like another world—a place out of time. Of course there are all the touristy bits you'd expect, the overpriced coffees thanks to the invasion of Starbucks, and the locals have really embraced the ideals of capitalism to the point that what's theirs is theirs, and what's mine is theirs seems to be the maxim of the day. Some of it, like the Jewish cemetery built on top of a row of shops, made me smile at the quirkiness of it, right up until I saw just how many gravestones were crammed into that tiny space. I started to think about what it really meant. Then there were other parts where the wealth of the city is on display with the rows of shop windows filled with Hermès, Dolce & Gabbana, Versace, and Bulgari. When you thought about the beggars on their knees two streets away it was kind of sickening, really, but that was the modern world all over.

I walked around for a couple of hours. That was all it took for me to stumble upon the underbelly of the city.

Walking down Karlova, this wonderful Brothers Grimm kind of street that leads toward the Charles Bridge, I was confronted by a naked woman doing her best to walk seductively down the middle of the cobbled path. She had that vaguely stoned look to her brown eyes. And yes, I was looking at them, it was the only place I felt safe to look. She seemed to be finding it increasingly difficult to walk—never mind seductively—in heels without breaking her neck.

A fat man with greased-back hair and a thick gold chain around his neck that made him look like something out of a seventies sexploitation movie was ten steps in front of her, walking backward, and filming the looks of passersby for his website and encouraging her to bend and twist, dip a little thigh, flash a smile, be coy, and cover up, open up.

Somewhere in the distance a brass band struck up the opening chords of the *Indiana Jones* theme. It couldn't have been more surreal, or more perfect.

It was nowhere near midnight and the bridge was on the other side of the tramlines, less than a minute's walk. I could see the distinctive tower over the rooftops. I decided to check it out while the puppeteers and artists were plying their trade, so I waited for the old red tramcar to pass, and then joined the crowd moving toward the bridge.

With the sun going down, the tower's arch had transformed into a Gothic picture frame, and inside it I could see the silhouette of the black castle and skyline on the other side of the river. I had to squint to see any of it clearly. I couldn't help but smile. A guy was on his knees acting out some sort of passion play with puppets of a cloven-hoofed George W. and a wild-haired Saddam with a unibrow fit to launch a thousand nightmarish ships. Who said political satire had to be cutting edge?

The first thing that caught my eye was the terrible restoration job. They'd obviously tried to purge two hundred years' worth of soot from parts of the old bridge, and left some of the gold on the statues looking like it had come out of a Christmas cracker. Tourists climbed up onto the wall to have their photographs taken with the various saints and patron saints that lined the bridge. I walked toward the middle and St. Christopher; after all, I was a traveler. I didn't realize I had been clutching Isla's medallion until I was standing on the wall, eye-to-eye with the statue. I hung her St. Christopher from the fingertips of the baby Jesus on the saint's shoulder. I recited a couple of lines from Mácha as a sort of prayer, and clambered back down before anyone could complain about the crazy tourist hanging off their national treasure.

As I turned, I saw a painting that stopped me dead in my tracks. It was of a couple standing outside of a shop window, meeting for the first time. The hope in their eyes was agonizing. I know, because it was the hope in my eyes the painter had captured. I couldn't see if the same look of love was in Isla's eyes because her head was tilted just slightly away as she looked into the window. All I could think was "be brave" as I walked up to the artist. He sat beside his easel, eating a meat pie with his hands.

"This painting, how did you see this?" I asked, pointing an accusing finger at the shop on the Westgate Road.

He looked up at me like I was mad.

I was beginning to think I was.

"I mean, this picture, that very minute, that's the most important minute of my life; what's it doing in one of your paintings?"

He continued to look at me, and then a slow smile spread across his lips as he recognized me. "It's you," he said.

I nodded.

"Oh, my God, it's you." He jumped up, dropping his meat pie and grabbing my hand to pump it. "I'm so pleased to meet you! You have no idea!"

I really didn't.

I felt like a character in some surreal black-and-white art house movie.

Once was coincidence, but twice, what was that? It certainly wasn't coincidence.

"I don't understand what's happening here."

"It's a funny story," he promised, but I doubted it. "I was away from home, living in this shitty studio apartment, when my girlfriend phoned me to tell me she was pregnant. . . . It was the happiest moment of my life," he said, still grinning. I have to admit it, his grin was infectious. I wanted to share his happiness. "I just went to the window and took a photograph of the world outside. I wanted to remember that exact moment, all of it, exactly how it happened. I always wondered what was happening down there."

"It was the happiest moment of my life, too," I said, thinking about it all over again. Thinking about how it felt to swallow my fear and walk across the street and say: *Hi, I'm Steve, I'm hoping you'll fall in love with me.* "I was finally being brave. I saw this woman, and I just knew I had to walk over there and tell her she was going to be the love of my life."

"That's wonderful! What happened? Did she fall in love with you? Tell me she fell in love with you! That would be perfect, two happily ever afters entwined in a single painting. I could call it *Four Hearts.* That's a great name for a painting. *Four Hearts.*"

I nodded. "She did." I didn't realize I was crying until he asked me what was wrong. "This was supposed to be our honeymoon," I said. I didn't say anything else; I let him read between the lines.

There was a moment in which the silence between our heartbeats was deafening, and then the painter understood the implications of the word supposed, and said, "Oh, shit, I'm sorry. I . . . what happened? Can I ask?"

"She saved someone's life," I said, "but no one saved hers."

I really was crying now, not just a single tear. The painter sat me down on the tarpaulin he'd laid out on the ground. I told him what I was doing, my pilgrimage, and about the old couple I'd met in Paris a few days ago. I don't know how long I sat there. I couldn't take my eyes off the painting. By the time I stopped looking at it, it was past midnight and the tourists had gone home.

"It seems to me this journey of yours is being steered, my friend. Call it fate, call it chance; you were meant to be here, tonight, because you needed to be here. I want you to have this," he said, taking the painting off the easel.

"I can't. . . . Let me give you something for it."

He shook his head. "You already did, believe me. Just by being there you gave me part of your life and made it such an important part of mine. Let me give it back to you."

I couldn't argue with that.

I held the painting like it was the most precious thing in the world as I walked back to my room in the old Dominican monastery, and hung it on the wall.

I lay in my bed looking up at the painting of when I met Isla Durovich for the first time. Four hearts.

But there were only three of them now.

At three-fifteen the next morning my watch stopped, and I couldn't get it going again. It was only a small thing, but it felt like the greatest tragedy in the entire world. I cradled it in my hands like a dying child, willing it to tick. It didn't.

I'd seen a place in the Jewish Quarter called Old Watches. It was a tiny antique place with a watchmaker who looked like a gnome with mad whiskers and madder eyes. I set out at first light. I couldn't sleep. I needed to get it fixed. I couldn't bring Isla back, but I could fix this. It's funny how little things become obsessions. I didn't care about my train to Vienna; I wasn't leaving until my moon-landing watch was keeping good time.

The morning air was brisk. There was rain in the air. Locals bustled toward the underground station, Staroměstská. It was too early for the shops; they were all boarded up or shuttered. It felt like I was seeing a secret part of the city, like watching a lover in bed, drowsy and not quite ready to face the world. I couldn't remember exactly where I'd seen the watch shop, somewhere close to the old Jewish cemetery and the synagogues, so I just wandered around for a while drinking in the architecture of dreams and desires that had fired those imaginations oh so long ago, marveling at just how beautiful the buildings were and wondering—not for the first time— what future generations would think of the modern monstrosities we left as our legacy with the ugly but functional lines.

The shop was open.

There must have been ten thousand watches and parts of watches in the window, all of them at least fifty years old, most a lot older, all of the working parts ticking away to different rhythms. I opened the door. A little bell rang. There was no room inside—there was a one-foot-square space in front of the watchmaker's counter and the rest of the shop was taken up by mechanisms. He looked up from the timepiece he had been tinkering with and waggled his bushy eyebrows. There were trays, all neatly arranged with bits of this and bits of that that somehow came together to make everything tick.

"What can I do for you, young man?" he asked, in perfect English. I hadn't been expecting that. I'd been all primed for five minutes of miming to get my point across.

I took my watch off and put it on the counter between us.

"It stopped last night, and I can't get it going again."

"Well, let's have a look at it, shall we?" He studied it, reached into one of the drawers beneath the counter and brought out a little tool to screw the back off of it. He put a jeweler's monocle in his eye. Using a fine pin he teased the mechanism, tutting like a mechanic about to tell me he could fix my car, but it was going to cost a lot because the gear box was shot, the manifold was blown, the gaskets were knackered, and a whole bunch of other technical terms that made no sense whatsoever to me was wrong with it. "I see what the problem is," he said.

"What's wrong?"

"It's broken." He grinned at me. "But don't worry, I can fix it. I assume you *want* me to fix it?"

"That's why I'm here," I said. "How much will it cost?"

"For you? Nothing, Steve," he said, taking the monocle out.

"You know my name? How?"

"I know all my customers' names, Steve. It's just good business."

"Yeah, right, sure, but *how* do you know my name?"

"I make it my business to. We're all cogs, my friend; we're all gears in the guts of the world. We tick, we tock, our orbits occasionally draw us close to one another, though more often than not they take us away."

"Have we met before?"

He shook his head. "Now, let's see about fixing this, shall we? Been losing a lot of time, has it? The spring's loose. I should probably replace it, but I'm not sure you want me to do that."

"Why not? I'm sorry, I don't really understand. If you need to replace the spring to make the watch work again, why wouldn't I want you to do that?"

"Because of the time that's stored up inside it. Change the spring and it's gone forever."

I shook my head.

"Gone?"

"Yep, gone, vanished, spent, left behind, lived through, no more, a memory."

"But that's what happens. Time passes."

"Oh, you know so much, do you? So how come you didn't notice your watch was saving time?"

"It wasn't, it was losing time."

"Losing, saving, you speak like you don't understand the difference," the watchmaker said, sniffing. He screwed the lid back on and pushed the watch into the middle of the counter between us. "It's all in there, all of that saved time."

I looked at it.

It wasn't ticking.

"You didn't fix it?"

"Did you see me fix it?"

"No."

"Then I didn't fix it. I don't think you want me to fix it. After all, there are two whole days stored in there. That's a lot of time to throw away. It's up to you, but I'd think long and hard about it. Two days. What's happened to you over the last couple of days, and more importantly, are you ready to give it up?"

What had happened to me? I'd met an old couple who'd reminded me of just how incredible it felt when Isla said yes, and I'd met a painter who had captured the single most important moment of my life. In less than forty-eight hours they'd given me back two of my most precious memories of Isla. There was no way in a million years I'd give that up; but it wasn't as though I'd just forget them, either. They were etched on my soul.

"Forty-eight hours," he said again. He picked up the watch and reset the time, rolling the hands back. "Think about it."

I took the old moon-landing watch off him. I could feel the gentle tick of the hands moving. I put it on. "Thank you," I said, and stepped out of the cramped little shop onto the Parisian street. I felt the padlock in my pocket. I wanted to go to the Les Pont des Arts because of Julio Cortázar's book Rayuela. Isla and I had joked about fastening a padlock to the bridge like lovers do. I knew what was going to happen. I'd throw the key into the river, then walk down to the subway and meet an old couple looking at a photograph of Isla and me, and I'd be as happy and sad as I could remember ever being, both at the same time. Then I'd move on to Prague to scatter another one of her ashes, her St. Christopher.

I looked at the watch Isla'd given me for my birthday. It was losing time. No. It was *saving* time. There was a difference. It was saving a little bit every hour until it was full. Then it would stop. And when it stopped, I'd go to a little watchmaker's shop in the Jewish quarter of Prague, and he'd say, "I know all my customers' names, Steve. It's just good business." This time I'd know how he knew my name, because we'd done this dance before.

If he gave me that choice again, fixing it, or using it, I'd keep on using it until I was ready to go on scattering the rest of Isla Durovich's ashes in Vienna—on a picnic blanket on the green in Bellevue Höhe overlooking the entire city—and Venice—on the Grand Canal—then Rome—taking in the breathtaking view of the Eternal City from Gianicolo Hill—and finally that little lake house in Garda that was just for us, our little dream house.

And when I was ready, I'd go on to the third battered paperback in my bag, but not yet, and I couldn't go back four years, six months, four days, thirteen hours, and fifteen minutes to the moment I'd had Tom of Finland tattoo "be brave" over my heart, and live it all again, because forty-eight hours was forty-eight hours. The watch couldn't save any more time. Not in the year I'd had it.

But I didn't need to go back. As tempting as it was to wish I could save the child myself, or go back to that day we first met and be brave all over again, I couldn't change things. This was the way it had to be.

All I needed to do was to let him rewind the watch on all of its saved time, and step out of his shop onto the moonlit Parisian streets. There would always be an old couple waiting for me on the platform with their Kodak moments, and a painter on a bridge tomorrow desperate to share the happiest moment of his life with me.

That was Isla's last gift to me, seconds saved here and there from our last year together that all added up to time to remember her.

Internationally bestselling author Steven Savile has written for Dr. Who, Torchwood, Primeval, Stargate, Warhammer, Slaine, Fireborn, BattleTech, Pathfinder, and other popular game and comic worlds. His novels have been published in eight languages, including the Italian bestseller L'eridita. *He won the International Media Association of Tie-In Writers award for his Primeval novel,* Shadow of the Jaguar, *published by Titan in 2010, and has been nominated for the British Fantasy Award on multiple occasions.* Silver, *his debut thriller, reached number two on the Amazon UK e-charts in the summer of 2011. Steven has also worked in computer games, writing the story for the hugely successful* Battlefield 3 *from DICE/EA. His latest books include* Tau Ceti *(coauthored with Kevin J. Anderson);* Each Ember's Ghost, *an urban fantasy set in his hometown of London; and the novelization of the computer game* Risen 2: Dark Waters.

Bedding

An Homage to "Straw" by Gene Wolfe

DAVID DRAKE

On Gene Wolfe: *Jim Baen published my first two Hammer stories in the October and November 1974 issues of* Galaxy *magazine. This led more or less directly to my subsequent writing career. Jim published "Straw" in the January 1975* Galaxy. *I read it there and realized how far I had to go to write as well as Gene Wolfe. That remains true.*

After the tumble I'd taken when the horse bunted me out of the way, I let Diccon do more than his share of stretching out the balloon to fill evenly. The boy was willing, full marks to him for that, and as strong as a draft horse. That was all this job required.

Fighting needed more, though. I've known draft horses smarter than Diccon, and I'm not saying that I've known any smart horses. The Captain was half his size, but the boy wouldn't last three seconds with him; and even banged up like I was, he wouldn't give me much trouble, either.

Siltsy moaned; he was coming awake again. Birgitta had bought all the lettuce cake in the village, but the biggest dose she could give Siltsy wasn't enough to let him sleep. The saber had cut so deep into his upper arm that it had cracked the bone. The drug might help with pain, but the ache wouldn't go away until he died.

The Captain was getting charcoal going in the brazier; I walked toward him. Siltsy must've seen the movement, because he sat up.

"Bagnell?" he called. He sounded like an old man. "You won't leave me here, will you? We're buddies, right? You wouldn't leave a buddy!"

"Hush," said Birgitta. She'd been wiping Siltsy's forehead with a wet cloth; now she slid it down to cover his eyes. "Just go to sleep, darling. Just go to sleep."

"Hey, don't you worry, Siltsy," I said. His face was red as fire; an infection must already have started biting. "You'll load for me on our next contract, but you'll have your job back after that."

Siltsy was going to lose the arm if he didn't die. Most likely he was going to lose the arm and then die. Even if he lived, a one-armed crossbowman wasn't much use.

But it wasn't my place to say that, not now and not ever. I wasn't afraid of Birgitta, but I don't pick fights where nobody's going to pay me.

The Captain had a fire already. I've never known a man with such a talent for lighting charcoal. It wasn't glowing, but I could see the air wriggle above the brazier.

He nodded toward the brightness in the east and said, "It won't be long now."

"It'll be at least an hour before we start getting updrafts," I said. "I've got some business to take care of."

"You're favoring your left leg," the Captain said. "Should Birgitta take a look at you?"

"Fat chance that," I said, but I kept my voice low. "She'd like to wring my neck for taking over as shooter. If she could've figured out a way to blame me for Siltsy, she'd have come at me with her halberd already."

"You could've taken the shot yourself instead of passing the loaded bow, you know," the Captain said. He spoke so softly that the only reason I knew what he was saying was that I'd been thinking the same thing ever since Siltsy went down.

"You're the one who kept me loaded!" I said, angry because half of me thought he was right. "I passed the bow to the shooter, because that was my *job*!"

I kept an eye on Birgitta, but she was so lost in coddling Siltsy that she didn't hear—or anyway, she pretended not to hear. Dropping my voice again, I said, "He wouldn't thank me, Captain. Not even now he wouldn't."

The Baron—that's what he called himself, anyway—had placed the five of us at the ford. Our crossbows would've had better targets from a flank, but he was looking at the two halberds and figuring that we wouldn't flinch the way his peasants with knives tied to poles would. He was paying, so we danced to his tune.

Four horsemen had come at us out of a stand of birches fifty yards away. There was a swale in back of it. They must've led their mounts, then swung into their saddles and charged straightaway. Maybe we should've seen them earlier, but things had gotten hot on the left. Anyway, we didn't.

Siltsy took the leader's horse in the shoulder. It reared. The rider kept his seat for a moment, but then the horse went down and the rider still had his feet in the stirrups.

Diccon and Birgitta were ready with their halberds. I took the bow from Siltsy and handed him the one I'd just loaded. He shot as I put my left foot in the stirrup of the empty and brought the cocking lever back.

He didn't miss, exactly, but he shot at the rider instead of the mount, and the fellow had a steel cap. The helmet spun off—I saw sparks where the quarrel glanced from just above the ear—but the fellow didn't drop.

The Captain used two swords, a straight one in his left to thrust with and in his right a yataghan sharpened on the inside curve. He could trim an anvil when he put all the strength of his right arm into a stroke.

This time he took the outside horse's muzzle off. There was more blood than I'd ever seen, and a gurgling scream that was louder than all the rest of the battle. The rider went backward over his crupper and broke his neck when he hit, though we didn't learn that till things had quieted down.

Birgitta had the butt of her halberd in the ground and a foot on it to brace it there. She leaned the blade straight at the middle horse. It shied, like they mostly do. By the time the rider got it under control, the best choice he had was to gallop back the way he'd come. That's what he did.

If Diccon had just done the same thing as Birgitta, there wouldn't have been a problem. Instead he had swung his halberd like an axe and missed his timing, like you'd expect from a newbie. A halberd's edge is out on a long pole and takes longer to get moving than an axe does.

Siltsy threw the bow, which didn't help, and put his arm up, which meant the rider's saber didn't take his head off. That probably would've been a mercy, but I might've done the same if it'd been me.

The horse slammed Siltsy one way and me the other, but not before I got the spike of the bow I was trying to load in under the rider's rib cage. I went ass over teacup, but the horse's saddle was empty when I got a look at it again.

Now the Captain shrugged and made a face that could've meant anything. "I suppose you're right," he said, but he *knew* I was right. He turned his head slightly and said, "Diccon will load for you. We won't make any other changes right now."

"Right," I said. That was going to slow our rate of fire, but the boy did okay with anything that didn't require thinking. I could train him up. "Leaves us short a halberd, though."

"I said we'll leave it there for now!" the Captain said, angry that I was prodding him about Siltsy, and angry about Siltsy, too.

Hell, so was I. We hadn't been buddies, whatever Siltsy said now, but we'd been some hard places together and come through the other side. Until this time.

"You could've made that shot, couldn't you?" the Captain said in his quiet voice again.

"I wouldn't have tried!" I said. "I'd have dropped the horse, the big target. If the rider decided to get up again when he untangled himself, well, I'd have another quarrel ready. *I* didn't have anything to prove."

And that was the cold truth of it: Siltsy had wanted to show us all that he was as good a shot as I was, that the Captain wasn't just keeping him as shooter for old time's sake. Siltsy was going to die now, because he'd been wrong about both those things.

The Captain made that sour face again. He looked to the east and said, "Start rounding up locals for the ropes. There's not much breeze now, but it's likely to pick up. I want at least eight on each rope."

"We can belay one rope around the well curb," I said, nodding. I'd paced the distance off last month, when we moved the balloon here to the village in two of the Baron's ox wagons. "That's as good as four men. But you're going to have to find them yourself. Like I told you, I've got business."

The Captain looked at me sharply. "You'd be better off just leaving, you know," he said. "Everybody would."

"Maybe," I said. "But I'm going to see her."

He shrugged. "I always did, too," he said to my back. "Which is how I know it's a bad idea."

I let myself back in without a fuss. Tige, the guard dog, was on the stoop, but he'd gotten to know me over the past three weeks; I think maybe he even approved. He didn't bark or even raise his shaggy head, though his tail shook the boards with quick, soft thumps.

Janelle's father—Janelle and Perley's—had been Speaker of the village, which meant he talked to the Baron when there was something to talk about. Pretty much that meant saying, "Yes, *sir*," but the title meant something anyway.

The house was wood frame, not wattle and daub, and had a half loft besides a shed for the animals so that the family didn't have to sleep with their livestock. Ordinarily, at least: Perley had been in the shed since I moved in with his sister.

He'd been trying to be the man of the house since their father died last year. I'd done the same when I was his age—but that age was ten, and there's a lot you don't understand when you're ten. I was glad he hadn't made a fuss when Janelle told him to move out for a while. Sure, he wasn't *that* little; but I didn't want to rub his nose in what was going on, either.

"Chris, is that you?" Janelle called. There was more relief than question in her voice.

The bedroom door was open, so she'd wakened since I slipped out and closed it behind me. She was sitting up in bed. When I came through the door she held out her arms.

I had the purse in my left hand. I set it on top of the chest beside the bed while I put the other hand beside her head. I kissed her hard, then straightened.

"You're a hero, darling," she said. She tossed the cover back; the mattress, waxed linen stuffed with straw, creaked as she moved. "Come, let me give you your reward." She giggled. "Your reward again, I mean."

"I've got to go, darling," I said. "You're a lovely girl."

"Well, you'll be back soon, won't you?" Janelle said. "After you've said good-bye to your friends."

"Love," I said, "I'm not coming back. The Baron doesn't want us around now that the trouble's over. He's given us fuel to get plenty far away, and it's healthier all round if we take the hint. Ah—I left a purse on the hamper there."

It was the equivalent of a gold piece, but I'd found it in copper so that she wouldn't have trouble spending it. It was half my own share of the contract—and more ready money than anybody else in the village had ever seen. Siltsy would have told me I was crazy, and even the Captain would raise an eyebrow.

I wouldn't miss the money once it was gone. And maybe I'd sleep better, or at least have less reason to sleep badly.

"You *can't* leave," Janelle said. Her voice was going up. "Chris, what if I'm pregnant?"

"Marry a local boy," I said. I almost said, "Marry Kettler," her father's hired man and now hers. He was a solid sort, and I could tell from his eyes when he looked at me that it was more than the farm that he resented me for. "I'd never make a farmer. I had enough years of it to know that for a fact."

I stepped sideways toward the bedroom door, still looking at her. She got up like I'd hoped she wouldn't and said, "Chris, you can't do this to me! You can't just leave!"

"Love, you don't know who I am or what I am," I said, not trying to keep my tone sweet anymore. "Whatever happens to you now, it'd be worse if I stayed. But that doesn't matter, since I'm not going to stay."

Janelle started screaming. There wasn't anything to be gained by hanging around, so I walked across the front room—walked fast, but I wasn't running. I had my hand on the latch just as Perley jerked the door open from the outside.

"Chris, what's the matter?" he said, looking as wild as his sister did.

I blinked when I saw his outfit. He was wearing a leather jerkin, cut to look like my jack but not boiled in wax to harden it, and a leather cap like mine, too. He had a harness strap over his shoulder for a bandolier, and from it hung the holstered revolver I'd given him when he agreed to go out into the shed at night.

I'd asked him to sleep in the shed "to keep watch on things," and I'd given him the gun. And, okay, it had been a dumb thing to do, but I *liked* the boy.

"Perley, go help your sister," I said, patting him on the shoulder. Then I was through the front door and heading back to where I belonged.

The Captain saw me coming but didn't say anything, just nodded from the car. Diccon brightened like a lamp being turned up and said, "I thought you was gonna stay, Chris. Gee, I'm glad you're not."

If it'd been anybody but Diccon, I'd have gone for him; but the boy really was that dumb, and I needed him for a loader. I just said, "Nope. We ready to lift, Captain?"

There were nine local men on the ropes. That would've been okay, but most of them hadn't come through the fight yesterday any better than I had. Well, peasant farmers had as much experience in working hurt as we floating swords did. They'd be all right for as long as we needed them to steady our rise.

"The fire's ready," the Captain said. He'd laid more charcoal on the brazier when the original sticks were well alight. "We just need to get Siltsy aboard."

"Right," I said. "Birgitta, get into the car. I'll lift him up to you."

"I'll—" Birgitta said. She was in a mood to argue with anything I said. But she really did care about Siltsy, and that shut her mouth when she took time to think.

"I'm taller than you are," I said, squatting by Siltsy across from her. He wasn't sleeping, exactly, but his eyes were closed and what he mumbled didn't seem to be words. "And you can't be both places."

"I can help!" said Diccon.

I raised an eyebrow to Birgitta. She grimaced and stood.

"Get in the car with me, Diccon," she said. "We need you to pull the balloon over the brazier when Bagnell and I get Siltsy aboard."

She had to make the choice, but again she'd made the smart one. The boy was strong and not particularly clumsy, but his own mother wouldn't have called him gentle. I'd seen him crack the handle off a stoneware tankard, just holding it in his hands.

The Baron and four of his men were mounted and watching from the other end of the ridge. They were making sure we were on our way as agreed.

There wouldn't be a problem, though I noticed the Captain had cocked both the crossbows in the car with him. The bows weren't a threat till quarrels were nocked; but leave-taking was a nervous business for both sides.

The Baron had captured horses and armor yesterday, but that didn't make riders out of footmen or a warrior out of the peasant he'd just promoted to House Man. It had been a great victory by his standards, but he'd lost people, too.

"Ready," Birgitta said.

I slid my arms under Siltsy, making sure I had his head cradled in the crook of my right elbow. His skin felt tight and as hot as a brass foot-warmer. I got up smoothly, using my knees to lift. My whole left side felt like it was being branded, but I didn't flinch. I stepped toward the car and Birgitta's outstretched arms.

"Chris!" a voice piped up behind me. "Chris Bagnell! Turn around!"

"I'll take care of this!" I said to the three in the car. I wasn't worried about the Captain, but Diccon had already lifted a bow with a quarrel in his other hand. In our line of work, you don't hesitate when somebody points a weapon at you.

"Turn around or I'll shoot you in the back!" Perley said.

Carefully, just like there was nothing else on my mind, I laid Siltsy onto Birgitta's arms. She was wary, but I was the one who knew what was going on, so she was backing my play.

"I'm going to shoot you!" Perley said.

Birgitta took the weight and lifted Siltsy out of my arms. I turned like any other time: not fast, not slow. There was the kid, six feet away, and there was the little revolver pointed right at the middle of my chest.

It was the old kind of steel that looks like silver but doesn't rust. He'd kept it polished with a chammy, just like I used to do, and I knew the five brass cartridges would shine like gold in the rising sun if we took them out of the cylinder.

"Where did he get that?" Diccon whispered. The Captain told him to hush. The Captain knew where Perley's revolver came from.

"If you don't come back to Janelle, I'll kill you, Chris!" Perley said. His face looked like he'd been crying, but it might just have been that he was so angry. "You've got to come back!"

"Perley, I'm not the right man for your sister," I said, keeping my voice as calm as I could. "She'll know that herself in a day or two, and so will you when you get a little older."

"You've got to!" The revolver was trembling, his whole body was trembling, but the muzzle never wobbled so much that it didn't point at my chest.

"I'm going to leave now, Perley," I said. I started to turn, and he pulled the trigger.

I moved fast then, but he kept trying to shoot me till I had his right arm behind his back and squeezed till his hand opened. He was screaming—with anger, not pain, though I wasn't being gentle.

I used the bandolier to bind his wrists. There was enough of a tail left to the harness strap that I lashed his ankles, too, leaving Perley on his belly and properly hog-tied.

I stood, leaving the revolver where it was. The cartridges had been dead long before the gun came to me; probably dead for centuries. Part of me hadn't really believed that, though; not till it was over.

"Don't let him loose!" I said to the men holding the ropes. None of them looked like they planned to, but it was simply to make sure. They were scared of what was about to happen to them, if I was any judge of expressions.

I turned toward the Baron and yelled, "Keep him tied till we're safely away! Otherwise he's likely to hurt himself!"

I walked to the car. Diccon must've pulled the balloon's throat onto the frame over the brazier as soon as Birgitta had laid Siltsy on the floor. He wouldn't have done that without orders, so the Captain wasn't taking chances. The bag was full enough that the car was getting light on the ground.

Usually I'd have half jumped, half swung over the wicker side, but I was weak as a kitten after the business with Perley. I barely got my feet off the ground and had to grab the shrouds to drag myself in. Even so I'd have landed on my face if the Captain hadn't supported me with an arm. The Captain has muscles like steel bars.

"I'll follow you, Chris Bagnell!" the boy shouted. He'd managed to roll onto his side so he could look at us, but he wasn't going to get loose on his own. "I don't care how far you run, I'll catch you!"

"Slack the ropes!" the Captain called to the local help. "Easy, now, *easy*!"

We started to rise.

There was a good breeze at three hundred feet. It was taking us in the direction I wanted to go: away. The village had been out of sight for more than an hour.

Birgitta was talking to Siltsy, though what I caught of her words didn't make any more sense than his own mumbling did. She must have seen more in Siltsy than I'd thought was there. Well, it was none of my business.

Diccon was dozing. He'd had quite a time last night, a big hero and money in his purse. I suspected he didn't have as much left of his pay as I did of mine.

The Captain was standing beside me. I hadn't noticed him move; I guess I was off somewhere else myself.

When I looked at him, the Captain nodded and said, "I'd always wondered where that revolver went." I could barely hear his voice, even as close as we were.

"It didn't weigh much," I said in the same kind of whisper. "Where did you get it? I never asked you that."

"Took it off a drunk in Gotham on my first contract," he said. He smiled faintly. "That was before the sack and the fire, of course. He had too much ale in him and decided we mercenaries were being paid more than we were worth."

I didn't say anything. I was thinking.

"Do you suppose the boy *will* follow?" the Captain said. "Boys say a lot of things, but now and again they mean them."

"He might," I said. "He's got a lot of grit. But it'll take him years if he does. The years'll teach him, and chasing me will teach him even more. Things will look different by the time he catches up."

I looked at him. I was smiling, too, but it felt lopsided.

"Anyway," I said, "they looked different to me. Didn't they, Captain?"

The army took David Drake from Duke Law School and sent him on a motorized tour of Vietnam and Cambodia with the 11th Cav, the Blackhorse. He learned new skills, saw interesting sights, and met exotic people who hadn't run fast enough to get away.

Dave returned to the United States to become Chapel Hill's assistant town attorney and to try to put his life back together through fiction, making sense of his army experiences.

He often wishes he had a less interesting background.

Dave lives with his family in rural North Carolina.

...And Other Stories

NANCY KRESS

On Gene Wolfe: *I have known Gene for thirty years, and his work for even longer. When I met him, I was a young writer and in awe of this man. Decades later—after we have taught together, visited each other, blurbed each other, cut up fruit salad together—I still am in awe. No one else has produced anything like Gene's body of work. No one else could.*

Yesterday I was in *Emma*. Unseen on Box Hill, as all servants are unseen, I unpacked hampers from the wagons and watched Emma flirt with Frank Churchill. Mr. Knightley glared at Emma. None of the other servants challenged my presence. Maybe they were too busy, or not allowed to talk among themselves while serving, or else the Hartfield servants thought I came from Donwell Abbey and Mr. Knightley's groom assumed I came from Hartfield. Or not. I never find out that sort of thing.

The grass on Box Hill was very green, soft and lush from English rain free of industrial pollutants. Emma was lovely in her absurd high-waisted muslin, and very bratty. I lugged the heavy hampers of food and blankets, china and wine, up the hill, but I was only there about thirty minutes before it ended.

I never know how long it will last, or where I will go, or when. Sometimes I'm already in Grandmother's house. Sometimes I'm shopping or at school, where I am mocked and shunned and friendless. Wherever I am, whatever I am doing, when the terrible summons comes, I have to race to Grandmother's library. Then she does it to me, and there is no way to resist.

"Lose yourself in literature," my asshole English teacher tells the class.

She has no idea.

Thursday I'm in detention when the summons hits. Two days of detention for truancy, again. I sit working on quadratic equations and then all at once my skin is on fire, my bowels are turning to water, my mind howls with an icy wind. There is no resisting it. I jump up, knocking *Advanced Algebra* off the desk, and race to the door, which is locked. Shaking the lock, I howl like a hyena, unable to stop.

"Caitlin!" shouts Mr. Emry.

I howl louder. The others in detention are not the kind students who pity me or the timid ones who shun me; kind and timid students don't end up in this basement room. The ones here laugh and point. I tear my hair, and Mr. Emry, trying to not look frightened, calls for Security. The moment the ex-cop hired by Wakefield High arrives to unlock the door from the outside, I am gone, evading his grasp, running down the hall and out of the school and down the street to Grandmother's gloomy Victorian house. On the way I shit my jeans, but that never makes any difference. I collapse in the library and then I am in *Anna Karenina*.

I recognize Anna from previous trips. She sits in the garden at Vozdvizhenskoe, sewing, her beautiful face clenched and sour. When I appear, she looks up. "Katerina, tea, please."

I go to fetch the tea tray from the kitchen. Everyone there accepts my presence; that is how Grandmother's curse works. Never any difficulty with language or duties, just the unrelenting hard work of a menial. She hates me. I know why, but it is not fair.

I carry the heavy tea tray to the garden. Count Vronsky has just returned from Moscow; he and Anna are quarreling. Their voices rise to a shout: "Oh, Anna, why are you so irritable?" I know that later she will take out her unhappiness on me, for witnessing it. Jealousy and regret and the boredom of exile have already changed her, and in a few more chapters she will return to Moscow, where she will be still more unhappy.

By night my shoulders ache with the hard labor of a servant in czarist Russia. My legs tremble so much I can barely stand. I find my bed and collapse into it, but it seems I am barely asleep before there arrives the early dawn of a Russian summer, and I must rise to carry cans of hot water, scrub corridors and dishes, empty chamber pots. *Anna Karenina* is not as back-breaking as parts of *David Copperfield,* but it is hard enough.

The irony is: I used to love to read.

I am at Vozdvizhenskoe the entire week. Vronsky and Anna make up, fight again, say bitter things to each other. Levin has just arrived to visit Anna when I am snatched back to the library. I lay on the floor, panting and stinking, in my freshly soiled jeans. Here, no time has passed.

"Welcome back," Grandmother says. She guides her feather duster around the tusks of a carved elephant. She and my mother, the love of Grandmother's life, bought it on their travels in India.

I will not cry in front of her. I will not.

"I think, Caitlin," she says in her measured, calm voice, "now that you are sixteen, you should drop out of school. It does not seem to be doing you much good. I will obtain the paperwork for you to sign."

I cannot speak yet, nor move. When I have enough strength to get up off the floor, I stagger to the shower. Every muscle in my body hurts.

The truant officer will, I know, show up here soon. I know, but I don't care. School, with its jeering classmates, is only another kind of torture. Twice I have not made it out of the building before my bowels gave way. Dropping out doesn't seem any worse than staying. Or any better.

The summons began when I was twelve, six months after my mother died. Since then I have scrubbed chamber pots in Victorian England, starved in a labor camp with Ivan Denisovich, slaved in David Copperfield's wine-bottling factory until my fingers bled, suffered a beating at Lowood Institute along with Jane Eyre. Three times I ran away from Grandmother. The first time I was thirteen and I got no farther than the park, carrying my sleeping bag and suitcase, before the summons hit me. The second time I was fourteen, and savvier. I stole money, bought a bus ticket, got as far as the next city. The summons hit and I tried frantically to hitchhike back to the library, my skin burning and my mind howling. When my bowels gave way, the kind woman who had picked me up took me straight to the emergency room. I jumped out of the car and staggered—was dragged, compelled, forced—to the library.

Three months later, savvier still, I went voluntarily to the ER and acted crazy, waving around a kitchen knife and claiming hallucinations. I was examined, committed, sent to a locked psychiatric ward. It was wonderful. Grandmother was not allowed to visit. Then another inmate sat in the day room reading *Les Misérables,* and I was with Fantine and the other women forced into prostitution to survive. Fantine sold her hair, then her jewelry, but could not stop the inevitable. I had no jewelry, and my hair was already cut short. I was had by ten men in four days.

"If you try that again," Grandmother said, "it will be *Les Misérables* again."

In the middle of that night, I set the library on fire. I poured gasoline siphoned from the lawn mower—we had no car—onto the parquet floor. I opened the window, went outside, and tossed in a flaming match, one of the long wooden kind used for fireplaces. The gasoline blazed for half a second and then went out. Two more matches. It didn't burn.

My grandmother appeared in the doorway in her long white nightdress, looking like a ghost, a phantom, a white demon from an icy hell. "Don't do that again, Caitlin," she said. "It won't help. You took her life away from me. So yours belongs to me. That's only fair. Now clean up this mess."

I screamed, "I didn't mean what happened to Mama!"

"Meaning is an illusion," she said and went back to bed, leaving me alone outside the window, staring at the pool of gasoline on the polished golden floor.

I drop out of school. I watch TV. I go for walks, but not very far. I read nonfiction. I'm in the kitchen, eating a ham sandwich and ignoring the dirty dishes piled in the sink, which I was supposed to wash last night, when the summons comes and I run to the library.

It's a medieval castle, further back in time than I have been before. Knights, ladies, servants gather in a great stone hall with banners on the wall and great smoky fires. Everyone is shouting, dogs are barking; it's chaos. Finally one huge knight climbs onto a trestle table and makes himself heard above everybody else.

"Now we have been served this day of what meats and drinks we thought on; but one thing beguiled us, we might not see the Holy Grail, it was so preciously covered. Wherefore I will make here avow, that to-morn, without longer abiding, I shall labor in the quest of the Sangreal, that I shall hold me out a twelvemonth and a day, or more if need be, and never shall I return again unto the court till I have seen it more openly than it hath been seen here; and if I may not speed I shall return again as he that may not be against the will of our Lord Jesu Christ."

More shouting. The king—Arthur?—rises from a throne at the head of the table. Everybody falls silent. The king says, "Alas, said King Arthur unto Sir Gawaine, ye have nigh slain me with the vow and promise that ye have made; for through ye have bereft me the fairest fellowship and the truest of knighthood that ever were seen together in any realm of the world; for when they depart from hence I am sure they all shall never meet more in this world, for they shall die many in the quest. And so it forthinketh me a little, for I have loved them as well as my life, wherefore it shall grieve me right sore, the departition of this fellowship."

"Girl," says a man in rough brown wool. "Get ye to yer work!"

I do, while the knights argue and the ladies weep and the king keeps saying, "Gawaine, Gawaine, ye have set me in great sorrow."

I am there eleven days. One hundred and fifty knights leave on the quest for the Holy Grail. A religious prophet turns up to say that no lady may go on the quest because all women are unclean, which puts the ladies in a more foul mood than they already were by the departure of their men. And I am left behind with them. Guenevere is the worst, alternately crying and raging at Arthur, at her women, at the servants.

Not that I see much of her. I thought servants' lives in *David Copperfield* and *Middlemarch* were hard—but this! Only *Les Misérables* had been worse.

Rough labor from way before dawn to after dark. Sleeping huddled on dirty straw in an unheated room, packed together for warmth in a cold winter. I get chilblains on my hands, which fester and burst, making it an agony to touch anything. The food is ample enough, but very poor: gruel with the dead insects from the grain bins still in it, bread so hard I chip a tooth. I lose weight, am cuffed alongside the head by the kitchen women, am screamed at by a lady who smells almost as bad as I do. One evening, a male servant is flogged bloody in the outer ward. I never learn what he did.

Almost, I am glad to return to the library, although I stare at the books on their orderly shelves with hatred.

"Welcome back," Grandmother says, polishing a brass tray inlaid with silver. She and my mother brought it back from their summer trip to Morocco.

"It isn't right to punish me like this," I gasp. "It was an accident!"

She doesn't answer.

I begin to think about suicide.

The next time, I don't recognize the place, or the people. I stand on the wide veranda of a house perched on rocks above a cold sea, dull green-gray and restless. The house, weathered gray, looms four stories above me. I shiver, not knowing what to do, until a young, handsome man in Levis comes out of the front door, holding a coffee cup. He has strong shoulders and a weak chin.

"Oh—you the girl from the village? To help clean for the party?"

And then I know that I am. "Yes, sir."

"Well, go on inside, you're shivering. Tackie's in the kitchen and he'll tell you what needs doing." He drains his coffee cup, sets it on the veranda railing, and bounds down the steps toward a sporty red Jaguar. I take the coffee cup into the kitchen. It's warmed by an old-fashioned stove. A boy sits at the table, eating sugary cereal. The boy looks up.

"Are you Tackie? I'm the girl from the village here to—"

"Clean, I know." He smiles, an unhappy smile. "Mama said you should first clean the bedrooms on the second floor for Aunt May and Aunt Julia. They're coming here to help with the party."

"Okay. Will you show me which rooms they are? And where the cleaning supplies are?"

"Sure." When he gets up, I see how thin he is. "What's your name?"

"Katie."

"I'm Tackman Babcock."

He brings a book with him, a thick and heavy book, old looking. I can't see the title. The rooms I'm supposed to clean are thick with dust, as if no one has been in them for months. They smell musty. I throw open the windows, dust and mop and find linens for the beds, remove old ashes from the fireplaces. The stationery on the desk is headed "HOUSE of 31 FEBRUARY," which makes no sense. I take the small rag rugs outside to shake them, since there seems to be no vacuum cleaner. Tackie is on the front porch, huddled in a sheepskin jacket, reading.

I say, "Aren't you cold?"

He looks up vaguely, snapped too suddenly from the world of his book, uncertain for a moment where he is. I recognize that feeling, from back when books were a delight to me. He says, "Oh. Katie. Did you talk to Mama?"

"No. Where is she?"

"In the kitchen. She wants to see you."

Mrs. Babcock is there with the handsome young man named Jason, and his hand is on her breast. When I come in he removes it, but not very fast. She is pretty, dressed in a silk bathrobe too light for the weather. I know immediately that she is on something. Her pupils are big as dimes, and she has that bright, jerky way of talking.

"Oh, Katie! There you are! If you could start with the bedrooms for my sister and sister-in-law, who—"

"I already did those, ma'am."

"Oh! Of course you did—silly me! Tackie told me. Well, then, the other rooms. Whatever looks like it needs doing."

"Yes, ma'am." Jason ignores me. I'm not surprised; I'm not pretty. Jason is just as transparent to me as Mrs. Babcock is.

I spend the rest of the day cleaning. The work is easy. Hot running water! Toilet brushes! Windex! Grandmother must be slipping.

In the late afternoon I go back downstairs. Mrs. Babcock and

Jason have disappeared into her bedroom. Tackie has reclaimed the kitchen, reading at the table.

I say, "What about dinner?"

"Dinner?" he says, as if the word is Sanskrit.

"Yes . . . *dinner*. Who usually cooks it?"

"Nobody."

I find the pantry and old-fashioned refrigerator well stocked. Tackie actually looks up from his book as I fry lamb chops, fix mashed potatoes, cook frozen green beans. His little mouth hangs open in astonishment and anticipation. I take a tray up to Mrs. Babcock and Jason. She, too, is astonished.

"Well, damn," Jason says, eyes on the lamb chops.

Tackie and I eat in the kitchen. He is a very silent child. Outside, the sea surges rhythmically in a rising wind. Finally I say, "What are you reading?"

He pauses, fork halfway to his mouth, as if this is a dangerous question. He says, "A book."

"What's it about?"

"Stuff."

"Can I see?"

Obediently, reluctantly, he hands it over. The pages are tinted yellow, a few dog-eared. *The Island of Doctor Death*. I hold back my snort; this is a long way from *Anna Karenina*. I glance at a random paragraph, and the kitchen disappears.

I am in another castle, standing in a stone corridor beside an open door. Inside the room a man in evening clothes stands beside another man strapped onto a table. The second man is naked; the first looks over him and straight at me. I run; there is no shout to halt, no pursuit. At the end of the corridor something comes around the corner and I scream.

It doesn't seem to hear. Huge, shaggy, half man and half beast, it lumbers past as if I don't exist, heading for the room I just fled.

What the fuck?

Cautiously I tiptoe back down the stone corridor. Condensation drips from the walls. Standing outside the room, I hear the book's dialogue.

"Do you mean that you *made* these monsters?"

"*Made* them? Did God make Eve, Captain, when he took her from Adam's rib? Or did Adam make the bone and God *alter* it to become what he wished? Look at it this way, Captain. I am God and Nature is Adam."

A hunchbacked . . . thing ambles past me and into the room. It doesn't see me any more than the first monster had, or the naked man, or the crazy torturer. Here, I am invisible. Pure observer.

So I observe. I watch Bruno, the former St. Bernard, free Captain Ransom. I watch Ransom in turn rescue the impossibly gorgeous girl Talar: Gisele Bündchen crossed with a Barbie doll. I watch her tell him about "a city older than civilization, buried in the jungle here on this little island," and I laugh aloud at the sheer exuberant schlockiness of Tackie's book. I watch them escape the castle of Dr. Death and set out for Lemuria.

Am I stuck in this book?

For a while, I don't care. I'm not hungry, not used like a slave, not beaten. Not even seen. Most of all, and for the first time since my mother died, I'm not afraid—until I realize I might be trapped here for good. Will my grandmother's black arts work if I am in a book within a book? *Can I get out?*

The moment I think that, I'm back in the kitchen of the House of 31 February, and Tackie has just started on his third lamb chop. I had chosen the moment of return, willing myself out of the story.

"Tackie," I say shakily, "do . . . do you ever go inside your book? Go where Captain Ransom and Bruno and Talar and the others are?"

He picks up a forkful of mashed potatoes drenched in too much butter. "No," he says, not looking at me, his thin little face flushed, "but sometimes the book people come out to me. I don't go in."

But I had. Ransom hadn't come into the tale of the House of February 31; I had gone into his. Maybe because Tackie is already a character in a story, and I am not? Before I can ask Tackie anything else, I'm back in Grandmother's library.

She is rearranging the collection of ivory and jade figurines that she and my mother bought in Thailand. Fabulously expensive, they sit on the library mantel, flanked by tall cherry bookshelves of leather-bound classics. "Welcome back, Caitlin," Grandmother says.

I am not as innocent as Tackie. I am experienced with this evil old woman. More important, I have had days of calm, safe invisibility: time to think and plan.

"No," I scream as if in pain, writhing on the floor. "No, please, Grandmother . . . not there, not again!" I burst into tears. It is surprisingly easy. "Send me to *Les Misérables* rather than there!"

She pauses, an exquisite carved Kinnaree goddess statue in her hand, her face first surprised and then sly. "It was difficult?" she says with mock, razored sympathy.

I sob louder.

I knew there was no chance she would ever have read *The Island of Doctor Death*.

My mother died when I was not quite thirteen. She had taken me downtown to shop for school clothes, a once-a-year expedition I always looked forward to with hungry longing. For one whole glorious afternoon I would have her complete attention. Me, not Grandmother, with whom Mother spent most days talking, laughing, and traveling, always traveling on Grandmother's trust fund while I stayed home with a succession of uncaring maids and a picture of the dead father I couldn't remember.

We picked out boots at Nordstrom, skirts at Saks, tops at a trendy place for teens. "After all," Mother said gaily, "you're going into junior high!" We stepped off the curb, both of us laden with packages. A silver Lexus sped around the corner, going too fast. Mother dropped her packages and shoved me out of the way. She was killed instantly.

At the wake I clutched a book, my only escape from grief, and my grandmother stared at me across the open coffin. That was the first time the icy wind blew into my mind.

What if entering Tackie's novel was a freak occurrence, something that never happens again?

The next day, I attack Grandmother with a fireplace poker. I can't reach her, of course; it's not like I haven't tried before. She shoots me a look of contempt, the summons comes, and I'm back on the veranda of the House of 31 February. But Tackie, clutching his book, is leaving. He's climbing into a car with a middle-aged woman and a gray-haired man, who carries his suitcase. The drug-addicted mother and slimy boyfriend are already gone. Only a pair of Tackie's aunts are left, May and Julie, and they don't stay long, either.

There are no other books anywhere in that huge, once majestic house. Only a stack of girlie magazines and a crushed cigarette pack in what I assume was Jason's bedroom. And I can't leave the house. I wander it, a ghost in a story that's already over, for three long days before Grandmother yanks me back.

This time I smile, stretch, and go to shower without speaking to her.

Next time it will not be *The Island of Doctor Death*.

I don't know what it will be. But Tackie Babcock is not the only fictional character who reads. I think of Marianne Dashwood praising Cowper, reading Shakespeare with Colonel Brandon. Of Anna Karenina, bending over book after book at Vozdvizhenskoe. Of Jane Eyre, reading away her loneliness at Gateshead Hall and Lowood Institute and Thornfield. Even in *Les Misérables,* although Fantine could not read, Cosette did. All I would have to do was find Cosette and dive into her book. Or anyone else's.

And then I would climb out when I chose, after staying as long as I chose. Because now I understand fully what I have always known in my guts and bones: The only escape from the illusion of stories is to go deeper into the story, *beneath* the story, where you yourself disappear and only the tale remains.

So I will hide in the stories under the stories, and there I will be safe.

Nancy Kress is the author of thirty books, including fantasy and science fiction novels, four collections of short stories, and three books on writing. For sixteen years she was also the fiction columnist for Writer's Digest *magazine. She is perhaps best known for the Sleepless trilogy that began with* Beggars in Spain. *Her work has won four Nebulas, two Hugos, a Sturgeon, and the John W. Campbell Award. Her most recent books are a collection,* Fountain of Age: Stories *(Small Beer Press, 2012); a YA fantasy written under the name Anna Kendall,* Crossing Over *(Viking, 2010); and a short novel of eco-terror,* Before the Fall, During the Fall, After the Fall *(Tachyon, 2012). Kress lives in Seattle with her husband, science fiction writer Jack Skillingstead, and Cosette, the world's most spoiled toy poodle.*

The Island of Time

JACK DANN

For Gene, who grew us all from a bean

On Gene Wolfe: *I know two Gene Wolfes. One is an affable, taciturn, witty convention companion, whom I can't resist hugging every time I see him. The other Gene Wolfe scares the living hell out of me. He's the one who writes science fiction and fantasy with the skill and depth of a Nabokov, Borges, or Joyce, a literary genius ferociously bending and twisting genre tropes into high art. A blessing on both your heads, Gene Wolfe!*

Your name is John Carter—Captain John Carter of Foster, Victoria—and you're twelve years old. Actually, you're twelve and three quarters, almost a teenager. It's a June night, and the Australian winter cold has settled deep into your bones, making you shiver as you stand in the sunken garden, just as you shiver when you're in your own bedroom: You're not allowed to keep the space heater on because it uses too much electricity.

Above you, an impossible eternity of distance above you, the gauzy span of the Milky Way is almost as bright as the moon. You've turned your head upside down to see the face in the moon before, but not tonight. Tonight you are desperate to become the *real* you . . . the grown-up you. Tonight you must focus; and so you stand under the starry sky, staring as hard as you can at the black expanse of the Southern Ocean until you sight the island landmass known as Barsoom. Although Barsoom can't be seen during the day, you know it's green and lush; the great gold and crystal spires of the city Helium on the river Iss reflect so much light that it's hard to look at them. You know that because you've seen them. Now, as you raise your arms and concentrate, as you silently call to the *real* you to come and help, to transform you, you can see the faraway city's lights twinkling and spinning. Your outstretched arms begin to ache as you shiver in the moonlight and await an answer to your call.

But there will be no answer.

Not tonight.

"Stop that, Jonathan!"

The lights of Helium blink out.

You lower your arms and turn around. "Stop what? I'm not do-ing nothin'."

Your sister Julia is wearing torn jeans and the navy blue sweater that your grandmother, may she rest in peace, knitted for her. Her blond-streaked hair is pulled back tightly into a pony-tail, and her ring-pierced lips look swollen and bruised. She's two years older than you and has breasts—you've seen them—but you would never know it by looking at her in that sweater.

"You know what," she says, poking you in the ribs. "You've just got to stop it. I heard Mother talking with the Dickhead about tak-ing you to see a shrink. Is that what you want?"

You shrug. "How would I know? I've never seen one, and you know as well as I do that the Dickhead wouldn't never allow it, any-way. He'd be afraid that—"

Your sister gets that closed, dangerous look. "Go back to the house before—"

You know you shouldn't argue with her, not after she's been hurt; but you can't help yourself. "Before what?"

She pushes you with both hands. "Before I—" And then she just walks away. You want to go after her, but she's all closed up. Angry and sad and somehow a little dead. So you take one last look out over the sea (but all you can see now are the ruddy lights of the drilling rigs off the coast of Barrie's Beach); and then you climb the stone perron, cross the manicured lawn with all its silly fluted topiaries, and quietly sneak back into the Dickhead's faux Greek Revival mansion. The rooms on the first floor all have high ceilings and chandeliers and marble fireplaces, which always impress guests, and, as the Dickhead is so fond of repeating: "It's good for business." But the maroon carpets are threadbare in spots, and you once heard someone say that all of the really good furniture and paintings had been sold long ago. Nevertheless, it's the most impressive house *you've* ever seen.

You take the stairs that lead into the servant's quarters. You skip certain steps because you know which treads creak; you know every inch of this part of the house, which is always "closed off," probably because your mother hates housecleaning and probably because it saves on fuel bills. Although your mother thinks that the Dickhead is rich—which is probably why she married him—he claims that all he's got left is the house and the cars and a small annuity, which will keep them all going until he sells his first novel for seven figures. You don't quite know what seven figures means, but you figure you'll find that out eventually.

When you reach the third floor, you duck under a low archway and carefully open the door so it doesn't squeak; then down the hall to your room, to safety . . . except that the Dickhead has been watching you all along. Watching you from your own window. Waiting for you in your room.

"What in God's good name are you doing out there at this hour?" he asks in his conversational voice, as if he were saying "Good morning."

He's wearing a heavy white bathrobe with his initials embossed on the chest pocket; your mother has one just like it. His bristly gray hair is neatly combed and still damp. Your mother tells you that he's very good-looking and his cleft chin is a sign of strength and resolve, but he reminds you of a silly, gangly guy you used to watch on television when you were a kid. His name was Mr. Cracker, and he lived in a house that was painted like a barber's pole. However, you suppose that the Dickhead looks nice. He has an old, crinkly, and happy kind of face, which makes you hate him all the more.

"Well, are you going to answer me?"

"Yessir."

"How many times do I have to tell you, call me Dick . . . or Dad."

You already have a father, and he's not dead, just gone away, so you say, "Okay . . . Dick."

"Now, tell me, what were you doing out in the sunken garden at this ungodly hour?"

"Nothin'. Just looking out, you know."

"Without a jacket? You're shivering even now."

You can't tell him that it won't work if you have too many clothes on. By rights you should be naked when you make what Tars Tarkas calls the *sak* of transformation. (*Sak* means jump in the language of Barsoom's green men; more about all *that* later.) But the *sak* of transformation works sometimes, even when you're just wearing pants and a shirt: no socks or underwear.

"Well?"

"Yeah," you say, sloping your shoulders, "it was pretty dumb."

"But why on earth would you go outside like that to freeze your butt off in the middle of the night?" He's earnest now, earnest and caring; and you know just what to say. But as you say it, you hope that your mother is awake, so he won't . . . linger.

"I dunno, sometimes I wake up thinking about my dad, and I get scared and then I find myself outside and—"

"Well, get undressed and try to get some sleep," he says in what you think of as his forgiving voice. But he's sly. You know that about him.

"You'll have to be up in a few hours for school."

You try not to wince as he gentles your hair and pats your face. He sees you into bed and pats you again. You pretend to fall asleep and don't open your eyes until he leaves, and then you listen to the floorboards creak as he slowly walks through the hallway. You hold your breath as he passes your sister's room, because you know she's not in there. You hear the doorknob squeak like a mouse as he opens her bedroom door, then silence—the silence of the stars; one beat, the silence of the moon; two beats, the silence of deep black you're-dead-forever water; three beats—and finally you hear the door close and the creak of footsteps fading down the hallway. You exhale.

"Darling?" It's your mother calling the Dickhead. "Are the kids all right?"

"Yeah," says the Dickhead, his voice soft but clear in the echoic darkness. "Jonnie couldn't sleep, poor kid. But he's all tucked up now."

"And Julia?"

You wait for it . . .

"She's fine, honey," he says with a chuckle, and you hear the sticky sound of their bedroom door closing.

Although you can't hear anything now, you *know* what he's saying.

"That little girl of yours is pretty near a grown woman."

"Pretty near," you whisper guiltily. *The Dickhead was pretty near, but he's gone now.*

You squeeze your eyes closed and dream of Tars Tarkas and the *real* you.

Tars Tarkas is three hundred and seventeen years old and weighs about four hundred pounds. He stands fifteen feet tall, has a vertical slit for a nose, a fanged mouth framed by four enamel-white tusks the length of your arms, and two crimson eyes that bug out of the sides of his head; if he needs to (and he often does because he's a green-blooded warrior chieftain), he can see in two directions at once. His scaly skin looks like rough-cut jade, and he's your very best friend . . . or, rather, he will *become* your very best friend once you grow up into what you're supposed to be.

You first met him on the school bus.

Well, you found his four-armed picture on the cover of a magazine scrunched under the cushion of your seat. The wrinkled, yellow-stained magazine was thick as a book and still smelled of lemon cordial. And there he was, the one and only Tars Tarkas—scimitar, spear, carbine, and sapphire-pommeled battle-axe in hand—holding back an army of slavering, reptilian centurions. Beside him, but not dwarfed by the jade-skinned Barsoomian, stood a sandy-haired, broad-shouldered Earthman. And right then and there—without even having to read the magazine—you knew who that Earthman was. It was *you*, the grown-up you, the real you. And there you were, standing tall and unafraid, army knife gleaming under the silvery light of the twin moons, protecting a half-naked princess—who looked just like your sister—from a leaping, two-headed Martian tiger.

Your sister told you to leave the dirty, old magazine on the bus, but you stuffed it into your book satchel. At lunch break you sneaked away to Pearl Park, sat under the gazebo near the stream, ate your peanut butter and jelly sandwich, and read the magazine until you knew it by heart. Then you buried it because now it was *yours*; you wouldn't need paper and pictures to remember who you really were. And no matter what the Dickhead might try to do to you, the real you (who stands six foot seven and can jump thirty feet in the air on Barsoom) would be able to protect your sister.

It doesn't matter that you are skinny and pimply and only twelve and three-quarters, because the real you and your companion Tars Tarkas have given their solemn word that they will come to help whenever you call. All *you* have to do is follow proper procedure: raise your naked arms at just the right hour, encompass the night sky, and remember the proper sequence of incantations taught to you by Tars Tarkas in the sacred language of his people, the green Thants.

But unless you do it right, unless your thoughts are properly focused and calibrated to the exact telegraphic frequency, you will just stand there like an idiot in your birthday suit; and there will be no *sak* of transformation.

No Barsoom.

No adventures with Tars Tarkas and the grown-up Captain John Carter.

And . . . no help here on Earth.

You've been crossing out the days on your free pocket calendar from JOHN'S MEAT EMPORIUM, FOSTER, and now it's the Queen's Birthday weekend, which means trouble because the Dickhead is home and prowling about. The weather has become unseasonably warm, and tonight—Saturday nights are *always* the worst—you hear the Dickhead's footsteps, the squeak and squeal of doorknob and door, and the consequent soft banging noises in your sister's bedroom. Quiet as a snake and angry as a two-headed tiger, you sneak out of your room. The Dickhead won't hear the *tap-click* of your bedroom door latch, not with all that stentorian breathing, and then you're free and breathing the cool, unstrangulated air of the sunken garden.

But you've no time for air and freedom.

You need to save your sister, so—difficult as it may be to concentrate—you raise your arms to embrace the star-spangled night and pray (in the sacred Thantian language) for the familiar, blindingly bright flash of transformation.

This time the gods of Mars grant your wish.

But something is terribly wrong. . . .

You're standing in familiar surroundings on a yellow, mossy plateau overlooking Helium. The huge city is in flames, its crown of gold and crystal spires shattered. Gaily colored, fire-bombing aerostats circle in the smoky sky above, two-masted catamaran warships crowd the River Iss, and armies swarm like ants around Helium's breeched fortifications. Although the wind is high at this elevation—keening and whistling through the stunted blood-colored trees and quartz outcrops—you can still hear the distant thunder of bombs exploding, arms clashing, and men screaming in blood-fury.

Your eyes burn and tear in the strong Martian sunlight as you look around Tars Tarkas's camp. There are no chariots, mastodons, warriors, women, or children to be seen. All the tents are gone, except yours, and the campfires are long dead. You turn your gaze back to the burning city. You are certain that your friends, human and Thant alike, are down there fighting the invading hordes of lizard men and white apes, and you must find them. They rode to battle upon their mastodons and eight-legged, white-bellied riding beasts, but yours is nowhere to be found. No matter, because your muscles—which are conveniently adapted to the much stronger gravity of Earth—give you the strength to vault and leap as if you were wearing seven-league boots.

As you've no time to waste, you dress quickly. You collect your saber, knife, and carbine (which shoots radium projectiles), and then you step outside and take a deep breath of the clean Martian air. Now you finally, finally *feel* like your true self.

You're the John Carter who saves his friends.

You're the John Carter who *will* save his sister.

And so you run, bounding over gullies and crevasses that ordinary Martian riders would have to go around, vaulting over hills, trees, and settlements. With every gravity-defying step you take, the clangor of iron and steel and the cries of men and monsters become louder and louder . . . and the clouds of dust and smoke kicked up by the fighting hordes and carried hither and thither by the wind become incrementally closer. After an hour, your legs begin to ache, you're out of breath, and a wall of dust and smoke looms up and over you. One step, two steps, three, and now you're right in the fray. Lizard men astride two-headed octopeds the size of hippopotamuses attack you, but you have no time to waste: You must find Tars Tarkas.

With lightning-fast sweeps of your saber, you decapitate the heads of the nearest octoped and, in quick succession, shoot three of the reptilian beast-riders with your carbine. Then you take a great leap over the other beast-riders and land just inside the breached fortifications. But you are almost knocked to the ground by a mob of deserters. You're surprised because the warriors are wearing the emblems, brassards, and purple and rose colors of Helium guards. You stop one of the deserters and ask him for the whereabouts of the Thant fighters. He looks at you, shakes his head, laughs, and then disappears into the dust-swirling miasma of fighting men and beasts.

You press forward toward an open area where the clash of weapons is the loudest. And it is there—in the slaughtery that had once been the Queen's private gardens—that you find Thant warriors fighting lizard men and white apes. Although greatly outnumbered, the jade-skinned Thants—unlike men—will not retreat.

And neither will you.

"Tars Tarkas!" you shout as you cleave and hew, as you and the outnumbered Thant warriors begin to turn the advance of these beast-riders and white apes into a rout. "Tars Tarkas!"

Your voice is hoarse. Your hands are slippery with blood.

"Tars Tarkas!"

"Ah, welcome, John Carter of Foster. I was afraid we would not look upon each other again."

You feel (rather than hear) his responding call; and you fear the worst, for you know that Tars Tarkas is loathe to reveal his telepathic sigil to anyone.

"But you must make haste, Earth friend, if we are to fight and— with the blessing of the great River Iss—die together in battle."

You leap across the gardens and fight your way past the Queen's treasury and the shattered halls of governance, but you're too late: No Thant (not even Tars Tarkas) standing alone without carbine or cannon could overcome a troop of lizard men astride their two-headed, shark-jawed octopeds. Before you can reach him, one of the octopeds bites through his lower right arm and slams him to the ground. But Tars Tarkas slashes at the creature with his other arms. The huge beast rears back, squealing in pain and dislodging its rider, who was positioning himself to take Tars Tarkas's head as a prize.

You shoot the stinking, flesh-hungry beast.

It dies open-jawed, revealing Tars Tarkas's dismembered arm, which seems to be reaching out to you from the rows of bloodied, needle-sharp teeth. Its dismounted rider rushes toward you. You barely have time to deflect his poison-tipped spear. But as you decapitate him with a roundhouse swing of your saber, you hear someone sound the call. A dozen Thant warriors materialize out of the smoke and dust; and as they slaughter the lizard men and their beasts, you try to carry your friend to safety.

"No, John Carter," Tars Tarkas says in a thick, raspy voice. He presses one of his remaining large, nail-less hands against his wound to stem the flow of blood. "I must die *here,* standing and fighting. Gird me to fight. Help me, Earth friend, as I would help you."

You tourniquet his wound with your belt and then gently lift him to a standing position. Leaning back against a blood-smeared wall, he grimaces—which is the Thant version of a smile—grips his sapphire-pommeled battle-axe in one hand and his scimitar and spear in the others, and says, "I suppose these will have to do. One of the octos ate my rifle, anyway." Then he shakes his head twice, a gesture of great sadness and serious import. "You came to help us in our time of need, but, alas, I will not be able to reciprocate. Your sister . . . you must save her yourself, you must—"

The white apes attack, and as you stand together fighting, you sense the instant that Tars Tarkas dies. You *feel* the whisper of good-bye, and you know that the greatest Thant warrior on Mars was not defeated by his enemies: His two great hearts simply stopped beating. And still, even in death, he stands upright.

But you . . . you fight on alone until a war hammer crashes into flesh and bone. *Your* flesh and bone.

And thus you fall back to Earth.

Back into the sunken garden . . .

Into the long sunlight of a winter afternoon.

You open your eyes and then turn your head away from the sun. You have a terrible, pounding headache, and your arms and legs feel stiff and tingly. You look toward the Dickhead's house and wonder what happened.

Every other time you've gone to Mars, even when you've spent days and weeks there, you'd always find yourself back on Earth within a few minutes (Australian Eastern Standard Time). This isn't Saturday night, and you *know* you're in trouble. No sense trying to sneak back into the Dickhead's house; you'll just have to think this through.

But you don't even know what day this is. It could be Sunday or next week. You can tell Mom and the Dickhead that you fell asleep and somehow got amnesia like Arnold Schwarzenegger in *Total Recall* or Gregory Peck in *Spellbound*. Or that you were abducted like the kid in *Ransom* . . . or that you ran away because you want to be an entrepreneur or a writer and don't want to go to school anymore; but then, hallelujah, you saw the light of reason (the Dickhead's reason) and decided to come back home.

Or you can just tell them that you were on Mars—they would believe that!

As you stand up, your mind suddenly reels with memory and grief. Now you feel it. Now you know it. Now you believe it.

Tars Tarkas is dead!

Although you feel small and weak and alone, although you feel every one of your twelve and three-quarter years, you walk big as life through the garden to the house. You open the front door with such force that the brass knocker bangs up and down. And as you stand in the checkerboard-tiled hallway, you feel exactly as you did when you heard Tars Tarkas's telepathic whisper of farewell.

You walk into the reception room.

"Hello? Is anybody home?"

You check the living room, library, study, kitchen, mudroom, pantry, and dining room. Then you run upstairs, up the curved staircase and through the hallway, past the guestrooms and entertainment center. *Click.* You open the door to your mother and the Dickhead's bedroom. You smell strong, sweet perfume: *Joy.* The mirror on the wall over your mother's dressing table is all cracked, and a triangular splinter sparkles on the carpet. Perfume bottles and your mother's favorite jade lamp are also all over the carpet. The bed isn't made, and your mother's bras, stockings, underwear, and dresses are strewn across the pink-and-black sheets. You don't see any of the Dickhead's clothes, though, and suddenly you're scared.

Something is wrong, very wrong . . .

You step on a yellow-lined notepad—what's *that* doing on the floor?—as you rush back into the hallway, pass under the archway and up three steps into the servants' quarters. You open the door to your sister's room. You know it's silly, but you're afraid that she's dead, that the Dickhead has hurt her again, only this time . . . this time . . .

The room is empty, the house is empty, and you imagine—silly as it is to have such thoughts—that the *world* is empty, and you'll be alone forever. You call out your sister's name, just to hear the sound of it.

"Julia."

You listen to the house sounds and call again, "Julia? Sis?" You want to tell your sister that you *tried* to bring Tars Tarkas back to help her.

If only . . . if only you could have returned to Earth as your true self this one time: But you *always* return as the small and weak and guilty you. And right now you wish that you could keep getting smaller and smaller and smaller until you just . . . disappeared.

You go back to the Dickhead and your mother's room. Something is niggling at you. The yellow notepad. You pick it up and see the indentations like writing without ink on the top sheet. You know the trick of reading secret writing, so you take the pad back to your room, sit down at your built-in desk and ever so lightly rub a soft number-two pencil over the indentations.

> *Dear Mother,*
> *I'm sorry I'm really sorry but I have to leave. You <u>KNOW</u>*
> *why and if you really don't ~~then you must be blind~~ well*
> *then I just don't know. Dick hurts me and he hurts Jon*
> *and I would have taken him with me if he hadn't already*
> *run away somewhere. You should get*

That's all you can make out, but it's enough, enough to let you know that it's all your fault and that she thinks you ran away and left her with the Dickhead.

You hear the door open downstairs.

You're shivering and your hands are shaking, but you go into your closet, reach up, up, stretching, and grab a hammer that you've hidden behind a bunch of stuff on the top shelf. It's just a regular hammer, not a war hammer like the one you carried on Barsoom, but it will have to do. Quiet as a cat, you slip out of your room and down the hall. Your only chance is surprise. You'll have to jump out and crack the Dickhead on the head before he knows what happened. Then you can . . . well, you'll worry about what to do once he's dead.

But it's not the Dickhead. You can tell by the *clattery-clack* of your mother's high-heeled shoes on the tiles. You see that she's alone, and you drop the hammer onto the carpet. When she sees you, she shouts, "Oh, God, oh, thank God you're all right," and she drops her keys, patent leather handbag, and groceries, and smothers you with a hug. Then she pulls away from you, but doesn't let go of your arms. Her eyes are glossy with tears, her usually clean and frizzy autumn brown hair is straggly and pulled back with an amberina comb, and her right eye and cheek are swollen and black and blue. "Where *were* you, Jon? I was so sick with worry." She hugs you again, and you can smell a kind of sour-sweet perspiration on her blue cashmere sweater.

"I . . . I didn't mean to be gone so long," you say. "What day's today?"

She looks at you the way she does when she thinks you're telling a whopper. "It's Wednesday. You've been gone four days. You must be starving."

You are kind of hungry.

"Where's the . . . where's Dick?"

Your mother gets a closed, almost sly look . . . just like your sister's. "You don't have to worry about— He won't be back. I promise."

"Cross your heart and hope to die?"

"Cross my heart and hope to die." She hugs you again and makes a wailing sound. When she's done, you pick up her groceries and follow her into the kitchen. You notice that there are dirty dishes in the sink: She's never left dirty dishes in the sink before.

"What about Julia?" you ask as you put the plastic grocery bags on the counter. Just saying her name makes you want to cry. But *you* don't cry, even though it's all your fault.

"Oh, she's out. But she'll be back soon." Your mother doesn't look at you when she says that. She takes a stack of frozen dinners out of one of the bags, puts them in the freezer, and then she looks at you. "Now, Jon, you must tell me where you've been. Did your stepfather try to . . . did anybody try to—" She sobs, and you don't want to worry her, so you tell her that nobody tried anything and you ran away because you didn't want to go to school. But you finally saw the light of reason and came back home. "But . . . where did you go? Where did you sleep? What did you eat?"

You make something up that doesn't involve Tars Tarkas—you can't say his name either without feeling like something hard has caught in your throat—and after dinner you promise that you'll never, ever leave her again.

Even though you know that's a lie.

The radium dial on your alarm clock glows 3:07 AM THURSDAY 14 JUN. Without bothering to dress, you get up and quietly go downstairs. You open the door to the garage, pull your 6061 aluminum-frame, eighteen-speed pearl white mountain bike off the wall rack, and then walk it back into the house and out the servants' side door. It's a chilly, moonless morning, and clouds obscure most of the stars. You look out over the Southern Ocean, but can't see Barsoom. Even if you could, there would be no lights spinning and twinkling in Helium. You turn away, walk your bike over the lawn to the laneway, and you're off, pedaling hard through the gears, now pedaling down O'Grady's Ridge Road, and then Fish Creek Road. Half an hour later, you come to your turn-off. You go around the big sawhorses blocking the dirt road that winds its way to a high perch overlooking the sea. From there you can see *everything*.

It's your secret place . . . yours and no one else's.

When you reach the embankment, you lean your bike against a gum tree, throw your pajamas down beside it, shiver, and then walk over to the edge. Although you've never been able to jump from here—the *sak* of transformation only seems to work in the Dickhead's sunken garden—you don't care.

You gaze at the night-black water in the distance below, whisper a prayer in the sacred Thantian language, and then, arms outstretched, you lean out into the cool darkness.

You couldn't save your sister.

Perhaps you can save yourself.

Jack Dann has written or edited more than seventy-five books, including the international bestseller The Memory Cathedral, *which has been published in more than ten languages and was number one on the* Age *bestseller list. He is a recipient of the Nebula Award, the World Fantasy Award, the Australian Aurealis Award (three times), the Ditmar Award (four times), the Peter McNamara Achievement Award and also the Peter McNamara Convenors' Award for Excellence, and the Premios Gilgames de Narrativa Fantastica. He has also been honored by the Mark Twain Society as an Esteemed Knight.*

Jack's latest novel, The Rebel: An Imagined Life of James Dean, *was published by HarperCollins Flamingo in Australia and by Morrow in the United States. A companion volume of stories entitled* Promised Land *has also been published in Great Britain. His other short story collections include* Timetipping, Jubilee, Visitations, *and* The Fiction Factory. *Recent publications include the short novel* The Economy of Light *(2008), the autobiography* Insinuations, *and a special reprint edition of his 1981 novel* Junction.

He is also the coeditor of the groundbreaking anthology of Australian stories, Dreaming Down-Under, *which won the World Fantasy Award in 1999. He edited the* Magic Tales *anthology series with Gardner Dozois; and the anthology* Gathering the Bones, *of which he was a coeditor, was included in* Library Journal's *Best Genre Fiction of 2003 and was shortlisted for the World Fantasy Award. His an-thology* Wizards, *coedited with Gardner Dozois and titled* Dark Alchemy *in Great Britain, was shortlisted for the World Fantasy Award. His latest anthology,* Ghosts by Gaslight, *coedited with Nick Gevers, which was listed as one of* Publishers Weekly's *Top Ten SF, Fantasy, and Horror Picks, won the Aurealis Award and the Shirley Jackson Award, and was shortlisted for the Bram Stoker Award.*

Jack lives in Australia on a farm overlooking the sea and "com-mutes" back and forth to Los Angeles and New York. His website is www.jackdann.com.

The She-Wolf's Hidden Grin

MICHAEL SWANWICK

On Gene Wolfe: The Fifth Head of Cerberus *is an important book for me. I was twenty-two years old, determined
to be a writer, and still eight years away from publication
when I first encountered it, and it radically expanded my
awareness of what fiction could be and do. Forty years
later, it can still be reread with astonishment and wonder.
As for Wolfe himself . . . he remains the best writer science
fiction has ever produced and almost certainly the single
best writer of our times. If I could, I'd arrange for his face
to be carved on a mountainside, sixty feet high. A writer's
income being what it is, however, this story will have to do.*

When I was a girl, my sister Susanna and I had to get up early
whether we were rested or not. In winter particularly, our day often
began before sunrise, and because our dormitory was in the south
wing of the house, with narrow windows facing the central courtyard and thus facing north, the lurid, pinkish light sometimes was
hours late in arriving, and we would wash and dress while we were
still uncertain whether we were awake. Groggy and only half co-
herent, we would tell each other our dreams.

One particular dream I narrated to Susanna several times before
she demanded I stop. In it, I stood before the main doorway to our
house staring up at the marble bas-relief of a she-wolf suckling two
infant girls (though in waking life the babies similarly feeding had
wee chubby penises my sister and I had often joked about), with a

puzzled sense that something was fundamentally wrong. "You are anxious for me to come out of hiding," a rasping whispery voice said in my ear. "Aren't you, daughter?"

I turned and was not surprised to find the she-wolf standing behind me, her tremendous head on the same level as my own. She was far larger than any wolf from ancestral Earth. Her fur was greasy and reeked of sweat. Her breath stank of carrion. Her eyes said that she was perfectly capable of ripping open my chest and eating my heart without the slightest remorse. Yet, in the way of dreams, I was not afraid of her. She seemed to be as familiar as my own self.

"Is it time?" I said, hardly knowing what I was asking.

"No," the mother-wolf said, fading.

And I awoke.

Last night I returned to my old dormitory room and was astonished at how small it was, how cramped and airless; it could never have held something so unruly and commodious as my childhood. Yet legions of memories rose up from its dust to batter against me like moths, so thickly that I was afraid to breathe lest they should fly into my throat and lungs to choke me. Foremost among them being the memory of when I first met the woman from Sainte Anne who was the last in a long line of tutors brought to educate my sister and me.

Something we had seen along the way had excited the two of us, so that we entered the lesson room in a rush, accompanied by shrieks of laughter, only to be brought up short by a stranger waiting there. She was long-legged, rangy, lean of face, dressed in the dowdy attire of a woman who had somehow managed to acquire a university education, and she carried a teacher's baton. As we sat at our desks, she studied us as a heron might some dubious species of bait fish, trying to decide if it was edible. Susanna recovered first. "What has happened to Miss Claire?" she asked.

In a voice dry and cool and unsympathetic, the stranger said,

"She has been taken away by the secret police. For what offenses, I cannot say. I am her replacement. You will call me Tante Amélie."

"'Tante' is a term of endearment," I said impudently, "which you have done nothing to earn."

"It is not yours to decide where your affection is to be directed. That is your father's prerogative, and in this instance the decision has already been made. What are your favorite subjects?"

"Molecular and genetic biology," Susanna said promptly.

"Classical biology." I did not admit that chiefly I enjoyed the wet lab, and that only because I enjoyed cutting things open, for I had learned at an early age to hold my cards close to my chest.

"Hmmph. We'll begin with history. Where were you with your last instructor?"

"We were just about to cover the Uprising of Sainte Anne," Susanna said daringly.

Again that look. "It is too soon to know what the truth of that was. When the government issues an official history, I'll let you know. In the meantime we might as well start over from the beginning. You." She pointed at Susanna. "What is Veil's Hypothesis?"

"Dr. Aubrey Veil posited that the abos—"

"Aborigines."

Susanna stared in astonishment, and then continued. "It is the idea that when the ships from Earth arrived on Sainte Anne, the aborigines killed everyone and assumed their appearance."

"Do you think this happened? Say no."

"No."

"Why not?"

"If it had, that would mean that we—everyone on Sainte Anne and Sainte Croix both—were abos. Aborigines, I mean. Yet we think as humans, act as humans, live as humans. What would be the point of so elaborate a masquerade if its perpetrators could never enjoy the fruits of their deceit? Particularly when the humans had proved to be inferior by allowing themselves to be exterminated.

Anyway, mimicry in nature is all about external appearance. The first time an aborigine's corpse was cut open in a morgue, the game would be over."

Turning to me, Tante Amélie said, "Your turn. Defend the hypothesis."

"The aborigines were not native to Sainte Anne. They came from the stars," I began.

Susanna made a rude noise. Our new tutor raised her baton and she lowered her eyes in submission. "Defend your premise," Tante Amélie said.

"They are completely absent from the fossil record."

"Go on."

"When they arrived in this star system, they had technology equal to or superior to our own, which, due to some unrecorded disaster, they lost almost immediately. Otherwise they would have also been found here on Sainte Croix." I was thinking furiously, making it all up as I went along. "They rapidly descended to a Stone Age level of existence. As intelligent beings, they would have seen what was going on and tried to save some aspect of their sciences. Electronics, metallurgy, chemistry—all disappeared. All they could save was their superior knowledge of genetics. When humans came along, they could not resist us physically. So they interbred with us, producing human offspring with latent aboriginal genes. They would have started with pioneers and outliers and then moved steadily inward into human society, spreading first through the lower classes and saving the rich and best-defended for last. Once begun, the process would proceed without conscious mediation. The aborigines would not awaken until their work was done."

"Supporting evidence?"

"The policies of the government toward the poor suggest an awareness of this threat on their part."

"I see that I have fallen into a den of subversives. No wonder your last tutor is no more. Well, what's past is over now. Place your hands flat on your desks, palms down." We obeyed and Tante Amélie rapped our knuckles with her baton, as all our tutors had done at the beginning of their reigns. "We will now consider the early forms of colonial government."

Tante Amélie was the daughter of a regional administrator in a rural district called Île d'Orléans. As a girl, she had climbed trees to plunder eggs from birds' nests and trapped beetles within castles of mud. She also gigged frogs, fished from a rowboat, caught crabs with a scrap of meat and a length of string, plucked chickens, owned a shotgun, hunted waterfowl, ground her own telescope lenses, and swam naked in the backwater of a river so turbulent it claimed at least one life every year. This was as alien and enchanting as a fairy tale to my sister and me, and of an evening we could sometimes coax her into reminiscing. Even now I can see her rocking steadily in the orange glow of an oil lamp, pausing every now and again to raise a sachet of dried herbs from her lap so the scents of lemon, vanilla, and tea leaves would help her memory. She had made it to adulthood and almost to safety before her father "inhaled his fortune," as the saying went on our sister planet. But of the years between then and her fetching up with us, she would say nothing.

It may seem odd that my sister and I came to feel something very close to love for Tante Amélie. But what alternative did we have? We only rarely saw our father. Our mother had produced two girls and multiple stillbirths before being sent away and replaced with the woman we addressed only as Maitresse. None of the other tutors, even those who resisted the temptation to sample father's wares, lasted very long. Nor were we allowed outside unaccompanied by an adult, for fear of being kidnapped. There were not many objects for our young hearts to fasten upon, and Tante Amélie had the potent advantage of controlling our access to the outside world.

Our house at 999 rue d'Astarte doubled as my father's business, and so was redolent of esters, pheromones, and chemical fractions: most particularly that of bitter truffle, for he held a monopoly over its import and used it in all his perfumes as a kind of signature. There were always people coming and going: farmers bringing wagons piled high with bales of flowers, traders from the Southern Sea bearing ambergris, slave artisans lugging in parts for the stills, neurochemists summoned to fine-tune some new process, courtesans in search of aphrodisiacs and abortifacients, overfed buyers almost inevitably accompanied by children with painted faces and lace-trimmed outfits. Yet Susanna and I were only rarely allowed beyond the run of the dormitory, classroom, and laboratory. Freedom for us began at the city library, the park, the slave market, and the like. Tante Amélie was a vigorous woman with many outside interests, so our fortunes took an immediate uptick at her arrival. Then we discovered quite by accident that she had opened a bank account (legal but interest-free) in hope of one day buying her freedom. This meant that she was amenable to bribery, and suddenly our horizons were limited only by our imaginations. The years that Tante Amélie spent with us were the happiest of my life.

For my sister, too, I believe, though it was hard to tell with her. That was the period in which her passion for genetics peaked. She was always taking swabs of cell samples and patiently teasing out gene sequences from stolen strands of hair or nail clippings. Many an afternoon I trailed after her, in Tante Amélie's bought company, as she scoured the flesh market for some variant of Sainte Anne's ape or rummaged in disreputable antique shops for hand-carved implements that might be made from—but never were—genuine abo bone.

"You think I don't know what you're doing," I told her once.

"Shut up, useless."

"You're trying to prove Veil's Hypothesis. Well, what if you did? Do you think anyone would listen to you? You're just a child."

"Look who's talking."

"Even if they took you seriously, so what? What difference would it make?"

Susanna stared nobly into a future only she could see. "Madame Curie said, 'We must believe that we are gifted for something and that this thing, at whatever cost, must be attained.' If I could make just one single discovery of worth, that would atone for a great deal." Then she lowered her gaze to look directly at me, silently daring me to admit I didn't understand.

Baffled and resentful, I lapsed into silence.

I did not notice the change in my sister at first. By slow degrees she became sullen and moody and lost interest in her studies. This, for an irony, happened just as I was growing serious about my own and would have welcomed her mentorship. It was not to be. A shadow had fallen between us. She no longer confided in me as she once had; nor did we share our dreams.

Rummaging in her desk for a retractor one day, I discovered the notebook, which previously she had kept locked away, recording her great study. I had never been allowed to look at it and so I studied it intensely. Parts of it I can still recite from memory:

> This implies a congeries of recessive sex-linked genes; they, being dependent on the x-chromosome, will necessarily appear only in women.

and

> Under the right conditions, activating the operon genes in the proper sequence, the transformation would occur very rapidly, even in adults.

and

> Colonization of the twin planets entailed an extreme constriction of genetic plasticity which renders heritability of these recessives at close to one hundred percent.

and most provocative of all

> All this presupposes that abos and humans can interbreed & thus that they spring from a common star-faring (most likely extinct) race. *H. sapiens* and *H. aboriginalis* are then not two separate species but specializations of the inferred species *H. sidereus.*

The bulk of the notebook was filled with gene sequences, which despite Susanna's tidy schoolgirl script I could barely make sense of. But I journeyed through to the end of the notes and it was only when I fetched up against blank pages that I realized that she hadn't added to them in weeks.

That was the summer when Susanna conceived a passion for theater. She went to see *Riders to the Sea* and *Madame Butterfly* and *Anthony and Cleopatra* and *The Women* and *Mrs. Warren's Profession* and *Lysistrata* and *Hedda Gabler* and *The Rover* and I forget what else. She even got a small part in *The Children's Hour.* I attended one rehearsal, was not made to feel welcome, and never showed up again.

Thus it was that when I had my first period (I had been well prepared, so I recognized the symptoms and knew what to do), I did not tell her. This was on a Sunday morning in early spring. Feeling distant and unhappy, I dressed for church without saying a word to my sister. She didn't notice that I was withholding something from her, though in retrospect it seems that I could hardly have been more obvious.

We went to Sainte Dymphna's, sitting as usual in a pew halfway to the altar. Tante Amélie, of course, sat in the back of the church with the other slaves. Shortly after the Mass began, a latecomer, a young woman whom I felt certain I had seen before, slipped into our pew. She was dressed in black, with fingerless lace gloves and had a round, moon-white face dominated by two black smudges of eyes and a pair of carmine lips. I saw her catch my sister's eye and smile.

I endured the service as best I could. Since the rebellion, the Québécois liturgy had been banned, and though I understood the reasons for it, the vernacular sounded alien to my ear. Midway through the monsignor's interminable sermon, something—a chance shifting of light through the stained-glass windows, per-haps, or the unexpected flight of a demoiselle fly past my head—drew my attention away from his impassioned drone. I saw the stranger stifle a yawn with the back of her hand, then casually place that hand, knuckles down, on the pew between her and my sister. A moment later, Susanna looked away and placed her own hand atop it. Their fingers intertwined and then clenched.

And I knew.

The components for a disaster had been assembled. All that was needed was a spark.

That spark occurred when Susanna returned from cotillion in tears. I trailed along in the shadow of her disgrace, feeling a hu-miliation that was the twin of hers though I had done nothing to earn it. Nevertheless, as always happened in such cases, as soon as our escort had returned us to our father's house and made his re-port, we were summoned as a pair before Tante Amélie. She sat on a plain wooden chair, her hands overlapping on the knob of a cane she had recently taken to using, looking stern as a judge.

"You spat in the boy's face," she said without preamble. "There was no excuse for that."

"He put his hand—"

"Boys do those things all the time. It was your responsibility to anticipate his action and forestall it without giving him offense. What else do you think you go to cotillion to learn?"

"Don't bother sending me back there, then. I'm not going to become that kind of person."

"Oh? And just what kind of person do you imagine you can be?"

"Myself!" Susanna said.

The two women (it was in that moment that I realized my sister had stolen yet another march on me and left her childhood behind) locked glares. I, meanwhile, was ignored, miserable, and unable to leave. I clasped my hands behind my back and let my fingers fight with one another. The injustice of my being there at all gnawed at me, growing more and more acute.

Angrily, Tante Amélie said, "I despair for you. Why are you behaving like this? Why can't I get a straight answer out of you? Why—"

"Why don't you ask her girlfriend?" I blurted out.

Tante Amélie's lips narrowed and her face turned white. She lifted up her cane and slammed it down on the floor with a *thump*. Then she was on her feet and with a swirl of skirts was gone from the room, leaving Susanna shivering with fear.

But when I tried to comfort my sister, she pushed me away.

The summons came later than I expected, almost a week after Tante Amélie's abrupt cane-thump and departure. Tante Amélie escorted us to Maitresse's austere and unfeminine office—she had been the company doctor, according to gossip, before catching father's eye—and with a curtsy abandoned us there.

Maitresse was a pretty woman currently making the transition to "handsome," very tall and slender, and that evening she wore a pink dress. When she spoke, her tone was not angry but sorrowful. "You both know that your place in life is to marry well and increase the prestige of our house. A great deal of money has been invested in you." Susanna opened her mouth to speak, but Maitresse held up a hand to forestall her. "We are not here to argue; the time for that is long past. No one is angry at you for what you have done with that young lady. I have performed for your father with other women many times. But you must both learn to look to your futures without sentiment or emotion.

"We are going out. There is something you must see."

Into the lantern-lit night streets of Port-Mimizon we sallied. This was a pleasure I had almost never experienced before, so that my apprehension was mingled with a kind of elation. A light breeze carried occasional snatches of music and gusts of laughter from unseen revelries. Maitresse had dressed us in long cloaks and Venetian carnival masks—undecorated *voltos* for us girls and for her a *medico della peste* with a beak as long as Pinocchio's—as was the custom for unescorted females.

The slave market at night was dark and silent. No lanterns were lit along its length, making the windowless compound seem a malevolent beast, crouching in wait for unwary prey to chance by. But Maitresse did not hurry her step. We turned a corner and at the end of an alley dark as a tunnel, saw a bright blaze of light and well-dressed men and women hurrying up the steps of a fighting club.

Maitresse led us around to the side, where we were let in at her knock. A dwarfish man obsequiously led the way to a small private waiting room with leather armchairs and flickering lights in mother-of-pearl sconces. "We'll have tea," she told the little man, and he left. While we waited, for what I could not imagine, Maitresse addressed us once again.

"I spoke of the trouble and expense that went into your educations. You probably think that if you don't make good marriages, you will simply be sold for courtesans. That was a reasonable expectation a generation ago. But times have changed. Male infants have become rarer, and even the best-brought-up girls are a glut on the market. Increasingly more men have taken to pederasty. The reasons are not well understood. Social? Cumulative poisoning from subtle alien compounds in the environment over the course of generations? No one knows."

"I will not give up Giselle," Susanna said almost calmly. "There is nothing you can do or threaten that will change my mind. She and I . . . but I imagine you know nothing about such passion as ours."

"Not know passion?" Maitresse laughed lightly, a delicate trill of silver bells. "My dear, how do you think I got involved in this mess in the first place?"

Our tea came and we drank, a quiet parody of domesticity.

What felt like hours dragged by. Finally, there came a roar of many voices through the wall and the dwarf deferentially reappeared at the door. "Ah." Maitresse put down her teacup. "It is time."

We entered our theater box between bouts, as the winner was being wrestled to the ground and sedated and his opponent carried away. Susanna sat stiffly in her seat, but I could not resist leaning over the rails to gawk at the audience. The theater smelled of cigar smoke and human sweat, with an under-scent of truffle so familiar that at first I thought nothing of it. As I watched, people wandered away from their seats, some to buy drinks, others retiring by pairs into private booths, while yet others . . . My sight fixed on a large man as he snapped a small glass vial beneath his nose. His head lolled back and a big loutish grin blossomed on his heavy face. I had never witnessed anyone sampling perfume in public before, but having seen it once I immediately recognized its gestures being repeated again and again throughout the room.

"Your father's wares," Maitresse observed, "are extremely popular." I was not sure if she wanted me to feel proud or ashamed; but I felt neither, only fearful and confused.

After a time, the audience, alerted by cues undetectable to me, reassembled itself in the tiered rows of chairs wrapped around a central pit with canvas-lined walls. The loud chatter turned to a dwindling murmur and then swelled up again in a roar of unclean approval as two girls, naked, were led stumbling down opposing aisles. Their heads were shaved (so they could not be seized by the hair, I later learned), and one had her face painted red and the other blue. Because they were both of slender build and similar height, this was needed to tell them apart.

Several slaves, nimble as apes, lowered the girls into the pit, then jumped down to rub their shoulders, chafe their hands, speak into their ears, and break vial after vial of perfume under their noses. By degrees the fighters came fully awake and then filled with such rage that they had to be held back by four men apiece to keep them from prematurely attacking each other. Then a bell rang and, releasing their charges, the slaves scrambled up the canvas walls and out of the pit.

The audience below came to their feet.

"Do not look away," Maitresse said. "If you have any questions, I will answer them."

The two girls ran together.

"How do they get them to fight?" I asked even though I was certain I would be told simply that they had no choice. Because were I in their place, knowing that the best I could hope for was to survive in order to undergo the same ordeal again in a week, I would not fight someone of my trainers' choosing. I would leap up into the audience and kill as many of them as I could before I was brought down.

"Your father creates perfumes for myriad purposes. Some cure schizophrenia. Some make it possible to work a forty-hour shift. Some are simple fantasies. Others are more elaborately crafted. Those below might think they are dire wolves fighting spear-carrying primitives, or perhaps abos defending their families from human ravagers. Their actions seem perfectly rational to them, and they will generate memories to justify them." As commanded, I did not look away, but I could feel her gaze on the side of my face nonetheless. "I could arrange for you to sample some of your father's perfumes, if you're curious. You would not like them at first. But if you persisted, after a time you would find yourself liking them very much indeed. My best advice to you is not to start. But once would not hurt."

I shook my head to blink away my tears. Misinterpreting the gesture, Maitresse said, "That is wise."

We watched the rest of the fight without further comment. When it ended, the survivor threw back her head and howled. Even when burly slaves immobilized and then tranquilized her, her mad grin burned triumphantly.

"May I stop watching now?" Susanna asked. I could tell she meant it to be defiant. But her voice came out small and plaintive.

"Soon." Maitresse leaned over the rail and called down to the pit-slaves, "Show us the body."

The pit workers started to hoist up the naked corpse for her examination.

"Clean her up first."

They produced a dirty cloth and rubbed at the girl's face, wiping away most of the red paint. Then they lifted her up again. In death, she seemed particularly childlike: slender, small-breasted, and long-legged. The hair on her pubic mound was a golden mist. I could not help wondering if she had experienced sex before her premature death and, if so, what it had been like.

"Study her features," Maitresse said dryly.

I did so, without results. Turning to my sister with a petulant shrug, I saw in the mirror of her horrified expression the truth. There came then a shifting within me like all the planets in the universe coming into alignment at once. When I looked back at the dead fighter I saw her face afresh. It could have been a younger version of my sister's face. But it was not.

It was my own.

————

Susanna said nothing during the long walk home, nor did I.

Maitresse, however, spoke at length and without emotion. "Your mother made many children. You"—(she meant Susanna)—"were natural. You"—(me)—"were the first of many clones commissioned in an attempt to create a male heir, all failures. When your mother was sent away, your father resolved to get rid of everything that reminded him of her. I argued against it and in the end we compromised and kept the two of you while selling off the others. I have no idea how many survive. However, the economic realities of the day are such that, were either of you to be sold, you would fetch the highest price here." She said a great deal more as well but it was unnecessary; we already well understood everything that she had to tell us.

When we arrived home, Maitresse took our masks from us and bid us both a pleasant good-night.

We went to sleep, my sister and I, cradled in each other's arms, the first time we had done so in more than a year. In the morning, Tante Amélie was gone and our formal educations were done forever.

Last night, as I said, I returned to my old dormitory room. It took me a while to realize that I was dreaming. It was only when I looked for Susanna and found nothing but dust and memories that I recollected how many years had gone by since my childhood. Still, in the way of dreams, there was a pervasive sense that the entire world was about to change.

"You know what to do now," a rasping whispery voice said. "Don't you, daughter?"

I turned and the she-wolf was not there. But I felt sure of her presence anyway. "Is it time?" I asked.

She did not reply. Her silence was answer enough.

I grinned for I now understood where the she-wolf had been hiding all this time.

Not so much awakening as taking my dream state with me into the waking world, I got up out of bed and walked down the hall to my husband's room. Then I paid a visit to the nursery, where my twin sons were sleeping. Finally, I went out into the night-dark streets to look for my sister.

The night is almost over now, and we must hurry to finish what we have begun. At dawn we will leave the cities behind and return to the swamps and forests, the caverns and hills from which the humans had driven us, and resume our long-interrupted lives. I have taken off my skin and now prowl naked through the streets of Port-Mimizon. In the shadows about me I sense many others who were once human, and I devoutly pray that there are enough of us for our purpose. In the back of my mind, I wonder whether all this is real or if I have descended into the pit of madness. But that is a minor concern. I have work to do.

I have freed the she-wolf from within her hiding place, and there is blood on her muzzle.

Only . . . why does the world smell as it does? Of canvas and bitter truffle.

Michael Swanwick writes science fiction, fantasy, and occasionally nonfiction. He has received the Hugo, Nebula, Theodore Sturgeon, and World Fantasy awards and has been nominated for and lost more of these awards than any other human being. Michael lives in Philadelphia with his wife, Marianne Porter. His latest novel is Dancing with Bears, *a post-utopian adventure featuring confidence artists Darger and Surplus, and he is currently at work on two new novels.*

His Web page can be found at www.michaelswanwick.com and his blog at www.floggingbabel.blogspot.com.

Snowchild

MICHAEL A. STACKPOLE

On Gene Wolfe: *He is a writer whom I have admired from afar. His work intimidates me. He has the uncanny ability to draw me immediately into his characters so deftly and with such a subtle hand that to merely glance at a page is to be sucked into a story for a chapter or three. It is sorcery, I'm fairly certain. It has to be, because I can study his work and can't crack it. While that's a bit frustrating, it's also a joy because it means his work remains a seamless pleasure in which I can truly delight.*

The gray fog tendrils swirled around the wound in the mountain's granite flank. Misty scraps twisted down into it. The haze obscured its black depths, but even its absence would not have let Kellach see much. Standing high on the wooded ridge as dusk came on, he could see little of the slender footpath leading down into the narrow valley. He saw nothing of where it came back up through the forest toward the hole.

"Just as well you've stopped here, friend. The valley will be as much your enemy in the night as what waits in that abyss."

Kellach turned slowly but did not raise his double-bitted great axe. The warmage stood half-hidden by a rock, and far enough away that he could cast a spell well before Kellach came into axe range. He wore a red cloak, which the dusk made the color of drying blood—save where iridescent crimson pulsed through webwork veins. He bore a slender sword, which could only function when stiffened by magick. Similarly, the brown leather jerkin and silken trousers could be sorcerously fortified, giving each the strength of the mail Kellach wore.

Since the warmage's words had carried no threat in tone or meaning, the Cengar elected to respond with caution over hostility. After all, if the man needed killing, later would serve just as well as now. "You wait here for the same reason?"

"I came as quickly as I could, but it appears she eluded me, as well." The smaller, wiry man smiled easily as he slipped from cover. White teeth split black mustache from goatee. "Both of us thwarted. We should make the best of it. I would have company over a fire this evening, and aid of that axe in tomorrow's endeavor . . . if you are of a mind of sharing my hospitality."

Kellach nodded.

The warmage pointed back down from whence he'd come. "On this side is a sheltered outcrop. Easy to defend, not easy to see, even for the maggot-folk."

Kellach glanced back. "Nothing hospitable back for a mile or more."

"Then you shall be my guest."

Kellach, taller, broader, and heavier than his companion, slipped along in the man's wake. The Cengar made less noise than the lonely breezes washing through the pines. Kellach did not carry much kit, and his mail rustled with a serpent's whisper. The forest, though old, was but an infant to the forests in which he had been raised, and these mountains mere molehills to the icy rock spires of his homeland. Here, in the north, noise would get a man noticed. In Cengaris, it would get a man killed.

The warmage stepped to the center of the clearing, and then spread his arms as if a noble welcoming a favored vassal. "Hardly a proper display of hospitality, but it must do. I, Praetor Azurean, bid you welcome." His cloak clung to him as a jealous lover might, and the hem snapped as if angered to be sharing the camp with Kellach.

Wood had been gathered inside a ring of stone, awaiting the kiss of a spark. A metal pot for tea, a cup for same, a different cup for wine, a thick sleeping carpet and blanket to cover, and a small folding chair had all been arranged on one side with measured precision. Back away, beyond the carpet, sat a small leather chest. Straps, now loose, would bind it; the brown skin had been worked with a variety of symbols arcane.

The man might have been making haste in pursuit, but was not so hasty that he could not see to his comforts. Kellach smiled, not surprised. Civilized northerners often entangled themselves in unnecessarily complex circumstances.

Kellach shrugged off his bedroll, waterskin, and a small satchel with a dwindling supply of trail rations. He piled everything by a small rock, then sat. He leaned his axe on the rock and unbuckled the wide belt that gathered his mail and supported a Haranite longknife. He set the belt with his pack, but did not doff his mail.

"That rock looks none too comfortable." Praetor looked at this chest. "I've got another chair in there, but I doubt it would support your weight. Some pillows, perhaps?"

Kellach shook his head, his emerald eyes tightening. "I will be fine. I would contribute to the meal. I can make the fire."

"No need for that, my friend." Praetor dropped to one knee and thrust a hand into the woodpile's heart. His eyes closed for a moment, then he yanked his hand away and slapped at a spark on his sleeve. His hand got it a half second before the cloak's tail did. Smoke rose from the wood, then flames licked up. "See: done easily."

Yet my way would not have threatened to catch my sleeve on fire. Kellach stood. "Let me fetch water."

"Yes, splendid idea." The warmage opened the chest and pulled out a small leather bucket. "This should hold all we need."

The Cengar caught the bucket and headed into the forest, assuming he'd be making more than one trip. The bucket might hold enough to fill the teapot, but not much more. He figured the warmage would have some ritualistic ablutions to perform. *If he wants a bath, he hauls his own.*

Kellach followed the trail Praetor had used coming from the west, then cut over a hill to the north and down into a ravine. A little brook trickled. Kellach ducked the bucket into a small pool. Instantly the pool lost two fingers' width of depth and ceased spilling downhill.

The Cengar's brow furrowed. He tugged on the handle to pull the bucket free, but the wet leather slipped greasily out of his grasp. Bending, he gripped the handle tight with both hands. Muscles bulged, but he couldn't shift it. He stepped into the pool, squatted, and lifted with his legs, again to no avail.

He grunted and tipped the bucket as if pouring water out. The pool's level rose and the stream flowed again. Kellach cautiously hauled the bucket out of the water. At best it should have held a quart, but weighed as if it contained five gallons. Kellach really didn't appreciate his companion having so casually tricked him. Deviltry— like the bucket and cloak—and trickery did not inspire trust.

He thought he had hidden his concern, but Praetor smiled broadly upon Kellach's return. "Amazing little thing, isn't it? The magick is aeons old. Sorcerers made those buckets to try to stem the flooding sea. Problem was, no one could lift the buckets. Eventually the buckets all burst—magick does have its limits—and the flood was unabated."

"Even if they could have lifted them, there was no spout to pour the water."

"Very good point, my friend." Praetor smiled, firelight playing over his short black hair. "But let us not be coy, shall we, since most likely, tomorrow, we shall be staunching each other's wounds. How much is the bounty on the girl?"

Kellach's dark brows narrowed. "Her parents sent me after her."

"Truly? How interesting." Praetor slipped off his swordbelt and coiled it round a hand. "Do you know how to read this?"

Kellach deftly caught the swordbelt. A number of symbols had been burned into it. Neither Praetor nor his belt were unique. The symbols identified schools and traditions of magick, as well as honors he'd been given. Kellach recognized a few of them. He grunted, then rolled the belt and lofted it back.

"I knew you for a warmage by your . . . blade." He'd almost said he'd known him for hiding behind a rock, but that would have been an unnecessary complication of circumstance. "Aught else means nothing to me."

"You've figured some things out, though. You know I am from Athanis, or perhaps Peris. Born in one, trained in the other. I am a student of the College of Ktheru, in good standing. You've heard of it?"

Kellach nodded, his long black locks brushing forward of his shoulders. "It is a school not without honor."

"Good. Then you know why I am out here, Cengar." Praetor's smile straightened itself. "You *are* a Cengar, though I can't read the clan from the plaid of your trousers. Well worn, though, so you are an adventurer or in exile. Strong, and your axe has more scars than you do, so well trained. Not a bandit, I think, but certainly a mercenary—now, or in the past, and certainly in the future."

Kellach's head came up. "A warmage who divines the future?"

The Athanite laughed. "That would be the trick, wouldn't it? No. War magicks create chaos. Divination seeks to impose order. They are an anathema. But, tell me truly, why are you hunting the girl?"

Kellach pointed back south. "She and her family were running. We shared a campsite."

Praetor arched an eyebrow. "You were not afraid?"

"Afraid? Of the snowchild? Why?"

"Is that what you call them? Here, in the north, they are fell things. In their presence milk sours in the udder, hens cease laying, crops wither. If a child is born white and misshapen and squiggly, he is left on a hillside to die. If he's lucky, that's what happens. If not, the maggot-folk find him and keep him as their own. But for one such as she, who changes as womanhood beckons, of them the tales are yet worse. They become witches of great power, with no schooling, no allegiance, and no discipline. They live alone, shunned, hated, feared; unless courted to work their magicks. Often they are vengeful. Those tales you must have heard."

"The only White Witch we fear is she who sends storms north to bury us in winter." Kellach slowly shook his head. "This girl, Serinna, is not that witch. Nor is she maggot-folk."

"I'd not be so confident of that, my friend." Praetor dipped water from the bucket into his teapot and set it to boiling. "I've learned much of the maggot-folk. There are those who claim they are what men once were, when the Sepheri ruled over this world. Others say they are what we will become, with our living in sin and with profligate use of magick. They say the gods are not pleased, and send us maggot whelp to remind us to mend our ways. Both sides are persuasive. I'm not certain what I believe. How about you?"

"Neither is what I am, so it is of no matter."

"Why, again, are you hunting her, then?"

"I slept while she was taken." Kellach stared hard at the warmage, watching his face for even the most fleeting sign of contempt.

Praetor stroked a hand over his beard. "Your honor demands you recover her more than any beseeching by her family. Very good. Be assured that you were not inattentive. The maggot-folk appear to have an innate facility with magicks that befuddle and fatigue. Curious that they did not kill you all, however."

Kellach shook his head. "No signs of struggle. Her mother believes Serinna agreed to go willingly."

"Saving you from harm. She would tell herself that, of course. She would have to believe it." The warmage's brown eyes tightened. "However, in my pursuit of her I have seen no sign of struggle or unwillingness to travel. Perhaps she did sell herself for your sake."

"I followed her trail, but saw no sign of you."

"No, of course not. You followed the trail here. I used other means." Praetor opened the arcane chest and removed a tea caddy, a small loaf of bread, and some cheese. He introduced several healthy pinches of tea into the boiling water, and then set it aside to steep. He tossed the small round of cheese to Kellach. "You can divide that in half. How much do you know of the Veils?"

Kellach drew his longknife and sliced the soft cheese disk in half. He exchanged a portion of it for half of the loaf. "I have heard of the Veils. I have seen magick." He actually knew more of magick than he'd admitted; and far more of it than would have made the warmage comfortable. Kellach saw no vice in letting the warmage draw his own conclusions—something that appeared to make Praetor quite happy.

"There are many Veils, my friend. Were I to look at you through the first, I could see that you carry no enchanted weapons and have no trace of magick lingering about you—your encounter with the maggot-folk notwithstanding." Praetor set aside the bread and cheese to pour tea. "It was through another Veil that I searched for the girl. She shines brightly—the sun to faint stars surrounding her. I could watch her course, and chose mine to cut her off. Alas, I was slow in my arrival."

Kellach accepted the tin cup of tea and set it at his feet. "Why do you seek her?"

"I do the bidding of my College. My masters decry the barbarity of infanticide, and the superstition that haunts the lives of these poor afflicted. When rumors of a snowchild, to use your more gentle term, arose—and they travel swiftly through the Veils—I was dispatched to find her, to offer her and her family support and succor."

"Is she not better off with her own kind, if that is her choice?"

Praetor sipped his tea and frowned heavily. "She is truly but a child, thus incapable of making such a decision. She does not know why they seek her. They desire her not as a companion. The maggot-folk are quite sterile, but they cling to a prophecy that says a white child will come to them. It will mate with their queen, or be taken for their queen, and produce a thousand whole and clean-limbed creatures of their kind. It will breed true and they will emerge into the daylight to reclaim a world that was once theirs."

"Or is destined to be theirs?"

"Very good. You actually listened." Praetor gave him a half-smile. "I appreciate that in a companion."

Kellach dipped a bit of the bread in tea to soften it. "If you listen well enough, even the emptiness will whisper wisdom."

"Cengar sagacity?"

"I've heard it many places. It is seldom heeded."

"Such is the fate of wisdom, alas." Praetor sat back in his chair. "I've noticed, my friend, that you've not given me your name. You are wise to withhold it from the Gifted, but we have broken bread together. We share a fire. Tomorrow we should likely die together. I should know your name."

"I am Kellach. I am a Cengar far from home." Kellach swallowed some tea. "Clan names would tell you nothing. I am my own man. My chasing the girl is a matter of honor."

Praetor extended his cup above the fire. "To men of honor, then, Kellach. May we save the girl from the fate into whose arms she has been cast. And do it without dying."

Kellach took the dawn watch and let the fire die. Praetor lay co-cooned in his cloak. Light pulsed through it in rhythm with the man's heartbeat. It swelled and fell with his breathing—though it covered him completely. While the cool morning air allowed Kellach to see his own breath, he saw no steam rising from the cocoon. *Yet the man breathes, so air must get to him.*

Having been raised in the south, amid snowcapped mountains where water was drawn from streams bleeding off glaciers, Kellach did not mind the cold. In fact, he found it something of a comfort.

He breakfasted on cold water and dried beef from his own supplies while he waited for the warmage to waken.

Praetor Azurean took his time in that. A momentary flash of disgust when he saw the fire had gone out revealed his dislike of the cold. The warmage made no complaint, however. The cloak reluctantly released him and he rolled to a knee. He warmed water for his tea by holding the pot in both hands, and even offered Kellach a steaming mug. Kellach declined with a shake of his head.

Praetor busied himself cleaning up their camp. He folded his chair down and slid it into the trunk as if the box had no bottom. The bucket was yet half full of water, so the man poured it out, then deposited it on top of the chairs. Everything else went in as well. Then the warmage buckled the lid on tightly. With a wave of his hand he split the chest in half, stacked one half atop the other, and pushed down. One half slid into the other, producing a chest half the previous size. He did this again and again until he'd reduced the chest to a small case the man could have hidden behind his hand. Then he slid his belt through a loop on the back. He brought the box around to his right hip, opposite his sword, and smiled.

"There: all set."

"You do not carry a staff or a wand?"

The warmage chuckled as he set foot on the path leading back to the ridge. "Hedge wizards and paltry warlocks might use them, but we who are Yag-Ktheru eschew them. Hard to use them in conjunction with a sword, no?" He raised his right hand and flicked his thumb against a gold ring set with what appeared to be an ancient coin. "Easier to focus through something like this. As you and I focus our physical strength through my sword or your axe, so I focus magickal energies through this ring."

They paused at the ridge. Fog completely filled the valley. No hint of the cave, no breeze stirred the fog. Higher clouds made it unlikely the sun would burn the fog off any time soon. Condensing moisture darkened the rocks and glowed from leaves.

Kellach started down first, filling his right hand with the long-knife. The trail was little more than a track for runoff, where thin soil had been eroded to bare rock. Traces of past rockslides required them to pick their way across the face of the mountain, switching back many times. The scrub brush up top and more lush forest below allowed them no more than a dozen feet of visibility along the trail, and often a quarter of that side to side. Kellach would never get to swing his ax in such tight quarters, but the longknife would more than suffice if they were attacked.

Though the warmage had not seemed a likely companion when they camped, he redeemed himself on the trail. They did not speak. He would stop when Kellach did, and study places at which Kellach pointed. They each listened hard, and sometimes Praetor closed his eyes, looking through the Veils for danger. He reported nothing unusual with a head shake, and they moved on.

They continued down to the valley floor, reaching it by mid-morning. Kellach refilled his waterskin in the stream there. Praetor filled a flask that—from a faint scent—changed water into something else. They worked up and down the stream for a hundred yards or so each way, looking for other trails. Kellach found one down-stream, almost directly below where the cavern mouth should be. Close by he discovered a small sandbar where the stream turned north and broadened out for a bit.

He crouched and studied the footprints. They belonged to two individuals. Because of the size he thought them a child and an adult. The adult had six toes on one foot, three on the other—and clearly had lost them through some sort of an accident. The child had a clubbed foot on the right.

Praetor joined him, squatting on the shore. "In that little pool, berry pits."

Kellach nodded. "Bird berries. They ate a few while resting."

"Harvester's wage, all fair." Praetor shrugged. "Though I doubt they have the intelligence to know the old ways and abide by them. They're little more than animals."

Kellach had heard that sentiment before, directed by brain-proud northerners at the Cengari people. He'd have challenged Praetor to justify his remark then and there, but it was neither the time nor the place for a steely discussion. Instead he grunted. "More reason to rescue Serinna."

"The girl, yes."

Working upslope from the sandbar they located the berry-pickers' meandering trail. It took them through several stands of bushes that had been picked clean. Multiple tracks overlaid one another, revealing more misshapen feet and many days' work to harvest all the berries. Kellach saw no more collections of pits, but did see evidence of brush having been cleared to allow the berry groves to expand. He'd not seen many animals do that.

Working their way up, they also came around toward the east. Given the maggot-folks' aversion to sunlight, they would be less watchful from that direction. As they reached the level of the cave mouth, they headed west and upward. Praetor slipped into the lead. He apparently found no alarms or ambushes through a Veiled glance, so he waved Kellach on. When the Cengar drew parallel, the warmage pointed with two fingers down below.

Kellach had seen maggot-folk before, but that hardly mattered. No two were the same. Corpse-white flesh with gray blemishes covered them. Excess flesh bulged here and there, though they weren't fat. It seemed as if their skin was exceedingly thick and hanging there as if waiting for its owner to double or triple in size. Naked save for a gold armlet on one's third arm—the trinket had likely once been a child's bracelet—and a rusty iron torc around the other's neck, one clutched a stone axe, the other a stone-tipped spear. The taller one had no hair, while the smaller had brown pigeon feathers woven into long white locks. They hunched in plain sight, largely immobile, not speaking to or even looking at each other.

Kellach glanced at his companion, then held up a hand and waggled his ring finger.

Praetor shook his head and covered his mouth with his hand. "Magick can be detected."

Kellach nodded. Praetor wasn't the first warmage of his acquaintance who hadn't hidden behind that bit of truth. *They don't mind killing. They mind getting wet.*

Though a large man, Kellach moved to the cave mouth with the fluid stealth of a shadow's sigh. He hid against a large plinth, close enough to hear the guards' raspy breath, waiting for his final rush. Kellach reversed the longknife, such that the blade ran back along his forearm, well past his elbow, the razored edge outermost. As he straightened, he cocked his wrist so the blade's tip pointed up near his right shoulder. With the knife thus hidden behind his arm, he stepped into the cave mouth and went to work.

No war cry. No time for the maggot-folk to raise an alarm. Kellach's right arm swept up, bending at the elbow. The blade slashed the first from breastbone to chin. Blood flew dark, the air full of the foul stench of a lanced boil. The Cengar twisted, driving the longknife back, stabbing the second through the throat. He yanked the blade free, more misty blood staining the fog, and shifted the longknife to a more conventional grip. He brought the blade back around, the return stroke biting deeply into the first guard's throat. More blood spurted from an open neck.

Both guards crumpled, mortally wounded before either hit the ground.

Praetor came scrambling along quickly, his face a shade paler than before. "God's breath you're fast."

Kellach slid the longknife back into its scabbard. "Fast or slow, killing is killing." He slipped the great-axe off his back and removed its hood.

The warmage pulled the gold armlet off the dead guard's third arm. "Opaniri in manufacture. Stolen, obviously."

Opanir existed an ocean away. Chances were that the mystery of how the bracelet got into the mountains of Zethanis would never be solved. Kellach found the mystery intriguing, but spared it no more than a fleeting thought. The bracelet was there, and the *how* of its being there would not change that fact. If he later perceived a value to learning the means by which it reached the maggot-folk, he would be relentless in hunting the answer down. Until such a circumstance arose, however, it mattered not.

Without giving Praetor Azurean the option of preceding him, Kellach headed into the cavern. It had begun life as a natural cave, but a dozen yards in showed signs of work. Generations of feet had worn paths smooth. Tools had widened passages. Bridges spanned crevasses, crudely hacked stairs and simple ladders provided access to side tunnels and catwalks. The maggot-folk had created their own little warren within the cave. It reminded Kellach of slum dwellings in the world's larger cities.

As they moved on, their way lit dimly by luminescent lichen and tiny globes glowing with wan magelight, Kellach noticed things he'd never seen in the slums. The maggot-folk had carved alcoves of various sizes and appropriate shapes into stone walls. Within each they'd placed a statue or marble tile with some god's visage on it. Some he recognized outright. Others he recognized by style—not knowing who they were but certain of where they came from. Opanir found itself represented well. Likewise statues of Imperial manufacture from before the flood and even a Sepheri totem or two warded the walls. Even more remarkable than the presence of the shrines was the pristine nature of their keeping. It contrasted sharply with the squalor the maggot-folk otherwise endured.

They slipped deeper into the cavern, remaining on the wider, well-traveled track, ignoring side passages that led to more residential chaos. A steady and solemn drumbeat drew them on. As regular as a martial beat, different notes lifted it above mere mechanical timing. It had purpose, but exactly what Kellach could not discern.

Their path took them gently down until, after a brief narrowing, it opened onto a vast chamber. The bowl-shaped floor featured a lozenge of a dark lake thrusting away from them, the shore studded with stalagmites. Only the occasional water drop falling from stalactites above disturbed the placid surface. Opposite the entry tunnel, a small stone dais stood flush against the wall. Dark tunnels led off and down to either side. Tall statues edged the dais, making it a communion place of gods easily recognized, ancient and forgotten.

Kellach dropped to a knee in the shadows and Praetor beside him. He found the statues unsettling, and not simply because some of them predated the Sepheri empire. Their sheer size, the weight of stone and their limbs, would have made it impossible to have gotten them into the chamber. The statues could have been broken down and hauled in, but Kellach saw no evidence of joinery. This meant that either they'd been reconstructed with sorcery, or sorcery had been used to move them to their new home. Neither prospect pleased him.

The maggot-folk filled the basin, surrounding the slender lake, some clinging to stalagmites to give them a greater vantage. They clearly had a hierarchy, for the most misshapen kept to shadows. Those who were easier to look at sat nearest the dais, their faces filled with ecstatic joy. To the right, several of the multi-armed creatures held and beat drums of various sizes. The musicians were well practiced, but Kellach noted something about how they moved. They swayed with the rhythm, their eyes closed. He suspected magick united their efforts and, in turn, would unite those below.

A soft golden light appeared in the tunnel to the dais's right. Two children emerged first, each wearing a golden helm with a spike. Small globes had been fixed to those spikes. They cast the gentle glow. The children, one as clean-limbed as could be expected among the maggot-folk, the other more comfortable moving apelike on all fours, kept pace with the drumming.

Serinna followed them, her measured steps in time with theirs. Kellach recognized her because the woman could be no one else, yet she looked entirely different from the girl he'd met before. Her long white hair had been washed and dried, combed free of brambles and twigs. A gold cloak clasp gathered it at the back of her neck. A simple girdle of gold links and white silk provided her only other raiment. The cloth lovingly caressed long legs—*naturally*, not with the clingy obsession of Praetor's cloak.

The bird berries had not been gathered for consumption, but had been crushed. Their indigo juice painted her body. Odd sigils decorated her forehead and abdomen, shoulders, arms, and thighs. Kellach had seen slaves similarly marked, but never with these symbols. He could not decipher them, but they all shared something that suggested they were feminine, perhaps part of a pair.

"She is magnificent."

Kellach glanced at his companion. From the way Praetor's eyes focused beyond Serinna, Kellach realized the remark had nothing to do with her physical beauty. He studied her through the Veils. His jaw slackened at what he saw.

"What do the symbols mean?"

"Life, gateways, potential." Praetor's eyes cleared. "Fertility symbols many of them, but some speak to incredible power."

The drumming grew stronger, though no louder. It vibrated through Kellach's chest. A ripple spread over the lake and rebounded in legion from the shore. Where the ripples collided against one another, water rose in fluid silvery bubbles, floating gently upward. At the center, where all the ripples came together, a larger droplet formed. Perfectly spherical, it rose slowly. The others began to orbit it and one another in an elaborate dance.

Then light approached from the other tunnel. Serinna looked expectantly in that direction. Two twisted warriors bearing glowing shields heralded a man's arrival. Tall, lithe, and well formed, he came naked save for a wash of gold covering him completely. Even his hair, which fell to his shoulders, was composed of impossibly slender golden threads that danced to the drumbeats.

The maggot-folk bowed their heads reverentially as he mounted the dais. He stopped center stage and gestured languidly with an open hand. The magelight from shields and glowing orbs flew immediately to him, plunging the cavern into darkness. Then a blue light limned him. It traveled out along his hand and leaped away in little sparks that buried themselves in the floating water spheres. There they divided again and again, as if a spray of stars, and the shifting blue light filled the chamber.

Serinna's joy shone brightly in her smile.

Praetor grabbed Kellach's shoulder. "You have to get the girl away. If he completes the ritual begun here, they will be united. Their power will be united. They will be invincible."

Kellach stared at him. "My axe cannot hew a path through that crowd."

"I'll scatter them, fool. Go. Go lest the world be overrun by the maggot-folk."

Praetor stood back. The warmage turned sideways. The cloak wrapped him like a wet sail around a mast. His image twisted slender as a snake, then flattened. It collapsed down into itself, vanishing with nary a sound and the faint scent of spoiled meat.

An eyeblink later lake water boiled beneath the big sphere. Turgid bubbles burst loudly, drowning the drums. Then, as maggot-folk turned to look, dark red tentacles coiled up and out of the water. They smashed floating globes and wrapped round stalagmites. Maggot-folk screamed in a hideous cacophony. They fled in a chaotic tangle of limbs and a riotous wave of broken gaits. They choked pathways, jostling heavily. Some fell back amid the stalagmites, others streamed past the Cengar, blind to his presence in their panic.

Kellach had already moved away from the most direct line of flight and leaped down into the bowl. He headed straight for the dais, but had to swing wider, away from the water. It sloshed out of the basin, dragging down some of the slower maggot-folk. Several clutched at stone spikes to avoid drowning, yelping for succor.

Praetor Azurean rose from the heart of the lake, glorious, supported by his cloak. A tentacle snapped out like a whip, exploding a hapless man who'd slipped in the water. The stink of corruption filled the air. Whether it came from the warmage or the dead man, Kellach did not care. He forced himself forward, happy to reach the dais.

Happier to be out of the tentacles' striking range.

The gold man stepped to the fore, muscles tense and veins pulsing beneath his flesh. Coruscating red beams flashed from his eyes. One missed, wilting a stalagmite, but the other caught Praetor full in the chest. His tunic smoked. For a brief flash Kellach caught sight of white ribs beneath cracked, blackened flesh. A tentacle wrapped around the warmage, closing the wound; then another whipped forward, cracking off a bloody cloud of barbed darts.

The gold man dodged most of them. Three, however, did strike home: arm, hip, and thigh on the right. The impact spun him away from Serinna, back toward his tunnel. She reached one hand toward him. The other covered her mouth.

Even though staggering and bleeding, the gold man struck back. He brought his hands up and around, conjuring a barbed golden ball. It spun furiously and launched itself at Praetor.

A pair of tentacles rose to ward it off. Gold thorns pierced the cloak. They caught as a burr might in fur. The ball surged forward, wrapping the cloak tightly around itself. Once firmly caught, it shot upward. The cloak ripped free of its clasp. The ball impaled itself and the cloak on a stalactite, striking sparks as it slowly spun down.

Praetor fell, but not far. Light burst from his ring, burning through the glove. His fingers wove and he hung there, in the air. Contempt twisting his lips, Praetor raised a hand, thrust it into the large water globe suspended above him, and hurled it at his opponent.

The gold man thrust a palm forward. It appeared as if he believed the sphere would splash harmlessly against his hand. And, indeed, a dozen yards in front of him, the water globe hit something. It exploded against that invisible shield, infinitely replicating itself into other spheres large and small.

Praetor laughed, and with the echoes of his mirth came waves of cold. The globes froze instantly, orbiting high and low, picking up velocity. Successive sheets of hailstones shot above and around the shield, converging on the gold man.

The gold man reacted, but any chance that he might fend off the assault died when a melon-sized ice chunk struck him full in the face. It cracked his gold flesh and carried away part of his scalp. He reeled. Other ice balls hammered him and battered him backward. He dropped to a knee and sought to rise again, but ice made for treacherous footing, thwarting him. Another large piece smashed into his chest. It pitched him against the marble statue of a god twice his size.

The gold man, streaking the god's white flesh with scarlet, slid to its stone feet and began a palsied twitching.

Kellach reached the dais in a leap. He grabbed the girl's arm before she could run to the gold man's side.

"Let me go." Her eyes blazed as she turned on Kellach. "He was to have been my husband."

"Are you insane, girl? Look!"

With the gold man's magick ebbing slowly, the golden flesh that had defined him ran like candle wax. Firm muscles sagged. Liver spots dotted pale flesh. The strong jaw weakened. The chin receded. The draining magick eroded deep wrinkles into the man's flesh. His eyes, visible now, had the clouded appearance of the half-blind.

Serinna sagged to her knees and Kellach released her. "No, he wasn't like that. He was in my dreams, my dreams ever since I became . . . became what I am. He loves me."

"He *loved* what you had become, child. He loved what you would give him." Praetor landed lightly on the dais. "You were his gateway to immortality. You have no idea the power that resides in you. He was not worthy of it. But I know one who is."

Kellach interposed himself between Praetor and the sobbing girl. "Serinna, to your feet. Run."

"Ignore him, child." The warmage shook his head slowly. "Did you think, Kellach, that I believed you were after no bounty? How much will her parents pay for her head?"

Kellach half smiled.

The Northerner blinked. "You were not *chasing* her, but following, *guarding*. You, the two of you, colluded in this escape. Oh, very well played, Kellach. But, mark me, girl, he is not the one you want as your protector."

Kellach raised his axe, the head at his right shoulder. "Leave now."

Praetor cocked his head. "Cengar, you know not what you are doing. You cannot stand against me." The warmage stepped to the side so he could see the girl. "Serinna, you are being paid a great honor. My master, the Kesath-Ktheru Quintus Fulvean—of the *Major* family, not any of the Minors—bids me bring you to him. He would reveal your true power. He would allow you to reach your full potential."

Kellach's lower hand twitched and his axe rotated. "By wedding your master?"

"Truth be told, I do not think he wishes to take a maggot-woman to wife. Bed her, certainly, and get upon her children of promise, without a doubt. She, in turn, would have a life of luxury beyond which this or any other warren would provide." Praetor raised his left hand, but kept his right close to the hilt of his sword. "There is something in this for you, too, Cengar. Last night, during my watch, I reported back on the circumstances of our meeting. Were you to somehow actually defeat me, you would have the whole of Yag-Ktheru hunting you. We are many and relentless. Let her go, and we shall let you go."

"Major house or Minor, I fear your master no more than I fear you. Run, girl, now."

Serinna vanished in a rustle of silk and gold, racing back into the tunnel.

"Cengar, *you* force me to do this. Remember that." Praetor Azurean's longsword slithered from its scabbard. Runes and sigils burned on the blade with molten brilliance. The warmage raised his blade in a salute. The thin metal quivered, and then Praetor lunged.

Kellach parried the blade down with the haft of his axe, and then punched forward with the steel cap on its end. The blow should have taken the warmage full in the face. It met empty air. As if he were a snake, the warmage bonelessly dove forward and beneath the axe. He did not bother to roll, but twisted on his knees and came up. Again he thrust, this time at the Cengar's back.

Had Kellach been fighting a *swordsman,* he would have spun, the axe sweeping out in a broad arc that would cleave the man in half. He might have been pinked by the slender blade, but Praetor's parts would have writhed on the dais.

Instead, the Cengar darted forward two steps before turning. His axe came up and around, parrying the lunge of a blade that had doubled in length. He knocked it high, and then drove toward the warmage. He closed fast, but Praetor leaped away more quickly.

The warmage hunched in a conventional guard, the blade having returned to its scabbarded length. "Yes, so very quick." The gold ring flashed. "And now I am quicker."

Praetor closed in, his blade aimed at Kellach's heart. The Cengar brought the axe up to parry, but the blade's tip curled back. The parry missed. The sword's tip then snapped down and thrust toward Kellach's belly.

The large man twisted to the left. The blade skittered over ring mail before catching in a link. The armor popped. The blade's metal shifted and curled in toward Kellach's guts. It pierced flesh, burning as if it were red hot. It sought to go deeper.

Kellach kicked out with his right foot, catching the warmage high on the thigh. The booted foot broke Praetor's momentum and knocked him back a step. The sword came free, the tip bloodied. The warmage smiled at that.

The Cengar didn't give him a chance to decide if drawing first blood was an ill omen or good. Kellach swept his axe in a cross-cut blow, waist-high. It should have split the warmage up from down. It would have, save that the axe struck the magick box at Praetor's right hip. The axe crushed the buckle and severed the tongue. Still, the blow's force pitched Praetor halfway across the dais. He landed heavily on his knees and caught himself with his hands.

His sword skittered farther away, to the dais's edge behind him.

Kellach made to spring at his foe. Praetor glanced up. He gestured. The ring glowed. The puddle beneath Kellach's foot froze slick. The large man slipped, smashing his left knee into the stone. The jolt carried up into his hip and numbed the entire leg.

"A slip and a fall. How ignominious. Felled by magick. By rights, I should finish you with it." The warmage struggled to his feet and retrieved his sword. "But you are a warrior, so a warrior's death I'll grant you."

Kellach growled and brandished the axe.

Hellish light flared from the sword's runes. "I'll cleave through it *and* through you."

Yet before Praetor had advanced a single step, a golden fireball shot past Kellach. It blasted the warmage from the dais and out into the lake. As Praetor splashed down, the dying gold man gave out with a satisfied grunt. It tailed into a dying rasp.

The warmage sank beneath the dark water.

Kellach levered himself up and limped to the dais's edge. He threw aside his axe as Praetor bobbed to the surface once before vanishing. *At least in the water my dead leg won't slow me.*

Praetor came up again, but this time sucked in as much water as air. Bubbles marked the spot where he went down. His gloved hand clawed through them as fingers disappeared. Kellach quickly bent, unbuckled his belt, shucked off his mail, and leaped into the lake with longknife in hand.

The cold water was no more than a dozen feet deep, and becoming more shallow with each heartbeat. More chilling than it was the sight of Praetor, churning the bottom muck, weakly digging at his belt buckle with gloved hands. Beside him sediment swirled, being drawn through a vortex into the box at his belt. As with the mages of old, he could not lift the flood it had sucked in.

Praetor looked up. His expression asked for mercy in equal measure with disgust at being trapped. He clearly hoped for better treatment than he'd offered.

Kellach thrust his longknife deep through the warmage's belly. He twisted, and then yanked it roughly free. The dying man's hands hung suspended. The dark leakage from his wound streamed down into the box.

Kellach peered at him for a moment. No pity, just a desire to make sure the man was truly dead. Satisfied, he stripped the gold ring off his finger and struck for the surface. As he climbed from the lake and pulled himself back up on the dais, he discovered he was not alone. Serinna had reemerged from the tunnel. She'd reached the gold man's side. A knife lay beside her.

Kellach recovered his axe and, dripping lake water, approached but did not intrude. The old man raised a hand and caressed the girl's cheek. Her tears had already made the sigils on her cheeks run, but the old man gave no sign of noticing.

She held his other hand while he yet breathed, and then a bit longer. She looked up at Kellach with red-rimmed eyes. "He waited his whole life for another like him. I was the only one who came. He killed the warmage to save *me*."

"And you brought the knife to save him." Kellach nodded. "His act saved me. I owe him a debt."

"You said you owed me one, too. That didn't stop you from leading that Yag-Ktheru here."

Kellach leaned heavily on his axe and rubbed at his knee. "As you asked, I convinced your parents that I would lead you off and murder you. As you asked, I followed you here to see you arrive without interruption. After you'd descended, I discovered that the warmage had tracked you."

"You should have killed him in his sleep."

"He slept." Kellach pointed to the cave's ceiling, where the cloak dripped like mucus. "His *cloak* did not. It was an evil thing. Your man here saw that."

"Ataldin was his name." She kissed the old man's hand, then laid it on his chest.

"Will you remain here?"

Serinna rose and spread her arms. "There no longer *is* a here. The sanctuary has been violated. My brethren have fled. They carry with them what they can, including the tale of what happened. They will go to other underrealms."

"Will you follow?"

She thought for a moment. "The stories you told me of snowfolk among your people. Were they true? Are there cities of them who are all like me?"

"I have never seen them. I trust those who said they have."

She smiled. "Is the debt you owe me sufficient to have you conduct me there?"

"The debt to you, no." Kellach shook his head. "The debt to Ataldin, yes." He handed her Praetor's ring. "As you grow into power, this may be of aid."

Serinna slipped it onto her right thumb. She held it up, admiring it for a moment, turning the crest inward so it would remain unseen. "Help me straighten his limbs and lay him to rest, then we are bound for these fabled cities of snowfolk.

"It will not be an easy journey. In the land where mountains stab the sky, there are things from which I have run. Those things stand between us and our goal. I do not know if those things would fear a snowchild, but I think it is best we contrive to make certain they do."

Michael A. Stackpole is a New York Times *bestselling author of more than forty-five novels, best known among them being* Rogue Squadron *and* I, Jedi. *He has won awards for game design, computer game design, novel writing, editing, podcasting, screenwriting, and graphic novels. He has an asteroid named after him (#165612). Because this planet lacks the means to convey him to that asteroid, he contents himself with writing, dancing, and playing indoor soccer (the latter two of which would be much easier on said asteroid).*

Tourist Trap

A Companion Piece to
"The Marvelous Brass Chessplaying Automaton"
by Gene Wolfe

MIKE RESNICK AND BARRY MALZBERG

On Gene Wolfe: *Gene has a worldview and a way of expressing it that is uniquely his own. He has never genuflected to the so-called needs of the field, but has, over the course of his admirable career, made the field genuflect to him and his unique voice. There are worse legacies.*
—Mike

On Gene Wolfe: *I've been reading Gene Wolfe since "Trip, Trap" appeared in an early* Orbit. *We began to publish at about the same time; he's been far more successful . . . but then again I am eight years younger. His magnificent short story "Cues" was the subject of one of my earliest essays, which was published in Andrew Porter's* Algol *pulp four decades ago.*
—Barry

I was just bringing Lame Hans his lunch when he looked up at me excitedly.

"What do you see?" he demanded.

"I see a lame man waiting for his meal," I answered.

He shook his head vigorously. "The *game*," he said. "What about the game?"

"Same as always," I said. "You're sitting in your cell, the computer is right outside it, you're playing white, and since the computer is an empty shell, you're playing black, too."

"*No!*" he yelled. "It moved on its own!"

"Hans, even if it still had a brain, it's not plugged in."

"I don't care! It moved its Knight to King's Bishop three!"

"Hans, it hasn't moved a damned thing since you hid poor Gretchen inside it when you and Professor Baumeister attempted to defraud the others. And we all know that she suffocated. That's why you're here."

"Just *look*!" yelled Lame Hans. He pushed his Queen's Bishop forward, leaving her Rook unprotected—and while he held his hands up in the air to prove he wasn't touching anything or leaning on the board, the Black Queen slowly slid on the diagonal and took the Rook.

"There's someone inside," I said with certainty.

"Look!" he urged me.

I pulled out the side panel, and could see nothing, but remembering how cleverly they had concealed Gretchen, I walked around the other side, removed that panel, found that I could see clear through to the far well, and then felt around inside it. There was no one there and, of course, no mechanical brain.

"Well?" demanded Lame Hans.

"I don't know how you did it," I admitted.

"*I* didn't do anything!" he shouted at me. "The machine's alive."

He pushed a Pawn forward, and the machine responded by taking it with its Knight.

"I am the best chess player in all Bavaria," said Lame Hans. "The machine is not only alive—it's brilliant!"

Brilliant, I thought, but did not say. If the machine was indeed brilliant, then why was Lame Hans in his ongoing competition ahead by one hundred and sixty games to twenty-two? Why, time and again, did the machine succumb to Knight forks and fianchet-toed Bishops, stumble into doubled Pawns two games out of three? The machine had its instances, to be sure—twenty-two of them in fact—but it was impossible to conceive of it as anything other than a dull refraction of Lame Hans's madness.

Or so I thought. The thoughts of a jailer are not, however, profound by nature, and it is possible that I misunderstood the situation. Perhaps the brilliant Lame Hans had created a machine *persona* cunning enough to deliberately lose eight-ninths of the time, thereby inflating the already enormous ego of its perpetrator. Summers were hot in Bavaria, at the time of which I am writing, even hotter than they are now, a peak of solstice that fried brains and damaged reputations. The thoughts of a jailer are not to be dismissed; we see aspects of prisoners that they do not see themselves.

"It is time for another game," Lame Hans said deliberately. "Please redistribute the board. I will not ask you this again. If your mind is to drift, let it be when you are not in my presence."

Clumsily—I have never quite understood the initial posting of the thirty-two chess pieces even after all this time—I bent to the task. Lame Hans regarded me indolently, perched in the shadows of the cell. He called it his "Plato's Cave." Under no circumstance have I pursued this subject. It has something to do with idealization as opposed to the grim actuality furnished within the Bavarian compass, but I am not a reflective person (no jailer possibly could be and keep his position), and I leave Lame Hans to his own speculations. With some difficulty ("Queen takes her own color; Knights adjoin the Rooks on the first line," I mumble subvocally) I completed the formation and pushed the board into proximity to the prisoner. Rubbing his hands, he contemplated the fresh formulation with delight. "Are you ready?" he asked.

"Of course I am ready. Go ahead."

"Not this time," Lame Hans said. "It is time now for you to play. You have the white pieces. Move."

The invitation was unprecedented. Hans had never before asked my participation. I admit that I looked at him with some confusion. "I don't understand," I said. "It is your move. Both times."

"This is the second series," Lame Hans said. He moved in spindly, erratic fashion from the deep shadows to the front of his cage. "In the second series there are two participants. The previous series has reached its conclusion. It was mediated that the winner would be the first to achieve one hundred and sixty victories, and I have now done so. The machine is therefore eliminated, and it is time for you to take its place."

This announcement was dismaying. I barely knew the rules of chess, as I have made clear—and in the role of human, entrapped opponent, Gretchen suffocated. While I am sturdier than Gretchen and considerably less naive, I have my own disability as well as only the shakiest command of chess. "I would rather not," I said. "This was never provided."

Perhaps I should explain the conditions. Bavarian tenets and folkways can be mystifying to tourists or the uninitiated. Through the years we have had occasional wavelets of visitors, some of them interested in mountain passages, others in hearty adventures in the local pubs and resorts. A few of them have been drawn by news of the legendary Lame Hans and his bizarre penitentiary in the aftermath of Gretchen's horrible but rather necessary death. We are obliged to enact this strange tournament for their edification and ours. It is a laborious and stultifying circumstance, but I assumed my role without complaint. It had been my plan to abscond to the North and somehow change my life, but I had been embarrassingly caught at the border and returned in chains and humiliation to the authorities and, after a perfunctory trial, to my rather peculiar fate. I had not objected. There were worse penalties. The delectable Gretchen, for instance, had been sentenced to the machine and subsequent suffocation. I had in contract been given privileges of the cell block and occasional periods in default during which Lame Hans had been subject to interrogation, and I had been permitted to sleep or otherwise amuse myself. Of course, there were limits to my own freedom, and my life contained no more possibility than that of Lame Hans.

The good aspect of totalitarianism is that it grinds all of its subjects into a monotony of feeling and circumstance. Everything feels pretty much like everything else after a while. There is a glittering similarity and a fascinating restriction of emotional range that, once accepted, tends to pass rather quickly.

"There was never any intention to enlist me in place of the machine," I pointed out. "I was never meant to be a participant."

"*Au contraire,*" Lame Hans said. Sometimes he lurches into terrible French, a language he comprehends as poorly as I do chess. "Provisions were clear. You would enter at the conclusion of the one hundred and sixtieth victory for either side. You are white and therefore on move. I suggest an aggressive game. King's Gambit? Of course it will be King's Gambit declined."

All of this rather tense and barely comprehensible exchange is taking place between a man in a musty corridor, barely pervaded by light, and another locked in a cell. The question of who is the prisoner, who the guardian, seems quite abstract at this moment.

"Gretchen suffocated," I observed pointlessly.

"So she did. Life itself is a dismal affliction, an imposition upon us. We breathe, we do not breathe; it is all the same. Like totalitarianism. Life itself is a species of suffocation. We are now on the clock. An imaginary clock of course, but no less determinant for all of this. I await your move."

I understood, finally, that the situation was somewhat more complex than I had previously thought. Bavaria is more than Bavarian: It is the world itself. This is a species of contemplation with which I had never been previously engaged.

In consequence and somewhat reluctantly, I moved the King's Pawn two spaces. I know this much at least, and of the necessity to bring out the Queen's Pawn on the subsequent move and the King's Knight shortly thereafter. In the wake of this rather daring accommodation, I survey the board glumly, awaiting Lame Hans's subsequent move. His eyes appear to glitter with purpose.

He moved his own King's Pawn, folded his arms, stared at me. "Mate in ten moves," he said. "By the way," he added, "all of this is in your imagination."

As if from a great distance, gasps and throttles come from somewhere behind him, deep in his cell.

Gretchen is suffocating again.

Mike Resnick is, according to Locus, *the all-time leading award winner for short fiction. He has won five Hugos (from a record thirty-six nominations), a Nebula, and other major awards in the United States, France, Japan, Croatia, Poland, and Spain. He is the author of seventy-one novels, more than two hundred and fifty short stories, three screenplays, and is the editor of forty-one anthologies. His work has been translated into more than two dozen languages, and he was the Guest of Honor at the 2012 World Science Fiction Convention.*

Barry Malzberg is the author of more than ninety books and three hundred short stories, and is a former editor of both Amazing *and* Fantastic. *A multiple Nebula and Hugo nominee, he won the first John W. Campbell Memorial Award for Best Novel.*

Epistoleros

AARON ALLSTON

On Gene Wolfe: *I first met Gene at the New Orleans Science Fiction and Fantasy Festival (NOSF3) in the early 1990s. I was a program participant at the convention and had a total of two or three novels in print at the time.*

I sat on a panel with several other writers with similarly short pedigrees, and just before the panel was to begin, a middle-aged man in the audience asked a question. "Do you mind if I come up there and join you? If I speak on a panel, I can write this trip off on my taxes." Seeing the blank expressions on all the panelists' faces, he added, "I'm Gene Wolfe."

Well, yes. If we could have levitated him up to the panel table, we would have. I have no recollection of what the panel was about, but I do remember that Gene was gracious, humorous, very well spoken . . . and tremendously nice to a collection of newbie writers who hadn't recognized him.

I didn't see him again until a Texas Book Fair several years later. The year 2000 marked the first time the TBF made an effort to recognize the genre of science fiction, and Gene, Elizabeth Moon, and I were among the guests. Again, Gene was erudite and gracious, as welcoming to fans and aspiring writers as he was to colleagues.

And, sadly, those are my only two protracted direct encounters with Gene. They've been just enough to answer something I'm curious about with every writer. Some writers are good at their craft, others indifferent or bad. Some writers are rotten human beings, or average, or fine folk. And there's often no correspondence between being good as a person and good as

a writer or bad as both. I'm delighted to say that Gene deserves
every accolade he's received as a fine writer and a great guy.

April 14, 1891
From Thaddeus Hobart, Salt Creek, Republic of Texas
To Chester Lamb, Chicago, Illinois, United States

Dear Chet:

By the time you read these words I will be dead and in Hell.

I don't begrudge my place in Hell. I earned it fair and square, and I'll be in fine company. But as for being dead, I will confess to being resentful of my fate.

I came to Salt Creek to do some gambling. There are no warrants out for me in the Republic, and this is the kind of town where cattlemen find themselves anxious for a last night or two of diversion before driving their livestock across the Red River and into Indian Territory. It is also a place where the Frenchies, soldiers and inspectors who come across the river to enjoy the entertainments their fort does not provide, are as willing to part with their Louisiana francs as the locals are to lose their Texas dollars.

Three nights ago, in a saloon named Bust, I joined a poker game with four cattlemen and a Spaniard named Rey. From his French manners and dress, this Rey showed himself to be a sissy. He had two ladies who were his companions, Frenchwomen, and one was with him that night. Rey had a poker face and a poker mind, and unlike the cattlemen he did not drink a drop. He and I cleaned the cattlemen out, and then I cleaned Rey out.

He did not take kindly to losing. He stared at me with eyes like they belonged on an alligator, and then he and his lady left without saying another word.

I did not know then that he began asking questions about me

that very night. I learned soon enough that he had found out about the bounties on my head, including the big dead-or-alive bounty from Kansas. I decided then to leave town, only to find that I was being watched and followed. It was not rummies working for drinks or farm boys anxious for a little fame keeping their eye on me. Money was not Rey's concern, and he had hired French soldiers, riflemen made hard in their battles with the Indians, to keep me in town. I can't ride to the edge of Salt Creek without having a rifle pointed at me by a damned Frenchman, and the town marshal has no interest in offering me aid on account of my reputation.

I don't know what Rey has in store for me. I'm not the shot I was when I knew you, and I don't think I'm in for a fair fight anyway.

So I'm asking you—no, let me be truthful. The promise you made to me back in '76, I'm holding you to that. If you find that I have met my end through treachery, I call on you to avenge me, so that as I sit among my fellows in Hell's halls I will be content in the knowledge that Rey will soon join me.

You know I am not a man of letters. I have been helped with the writing of this note by Cletus Simmons, a farmer hereabouts. If I do not write again, you will know that I am dead. When you come to Salt Creek, enquire of Cletus Simmons concerning my fate and he will set you on the right trail.

I think I will not see you again.

Your friend,

Thaddeus

June 1, 1891
From Chester Lamb, Salt Creek, Republic of Texas
To Morris Levitt, Chicago, Illinois, United States

Dear Morris:

In the event that my previous letters have not all reached you yet, I will summarize my travels reported in that correspondence.

After receiving your telegram and its terse explanation of Thaddeus's letter, I did depart New Orleans in haste. I traveled by boat to Houston. From there I secured passage by coach to San Antonio, then northward as far as Dallas, a journey of some days. It was from Dallas that I dispatched my last letter to you. I also confirmed, by telegram, that there was still no sign of Thaddeus in Salt Creek.

No stagecoach service exists from Dallas to Salt Creek, so I secured a horse and a mule. The horse, a palomino, which is, I confess, a bit of a nag, is named Becky and is of good disposition. The mule is neither a Becky nor a gentle soul.

I traveled the route of the Chisholm cattle trail northeast toward my destination. I had no company at first. This proved a blessing as it allowed me to issue complaints, sometimes in the most profane terms, as my backside, out of practice with the saddle, ached abominably.

My appreciation for solitude ebbed as I neared the Red River, however, since that waterway marks the boundary between the Republic of Texas and Indian Territory. The Indians settled on this side of the river, chiefly Cherokee, are considered allies of Texas, and those on the other side enemies of the French. So there is fair safety for English speakers in these parts, but young bucks on a cattle raid can make any encounter a dangerous one.

To my relief, though, two days out from Salt Creek, I overtook a longhorn cattle herd, that belonging to a Mr. Danton of San Antonio. His son, Young Mr. Danton, was trail boss. His cowboys were moving about two thousand head, and he was congenial. I contrived to ride with his crew for the sake of safety. The territory, lightly settled, alternated between grasslands good for grazing and piney woods around which we navigated, and we did not once encounter a band of rustlers or marauders of any stripe. Only the summer heat, growing daily, contributed to misery.

We were one day out from Salt Creek when two more riders bound for the same destination overtook us and elected to ride with us.

One was a younger man, perhaps one or two years past twenty, lean and hardy-looking as rope. He had an affable smile, yet he dressed in black from his crisp cowboy hat to his boots, and he wore a two-pistol rig about his waist. I took all these affectations as signs pointing toward a career, or at least ambitions, as a gunman. He rode a chestnut stallion with lovely lines and a large white spot shaped like a diamond on his chest, but the man had no relief horse.

The other man was forty or older, my age at least, a leathery *mestizo* with drooping mustachios. His features and eyes gave away no indication of what he might be thinking. He was dressed in less ostentatious garments than his companion; his duster coat, shirt, trousers, chaps all in varying shades of tan or brown, and his accoutrements, including cowboy hat, gun belt, and boots were all worn but well maintained. His gun belt carried only a single holster, on his left hip, and he had a fringed buckskin sheath for his carbine tied off to his saddle. He rode a compact gray mare, heavily spotted along its haunches, and its near twin trotted along in docile fashion a short distance behind, requiring no lead rope.

Over time, this villainous-looking pair chose to gravitate toward me. They drew abreast of me, the younger man to my left and the older to my right.

The younger man was the first to speak. "Headed up to Salt Creek, are you?"

I nodded. "I am."

"What's your name?"

"Lamb. Chester Lamb of Chicago."

Our conversation was delayed for several moments as he laughed. His merriment engaged his whole body and he was forced to wipe tears from his eyes. *"Lamb?"*

"That is my name." I was well used to his sort of humor.

"Well, I suspect you're a right tough *hombre,* then, because you must have been set on all your life by folks amused by your name."

I gave him a companionable nod but did not elaborate. "What's your name?"

"I am the Baghdad Kid."

Now it was my turn to laugh, but I did a much more manful job of suppressing the urge. "You're not claiming to be from Mesopotamia, I trust."

His expression became one of scorn. "Naw, not *that* Baghdad. Baghdad, Republic of Texas. Down Austin way. I'm the most famous man ever to come out of Baghdad."

"I am happy to acknowledge the truth of that." I turned to the other rider and found him staring intently at me.

He spoke before I could. "You are the Chester Lamb who wrote accounts of the Kaiser's War against France?" He spoke with only the slightest trace of a Spanish accent.

"Yes. I returned home less than a year ago."

"I enjoyed your dispatches." He urged his horse nearer, leaned my way, and extended a hand for me to shake. "Luis Vasquez of Laredo."

Morris, there might be an infinite number of Luis Vasquezes from Laredo, but there is only one with any reputation of consequence, which prompted my return question as I shook his hand: "Captain Vasquez of the Texas Rangers?"

He shrugged. "I am no longer with the Rangers."

As dangerous as the Baghdad Kid might believe himself to be, Vasquez was more so in actuality. It was a testament to his skill that after so many years of his violent way of life, he still possessed the majority of his own teeth.

He pressed on. "Why do you come to Salt Creek? It is not a town for news."

I took a moment to compose my reply. "I'm not here on assignment. I took leave from covering the centennial celebration of the end of the French Civil War to come here. I've come to enquire after an old friend. He sent me a letter suggesting his life might be in danger."

Vasquez looked past me at the Kid. I found him staring back at Vasquez, his expression startled.

Then the Kid fastened his attention back on me. "You don't mean Thad Hobart."

"I do."

"I'll be damned. How do you know him?"

"I owe him a debt. I met him on the occasion of my first visit to the Republic, fifteen years ago. I had written an account of murders a gunman named Dexter Trout had committed. Trout sought me out and found me on the streets of Fort Worth. I am not a proficient pistol duelist, but fortunately for me, Thad shot Trout. Thad's intent was not entirely altruistic, for there had been bad blood between them, but I swore to repay him if need ever arose."

The Kid nodded. "He's my uncle."

"So you're a Hobart?"

"Naw, I'm a Pfluger. Henry Pfluger. But my ma was a Hobart before she married my pa."

I turned to Vasquez to see if he would grace me with an explanation of his relationship to Thaddeus, but he merely stared at me with his emotionless, earth-colored eyes and said nothing.

So Thad had written each of us, and perhaps more individuals besides, to call in markers. I wondered how many of us it would take to avenge him.

[Omitted.]

Morris, Salt Creek is a cow town whose sole geographical feature of merit is a broad fordable spot in the Red River. Picture a thick cluster of wooden buildings, the oldest of them built forty years ago, spreading southward from the river, with beaten-earth streets for livestock and wagons, wooden sidewalks for men and women. Those buildings that are not homes for the town's citizens are chiefly businesses catering to the tastes of cowmen and soldiers: bars and gambling halls, hotels and barber shops, houses of ill repute, shops and dining establishments, bathhouses and stables. There is a telegraph office but no newspaper, a school but no library. Surrounding the town are broad pastures where the cattle may be rested and grazed before crossing into Indian Territory, and beyond them are outlying farms.

At first, it seems to be an unremarkable town, but it is actually a place of some tension.

The river is the border between the Republic of Texas and the French-controlled Indian Territory. Though technically a part of the vast Province of Louisiana, the Territory is a lightly settled and lawless place, most of its occupants being red men driven out of the United States after enactment of the Indian Expulsion Act of the 1830s. Possessing no affection for the Americans or the French, the Indians get along tolerably well with the Texans and do not visit much violence on this side of the border or against cowmen driving their herds up to the Kansas railheads. But the presence of that uncontrolled population does mean occasional danger for the townsfolk.

More tension derives from the two camps just downstream from the town, one on either side of the river. On the far side lies a French fortification properly named Fort Beauchamp but referred to by the Texans as Fort Cow. A squat and homely thing of wooden palisades and buildings made of uneven stones and mortar, it safeguards the French inspectors who levy tariffs on cattle entering Indian Territory; the French take possession of one cow per two hundred in a herd. This practice often produces conflict, for the French choose when they wish to examine a herd and can keep a trail boss and his cowboys waiting for days. A trail boss out of favor with the French can be the regular victim of this tactic. Delays might also be brought on by inspectors accepting bribes from one trail boss to inconvenience another. Coalitions of businessmen in Salt Creek, it is rumored, bribe the inspectors to hinder a herd's progress to promote the town's economy. On the other hand, trail bosses might offer bribes of cash or cattle to the inspectors to speed things along. It is a complicated business.

The cattle taken by the French are collected at intervals and sent along the same Chisholm Trail to Kansas for sale by the French.

Those herds are preyed upon by rustlers of all stripes, especially Texans and Cherokee.

Nor could the French have a fort here without incurring a Texan response. On the near side of the river, directly opposite Fort Cow, lies Fort Montague, similarly an architectural tragedy, its Texan garrison charged with eyeing the French while the French eye them. So a state of mounting agitation exists between the French and the Texans here.

[Omitted.]

We arrived in Salt Creek the day following my introduction to the Baghdad Kid and Vasquez. We three and Young Mr. Danton rode ahead of the herd. As we reached the town's outermost buildings, Danton made his farewells and rode on alone to visit the office where he would request an inspection of the herd.

The three of us continued, making, I am sure, an unusual picture: a raw-boned youth intent on achieving fame as a killer, a sleepy-eyed *vaquero* whose passivity concealed a history of mayhem, and a Northerner who might most charitably be described as a "dude." Astride my swaybacked nag, in civilized dress, a leather duster coat thrown over it all, a bowler hat atop my head and gold-rimmed spectacles before my eyes, my hair graying and my features mild, I was, I am certain, the least dangerous-looking man in Salt Creek that day.

We enquired after the location of the saloon named Bust and rode there. Contrary to my expectations, it was a reputable-looking wooden building of sound construction, one story in height but spacious, with glass in the windows. Dark orange curtains within shielded patrons from the sun, the building front being west facing. We watered our horses and mule from the trough outside, then hitched the beasts and entered through swinging wooden doors.

In the main room beyond, a massive, dark wood bar dominated the left wall. Square tables lined the other walls. Wooden partitions separated the tables along the back wall, and curtains, matching those of the windows, on rods allowed those tables to be screened off for privacy individually. None was so shrouded at this hour.

There were more tables in the center of the floor, but widely spaced, and I suspected that the spaciousness was meant to accommodate dancing. Against the right wall, where a table might otherwise rest, was an upright piano, its surface scraped and scoured, suggesting that it dated back to the Texas Revolution or earlier.

The business was lightly occupied at this hour. Seated at one table beside the piano, French soldiers argued in their own language about the virtues, real or imagined, of a young lady named Sally. Their red pants and blue coats made them the most colorful patrons present. Three cowboys, none of them young and all of them surly of manner, held cards and exchanged silent looks around a central table. The bar itself was unoccupied except for its keeper, a round-bellied man, his whiskers nearly white.

As we entered, I heard a growl from near my right foot. There lay a hound dog, dirty yellow in color, eyeing us as if considering whom to bite first. But it did not so much as stir a muscle as we passed, and ceased growling when we were a few steps beyond.

We moved to the bar and took stools there. I set my bowler on the bar beside me, while the Kid and Vasquez kept their hats atop their heads in the fashion of Texans.

I engaged the bartender's attention. "Your maître d' is not entirely friendly."

He left off polishing a glass mug. "My what? Oh, Mustard. He don't mean nothing. He loves all ladies and hates all men, but he don't actually bite. What'll you gentlemen have?"

Vasquez and I chose beer. The Kid ordered a white mule. Perhaps he considered rough, unaged whisky the drink of mean-spirited gunmen. I saw Vasquez suppress a laugh as the Kid made his demand.

My companions, perhaps trusting that my profession would afford me some ease in investigative conversation, left it to me to begin enquiries. When the bartender returned with our drinks, I asked, "Why is this establishment called 'Bust'?"

He smiled, clearly happy to answer a question he'd dealt with many times before. "It's where you end up. You know, Kansas or Bust, Nuevo Mexico or Bust, Florida or Bust. This is Bust."

"I'm Chester. This is Vasquez, and that's the Baghdad Kid."

The bartender did not react to that last name, so it appeared that the fame of the Kid had not yet spread as far north as the Red River. The bartender merely nodded. "I'm Tubb. Edgar Tubb, owner and proprietor. You here with Danton's drive? You don't look like a cowpoke."

"I'm here looking for an old friend. By chance, are you acquainted with a man named Thaddeus Hobart?"

He nodded again. "Spent some time here and in the gambling halls. He left awhile back, I think. Haven't seen him in nearly a month. That your friend?"

He seemed sincere and unconcerned, but his answer puzzled me. It suggested Thad had not perished in a public duel. Yet if he had escaped Salt Creek, surely he would have written or telegraphed my home in Chicago to let me know of his fate.

"That is indeed the name of my friend." I turned to my next avenue of investigation. "Do you know a Cletus Simmons?"

"I surely do. He and his daughter have a hardscrabble farm west of town. Saw his buckboard go past a little while ago. I imagine he's buying supplies. Might still be around."

The Kid stood. "I'll fetch him."

"You don't know Salt Creek, nor would you recognize Simmons by sight." I turned back to Tubb. "Do you have a boy you could send for him?"

"Well, yes." He frowned and his voice suggested he did not find the request to be a convenient one.

I drew forth a coin and set it on the bar before him. "For your boy's trouble."

He swept it away—I suspected the boy would see no part of that payment—and his smile returned.

The three of us retreated to one of the partitioned tables with our drinks. We had ordered and received a second round before the boy, an Indian lad of perhaps ten, returned. He led a very lean man whose hair and mustache were a dense gray, his garments a hard-wearing brown. When the boy pointed to us, the man gave us a look of trepidation before turning our way. The hound growled as he passed and the man shied away from the beast.

I gestured for him to join us and made introductions all around. In a voice beginning to go dry and thin with age, he confirmed that he was Cletus Simmons. He took off his hat and held it against his chest, twisting its brim as if unaware he were doing so.

I took little time to reach the subject. "Can you tell us where we can find Thaddeus Hobart?"

He looked around, his expression unhappy, before returning his attention to us. His voice dropped to a whisper. "I'd take it as a kindness if you would speak a little more quiet. Yes, because Thad told me some names, yours among them, I can tell you of his whereabouts. Anyone else, I'll deny ever having met him."

The Kid frowned at that statement. "Did he do you wrong?"

Mr. Simmons took a moment to array his thoughts. "Yes, he done me wrong, but that's of no matter now. You will find it easy to visit him. Because he's stone dead in an unmarked grave on my land."

Vasquez, the Kid, and I exchanged a glance. Vasquez was the first to respond. "How did he die?"

"Shot in the back by a man named Rey."

I sighed. There was to be no happy ending for Thaddeus Hobart. "Tell us the whole story."

There was nothing remarkable, only pettiness and tragedy, to the tale Mr. Simmons spun. Thad had initially approached him to write letters to us and two other individuals—both of them gunmen Thad had ridden with . . . men quite famous in their own right for crimes and exploits. It seemed they had not responded, or at least not yet responded, to Thad's entreaties. Thad had paid Mr. Simmons well for scribe duties and his silence.

A few days after the letters had been posted, Mr. Simmons heard a pounding upon his farmhouse door and a pained voice crying, "For God's sake, help me!" He unbarred the door, and Thad, in a state of collapse, fell into his home. Thad gasped out a few words of explanation, saying he had made a break from Salt Creek on foot, undetected by the soldiers watching him, but then he had been pursued by Rey. Rey had shot him in the back, leaving him to die. After those words, Thad had indeed perished. Mr. Simmons had buried him, telling no one of these events out of fear that as the sole person who knew the name of Thad's killer he might himself be murdered.

The news cast an air of gloom across me. Vasquez evidenced no emotion on the subject. The Bagdad Kid, on the other hand, seemed jubilant. "I'm sorry about Uncle Thad, but hell, I get to kill me a *bad man*."

I kept my attention on Mr. Simmons. "This Rey—is he still in town?"

Simmons nodded. "He comes to town every night with one of his whores, or both. But their quarters are at Fort Cow. I think they're friends with the commander."

"So he'll be here tonight?"

"He will. *Right* here. He comes to Bust most nights."

"Thank you, Mr. Simmons." I extended my hand to him. "We won't speak of your involvement."

"Thank you." He shook all our hands, then rose.

I added, "With your permission, once we've settled this situation, we may visit your farm to pay our final respects to Thaddeus's grave."

"Oh." He seemed to have been made uncertain by that request. "Of course. You'd be welcome." He hurried from the saloon, receiving another growl from Mustard.

Vasquez, the Kid, and I spoke then in hushed tones about what we needed to do. Clearly, a murderous attack from behind called for vengeance. Vasquez, pragmatic, suggested a solution suited to the Code of Hammurabi—shoot Rey in the back. But as dishonorable as Rey had been, I could not quite agree. Such an assault constituted a grave sin.

Nor would the Kid have anything to do with such a plan. He told us, "You don't get the right kind of fame shooting people in the back. It's going to have to be in front of God and everybody. Three duels. Me first, since Uncle Thad was my blood kin. If Rey survives—and he won't—Vasquez. And if the Spaniard survives Vasquez—which he won't—Chet kills him."

Such a strategy did seem to stack the deck against Rey, and yet it was fair. Each of us would be taking the same risk. Rey could not complain of unfair treatment. So I assented, as did Vasquez.

The Kid pressed on. "Chet, do you even *own* a gun?"

I patted the pocket of my waistcoat. "I have a derringer."

His face fell as though I'd confessed to being proficient only with thrown rocks. "Oh, dear God. See here, I'll bet you a dollar that Mr. Simmons ended up with Thad's Peacemaker. We'll set the duels for tomorrow noon but fetch you that gun before then."

"Done."

We then set out to stable our animals and secure rooms at the Station Hotel, a well-maintained business with a dining room, and we prepared to confront Rey that night.

[Omitted.]

On our return to Bust that evening, we found the establishment well occupied with patrons. Every stool at the bar was engaged, and most of the tables as well. A fair-haired man sat at the piano, hammering at its keys, producing a noise suggesting that the instrument was being rolled down a flight of stairs. There were women present, their dresses colorful and in some cases decorated with what looked like dyed ostrich feathers, offering dances, saloon companionship, and doubtless other services to the cowmen present. Oil lanterns hung from rafters cast a warm glow.

Mustard was in his usual place and offered his usual greeting. The Kid shook his head over that. "After I kill Rey, I may have to do something about that hound."

"Unlike Rey, he's done you no harm." I led the way to an unoccupied table away from the wall and set my hat aside. When Tubb approached, we repeated our orders of earlier in the day.

I also requested of Tubb that he point out Señor Rey when he arrived.

Tubb chuckled at that. "You'll know him when you see him."

A few minutes later, a hand—a white hand of diminutive proportions—pushed open one of the swinging doors and held it. Another individual, not so fair, strode through and paused.

This did indeed have to be Rey. He was a tall man, dark-haired, his skin the olive tone of Mediterranean natives, his features accentuated by a narrow black mustache. He was handsome enough to tread the boards as a leading man of the stage.

His mode of dress was indeed French and current. From neck to ankle he was in iron-gray silks, a well-tailored suit, with silver buttons holding his waistcoat closed and a silver chain indicating the pocket that held his watch. Though his trouser cuffs largely hid his footwear, it appeared he was wearing boots of gleaming black leather. He deviated from proper fashion in three significant ways. He wore no hat on his head, none at all. His suit jacket was cut short. The reason for that was the better to permit access to the gun belt he wore, a polished black rig matching his boots. From its holster on his right hip protruded the ivory grip of a revolver.

The individual who followed him into the saloon, the one who had held the door for him, was a woman. She had dark hair arrayed in a tight coif and topped with a bowler hat. She was dressed as if for riding. Her fitted red silk skirt, its smallish bustle of the current style, matched her tailed coat. Her white blouse was high-necked and topped with a most delicate lace collar. The fairness of her skin suggested a diligent avoidance of the sun. Her bosom was full, her posture erect. She surveyed the room with dark eyes that, like a cat's, demonstrated much attentiveness but did not betray her thoughts. The door she had briefly gripped swung shut behind her.

I felt a brief surge of annoyance. To me, Rey had just proven himself to be a bounder: Not only did he bring a well-born female companion to a place like this, he permitted her to hold the door for him rather than hold it for her like a gentleman. But I ignored my own feeling.

I glanced at Tubb for confirmation and found him already staring at me, nodding: This was indeed Rey.

Rey and his lady evaluated the few tables still unoccupied. My eye was then drawn to a curious detail: Mustard the hound lay in his accustomed place, and at this moment he offered brisk wags of his tail rather than his usual growl.

Before Rey could make a choice, I rose and approached him. I gave him a little bow. "Señor Rey? Allow me to beg the pleasure of your company, and that of your companion. My friends and I are newly arrived and would be delighted to spend time in the company of someone as extravagantly original as yourself."

He paused, considering my offer, and then gave me a little nod.

I led them back to our table. Vasquez in the meantime had secured an additional chair so that all five of us might sit. While we seated ourselves, I noted that Rey did not hold his lady's chair for her, and I made introductions.

Rey's reply, in a voice so faint that the three of us were obliged to lean forward to catch his words, was minimal in its detail: "Mademoiselle Sophie Garand." With a gesture, he indicated his companion, though he had not hitherto acknowledged her.

I had a polite line of enquiry in mind, one that would steer our conversation to the matter of Thaddeus Hobart. My intent was foiled by the Kid's forthrightness and indignation. He had begun to flush red even as Rey was taking his chair, and now, point-blank, he asked, "Are you the son of a bitch who killed Thaddeus Hobart?"

I endeavored not to wince. I discerned the volume of conversation at the tables nearest ours began to diminish, though it appeared that not everyone in the room had heard the Kid's words.

For a moment, it seemed that Rey himself was among those who had not heard them. But presently he did turn his head to acknowledge the Kid. Unruffled, no emotion marring the manly beauty of his features, he offered a second nod. "The man Hobart is no more, and it was at my doing." Again he spoke so quietly that we had to strain to hear him. Now, at last, a touch of an accent was evident in his speech, yet it was French rather than Spanish.

The Kid looked confounded that Rey would admit so readily to the deed. "And you shot him in the *back*?"

Rey offered an eloquent shrug of his shoulders. He whispered, "By that means I did not have to look on his abhorrent features. I am left to wonder about his family, whether he was the handsomest of his line, the others being obliged to remain within mud pens and eat slop."

The Kid's brows lowered during that statement, and his response was more decisive than I expected. He whipped up his right-hand revolver, aimed it point-blank at Rey's chest, and let loose with a blast.

Caught off guard, I jumped nearly out of my skin, then grabbed in awkward haste for the derringer in my pocket. Rey would be dead, of course, but he might have friends in the crowd, and a display of guns, including even one such as mine, might be the only way now for the three of us to leave this establishment alive.

An instant later, Vasquez drew and fired. Shouts of alarm filled the air, all but drowned out by the reports of the revolvers. The stink of gunpowder burned at my nostrils.

And still Rey did not fall. In the moment after my companions' weapons discharged, he merely continued staring at the Kid, impassive.

Then he reached for his hip.

The Kid and Vasquez fired again, and this time my shot joined theirs, the derringer kicking in my hand. I had a bead on his face—specifically, on the center point between the man's eyes. At this range my shot could not miss its target.

Yet no mark appeared on Rey's face. No discoloration spread on his waistcoat or the blouse beneath it. I became dimly cognizant of the fact that, in the direction my companions and I had fired, one of the establishment's windows had shattered a moment earlier.

Rey produced his revolver. Yet he did not aim it at any of us. He shrugged, spun the weapon around on his finger, and holstered it once more.

A silence, and I do not exaggerate to call it a shocked silence, fell across the establishment. Many of the patrons were on the floor, having thrown themselves there to avoid stray gunfire. Now the braver of them began to rise. But all eyes were on the five of us.

I caught a glimpse of Mademoiselle Sophie's face. It wore an expression of sadness, but there was not the slightest hint of shock to it. She had known events would transpire just this way.

A thought, a terrible thought, emerged from the fog that had suddenly gathered in my mind. No man could withstand five point-blank gunshots . . . none but one specific breed. My heart sank.

Now Rey spoke in his whisper. "Thaddeus Hobart was a thief, a liar, and a wastrel. A man without cause or principle. He deserved far worse than I gave him."

Vasquez, shock evident on his face, the first strong emotion I had seen him demonstrate, slowly lowered his gun and, with what seemed like great reluctance, holstered it. That reminded me of the bizarre tableau we all presented. I put my derringer away.

The Kid seemed to be in a greater state of shock than we were. "You—you—"

Stray thoughts flitted through my memory: a military camp I'd seen during the Kaiser's futile war against the French, abandoned except by corpses; the curious death, a century ago, of Benjamin Franklin; tales by the score from the implacable expansion of the French Empire. I addressed the man I had just shot. "Your name is not Rey and you are not Spanish."

He turned his attention to me. "Correct."

"You're French and your name is Renault."

"*Oui.*"

Finally there were other voices to be heard in the room—indistinct murmurs, with "Renault" and "paladin" the only comprehensible words. Two of the cattlemen at the bar bolted, making it outside and into the dark before the hound had time to growl at them.

Renault spoke again. All attention was now on him and everyone heard his whisper. "I say you are men of no worth. No honor. Pigs like your friend Hobart. But I give you a choice. Three days from now, at noon, I will return here. In the street outside, if you dare face me, I will shoot you each in the heart. If before then you wish to demonstrate your true natures and flee, do so. Since you have no honor left, running away can do it no harm." So saying, he rose, the economy of his motion such that he did not move his chair in the least.

Mademoiselle Sophie rose as well, and preceded Renault from the saloon. Then they were gone, and low conversations sprang up around the room.

The Kid finally remembered to holster his weapon.

Mr. Tubb appeared beside our table, his face pale and his expression grave. "I think you gents are done drinking here for the night," he assured us.

The three of us walked in a sort of daze back to the Station Hotel. Before we ascended the stairs, Vasquez demanded of the night clerk a bottle of liquor, any sort. With it and three mismatched cups, we entered my chamber. His face pale, Vasquez poured for us, filling the room with the odor of strong tequila.

I gulped at mine, surviving a stronger than normal liquor burn.

The Kid urged Vasquez to fill his cup to the lip. He received his drink and turned to me for more explanation. "Am I crazy? Or was that a damned paladin?"

I sat on my bed, which under my weight creaked a complaint of its years. "Yes, Kid. Renault is one of the Twelve Peers, the agents of God or Satan who have guaranteed the ascendency of the French Empire across the last century." Finally the significance of the date that Renault had proposed for our duel revealed itself to me. "And I fear we have become the victims of a cruel deception."

The Kid crossed himself, as though the gesture would do him any good under these circumstances, and took the chair by the window. "Why is he *here*?"

"I think I've just grasped the reason, Kid. It relates to the centennial celebration of the end of the French Civil War. In fact, I'm certain of it." At the Kid's blank look, I continued. "When Charles the Tenth deposed Louis the Sixteenth and assumed the throne of France, he did so with the help of the paladins. Then they exterminated the leadership of the revolutionaries who had plagued the noble class for the previous two years and set about securing France's fortunes as the most powerful nation on the earth. Unstoppable killers who could strike down the leadership of any army, any nation . . . and the revolutionaries were put down, to the day, one hundred years before the date of our appointment with Renault."

Vasquez, who had remained standing, finally spoke. "Renault staged this. He drew us in and will kill us, men well known in Texas. A message to all the Republic. 'Stop pushing at the borders. Stop protesting our tariffs. Be good boys.'"

The Kid shook his head. "But the Frenchies don't much care what goes on in this part of the world."

I tipped my cup to him in mock salute. "That's exactly it, Kid. This action signals a change in that policy. With their European borders secure, they must now be turning their attention to strengthening their colonies in the New World. Perhaps in Africa and Asia as well." I considered that. "It may be that at this exact moment, eleven other traps have been sprung all over the world, one paladin at the center of each. A few days from now, news dispatches from Indo-China, the Congo, the South Seas, and other places will join the poor account of our deaths."

Vasquez looked at me. "Why will ours be a poor account?"

I smiled. "Because I will not be writing it. It will be some lesser chronicler."

Vasquez tossed back some of his villainous tequila and frowned, which seemed to cause his mustachios to droop even more. "If the French do quiet down the borders, what comes next?"

"In the New World, expansion into New Spain, I suspect."

"That don't matter." The Kid waved away my political speculation. "How do we kill Renault?"

I shrugged. The tequila was beginning to settle my nerves. "There is a horrible consistency to the stories about the paladins. No physical violence harms them, or even leaves a mark, as we ourselves saw. It is said that bullets and blades seeking them find other targets instead. Thank heavens our bullets did no harm to others at Bust. The paladins never eat nor drink in public—it is said that they fear poisoning. They are all named after the champions of Charlemagne, a French king out of both history and legend, and it is sometimes said that they *are* those original paladins, brought back from the dead."

Vasquez smoothed his mustache as he pondered. "And they are all more than a century old, yes?"

"Yes, the only men to be so blessed."

"So we have a choice." Vasquez's voice sounded very matter of fact. "Stay and die, or run and be dishonored."

We were silent for at least a full minute after that pronouncement, each of us lost in our own thoughts.

Finally the Kid spoke. "Well, I got me no wife or children

depending on me. And Renault still killed my uncle. Hell, maybe I'll get in a lucky shot. One that doesn't find another target."

Vasquez nodded and drew his hat a little lower over his brow, giving him a rakish look. "I don't think much of being called a coward." He and the Kid turned their eyes to me.

"I have no wife or dependents, either. More the fool I." I shrugged. "I will admit that I am not comfortable in the role of a maker of news. My job is to chronicle the actions of others. But I think I'll stay. I'll send my friend Morris accounts of the next few days, providing minute detail. Perhaps he, in studying my accounts, can find some fact that will help others confront the paladins in the time to come. And I'll have the opportunity to write myself a first-class obituary."

Vasquez, for the first time, laughed.

The two of them returned to their own rooms, and I set about penning this account for you. But now the hour grows late and I must rest for the trials I am yet to endure.

As ever, I remain your friend,

Chester

June 2, 1891
From Chester Lamb, Salt Creek, Republic of Texas
To Morris Levitt, Chicago, Illinois, United States

[Omitted.]

It was clear that everyone in town had heard what had transpired at Bust. Townsmen and cowboys, it seemed, shared a similar superstition about associating with men under a death sentence, so the three of us were largely left alone, barely receiving a word from anyone we addressed.

After noon, we elected to ride out to the Simmons farm and pay our respects to Thad's grave. A hardscrabble farm it was indeed, its farmhouse the sort of low, sturdy shelter built to withstand Indian raids. Ill-tended fields suggested that one old man and his daughter were insufficient to wring a full bounty from the soil.

Mr. Simmons was not to be seen working his fields as we rode in. He emerged from the house to greet us and led us past the chicken coop and barn to a low hill whence a single grave marker, a neatly whitewashed wooden cross, protruded. Painted upon it were words of bereavement:

IN LOVING REMEMBRANCE

ABIGAIL SIMMONS

BORN 1850

TAKEN FROM US JANUARY 3RD, 1886

Beyond that grave, a few steps down the far side of the hill and thus not visible from the road, was another grave, an unmarked mound of recently turned but hard-packed earth. There we said our good-byes, each in his own way.

Vasquez stared skyward and remained mute for a minute.

I looked at the grave and told the departed, "I'm too late to help you, but I will try to oblige people to remember your good with your bad."

The Kid crossed himself and said, "Yeah, it was me who stole your straight razor, I hope you're not still mad about that."

Whereupon we all, Simmons included, restored our hats to our heads and turned back toward the farmhouse.

During the walk, the Kid caught Simmons's attention. "Been meaning to ask you. Me being Uncle Thad's sole heir, and Chet here in need of something more formidable than his little sissy gun for when we all get killed, I'd like to have Thad's Colt to lend to him."

"Oh." Simmons walked in silence for a few moments. "I can't give it to you."

"Why?"

"I buried it with him. His boots, too."

"Naw, you didn't." The Kid sounded incredulous.

"I'm a man of peace, Mr. Pfluger. I think tools of murder should be put in the earth and forgotten."

"Well, we'll just dig it up, then."

Mr. Simmons turned a horrified look upon the Kid. "That's a grave! Holy words have been spoken over that spot. God himself would smite you."

"God'll forgive me. He knows you didn't have permission to bury my gun."

"You may not dig up that grave." Mr. Simmons's breath came fast and heavy now, his voice raspy.

Vasquez and I, trailing behind the Kid and Mr. Simmons, exchanged a look.

We reached the farmhouse and the Kid, still friendly, clapped Mr. Simmons across the shoulders. "You just go on inside and fetch me Uncle Thad's sidearm. I don't hold it against you for taking it. A farm like this needs defending. And you can keep his boots. But Chet here needs the gun, so you just go get it."

Mr. Simmons moved as briskly as if the Kid had held a branding iron to his backside. But when he entered his home, he shut the door and we heard its bar fall into place, leaving us staring at a small squat fortress with heavily shuttered windows.

Then Mr. Simmons began shouting through a peephole in the door. "I've got my shotgun and your business on my land is done. I recommend you move on."

The Kid cupped his mouth to shout back. "One Colt is not worth making enemies for, Mr. Simmons."

"Move along, Mr. Pfluger, or I *will* open fire."

That seemed clear enough, and we were indeed in the open. One Colt was also not worth dying for. So we mounted up and headed back toward town.

But we rode only until stands of trees blocked our view of Simmons's land. We found a clearing in a small stand of trees a few yards off the road and elected to wait there for nightfall.

Each of us had been made suspicious by the same few facts. Mr. Simmons had been afraid that someone might learn he knew the identity of Thad Hobart's killer, yet he was willing to anger three men who knew that secret. No dirt-poor farmer would bury a man in his boots and with his firearm when such things, if not desired, could be sold. Thad's grave had not settled as much as a month-old burial should have, in my inexpert estimation.

Finally, there was the question of his daughter Eliza. In town, she had been described as well grown, of marriageable age. A mostly grown daughter is, in the absence of her mother, the woman of the house. She had not emerged to greet us, to offer us refreshment. Perhaps Mr. Simmons had ordered her not to show herself, for she might be pretty enough to incite violence from rough men. But this one minor implicit insult, added to the other details, made our curiosity even greater.

[Omitted.]

After dark we returned on foot to the farmhouse, and it was the Kid who conceived our plan. "You and Vasquez move quiet as lizards to either side of the door and wait. I'll draw him out."

We did so, and he crept off in the direction of the chicken coop. Minutes later, the noise of the chickens began to rise. To it the Kid added an authentic animal cry, a coyote's whining howl.

There were no voices from inside the farmhouse, but of a sudden we heard the door being unbarred. It swung inward and the business end of a shotgun emerged, held in two strong hands.

I grabbed the barrels and swung them skyward while Vasquez stepped in and planted a blow of his fist to the man's midsection. There was a tremendous expulsion of breath and the man fell, leaving me in sole possession of the shotgun. "Got him," I shouted in the Kid's direction.

Lantern light spilled out over the prone man, who was dressed in a long nightshirt. He did not seem so skinny as before. Too, his hair was darker, with no balding patch at its crown. Curious, Vasquez bent down to roll him onto his back.

The Kid hurried up just in time to see the light fall across the man's features. This was not the face of Mr. Simmons. The Kid looked down upon him and voiced the man's name. "Uncle Thad!"

We dragged Thaddeus inside and seated him, roughly I must admit, in the rocking chair by the unlit fireplace. Vasquez kept him covered with his revolver while the Kid and I went exploring. It did not take us long to discover Mr. Simmons and his daughter, trapped in the root cellar, a heavy hope chest and wooden crates dragged into place atop the wooden trap door that provided access to it.

Eliza Simmons was indeed pretty, a dark-haired farm girl of fifteen, clearly not intimidated by the presence of rough men in her house. She was most anxious to visit vengeance on Thad if only I would yield her father's shotgun to her, which I would not.

Mr. Simmons explained. "Thaddeus has been here since the night I said he came with a bullet in his back. The bullet was a lie, a story he told me to tell. He kept Eliza under his gun and said he'd do her harm if I didn't spread the story he told and write the letters he wanted writ."

We turned our attention to Thad. He looked very uncomfortable, his once-handsome features now twisted into an expression of considerable unhappiness. He had put on some weight since I'd last seen him years before, a middle-aged thickening of the torso, but his hair was still dark. At this moment, his face glistened in the lamplight with perspiration, and his eyes sought ours in a plea for understanding. "I wasn't going to hurt her none, despite anything I said."

"I'm not going to promise not to hurt *you*," Vasquez assured him. "Why did you bring us here, Thaddeus? Why have you condemned us to die at the hands of that thing?"

"I was the condemned one," Thad said. "In a Louisiana prison.

Awaiting execution. They came to me with a plan. I knew a lot of famous folk. They had a use for famous folk. I'd just tell a story, Thaddeus Hobart would be known to have been killed, I'd have some money to set up a new life in Quebec or one of the Frenchie islands in the Pacific Ocean, with no bounty over my head ever again. I'm still waiting for the money."

The Kid, who had been pacing, ceased his ambulations and turned to Thad. "I'm your kin, damn you. Now I'm in a bind I can't back out of."

"I'm sorry, kid," his uncle told him. "They insisted on you by name. You, Vasquez, Lamb, and others. They *insisted*."

The Kid nodded as if mollified. "Well, I guess that's all right, then." Whereupon he drew his revolver and shot his uncle in the face.

I'll admit it caught me almost as much by surprise as it did Thad. I can only imagine my own expression. Thad's face registered astonishment, and then blankness as blood began to trickle from the hole at the bridge of his nose. Eliza offered up a brief shriek. I moved to catch her but she did not swoon.

Thad slumped, and then slid from the chair to the earthen floor.

The Kid turned to Mr. Simmons. "I think I told you I wanted his sidearm."

Mr. Simmons hastened to fetch it. He returned with the gun, a wood-handled .45. With it Simmons brought Thad's gun belt and boots.

We spent awhile digging up Thad's empty grave and putting it to use as it had originally been described. Afterward, we said nothing over it, our last words to Thad having been uttered that afternoon. We returned to Salt Creek, a morose trio of men.

That, Morris, is the truth of the situation. We're all going to die for the sake of honor and a lie. I will admit to feeling a touch melancholy.

But despite my self-pity, I remain your friend,

Chester

June 3, 1891
From Chester Lamb, Salt Creek, Republic of Texas
To Morris Levitt, Chicago, Illinois, United States

[Omitted.]

I spent the last full day I would enjoy in this life in pursuit of my profession. I began asking questions about Renault and our situation.

I knew better than to ask about Renault's history. The Frenchies had taken measures to obscure details of the careers of the Twelve Peers. My estimation was that this had been done to protect the paladins: The less that was understood about them, the lower the odds that anyone could ever visit revenge upon them.

I knew some of the details surrounding the death of Benjamin Franklin, for this is the sort of story that schoolchildren ghoulishly tell to their younger brothers and sisters, thrilled to know something bizarre about a historical figure. But to refresh my memory, I visited the local school and asked questions of a Mr. Wainwright, the schoolmaster.

Franklin, the inventive, inquisitive Founding Father, served as the United States ambassador to France during our own revolution and for a time afterward. He returned to France in 1790 at the behest of his friend, the Count of Mirabeau, who was staunchly allied with the revolutionists. Franklin, who provided counsel to the revolutionaries and sought international support for their cause, did not die with the count or the other remaining leaders, but was found some days later in a house in Passy.

The body of the great man was discovered in a salon room into which so many boxes and crates had been carried, then arranged into long rows and stacks, that the room was a veritable maze of passages almost too narrow to navigate. In one of these passages lay the body. Injuries to his chest and back, suggesting that a sword had been shoved through him, were clear evidence of the cause of his death. A calling card lay on the floor at his feet, bearing only the name *Renault.*

But the truly curious detail of death was what Franklin wore: a steel helmet, its visor utterly lacking eyeholes, and that locked into place on his head. The helmet had little defensive value, as it exposed his neck, mouth, and ears. This object earned Franklin the sad sobriquet of "the American man in the iron mask." Historians, schoolchildren, and even authors such as Poe have speculated wildly as to why the killer locked the man into the helmet.

In light of my own appointment with Renault, I wondered if there was something in the event of the Franklin murder that would afford me some useful information, but, like countless others before me, I could divine nothing from it.

My other enquiries related to Renault's movements in and around Salt Creek. I asked after every detail that could be recollected of the man.

He was indeed staying at Fort Cow, with his two ladies, Mlles Sophie and Laurette, as guests of the garrison commander. Frenchies for whom I bought a few drinks said that they did not believe Renault and their colonel were friends. Renault had presented papers to the colonel upon arrival and had subsequently been treated as an honored guest. Once his true identity had been revealed, Renault had been viewed with some fear by the Frenchies as well as the Texans.

It was said that he walked so quietly that floorboards did not creak under his feet. Knowing the stories of the paladins and their ability to steal into guarded fortresses, I had no doubt of the truth of this.

His wardrobe was limited. In Salt Creek, he always wore the same sort of gray suit, accommodating a gun belt. It was said that he had garments more suited to formal occasions but had never needed them in this rural town. His clothes, though stylish, were not unique. I had seen many people in town, including off-duty

French officers and a few lofty-minded Texans, wearing similar ensembles. I inferred that one or more local tailors catered to French tastes.

From men who visited Bust regularly, I learned a curious fact. Renault, before his identity as Rey had been discarded, had joined many groups of card players and had been involved in many conversations. It seemed that those who spent the most time speaking with him grew weary of doing so. A German-born storekeeper, who was delighted when I conducted my conversation with him in his native tongue, explained it best: "It is as when I first came to Texas and was always surrounded by speakers I could not understand. I strained to understand, as if listening hard would make me grasp the English words, and I went to bed tired of mind, not just body, each night."

Texas soldiers, defiantly drab in their brown roundabout coats and trousers, told me that Renault seemed to remain true to his French companions; he never cast an eye upon the local ladies.

During one of my conversations with garrulous soldiers, I saw, through the window of Bust, Renault himself walk past on the near sidewalk. Again clad in his grays, he was in the company of a young woman I had not seen before, this one golden-haired. She was equal in beauty to Mademoiselle Sophie, and was dressed in the Franco-Mexican fashion in vogue in Ciudad de México. The cut of her walking dress was French from the lace that trimmed her sleeves and collar to the garment's diminutive bustle, but the garment's colors were Mexican: broad, vertical bands alternating between a potter's red-brown and an earthy yellow, heavily printed with rosettes and other geometric designs. I inferred that this was Laurette.

Townsfolk changed direction or left the sidewalk altogether so as not to crowd Renault. I noted that Laurette, too, was a woman who did not smile in Renault's company, and I wondered at that fact. Two beauties associated with a powerful, handsome agent of the world's greatest power, and yet they seemed to experience no joy.

Some minutes later, the soldiers having left my table, Mademoiselle Sophie herself entered the establishment unaccompanied, closing and lowering her parasol. Her own walking dress was white, so fine that it almost shone, with an abundance of lace at the neck and wrists. Her hat seemed to consist mostly of wide brim and was worn at a canted angle as if meant to help snow slip from a northern roof. The hound Mustard, unmoving, wagged his tail for her. She offered him the briefest of smiles before looking around the room and catching sight of me.

She approached my table. I stood, offering her a slight but cordial bow.

"Mr. Lamb, may I have a word?" Her English, unlike Renault's, bore only the slightest of accents.

"Of course." I moved to seat her, and then took to my own chair again. Tubb approached to ask if she wished something to drink, but her reply was a slight shake of her head and a barely detectable shudder.

When Tubb was gone, she returned her attention to me. "It seems you have little time left."

I patted the pocket of my waistcoat where I kept my watch. "Twenty-two hours and a few minutes."

"Would you care for more?"

"More time? Of course."

"You can have it if you wish."

"How?"

"In tomorrow's duel. Simply do not fire on Renault."

"And he will spare me?"

"Yes."

"Why would he do that?"

"He admires your craft. Your profession."

Ah. I was not in Salt Creek to die. I was here to report on this event, to lend it credibility with my skill and my reputation.

Mademoiselle Sophie had not stated so exactly, so I concluded that she was not supposed to. My professional instincts would not allow me to leave such a momentous thing entirely unsaid, however. I fixed her with a stare. "And would Renault take it as a favor if I did not submit my next story? It concerns Thaddeus Hobart. Where he has been in recent weeks. How he is truly in his grave at last."

She straightened, her posture going from perfect to rigid. It took a moment before she could entirely drive the look of surprise from her eyes. "Yes. He would."

"If I am to write about Renault, using all my skill, I will wish to characterize him with scientific accuracy. Renault, and you, and Mademoiselle Laurette."

That earned me a brief laugh. "Renault cannot be described scientifically."

"Many people I have spoken to"—a blatant lie, for I had not broached this subject with anyone—"wonder how it is that you and Mademoiselle Laurette do not fall on one another like wildcats, competing for sole possession of Renault's affections."

Her sigh was barely audible. "The most lurid assumptions make the best conversation, do they not? Laurette and I are at peace with one another because Renault is neither my lover nor hers. He has never touched me."

I might have been startled by her frankness, but she was French. I pressed on. "So he is a true gentleman."

She did not reply. She changed the subject—returned it to its original course, rather. "May I report that you have accepted his offer?"

"I'm still considering it. It would seem to be a tremendous compromise of my moral character."

She offered me a little Gallic shrug. "Yes. But all life is compromise. Only death is uncompromising. I will go now."

I stood, and she made her departure.

Eventually I walked to my hotel, dined alone, and returned to my chamber to pen this letter and ponder my fate.

Morris, I cannot prevent the deaths of the Kid or Vasquez. They can do so by choosing flight and dishonor, but I suspect they will not.

I could flee as well, though I have not in all my life done so and would not cherish being correctly branded as a coward. And I have a second option for life. All I need do is fail to add my efforts to those of these two men of courage, and afterward advance the causes of the foreign power that has contrived to kill them.

Telling the actual truth of Renault's manipulations in print will change nothing. Cowardice is cowardice. The French have us in a box.

This may be my last letter to you.

I remain, as ever, your friend,

Chester

June 5, 1891
From Henry Pfluger, Salt Creek, Republic of Texas
To Morris Levitt, Chicago, Illinois, United States

My dear Mr. Levitt:

You do not know me. I am acquainted with your friend Mr. Chester Lamb. He knows me better by another name, that of the Baghdad Kid. I shared with Chet an unfortunate destiny, one I know he wrote you of, a destiny that was resolved just yesterday.

Chet may have told you that I am an unlettered man, which is God's own truth, but I am speaking these words at various times to Mr. Cletus Simmons and to his most kindly daughter, Eliza, who are making them into proper English and putting them to paper on my behalf.

I regret to inform you that Chet is sore afflicted and may not survive what has befallen him. If he recovers, we will celebrate, but if he does not, I think it best that his friends know that he died doing admirable work. I would urge you, when Chet's final disposition is known, to pass word of it to his people if you know them.

Two days ago was the day before our appointed meeting with the paladin Renault. Each of the three of us spent it in his own way. I chose disreputable company. Vasquez chose to wander out into the pastures surrounding Salt Creek and practice his gunmanship, a far more admirable choice than mine. Chet walked about Salt Creek asking questions and writing accounts that went on for page after page.

Yesterday was the day of the duel. In the morning, I awoke well in advance of the appointed time and, receiving no response from my knock at Chet's door, descended the stairs to ask after his whereabouts.

I found him and Vasquez both in the dining room. Vasquez, it seemed, had just arrived. He was still standing, making no move to sit, and he was dusty and tired looking.

Empty plates on the table showed that Chet had eaten a final meal. Also on the table was a pasteboard box the right size to hold Chet's writing papers. Chet was freshly shaved and cologned, dressed in his suit, like he was going courting, and he held a burlap bag before him. There were a few other folk in the room, watching Chet and Vasquez but pretending not to.

I greeted my fellow doomed souls with a big smile and cheerful words. "It seems like a fine morning to die, don't it?"

Vasquez seemed neither perturbed nor annoyed by my bravado. Chet merely smiled. He withdrew a shotgun from the burlap bag. It was Mr. Simmons's shotgun, which I had last seen two nights previously, but now it reeked as though it had been recently fired. I felt the others in the room stir nervously as the weapon made its appearance.

Chet set it on the table beside his box. "Yes, a fine day to die . . . or to live. Tell me, Kid, can you dance?"

I took the other chair at his table. I'll confess I probably looked a mite confused. I told him, "Of course I can dance."

He reached into his right vest pocket and withdrew his little derringer pistol, moving it to his left suit pocket. "Something European? Not a hoedown dance."

From another man I might have taken offense, but this being my last day on earth, I decided to let his comment pass. "I can waltz," I said. "A little."

Now, from the burlap bag, he took another weapon. This was a Colt .45 with ivory grips. As Chet looked it over to assure himself it was loaded, I peered closely at it. This was Uncle Thad's gun; I could tell because the filed-down hammer was distinctive, but someone had changed out Thad's wooden grips for ivory. The new grips looked secure but had not yet been perfectly fitted to the butt.

This weapon Chet put in his right-hand suit pocket. While doing so, he told me, "You may be able to save our lives with that waltz."

"That's foolish talk," I assured him. "No one was ever saved by a waltz."

He ignored my words and handed the bag to Vasquez. "I won't need the extra shells."

Vasquez slung the bag over his shoulder. "I'll be going," he told us. He held out a hand to me. "If we don't see each other again—"

I could feel my mouth hang open. "You running out on us, Vasquez?"

"No. I'm off to die my own way."

"Oh. Well, that's all right, then." I shook his hand. "See you in Hell, compadre."

"Good luck," he said. He turned and left, his boots clattering across the wooden floor.

Chet pointed at his collection of plates. "Will you be breakfasting?"

"Naw, I shoot better on an empty stomach." I did take a cup of coffee while he finished his own cup. And he spoke quiet-like so the other folk around would not hear, explaining what he wanted me to do.

"It's simple," he told me. "We'll be conducting our duel inside

Bust rather than outside. I found out in my investigations that he is very prompt, so we'll get there in advance and make preparations. We will all talk at one of the tables for a short while. Then I will recommend that you dance with whichever of his ladies is present. You'll lead her from the table and dance while Renault and I conclude our talk."

I thought about where he was going with his plan. "So when I'm directly behind the Frenchie, I shoot him in the back? I don't much like that."

"No. It wouldn't kill him in any case. And his companion, if she's sufficiently loyal to him, might hurl herself in the bullet's path; a tragedy. No, I want you to do this. I will slowly draw forth two guns and point them at the ceiling."

"Renault will cut you down before you get the first one in hand."

"I'll bet you twenty dollars you're wrong."

"Done." I shook his hand.

He went on. "Who do I pay when we're both dead?" Seeing my expression of consternation, he continued. "I will fire the weapons straight up. At that moment, I want you to seize Renault's companion, carry her outside, and shut the front doors—the main doors, not the swinging doors—behind you so no one can see inside. And I want you then to keep every soul outside for five minutes, on pain of death if need be, before you reenter. You must do this in spite of orders, pleas, or any sound you might hear from within."

"No," I told him. "Let a dude do my fighting for me? It ain't manly." Miss Eliza is now trying to fix my words so they will be more genteel, but "ain't" is what I said and "ain't" is what I meant.

"It's very manly to eliminate a great evil," Chet responded. "Even if you are not the one pulling the trigger. Do you want to be thought of as a man who died well, or a man who did a great good and lived to tell about it? And which of those two sorts of men do the ladies prefer?"

I'll confess, he had a powerful argument. So I told him, "All right. But you have to write in a story that I weren't chicken."

"Done."

Once our coffee was finished, we took the short walk over to Bust, Chet with his shotgun under one arm and his box full of papers under the other. He had his derby hat on but had no hand free to tip it to the ladies. Me, I found myself tapping the butts of my guns again and again to be sure they were still in place, though cords over the hammers held them so.

The people on the streets and sidewalks saw us coming. It turned my stomach, the way they put on faces of sadness but gathered around to see us be gunned down. It kind of made me think that I was like an actor or a cowboy for show and I had to think about maybe doing something more worthwhile if I survived. Like maybe run a bawdy-house.

When we walked into Bust, there weren't many folk present. The piano player was not there, which would make it less likely that I would shoot him out of righteous anger. There were no bar girls present. I saw Tubb behind the bar, a dude who looked like a banker in front of him, and three cowpokes sat at one table. They all left off talking when we walked in. They just stared at us.

He didn't need to, but Chet raised his voice to shout, "The Kid and I do not choose to permit any Frenchie to tell us where to die."

The banker raised his beer and saluted us with it. "Well said."

Chet went on. "So we choose to die here instead. We have no wish for you to witness our final agonies, however, so I will oblige you all to leave now. Or the Kid and I will shoot you."

That was kind of a surprise, but I put my hands on my Colts. I also chose to look mean, though I know I look mean under most any circumstance.

All five men stared at us. They looked as confused as if Chet had been speaking Chinese. But they did not move.

I felt obliged to help them along. I drew my right-hand gun and aimed it down at that ornery hound. "Git, or he's the first one to go."

The men stood and left, carrying their cards and drinks. Tubb picked up his hound, the beast growling in his arms, and walked out.

When they were gone, Chet went into action. Seeing what he was about, I helped. He put his shotgun and his paper box on one of the back-wall tables, then closed the main doors. We went from window to window, drawing the curtains closed, casting the bar into deep shadow.

I set about lighting the lamps used at night. Chet meanwhile went down the little back hall that gave access to the storeroom and back door, and I heard him unbolt that door. He returned and sat at the table he'd chosen, against the wall, directly before Simmons's shotgun and his box. He waved me over and I sat beside him.

Time passed. Two, three hours, felt like, and I imagined I could hear the ticking of Chet's watch, but he assured me that no more than two minutes had gone by.

The sound of talk rose from outside as the people of Salt Creek became impatient for someone to die.

Then the buzz of talk grew quiet again, and the door swung open. Miss Sophie preceded Renault in and then closed the door once he was through. Miss Sophie was all in black today, her hat looking like a funeral veil ought to be draped from its brim.

Renault took a slow look around the saloon, then stared at us, one eyebrow raised like he was about to ask a question.

Chet, cheerful, like this was a meeting of old friends, waved them over. "Come, sit with us for a minute before you kill us. It's the civilized thing to do."

Renault shrugged, and then moved to our table. He sat opposite Chet, beside the wall. It pleased me that Miss Sophie sat opposite me, giving me something nice to look at.

Renault looked at the shotgun and the box. "You are most peculiarly armed." Like the other time, it was hard to make out his words.

Chet nodded. "Especially since you know that the shotgun's not going to kill you."

Renault nodded, too. "Yes."

"Yet at this moment, you are in greater danger than you have ever known."

"I do not think I am."

"I'll tell you why, Renault. But I don't wish to distress your companion." Chet frowned like he was thinking of something new. Then he turned to me. "Kid, do me this one last favor and ask Mademoiselle Sophie to dance."

"Why, surely." I rose.

Now Miss Sophie spoke. "There is no music."

"Aw, hell." I held out my hand for her. "Even when the piano player's here, there's no *music*."

She looked at Renault and he nodded. She took my arm and rose. I led her out into the middle of the floor and put my hands the way they were supposed to go for the waltz, though I hadn't danced that way since I was fourteen and my ma was teaching me.

I hummed the music my ma had hummed for me, and we danced. Miss Sophie seemed not to enjoy it too much, and kept her attention on the table whenever she could. That made the dance a mite awkward, as I needed to watch Chet. Then it occurred to me to look in the bar mirror whenever I faced away from the table, so I could always have it in view.

As he said he would, and talking in tones I could not hear, Chet reached, slow and sure, for Thad's Colt and brought it out, aiming it at the ceiling. To my surprise, Renault did not gun him down, even when Chet reached for his little dude gun and pointed it the same way. Then he shut his eyes like someone handling a firearm for the first time and fired both weapons into the ceiling.

I stooped, caught Miss Sophie up on my shoulder, and carried her outside. This was not easy, because she fought at every step, hollering French words that no longer sounded genteel. Getting through the door and then hauling it shut behind me was a chore, as Miss Sophie clung to every surface we passed.

Once outside, I was confronted with a mob of curious faces, some of whom looked as though they might take exception to my mistreatment of Miss Sophie. I contrived to stand where she could grab at nothing, and I drew one of my weapons and pointed it at everyone's faces. "First man to move, I shoot," I assured them. "First woman to move . . . I shoot in the foot."

They believed me, all right. Then, all of a sudden, Miss Sophie slumped, though the instant before she had not even begun to run down. I assumed that all her exertions had overcome her, as it would me if I wore garments pulled as tight as hers. I compelled two townsmen to take her from me and they commenced to try to awaken her, though without success.

For the full five minutes I held them at bay, and then, once the banker I had earlier expelled from Bust assured me the time had passed, I holstered my weapon and reentered the saloon, swinging its main doors wide open so others might enter. The crowd followed me.

My expectation was that I would find Chet dead and Renault ready for another duel. But that was not what I saw.

Both Chet and Renault lay on the floor, yards apart. From where they lay it was clear that they had been facing each other when both had been felled.

Chet had his shotgun across his chest. He still breathed, and there was no mark of violence upon him, but his eyes were closed and he could not be compelled to awaken.

Renault, on the other hand, was stone dead, so mutilated that it was clear that blasts from both shotgun barrels had struck him in the face. So gruesome was he that townsfolk tried to prevent their ladies and children from seeing his remains. I had not heard the shotgun discharge, yet here was indisputable proof that it had.

Renault's revolver lay near his hand, except that it was not his revolver, it was Thad's. Where Renault's gun might have gone I had no idea. From the weapon's condition we assured ourselves that it had been discharged, one cartridge having been fired. I did not mention that I had seen Chet fire that round.

I admit I could not fathom what had happened, even knowing more about events than the townsfolk. Chet had somehow taken and hidden Renault's weapon, had given Uncle Thad's Colt to Renault, had persuaded the Frenchman to stand in the center of the room, had killed Renault with a silent shotgun, and then had fainted. I did what my ma and pa had taught me as a child, and I stayed quiet.

In all the confusion, Vasquez joined us. He and I took charge, gathering up Chet's possessions and Uncle Thad's gun. We conveyed Chet to our hotel and summoned a doctor. Not long after, French soldiers came, demanding to take possession of Chet. But the two of us, joined by Texas soldiers and then townsfolk, our guns outnumbering those of the Frenchies, persuaded the intruders to leave.

I will notify you when I know Chet's fate.

Mr. Simmons informs me that I should end this letter with the words "your obedient servant," and I have informed him that such words are not for men. So I will say instead that I am,

Chet's friend,
Henry Pfluger

June 7, 1891
From Chester Lamb, Salt Creek, Republic of Texas
To Morris Levitt, Chicago, Illinois, United States

My dear Morris:
When I last wrote you, it was to let you know of my thoughts and activities the day before I was to die in a duel. After writing you, I prayed, then undressed and went to bed.

Some time later, I woke out of a fitful sleep with a thought fully formed in my mind.

The thought was the sum at the bottom of a column of numbers, except that the numbers were facts I had not hereto added together. I will remind you of some of them.

A hound who hated all men yet wagged its tail as Renault and Mademoiselle Sophie passed by.

The faintness of Renault's voice, which required an effort to hear.

His lack of gallantry toward his ladies, his willingness for them to do all labor for him.

"He has never touched me."

His lack of vulnerability to bullet or blade.

The ghastly image of Benjamin Franklin's body, the metal mask shielding his features from onlookers.

The sum of these facts formed a new number, a new idea, and at that moment, I thought I knew how to defeat Renault.

Yet victory was not assured. My only assurance was that if I fled Salt Creek, or agreed to collaborate with Renault, then I would survive.

After a time, I determined that I could regard only with contempt the Chester Lamb who would decide in favor of assurance under those terms. I dressed in a hurry, took myself to Vasquez's room, and knocked. He emerged, alert.

I told him my thought, and he assured me that pursuing it could not make his fate any more uncertain. I issued to him a series of instructions, some of them so ghastly that he had to fortify himself with another swallow of tequila. But he did dress and depart.

I returned to my chamber and commenced the task that would prevent me from joining Vasquez. I began to write. I wrote in haste and without consideration for style or brevity, for time was short.

Hours later, I collected the results of my labors in a pasteboard box, added my bottle of ink and a pen, and returned to my bed, where I was finally able to drift off to a short but restful sleep.

I awoke with the dawn and made preparations for what would be either my last day on earth or Renault's. That is to say, I shaved, dressed, ensured that my derringer was loaded, and wrote a set of letters that would be posted in the event of my death. I descended and ate a hearty meal in the dining salon.

As I was drinking my last coffee, I saw Vasquez and Mr. Simmons through the window as they arrived on the buckboard. Simmons stayed with the wagon, his expression mournful, while Vasquez alighted. Moments later he was before me, grubby and weary but reporting success with every errand he had been charged to complete. As proof in part, he presented me with a bag containing Simmons's shotgun and Thad's Colt with its new grips.

The Kid joined us then. He tells me he has faithfully recounted all that he observed from that moment to the point I was carried to the hotel, so I will not revisit all those details.

You will recall that the Kid danced away from my table with the Frenchwoman.

In the moments after that, Renault stared at me again. "You have given us privacy so that you might accept my offer without that one overhearing?"

"No. Your offer is for men without honor."

His face registered no disappointment. "Then you truly think I am in some danger."

"I do," I assured him. "Which I will demonstrate. But first, tell me—are you so fast on the draw that if I were to hold my weapons aloft, pointed at the ceiling, you could still draw and gun me down before I had you in my sights?"

"Yes." There was no arrogance or even confidence in his tone. He answered as if I had merely asked him whether the sun was up.

"Will you, then, give me that small head start? Allow me to have my guns in hand so that I might die like a man?"

"Yes."

"Thank you. I am reaching for them now. I will not turn them on you until we are both ready." So saying, I slowly withdrew Thad's Colt from my pocket and held it pointed upward. I repeated the action with my derringer. "Would you mind if I cocked both weapons before we do this?"

He gestured like a host offering a sideboard full of delicacies. "Be my guest."

"Thank you." I cocked the Colt, then the derringer.

"Now, Monsieur Lamb?"

Instead of responding, I clamped my eyes shut and pulled both triggers.

I did not aim my weapons before doing so, and because I gave no hint that I was ready to be shot, Renault had not even begun to move before I fired. Tremendous reports sounded in both my ears from inches away, deafening me. The rounds from the weapons crashed into the ceiling—or so I assumed. I did not hear or see them do so.

I stood, knocking my chair back into the partition, and sidled past the Kid's chair. Keeping my legs pressed against the tabletop so that I would always know where I was, I moved around the table, past Mlle Sophie's chair, and sat where Renault had been.

He was not there now. There was, in fact, no warmth in the wood beneath me to indicate anyone had recently been seated there.

I waited for the gunshot that would kill me, all the while hoping it would not come. And it did not.

I set the guns aside on the table and dragged the manuscript box to me. My eyes still shut, I threw off the box top. Within, by touch, I located the bottle of ink and the pen I had placed therein. They lay atop the papers I had written the night before, and I also assured myself that those pages were oriented correctly.

By touch alone, I unstoppered the bottle, dipped in the pen, and scrawled two words at the bottom of the topmost piece of paper. I transferred that sheet to the bottom of the pile of pages. Then, by memory, I began reviewing the words I had previously written and those I had just added.

I have those pages still, so I can quote them exactly.

While the Baghdad Kid and Renault's lovely companion continued their oddly graceful dance to music only they could hear, I maintained my grip on my firearms and smiled at my opponent. "I am as great a sorcerer as the one who made you, Renault," I told him.

His tone remained indifferent. "Summoned me back from my reward, you mean."

"Made," I insisted. "And the final step in my own enchantment will be the pulling of these triggers, an action even you are not fast enough to forestall. No—do not move, for I have you at my mercy, and I know your secret.

"You are not real, Renault. You do not exist. Ah, I see by your expression that I have struck to the pink. Your maker created twelve ideas, gave them volume and color and motion, but you do not exist as a physical thing. That dog, Mustard, could not hear or see or smell you, hence it wagged its welcome only to Mademoiselle Sophie as she passed. You barely whisper—we lean close, anticipating words, and we hear them, but it is only our own attention that makes this possible. Were you to be alone, all alone, with no one able to perceive you, you would fade away to nothing, which is why one of your ladies is always present. It was the sad mistake of Benjamin Franklin that he discerned part of your nature, but not all—he did not realize that hearing you would doom him as much as seeing you, and so you slew him."

He shook his head, a flicker of true fear beginning to manifest in his eyes. "Someone who is not real cannot kill—"

"It is the belief of your victims that kills them, not bullets that do not exist from a gun that is not real. As the faithful can sometimes bleed spontaneously from their palms, side, and feet in emulation of

Christ's suffering, your victims accept their deaths and so manifest bullet wounds—wounds which, if opened, would yield no bullets."

He was silent. At such a time, I would expect a mortal man to demonstrate frantic thinking in search of a way out, but he did no such thing.

"But do not grieve," I told him. "Life is not your state, and death is not your fate. As you are unreal, so you are imperishable. You simply go to a place where you can no longer do harm." So saying, I pulled the triggers of my weapons.

A tremendous roar shook the saloon, buffeting my ears, and the smell of gunpowder filled the air. And in that moment, Renault faded away like a specter glimpsed from the corner of the eye as one awakens.

Renault stared about himself, his expression one of wonder.

The estate was not great of size. He could see it to its borders in all directions, marked by a battlement-topped stone wall so high and featureless that he knew he would never be able to climb it. He was trapped here, contained until the day he might be needed once more.

But to be bound in such a place . . . To the south of the grass-topped hill on which he found himself was a village tucked away in a well-watered valley in the rolling land. Distant voices of singing came to his ears. All around him, the slopes of the hills were covered with vines heavy with grapes. And on the hilltop to his north, a house—a mansion of many wings and stories, white walls reflecting the bright summer sun, roof capped with rust-brown slates richly contrasting in color with the vines.

Renault took it all in. Then, for the first time in the century of his existence, he allowed himself the shadow of a smile.

———

My ears ringing but my heart light, I touched the pasteboard box that
now held Renault, his mysteries and his dangers, within. His fate was
sealed, with the fate of his fellow paladins soon to follow.

I sat back to await the return of the bartender. A brandy would be
my modest celebration. And perhaps a cigar.

At the very end of the page are the words I penned while my eyes
were closed, their letters awkward and overlapping but legible:

THE END

I was in the act of stoppering the bottle of ink when a great wea-
riness and darkness overcame me. I collapsed onto my manuscript
box and lay as insensate as the dead.

Why did I falter so? I do not know—such matters are, for the
time being, beyond me. It seems possible that the same mental exertions that allowed us to hear Renault's words were duplicated in
the act of imagining him out of existence, and stole strength from
me much as a sudden illness might. I did discover later that Mlles
Sophie and Laurette, the first outside with the Kid and the second
back at Fort Cow, also collapsed at about the same moment, each of
them taking a full day to recover.

In the first moments of my long sleep, other events I had set into
motion transpired.

Behind the saloon waited Vasquez and Mr. Simmons with the
buckboard. As soon as he heard my gunshots, Vasquez consulted his
pocket watch and waited for one minute to the second. He informed
me later that it was the most nervous minute of his storied career.

When that time had elapsed, he retrieved a dire object from under the blankets in the wagon bed—Thaddeus Hobart's body. In the
long hours of the previous night, Vasquez had pressed Mr. Simmons and Miss Eliza into service. They had dug Thad out of his

grave, removed his outer garments, and cleansed him of the dirt we had heaped upon him—a gruesome, cheerless series of tasks.

Eliza and her father had entered town with the morning light and made purchases with money from me and Vasquez: gray garments closely resembling Renault's and a pair of ivory pistol grips. Meanwhile, at the farm, Vasquez performed the most grisly act of all, firing both barrels of the shotgun into Thad's face.

Yes, Morris, you do not have to convey to me your discomfort at these words. Please weigh my plan against the benefits it has brought us, and will continue to bring, before issuing your final judgment.

At the farm, Vasquez and the Simmonses assembled these components into a credible simulacrum of Renault's body, a replacement for the body I believed did not exist in physical form. Then Vasquez loaded the body onto the wagon, the revolver and shotgun into the bag. He and Mr. Simmons drove into town.

Now, one minute after the gunshots, Vasquez carried the body through the back door of Bust, bolting the door behind him. Mr. Simmons drove on.

Vasquez deposited the body on the floor. In those same moments, the Kid, out front and knowing nothing of these activities, held the citizens of Salt Creek at bay with his guns and force of will.

Finding me unresponsive at my table, Vasquez still nobly did as instructed. He took Thad's Colt from my table and placed it near Thad's hand. He returned my derringer to my pocket. He carried me to the floor opposite the false Renault and deposited me there, then lay the shotgun across my breast. Finally, he returned my ink and pen to the manuscript box. He concealed himself in the storeroom to wait.

There it was, my solution. It had seemed to me that even if my speculations were entirely correct, if the townsfolk came into Bust and found me there alone, with Renault gone, they would never believe him dead. This, perhaps, would allow him to return. My thought was that if all saw a body they thought was his, they would believe Renault truly dead, leaving him no place on this earth to return to.

Mademoiselles Sophie and Laurette did not awaken until after the body was buried and so were unable to issue denials that it was his.

I knew none of these details. For three days, I lay unmoving. I am informed that during this time the Baghdad Kid wrote you with dire misgivings about my fate. Yet I recovered.

News of my mysterious accomplishment did reach the capitals at Austin, New Orleans, and Washington in rapid fashion. Upon my regaining consciousness this morning, I was informed that as soon as I was fit to travel, I would be escorted by a unit from Fort Montague to Austin and a conference with President Hogg at the new Capitol building.

So now I, possibly the most valuable man for thousands of miles in any direction, am packing for a trip to the Texas capital, where I will tell my story.

Nor, if mishap befalls me en route, will the secret of Renault's death be lost. You have this letter, and other letters of instruction I have written have now been dispatched to trusted friends to be opened in the event of my death or disappearance. The paladins are doomed, and the stranglehold the French Empire has on the world is, though they know it not, at an end.

What, you ask, of the other participants in these events?

The Baghdad Kid carries one of my letters with him. He has chosen to stay at Salt Creek for now. He enjoys the attention the townsfolk lavish upon him, but the confusion in his eyes suggests he now considers steering a new course with his life. From his spoken thoughts, I would not venture to say it will be a better course, merely a different one. He has given me Thad's Colt in payment of the bet he owed me.

Vasquez rides with me. He asserts that soon I will be at the center of calamity, and it is at such places that profit can be made. I suspect he is correct, but I think, too, that he longs to put my methods to the test against other paladins. He wishes to see this part of the world shake itself free of the Empire.

Mademoiselles Sophie and Laurette chose to depart Salt Creek but also eschew French-controlled territories. Their brief words on the subject suggested that they are delighted to be free of Renault but might have cause to fear French punishment. Laurette is bound for Nuevo Mexico in the hope of making a new life there. Sophie, greatly daring, has chosen to dress as a man and will accompany a cattle drive bound for Kansas. Her destination from there is Chicago. If, Morris, you are reading this letter and a comely Frenchwoman has placed it in your hands, it is she, and I ask of you that you use my resources and your influence to help her begin her new life.

As for me, the life I knew is over. From now until the last paladin is gone, I will be too valuable to the Republic of Texas and the United States of America to control my own destiny.

Too, I have noticed changes in myself. With each room I enter, some part of my mind tells me, were I to pluck the Colt from my holster, I could in an instant calculate the exact angle, elevation, and timing I would need to place a bullet in the heart or brain of every individual I saw. I had not that facility before.

Renault is within me. And, too, I know he is in the pasteboard box I carry among my possessions. I confess that the link between us makes me fear that someday I, too, will find myself trapped in leaves of paper, never to escape.

Au revoir.

Your friend,

Chester Lamb

Aaron Allston is a New York Times *bestselling novelist known in particular for his work in the Star Wars universe. Before making fiction his full-time career, he wrote role-playing game supplements, contributing to the Dungeons & Dragons, Champions, and GURPS lines. He has been inducted into the Academy of Adventure Gaming Arts and Design Hall of Fame. He teaches writing workshops across the United States.*

More information is on his website: www.aaronallston.com.

Rhubarb and Beets

TODD McCAFFREY

On Gene Wolfe: *Gene Wolfe's* Book of the New Sun, *including* The Shadow of the Torturer, The Claw of the Conciliator, The Sword of the Lictor, *and* The Citadel of the Autarch, *reinvigorated and defined a whole genre, raising the bar for all who came after him and uniting his works with those of Dickens, Lewis, Swift, and Tolkien. Gene's style and wit and his willingness to invent new words that seem like they* ought *to exist is charming to read and frustrating to emulate. Truly he's one of the genre's great treasures.*

The elfish girl walked spritely up the path.

"Gran!" she called, stopping for a moment to peer ahead and then starting forward again with a skip in her step. "Gran, where are you?"

There was no sign of him in the front of the stone cottage.

"Eilin?" an old voice called in surprise. The doddering old man, steps quick but wobbly, rounded the corner from the back of the cottage. He had a guarded look on his face and then smiled as he spotted the girl. "Eilin, what brings you here?"

"My lady was worried," Eilin replied, peering up at the silver-haired man. "She didn't see you in the garden."

"Oh, I was around back, just pottering."

"Pottering?" Eilin repeated. It was a strange word, like so many of the other words he used.

"Aye, nothing more," Gran replied, gesturing toward the front door. "Come in and I'll put on some tea for ye."

Eilin nodded, not trusting her face. Gran was forever going on about "tea," but it was always hot water poured over strange roots and never quite the amazing brew he made it sound like. She glanced back over her shoulder down the path she'd taken. Finding no respite—no signs of her lady mother beckoning her back imperiously—Eilin knew she had no choice but to accept her gran's offer.

"And what brings you here on such a fair day?" Gran asked as he opened the door to his cottage and bowed her in.

"My lady mother—"

"Ach, lass, that's what ye *said*," Gran interrupted. "I meant the real reason."

The silver-haired man followed her into the cottage, waved her to her favorite seat, bustled about near the stove and came back, beckoning for her to stand again, while he settled in the one plush chair and settled her on top of him.

"Was it the spiders?" Gran asked softly as she rested her head on his warm shoulder.

"No," Eilin said in a half-drowsy voice. Her lady mother said that they kept Gran because he was so good with children. Perhaps it was true: Eilin could never listen to his singsong voice for long before falling asleep on his lap. "Not spiders."

"The prince, then," Gran decided.

"The baby, actually," Eilin allowed. Her brother the prince was no more a pest after she'd discovered that he was more afraid of spiders than she—one night harvesting the worst of them and then laying them over him as he slept cured the prince of any desire to annoy her—which was as it should be.

A whistle from the kettle on the stove disturbed them and Eilin allowed herself to be manhandled as Gran stood, deposited her gently back on the warm chair, sauntered over to the stove, and poured steaming water into a clay pot.

Eilin's nose crinkled as the strange smell came to her. *Another of Gran's terrible brews,* she thought.

How long had it been now? Twenty years? Forty? More? Once his hair had been red, his eyes keen, his face fresh like a new apple. Now it was lined, his eyes were dimming, his hair all white and lanky. Even his body seemed smaller than once it had been, as though time had forced it to curl in obeisance.

Changelings never lasted very long. She'd only just gotten him properly broken in and now he was all worn out.

The smell shifted and Eilin sniffed again, her eyes open and senses curious. This time Gran's brew did not smell so bad.

Gran came back with two mugs on a tray and set them near the sofa. He scooped Eilin back up, settled himself, and pulled a mug over in one hand.

"If you'd care to try . . ." Gran offered.

"Of course," Eilin said, never one to refuse a graciousness. She sniffed, took a quick, thin sip and—amazed—her eyebrows rose in pleasant surprise. She took another sip, a bit deeper but only just—the liquid was piping hot.

Gran chuckled at her evident pleasure.

"Rhubarb and beet," Gran said. He took the second mug for himself.

"What's it for?"

"It's for the unicorns," Gran said.

Eilin took another sip. It was always unicorns with Gran. Always the same joke.

"Do you think they'll like it?" Eilin said, deciding this time to play along.

"We'll see," Gran said, taking another sip. "We'll see."

"Tell me about the unicorns," Eilin said as she'd said most every day she came to the cottage. She sipped her tea and wondered why in the Elvenworld Gran could ever come to the notion that unicorns might drink such brew.

"What's to tell?" Gran teased her.

"No one can see them," Eilin said, repeating his old story. Days and years he'd told her, put her to sleep with his singsong, sad, sorry voice telling her about the unicorns.

"No one can see them," Gran agreed. "Their horns take them from Elvenworld to our world and back."

"They brought you here."

"When I was just a lad," Gran said in agreement.

"And now you're here and you'll never leave," Eilin finished. She leaned back, resting her head on his warm shoulder companionably. "You belong here, with us."

"Forever in Fearie."

"With the Elves and the unicorns, my lady mother, lord father, and the prince, my brother," Eilin concluded. "This is your home and we love you."

"I had a home," Gran reminded her, his voice going soft and a bit hoarse, "and those who loved me."

"Long gone, time slips differently here," Eilin reminded him.

"Drink your tea," Gran said, raising his mug to his lips and draining it impatiently.

For once, Eilin did as he said.

"No one can ever see a unicorn," Gran said to her as she drifted off into pleasant slumber.

It was weeks later when Eilin came again. Her brother the prince had discovered thorny roses and had tormented her by hiding them in her bed as she slept.

The pricks and pains of the thorns had sent her crying to the comfort of Gran's cottage in the distance.

"Gran!" she cried. He had the greatest cures and poultices; perhaps he could pull the sting out of her. "Gran!"

No answer, no movement from the cottage. Alarmed, Eilin picked up her pace.

No sign.

She ran around the cottage to the back, crying, "Gran!"

"Sssh!" Gran called from the far end of the garden. "I'm here, no need to shout!"

"What are you doing?" Eilin asked, eyeing the green growth and dirty ground in surprise.

"Just tending my garden, princess," Gran told her, rising from his knees to stand and then bow in front of her.

"My brother the prince used thorns!" Eilin cried, raising her pricked palms toward him and then pointing to the gash in her neck and the others on her arms. "He put roses in my bed."

"I can help you," Gran said, nodding toward his cottage. "A bit of brew, some cold water, and you'll be right as rain."

"And how is rain right?"

"It's right when there's a rainbow and the air is clear of dirt and full of freshness."

Eilin nodded. Rainbows were expensive outside of Faerie; her father had the drudges work until they expired to find the treasure required for each rainbow. Gran had once called him too vain for his own good, but Eilin could only think of the pride of the kingdom and the bounty of the Elvenworld. The drudges were only human, lured by the same gold they died to provide, no matter to her father the king or even to Eilin herself.

Gracefully, Gran followed her to the cottage and bowed her inside, gesturing toward his comfortable chair. She sat waiting in pain while he pottered over the stove and set potions to brew.

Presently he was back and had her in his lap again, gently applying his hot brew and holding pressure on her pale white skin until the thorn punctures closed and the pain went once more.

"Do have you more tea, Gran?" Eilin asked as the last of the pain faded into dim memory.

"Tea?" Gran asked as he put his potions and clothes to one side.

"The purple tea you made," Eilin said.

"Unicorn tea," Gran said in a questioning tone.

"Yes."

"No one can see unicorns," Gran said, half-teasing her.

"The tea was good," Eilin said, feeling her eyelids drooping as the rise and fall of his chest and the warmth of him calmed her.

"The tea will make your stings come back," Gran said. He took a breath, and then continued. "Let me tell you about the rainbows."

"There were three that day," Eilin said, recalling his words from so many times before. It was a marvelous story; Gran told it so well and Eilin always filled with pride at the brilliant trick her father had played.

"Three rainbows and only one with gold," Gran said by way of agreement.

"Fool's gold," Eilin remembered, a smile playing on her lips.

"Fool's gold," Gran agreed. "And the fool was me, parted from friend and family by the faint hope that I could find enough gold to save them—"

"—from the famine," Eilin finished, her eyes now closing. "The unicorn ripped through that day, ripped from our world to yours three times."

"Ripped indeed," Gran agreed, his tone tightly neutral. "But no one saw them."

"Unicorns are invisible," Eilin agreed, closing her mouth at last and snoring gently on the old man's chest.

"Clear as the water they drink," Gran said softly to himself while the little elfish girl slept on.

"Gran!" Eilin shouted as she traipsed up the path to the cottage. Drat the man, where was he? "Gran!"

He usually replied by now, doddering out from his cottage or around from the silly garden on which he so doted. He was being slow and she'd make him bow so long in penance that his back would hurt. Well . . . maybe not *that* long.

"Gran!"

No sign of him in the cottage. He was old, Eilin remembered, and picked up her pace. Disposing of bodies was something she never liked, and then there'd be the bother of having to find a new human—she sprinted around the corner, looking for him kneeling over some of his silly rhubarb or his beets, but he wasn't there.

His garden opened up on the fields of cloudgrass—the favorite food of unicorns. Gran had insisted on it as inspiration, and the best location for the sun his plants required.

Every now and then over the years, she'd find him looking at the fields of cloudgrass, waving white and brilliant, watching as clumps were eaten by invisible grazing unicorns.

"What do unicorns eat?" Gran had asked early on when he still dreamed of escape from the Elvenworld.

"They eat cloudgrass and drink clear water," Eilin had told him expansively. "That's why they're invisible."

"And how they can cut between the worlds?"

Eilin didn't know and, as it was inappropriate for a princess to be ignorant, she said nothing.

Eilin gazed from Gran's garden to the field and her jaw dropped as she spotted the path. She followed it with her eyes, even as she willed her feet into action.

"Gran!" she cried, racing into the cloudgrass fields. She couldn't see him; the grass was nearly taller than her. She'd forgotten that most days when they'd gone into the fields she'd been riding on his shoulders—Gran being her very own special two-legged beast of burden.

"Gran!"

In the distance she heard thunder. Unicorns were racing. She saw lightning where their hooves struck hard ground.

They were stampeding. Soon enough they'd bolt and tear holes between the Elvenworld and the slow world of humans.

Was Gran hoping to catch one? How could he—they were invisible!

"Get on!" A thin reedy voice came to her over the winds and the thunders. "Ride on, go on!"

"Gran!" Eilin cried. "No, Gran, you'll never catch one!" He'd be trampled for certain, unable to see the unicorns, unable to dodge their panicked flight.

"On with you! Thunder and lightning!" Gran's voice, exultant, came over the noises and the cloudgrass.

Eilin remembered a knoll nearby and raced toward it. It was only a few quick strides for Gran, but for the little elfish girl it was nearly a hill.

At the top she could see over the cloudgrass, across the fields and—there!

"Gran!" Eilin cried. Oh, the fool, the fool!

He was riding a unicorn, his weak old arms tightly clasped around its neck, his bony legs gripping its withers tightly, and in one hand he held a long-stemmed rose, waving it wildly, striking the unicorn's hindquarters—the unicorn's *purple* hindquarters.

Rhubarb and beets, Eilin thought to herself with sudden clarity. All those years he hadn't given up hope, he'd merely been planning. Oh, clever human!

He'd raised the beets and the rhubarb for the unicorns. Fed enough, the usually invisible hide took on a faint purple hue. Coaxed with a gentle voice and the sweet and the sour of the rhubarb, it was no trouble to bring one of the unicorns to within hand's reach.

"Gran!" Eilin cried, her thin voice dying in the winds. "Oh, Gran, take me with you!"

The old man didn't hear her.

"Gran!" Eilin cried at the top of her lungs, realizing at last how much she loved the old human. How he'd been the only one to hug her to him, the only one to ever care the slightest about *her* as a person. "Gran!"

Thunder. Lightning tore through the sky and suddenly, the wicked electric-blue glow of lightning burst from the purple-veined horn of the unicorn Gran rode.

In an instant, the Void was torn and the far human world sprang into view. The unicorn, goaded unerringly by Gran, leaped through, and the tear closed.

A final burst of lightning and thunder rolled through the skies— unicorn and rider were only a dimming memory in the elfish girl's eyes.

Todd McCaffrey wrote his first science fiction story when he was twelve and has been writing on and off ever since. Including the New York Times *bestselling* Dragon's Fire, *he has written eight books in the Pern universe, both solo and in collaboration with his mother, Anne McCaffrey. His work has appeared in many anthologies, most recently with his short story "Coward" in* When the Hero Comes Home *(2011), and with* Robin Redbreast *in* When the Villain Comes Home *(2012), and the mini-anthology* Six. *His latest book,* City of Angels, *is currently available as an e-book in both Nook and Kindle formats. Visit his website at www.toddmccaffrey.org.*

Tunes from Limbo, But I Digress

JUDI ROHRIG

On Gene Wolfe: *During my stint as publicity coordinator for the 2002 World Horror Convention, I had the honor of dis-covering that guest of honor Gene Wolfe was not only an amazingly talented writer, but a crafty pirate who could break out in silly singsongs at the drop of a hat. (And in his case, a rather dapper hat.) Our friendship grew from there, based on our mutual fondness for wolves, mermaids, inter-esting words, Chicago Cubs baseball, the Li'l Pirate, and wooden pencils.*

The title of this story, "Tunes from Limbo, But I Digress," first popped into my head several years ago. When I shared it with Gene, he told me, "Hurry up and use that or I'm going to steal it." Luckily he didn't. And luckily, I saved it for the right story. What also found its way into "Tunes . . ." (a tromp inside his Home Fires *world) was an offhanded comment he made when I asked him how he liked his new laptop. After a low grumble, he said, "I would have been better off buying a really good pencil." And for a writer that would be a Palomino Blackwing 602.*

One thing I have learned from the man my daughter and I call "Raggedy Man" is to be constant in my pursuit of ripe story titles. (Good golly, look what grew from the one he wanted to pilfer!) And that this same extraordinary writer will rationalize appropriating any writing instru-ment if he takes a liking to it. (Or lead others to purloin one for him. I mean, what would you do to earn a Gene Wolfe approving chuckle?)

Dear—

What do I call you when I don't know who you'll be?

If only the Fates allowed me to address you face to face as we plummet through space on the *Domum Ignes*. You could help me to untangle what's happened. An accident, the ship's doctor tells me, his fumbling explanation to my once prevalent headaches and confusion perhaps, but not the lingering visions.

They arrive in bits and pieces mostly. A sudden smell or taste. The flash of an idea. A picture. Unexplained feelings and urges. Dreams. Remembrances of what we've left behind on our humble planet? I don't know.

Yet there they are: crackling flames from an open hearth blushing my face while my outstretched frozen fingers thaw, or sugar-sand beaches with frothy ripples tickling my toes while an unhurried wind peppers a salty mist. In my unfolding palms, I could tender a delicate bud of spring's promise or a plump fruit of autumn's harvest as well.

Then it all disappears.

In a way, I'm oddly reminded of a game played long ago on a rainy afternoon. Except here Colonel Mustard didn't use the candlestick in the conservatory to commit any crime. Though there are indeed pieces to this puzzle: Hayward Madden and his diplomatic entourage, each entubed in suspended animation, to be revived when we finally reach the treaty zone at the Gates of Johanna; Captain Tynan-of-Hod, crewmember; the Admiral's library; a smuggled pencil; and . . . Threeve, a Même.

Me.

The title of my *function* stems from the words *même récit,* referring to what I do, not who I am. I read our most precious cargo of slumbering diplomats their own life histories while they are in stasis. It isn't all that complicated, but here's the twist: They don't simply listen or absorb the information. The electrodes attached to the ridge on each Tuber's cerebral cortex—the superior temporal gyrus—

processes and transmits auditory information *from* them to the receiver d-comm implanted in my own device. In essence, we enjoy verbal interaction, though only one of us is fully awake.

Hayward—as he is so good to do—once boiled down the process for me: "On Earth, there are these beautiful black birds with red patches on their wings. They line the open fields, perching on a fence post or atop a bush and mark their territory by calling out 'I'm a red-wing blackbird and this is where I live.' That's what rendering is, Threeve. You come each day and help me to remember 'I am Hayward Madden, a representative of the North American Union, on my way to negotiate a truce with the Os.'"

And yet as a Même, I do more than simply regurgitate information. After I settle myself comfortably in the slingseat adjacent to the individual's tube, I shut my eyes, clear my mind, and focus. Spreading my hand along the benumbed metal casing, imagining the warmth from my fingertips penetrating the barrier, conveying my touch, helps me orient myself. Then, sans scouring the d-comm files, trusting my memory alone to refresh nuances of facts and feelings, I tip my imaginary Sheltonian wild violet bone china teapot and let the relaxing aromas of ginger and lemon balm swirl warmly in the air.

Conversation. That's all it will be. Between friends.

Though we may be nowhere near land or soil or even a planet, I infuse our homogenized air with civility, re-forming this artificially illumined cocoon into a lush garden: a prickly rosebush over there entwining its thorny arms around a wooden trellis, its vibrant velvety buds unfolding in delicate measures. And dangling over the top of the painted slats are plump purple lilacs. From time to time a mockingbird pops up, heralding a greeting in whatever tongue moves him, or a feisty robin redbreast skitters along the grassy green carpet. Sometimes I can almost hear the low rumble of thunder and catch a whiff of approaching rain.

And who's to know?

Besides Hayward, that is.

"They're gonna find you out, Sleeping Beauty. Then what?" he'd scolded on my last morning of true innocence. But before I could protest, he broke into one of his silly singsongs. "'And the Raggedy Man, he knows most rhymes. Tells 'em to me, if'n I be good sometimes.'" Then he laughed as much of a laugh as any Tuber could. "My mother used to read the poem to me before I went to sleep. James Whitcomb Riley. He wrote children's poems. Well, mostly children. I'm hardly a child, but could you find it and read it all to me, Threeve?"

"If the d-comms have it, I'll be happy to," I said.

"Try the *library*, if you can find the darned thing. The Admiral— kindly or wisely, I haven't exactly decided which yet—lugged along some pulpies, a collection inherited from a lawyer father. You know . . . *books*?"

"I'm aware of the library," I assured him. "It's small, though, so I can't guarantee this Riley will be there." I withheld from Hayward the fact the Admiral was no longer at the helm.

"Have it tomorrow, will you? And don't open it before you get here. Will you do that for me? I want to walk you through experiencing a book. It's not a mere collection of words, you know. My mother taught me that." He quieted for several seconds. "I doubt she's still alive."

I know I must have grimaced when he ventured into a forbidden area. Prime taboo subjects are time and . . . termination. I reasoned my own silence could allow his thoughts to move ahead, but they didn't, so I thrummed the tips of my fingers on his tube to signal my imminent departure. "That's all for today, Hayward."

"It can't be. I don't remember talking about my folks or sports. I'm athletic like my mother. She was in the military. Fought the Os with the Admiral's mother and managed to return in one piece when most did not."

"Your parents always top the list—"

But he was on his own mental track, his own bullet train, swooshing ahead in high gear. "I was one of the last Olympians, you know. Won four medals in swimming. Breaststroke, freestyle, butterfly, and individual medley. Not all gold, but two of them were."

Of all my assigned Tubers, Hayward's memory rendering often pushed past our time limit because his being the oldest meant he had more memories and experiences. Railing—getting him started—was never a problem. All I had to do was sit down and engage him. But protocol is strict. I had to meet my quotas, still have time to update the records, and fetch his blasted book.

"I'll be back tomorrow," I said. "Do you have a dream sequence in mind?"

"I feel restless tonight. Set the dials for brackish winds in my face and the snap of sails in my ears. Come with me, sweet Threeve-of-Kenning. There's room for one more in my little Bermuda rig."

"As tempting as that sounds, I'll have to pass. I don't think I can swim."

"I'm betting you could, but I'll wrap my arms around you and keep you safe."

"Be careful, Hayward. Tynan might get jealous."

"That's right. I forgot you were a contracta. And with your supervisor, no less. Conflict of interest. Clearly. But he doesn't have to find out. You could claim you needed to tend the vegetation in the Lada Garden or something. Tynan's not the farmer type, so I doubt he'd check for you there. We could have such fun. I could teach you songs and maybe even whisper a poem or two in your ears. I know plenty more of the bawdy ones you like."

If his physical features hadn't been frozen in place, I know his bushy eyebrows would have wiggled.

"Good night, Hayward."

"Sleep tight."

"Don't let the bugs bite."

In reality, there were no dials to set or buttons to punch or even "dream sequencing." I'd made it up, and he was all too easily hooked.

Since Tubers wear their unique personalities like battle decorations, the fib could not be employed with blanket utility, meaning I would never consider it for Lieutenant Commander z'Bette Cooney.

"I. Do. Not. Dream." Words popped from her. Abrupt and annoyed. As though with my arrival, I'd swung open the door to her private room without politely knocking.

"This is not a dream," I said.

"I am fully aware of what's happening."

I closed my eyes and sucked in a breath through my nose. "I understand you were a deep diver when—"

"We already covered that nugget of my life several times. Move on."

As always, I kept my words steady and calm. "Before signing on, you mastered three extra languages—"

"*Mettre fin à cette.*" Her angry words cut me off.

"*Vous voulez parler français?*" I replied.

If a mind could growl, hers did. In several languages, not just French. While Hayward's mind overflowed with words and ideas, Cooney seemed to pride herself on clamping hers shut and sealing it. I, on the other hand, was insanely determined to prod and poke at her softer edge. She had to have one.

Luckily for me, rendering is not an option; it's mandated. I straightened my back and placed one hand on my d-comm unit and the other flat against Cooney's cold metal tube. "You are Commander z'Bette Cooney, a soldier of the North American Union—"

After she repeated the basic information, I eased into reminding her of her talents and accomplishments, which were numerous.

"Fewer than a dozen people have ever gone as deep as three hundred meters on a self-contained breathing apparatus. You're one."

For the first time, I noted what could have been a waft of joy or happiness. I know technically Mêmes register words only, generated by the probes attached to the Tubers' brains, but . . . well . . . since my accident . . . I . . . *sense* things. It's difficult to explain exactly.

After a couple of hours sparring with Cooney, I was more than ready to indulge in a bit of relaxation, and since the ship's library was near where I quartered, I swung by there. Though most everyone knew about the cabin of pulpies, few felt worthy of even touching them. I was an exception. Too often Hayward's silly singsongs referenced leafy trees, fragrant flowers, chatty birds. The images niggled my senses, like the name of something you can't quite recall, but it's there on the tip of your tongue, just out of reach. While his words zipped through the air, almost animating themselves, the d-comms provided only bland explanations and sparse graphics. I thought whatever was in those pulpies might sate my inquisition.

The first book I opened puffed out a curious odor. Paper. I liked it at once, even before I smoothed my fingers over a page, which elicited such a pleasurable experience, I couldn't stop. And it was as though I could inhale each syllable, making my mouth water. Which drove me to taste each word as I pronounced it aloud, perking my ears. The same ears Hayward promised to whisper bawdy things into.

The vibrant images in the pulpies proved a hose-blaster: lofty trees with scabrous barks, their leaves rustling and crinkling in greens and golds and reds in chilling winds; reedy stems rising from loamy carpets, threading themselves around stilted fence posts and knotty trellises, sporting multihued and fragrant blossoms like glittering jewels; a covey of feathered birds, their beaks atwitter with a cacophony of chits and chatters, resounding happily in melodies tendered to unseen deities.

Books. Each page—Oh, how do I tell you?

Of course, I couldn't tuck these immensely stirring feelings in some payload bay or under my cot. My ecstasy spilled over into my relationship with my contracto. I sought the same satisfying and nourishing experience with the dark-eyed, black-haired Tynan that I'd found in the books.

My fingers didn't *touch* him anymore. They *caressed* his smooth, warm flesh. My nose poked in his long, clean hair, inhaling the fresh soap intermingling with his sweat. I longed to lick his eyelids and have him devour all of me with a searching mouth.

But he took it all the wrong way.

"I see you stroking their tubes. What is that? Threeve's foreplay?"

"Stop it."

"Then what is it?"

"Nothing dirty."

A superior scolding glower shoved aside his usual playful twinkles. "Then what?"

"Touch."

"Touch? You *can't* 'touch' them. You could contaminate them."

"With what? This ship is my home and my prison in one fell swoop."

"They have auto-stimulators."

"Which are not human fingers. Not 'touch.' Don't you see?" He didn't flinch when I trailed two fingers from his temple down his cheek and along his hard jaw. " 'Touch,' " I whispered. "They long for skin on skin, flesh on flesh. Just like we do."

"It doesn't follow protocol."

"No, it doesn't. It follows human"—I formed my fingers into claws and clicked the tips together several times—"*feeling.*" I had stretched out the last word. Let it roll off my tongue.

"That dirty old man!"

"What?"

"It's Hayward, isn't it?" Angry red splotched Tynan's cheeks. "What? Did he sweet-talk you with the pulpies' pretty words? I can see the two of you as he 'crumples the lace that snows on your breast.' Or how on his 'palette is a tint of your lips.' Nonsense like that. Crap from the Admiral's books. I should disservice the old bastard and be done with it."

"No! It's not like that. It's not!"

But no matter what I said, how I tried to explain, Tynan refused to hear me, to comprehend my words. I swore then I would mask the feelings I experienced with the Admiral's treasured books from Tynan and everyone else.

Except Hayward.

"I found the Riley book, Hayward, but you really don't have to explain to me about the experience of them." I smoothed my hand over the ragged embossed cover and the frayed grosgrain ribbon binding it closed. "I . . . know."

"But you didn't open the Riley, did you?"

"No."

"Clearly you've been in some of the others."

Too quickly, the conversation with Tynan flitted through the mind I was attempting to keep clear. But it was useless for me to offer empty denials or feeble rationalizations. Hayward could read my thoughts almost as well as I did his.

"'If you can think—and not make thoughts your aim . . .'" He spoke slowly, then paused. I thought it was for my confession, but it was really so he could skip over a line in the Kipling poem. "'If you can bear to hear the truth you've spoken / Twisted by knaves to make a trap for fools . . .'"

A crushing wave of sadness descended first inside my chest before radiating outward. Slowly. Deeply. But I couldn't explain it or truly identify where it was coming from.

"Untie the ribbon, or what's left of it, and open the book carefully."

"What page?"

"You'll know."

There was something stuck inside, bulging it a bit at the seam, but not protruding from the top. Opening the book gingerly, I found a long, slim leather pouch resting in the crease, indenting the pages as though pocketed in its own snug little place. "What's this?"

"Sometimes people press flowers or ribbons in pages, marking special places."

"This Raggedy Man must have been special to the Admiral, too."

> *O the Raggedy Man! He works fer Pa;*
> *An' he's the goodest man ever you saw!*
> *He comes to our house every day—*

But as I skimmed the text, I noticed the faint squiggles between the lines. Of course, I couldn't keep my hand against Hayward's tube and raise the book to better determine the smudges. They were words, too. Not printed ones, but ones scratched in with something that didn't damage the paper page, but rested lightly in a faded dark gray color.

"Ah, yes. Threeve experiences yet another beauty of the printed word: reading between the lines." Hayward didn't laugh. It was more of a chuckle that reminded me of Tynan. After the first time we'd coupled following the accident, he'd flicked a tendril of red hair off my nose and chuckled when I questioned our varying from procedure in his inseminating me for yielding. Maybe that's why I thought he would understand about "touching." About feelings. About the books.

Abruptly, I shifted the Riley and the pouch slid into my lap, exposing the tarnished zipper running down its side.

"Threeve, dear, open the pencil case."

"Pencil case?" I rested the book on my knees and unzipped it. Out tumbled an orange oblong plastic object with two small holes along with three dark gray sticks with sharp black points on one end and metal flattened squares with soft black protrusions on the other. Etched along the side of each were other words: PALOMINO BLACKWING 602.

"You use them to write with," Hayward said. "Pencils. And these are the very best. Used by writers and composers back in the day. The black point colors the page directly. Try it."

"Try it? You mean—"

"Look at the pages, Threeve; though I suspect you'd already noticed."

"I thought they were shadows or something. I—" Something so foreign, yet how had I instinctively perched the pencil between the exact fingers required?

How had I known?

My inkling to conceal what was happening from Tynan proved a solid decision, but keeping mum and finding time and a quiet place to read and write proved far from easy. For one thing, Tynan enjoys a heightened sense of smell. That poses a problem during intimate moments. He has a thing for hands and especially fingers. He began dwelling on mine, kissing my palms and rubbing them together against his nose and cheeks.

"What long digits you have, Threeve."

I recall doing my own chuckling because of a child's fairy tale I'd read. "Better to touch you with."

But he was far from amused, and after that, I became diligent about washing my hands following any prolonged handling of the pencil.

Hayward was no help at all. In fact, the next few days he hurried me through his renderings, his usual jocularity diminished. He kept badgering me about what else was written between the lines, what else I'd read.

In what little free time I had, I'd been so engrossed with the shapes and forms of the squiggles and loops and trying to emulate them, I had neglected to let the words impart their meanings. I'd perused the actual printed words of the stories and poems, but I'd obviously missed the most important part.

Finally, I curled up on my bunk with the well-worn collection of

James Whitcomb Riley's poems. Had Hayward not quoted them to me, I might have struggled with the language. Not so with the penciled-in musings between the lines.

Woven amidst the poetic hum of "The Used-To-Be" were the heavily underlined lamentations of the Admiral. Yes, *lamentations*: "There lies a land, long lost to me—"

Reading it both broke my heart and spawned an eruption of that niggling sensation again. As though I, too, yearned for some vanished place. But how? How could I possibly wrap my brain around the Admiral's homesickness?

Damn him. Damn Hayward. What right did he have exposing me to sights and sounds and feelings I would never have wondered about? Or missed.

The *Domum Ignes* was the only home I could remember. So why was it that my life, safely cocooned in my own tube, in my own stasis, no longer seemed enough?

"Imagination, the sharpest of all senses," the Admiral had penciled in between. "Dull down the taste and smell and sound and feel and sight—suspend them all—and still they live inside. Or so we are to imagine."

I had no clear recollection of a bee buzzing my ear or feeling its sting or tasting its sweet honey. But somewhere inside was . . . something. Just my imagination?

The book fell too easily open to the poem "The Man in the Moon."

> *Said the Raggedy Man, on a hot afternoon*
> > *My!*
> > > > *Sakes!*
> *What a lot o' mistakes*

Just after the words "Might drop a few facts that would interest you" came the familiar dark scribblings of the Admiral.

They are clearly madly in love. Sometimes I think when the two of them are within an arm's reach of each other, lightning will flash, singeing us all. And it makes me yearn for the day when my own true love and I can finally be together again.

I know this is no place to spill my secrets, but with the two people I care about most both in suspended animation, I have no other place to . . . to . . . to what? Rend my heart? Is that emotion even allowed for one in my station?

Hayward would know. Or Z. But I am no Même. Communication at this juncture would violate protocol.

Oh, to be able to steal away in some corner of this vessel and . . . touch our lips? A tiny taste is all I'd want. Something to tide me over. Not that you would settle for that, would you? And yet you settled for this bargain. After all these dreary months, I understand what you meant when you said it would be an uncertain hell for me, having you so close and yet so unreachable. But, my dear sweet one, I sustain myself with the vision of the two us . . . more equal? Is that what I desired or was that you? I don't really remember. Did it matter that much, our age differences?

Oh, that the Fates could have dealt us a hand like the young lovers. Like Tynan and Threeve. Only you and I will never know the same celebration of their love for we can never yield a child like they are—

A hot poker couldn't have burned my hand with any more intensity as I flipped the book away.

A child? A baby?

———

That night as we cuddled together in his bunk, Tynan planted kisses to the palms of my hands again with such a winsome smile. I wanted to bury myself in the folds of him. "My darling," he whispered like a man drunk on spirits. "My sweet, dear love."

And I tried to feel worthy of such unfettered affection.

Once we had been so close the Admiral felt our electricity. Where had it gone? And why? Because I'd lost our baby?

It was insane, I know, but I had to unscramble all of these puzzle pieces.

I left his bunk and walked, stopping at Hayward's tube. Tonight, I couldn't conjure up my china teapot swirling with a warmth of ginger and lemon balm. I wasn't seeking calm. I needed answers he had withheld from me.

And . . . I yearned to touch my friend.

Only I couldn't wake him.

Momentarily laying my hand on the edge of Cooney's tube on my way out, I heard her call. "Mary? Is it you? Have you finally—"

I waited for her to continue, but it was as if she were clearing her throat and her mind at the same time. Tossing a blanket over her mind to shield herself.

"Don't stop," I said. When she didn't immediately respond, I slammed my fists atop her tube. "Dammit! Answer me. Why did you think I was *Mary*? Who is she?"

She shifted into her haughty military voice. "Sit down, and for once, let me tell *you* a story."

And I slid into the slingseat.

"Once a time ago, our Earthly ships carried soldiers and weapons to battle the Os for their source of energy. But the men and women who fought those wars had no idea of the cost. Heaven knows there were enough people then. Too many, in fact, so if a few died, well . . . there were plenty more where they came from.

"Engineers and scientists thought they'd bested the beast known as deep space travel. Oh, sure there were a few glitches here and there, but on the whole they'd slap a piece of chewed gum here and there and pray nothing really bad happened.

"Only it did.

"The cognitive capabilities of those soldiers-in-stasis couldn't be brought back to fully functional levels. Oh, their bodies worked, but their minds had been wiped clean of years and years of training and experience. They were the walking dead. Zombies. Real ones.

"But desperate men are not above desperate actions, so the government latched on to the easiest solution they could find. There was this trendy process, initially rejected by the government, but whole-hog embraced by the wealthy. Brain transfers. Human brains—complete with memories and personalities—could be successfully scanned, uploaded into storage pods, and then downloaded into a host body with few physical or mental complications. The rich had their loved ones resurrected for as short as a holiday or special occasion like a birthday or wedding, or as long as several months or even years. Naturally, the exorbitant fees varied according to duration or need or whim, but the wealthy had noras. Lots and lots of noras. But when the dwindling energy sources took a dive-bomb hit on the economy, those left with any means at all simply moved on to other less flagrant frivolities.

"Then the European Union's coffers ran dry just like the NAU's. All due to energy exploration fiascos and that stupid, stupid war with the Os they never fought to win. And why?

"Energy.

"And just when it looked as though the government couldn't possibly beat their heads to bloody pulps against their lowest-bid walls any longer, a major breakthrough in brain-wave research and chemically induced hypothermia occurred.

"Well, fire up the booster rockets and load the payload bays!

"But no, not yet. Before deep space voyages could be tackled again there was one more stumbling block requiring tweaking. An additional *sense* won solid scientific recognition, and yet proved the

nastiest little bugger for successful stasis. No machine could ade-
quately stimulate it, which seems ironic when you think about it."

The Admiral's words flitted through my mind. "Imagination," I
said.

"Bingo."

"And that's what a Même really does," I added. "She stimulates
the imagination, but uses facts."

"Twists them sometimes even. Especially with *difficult* Tubers,"
she said.

For the first time, my fingers felt warm against her tube, and it
yanked me back to the reason I'd crept here in the first place. "Commander Cooney, I—"

"Call me Z."

Z. The Admiral's friend. I should have put that together at once.

"This hasn't worked out very well for you, has it?"

I didn't know exactly what she meant.

"I understand your accident was pretty bad. And even now
things aren't working out like they wanted."

"*They?*"

"Yeah, the lowest bidders."

And while I sat there, Z told me another story. One about impossible choices.

> *And the Man in the Moon, sighed The Raggedy Man,*
>> *Gits!*
>>> *So!*
>>>> *Sullonsome, you know,*
> *Up there by hisse'f sence creation began!*
> *That when I call on him and then come away,*
> *He grabs me, and holds me and begs me to stay!*

I thumbed through as many books in the Admiral's library as I
could, searching to verify Z's story. What I found were remem-

brances of a cabin deep in the woods. Snow so deep and cold, the Admiral noted how their crunching boots echoed empty and forlorn. How it seemed impossible to taste the ginger and lemon balm tea steeped in the six-cup Sheltonian wild violet bone china teapot. And how the crackling fire blushed their skins as they made love one last time before the *Domum Ignes* would take them far away to a distant place. One lover asleep for the years it would take them to reach the Gates of Johanna; the other aging naturally, which, if they had calculated correctly, would find them at nearly the same age on arrival.

Sharpening my pencil—using both holes in the orange sharpener, first for the wood, then for the graphite—I poised its long point against the book to begin fixing the pieces of the puzzle together, hoping that in writing it down, *I* might understand.

Several months ago, an explosion ripped through part of the galley, severely injuring the Admiral and Threeve. The ship's doctor and Tynan were left with a conundrum best left to the wisdom of Solomon. The Admiral had incurred irreparable damage to the back and chest, while Threeve suffered severe head trauma. Three days later, the Fates skulked away into the unknown with a spontaneously aborted fetus and his mother who never woke from her coma.

> *And, nestled in her palm, did seem*
> *To trill a song that called her "Dream."*

Yes, you see, don't you? You've already read between the lines of these words scratched between the lines of a poet's mirthful musing.

Though the Admiral's brain was downloaded into a Même's, it wasn't exactly a success.

Maybe somewhere, in one of the lobes, Threeve's and Admiral *Mary*'s extraordinarily gifted minds battle it out near their own gates to the future.

Hayward has yet to slip and call me Mary, but like my friend Z, he knows. Our minds connect daily.

I do wonder how it must feel for him when I utter the words "Raggedy Man," because in those niggling moments, I taste the name Mary had whispered into *his* ear so affectionately. When the snow was outside and two lovers were cozy in.

It's easier to curl up beside Tynan now, because I understand what he has endured and yet stands to gain or lose should this conflicted mind remember wholly— I nearly wrote "who I am," but at this point, who do I root for, Threeve or Mary?

Yet there is that itch again. As though I could be . . .

Hoosier writer Judi Rohrig's own affection for pencils began when all she could do was sniff the wood and nibble on the easer. Later, she scribbled little stories about cowboys and spies. Even later, she penned essays, interviews, newspaper columns, and news while continuing to jot down more twisted tales (but fictional, totally fictional!). Those writings found publication in Masques V, Furry Fantastic, Pandora's Closet, Spells of the City, Extremes V, Dreaming of Angels, Personal Demons, On Writing Horror, Mystery Scene, *and* Cemetery Dance. *Her short story "Still Crazy After All These Years" has been chosen for* All American Horror: Best of the 21st Century, First Decade. *The Horror Writers Association honored her with the 2004 Bram Stoker Award for Nonfiction for* Hellnotes. *Rohrig welcomes friends to her Facebook home at www.facebook.com/judi.rohrig and her blog at www.judirohrig.blogspot.com.*

In the Shadow of the Gate

WILLIAM C. DIETZ

On Gene Wolfe: I haven't had the good fortune to meet Gene Wolfe in person, so I only know him through his work. The Claw of the Conciliator was the first Gene Wolfe novel I read. I remember buying it back in the 1980s, based mainly on the cover art. It was only after I got it home and began to read that I realized I was holding something special. So special that I remember describing scenes to my wife, who, being used to such diatribes, nodded and said, "Yes, dear."

That was an important time for me because it was during the lead-up to writing my first book (in 1984) and a time when I was paying special attention to the craft of writing. The Claw of the Conciliator hooked me, and I'm still hooked, so it's a thrill to write a preface to one of my favorite stories.

There can only be one ending for the book *The Shadow of the Torturer,* and that is the one Gene Wolfe wrote. But for many years fans have wondered what took place in the brief interval between the end of *Shadow* and the beginning of *The Claw of the Conciliator.* Here's one possibility.

Seen from a distance, the wall looked like a snake. A black serpent that squirmed across the land dipping here, rising there, to eventually swallow its own tail somewhere on the far side of Nessus. Most people supposed that the wall had been built to keep people out.

Hethor, who had seen such structures on other worlds, knew some were built to keep things *in*.

Eventually, as the group got closer, the barrier became a black cliff. A wall so high the top of it was partially obscured by clouds. It was an awesome construct. Or would have seemed so had it not been for the fact that Hethor had seen cities that floated on air, oceans with the capacity to think, and rocks that could sing.

As the theatrical troupe neared the wall, Dr. Talos was in the lead, along with a beautiful actress named Jolenta, a carnifex named Severian, and a woman named Dorcas. The giant Baldanders followed behind, pushing a huge barrow loaded with props. And finally, in the most humble position of all, was Hethor.

But contrary to what the others believed, that was the place Hethor preferred, a position from which he could watch without being observed. And, as the troupe joined the stream of traffic that led toward the gate, Hethor took a particular interest in their backs. Especially the executioner's back. Because it was his job to kill the giver of death. Not to please himself, but on behalf of a woman named Agia. It seemed that Severian had been required to execute her twin brother, and she was after revenge.

Plus there was the matter of the item contained within the headsman's sabretache. Something Agia referred to as "a sentimental trinket," but Hethor suspected was of considerable value, and might mean more to his client than revenging her brother's death. Ultimately, once the object was cupped in Hethor's hand, it was *he* who would decide its fate.

The role of assassin was beneath him—or had been until recently. Now, having been forced to leave his ship without permission, he was on the surface of a backward planet without the means to support himself. So he had agreed to murder Severian. But *how*? It was no small thing to kill a professional killer. But if Hethor was to collect the second half of his fee, he would have to find a way. Perhaps the greatest problem was not the man so much as the weapon he carried. A beautiful sword called *Terminus Est*. By quickening his pace Hethor was able to draw even with Severian. "I will carry your sword, Master."

The carnifex turned to frown at him. He had a straight nose, sunken cheeks, and dark hair. He was dressed in a long cloak the color of which was fuligin, a black so black its folds were rendered invisible. "No. Not now or ever."

Hector looked down to his dusty boots. "I feel pity for you, Master, seeing you walk with it on your shoulder so. It must be very heavy."

Severian's expression softened. "Thank you, but no, it isn't as heavy as you might think."

Hethor was about to respond when the group rounded the side of a hill and Piteous Gate appeared in the distance. The road led straight to it and was crowded with people, animal-drawn carts, and heavily laden wagons. And that was enough to rouse Dr. Talos. He was a small man with fiery red hair and a quantity of gold teeth. Having seen the wall, and apparently inspired by it, he began to lecture those around him. All of which was quite boring insofar as Hethor was concerned. As for the sword, well, Severian was human. And humans must sleep.

At that point a man named Jonas appeared. He was mounted on a merychip and spoke to Severian. Hethor knew Jonas, and fell back lest he be recognized. And for that reason he was unable to hear what the men said.

Fortunately, once the conversation was over, Dr. Talos spoke to Jolenta, and Hethor was close enough to hear. "I think the angel of agony there, and your understudy, will remain with us awhile longer."

Hethor took that to mean that instead of returning to the center of Nessus as originally planned, Severian was going to pass through the gate with the rest of them. Hethor felt a stab of fear. He understood the gate better than his companions did. Here was a world without a port . . . a place so backward that it was listed as "primitive" on the charts. Still, it hadn't always been so. And one didn't need to look far to find ancient devices still in use. Were the gate's detectors in working order? Or had they, like so many things on the planet, been allowed to fail? His life could depend on the answer.

They were very close to the wall by then—and Piteous Gate was straight ahead. Looking into it was like looking into the entrance of a well-lit mine because the wall was extremely thick and honeycombed with corridors, rooms, galleries, hallways, chambers, and chapels. And one could expect those spaces to be thickly populated with men, women, and creatures that possessed features belonging to both. Hethor heard Severian ask about them.

"They're soldiers," Dr. Talos answered. "The Pandours of the Autarch."

And there was more, but as Dr. Talos spoke, the man named Jonas guided his merychip in close, forcing Hethor to fall back once again. Should he turn back? And look for other employment? Or follow Severian into the tunnel-like maw? After a moment's hesitation, the would-be assassin chose option two. The one that would line his pockets with money and, depending on what lay hidden within Severian's sabretache, could provide him with something of even greater value.

It was, as Hethor quickly discovered, the wrong decision.

There was a commotion up ahead as some members of the throng attempted to turn back. That frightened others, including a Waggoner, who was headed south. The man's lash flew, the metal tip kissed Dorcas's cheek, and she uttered a cry of pain. Severian went after the lout. Having been jerked from his seat, the Waggoner fell to the ground, where he was crushed by a succession of heavy wheels.

No sooner had that horror been realized than Hethor saw the reason for the stampede. At least a dozen beast men were charging straight at him! They had horns, and as one of them opened its mouth Hethor saw teeth that looked like nails and hooks.

Hethor turned to run, but the beasts were on him in a matter of seconds and quickly bore him away. Hethor struggled and called for help, but to no avail. A door opened and slammed behind them.

Inside, one wall of the chamber was taken up with windows that looked out onto the chaos outside. A sad-looking collection of what Hethor supposed to be pickpockets, bandits, and other criminals lined another. Most of the dejected prisoners were seated on the floor under the watchful gaze of a horned guard. It was a holding room, then, a place where those who had been sifted out of the passing crowd could be held until soldiers came to fetch them.

That was when a stern-looking man entered. He wore a tonsure, signifying his rank, and a robe so long that it brushed the floor. The man gave orders in a language that consisted of grunts and growls. The beast men put Hethor down and searched him . . . and there was plenty to find beneath the loose-fitting clothes. A pair of brass knuckles clattered to the floor, quickly followed by a double-edged dagger, two mirrors made of shiny metal, a copper vial that was filled with poison, a square of folded cloth, a crust of moldy bread, and matches in a brass box. One of the beast men uttered a grunt, and the human nodded.

"Well done. My name is Savek. And you are?"

"H-H-Hethor."

"Well, Hethor, you were brought here because you carry proscribed materials."

"Everyone h-h-has a right to defend themselves," Hethor replied. "And I use the knife to slice bread."

"I wasn't referring to the dagger," Savek said, as he bent to retrieve the mirrors and cloth. "I was talking about *these*. Where did you get them?"

"Beyond the western sea," Hethor lied. "That, oh lord, is w-w-where maidens with gleaming hair pour sweet nectar, where flowers perfume the air, and the bazaars of O-O-Opar open their arms at night. Dreams can be bought there—and potions such as to stir the blood! Even as s-s-stars fall from the sky, light-filled orbs float suspended in the air, and blind men see."

"So you purchased the objects," Savek said impatiently.

"Y-y-yes, lord. If it pleases you."

"It does *not* please me," Savek said, "as you are about to learn."

Savak waved a hand and the beast men took Hethor away.

Severian was furious. Having been denied the opportunity to torture the careless Waggoner, he turned to find that Dr. Talos, Jolenta, Baldanders, and precious Dorcas had disappeared. But there, no more than half a chain away, was Hethor. His feet were walking on air as two beast men carried him away. And though of no great concern in and of itself, that raised the possibility that the others had been abducted as well.

Severian shouted at the beast men soldiers to stop, but either they couldn't hear him over the surrounding tumult or chose not to acknowledge him. A door swung open, Hethor was taken inside, and the barrier closed again. Fearful that a similar fate had befallen Dorcas and the others, Severian hurried forward.

"Out of the way!" he shouted. And the combination of his commanding manner, the fuligin cloak, and the drawn sword was sufficient to clear a path to the metal-strapped door. The sword made a thumping sound as the hilt struck dark wood. "Open up!" Severian demanded, as he tugged on a bronze handle.

There was no response at first. Then a head-high door within the door opened to reveal a leering face. It had a low brow, pink-hued eyes, and a hog-wide nose. But the creature's mouth was disturbingly human, as were its ears.

"My name is Severian . . . I am a Journeyman of the Seekers of Truth and Penitence. Let me in."

The beast uttered a grunt, the window slammed closed, and Severian was left to fume for at least a minute before the larger door opened. Having returned *Terminus Est* to its scabbard, Severian stepped inside. His eyes swept the chamber, saw the prisoners, and checked them one by one. Dorcas was nowhere to be seen, nor were the others.

"My name is Kevas. I am the Assistant Exsecutor here. Can I be of assistance?" The voice was light and delightfully melodic.

Severian turned to find himself looking at a woman with black hair, a high forehead, and large, luminous eyes that seemed to peer right through him. "My name is Severian. I saw your soldiers snatch my servant off the street and bring him here. His name is Hethor. And I'm looking for the rest of my party as well. That includes a small man with red hair, a giant, and a woman almost as beautiful as you."

That was a lie, since Severian had never seen a woman as comely as Jolenta, but he figured a little flattery couldn't hurt. But the compliment had no visible effect on the Exsecutor. Her eyes were like deep wells. "There was a man," she said softly. "My superior is about to question him. As for the others, no, they aren't here."

Severian considered that. Dorcas was out on the road somewhere. Dr. Talos and Baldanders would look after her, to some extent at least, but not with the care that he would. So part of him wanted to leave right away. But what of Hethor? For some reason Severian was reminded of Triskele, the three-legged dog he had rescued, and even dreamt of the night before. Could he leave Hethor with the beast men? No, he couldn't. Time was of the essence, however, so he hoped to find Hethor and free him as quickly as possible. "I would like to see Hethor. Now, please."

The luminous eyes stared up at him. And as the clean scent of her found his nostrils, Severian could imagine how her soft melodic voice would sound interposed with the piteous screams of a well-flayed client. A musical counterpoint of sorts. A duet unsung.

"Your servant was carrying proscribed artifacts. Was he carrying them for you?" she asked. "Perhaps you aren't seeking the man so much as the items he carried."

Suddenly Severian was in a trap, or teetering on the edge of one, and wondered what if anything Hethor had confessed to. He sensed movement, but it was too late. A pair of beast men stepped in to grab his arms. Severian chose not struggle, lest doing so seem to confirm his guilt. "I am a member of the torturer's guild," he said, mustering all the dignity that he could.

"*And* a subject of the Autarch," Kevas said primly. The grunts and growls that followed meant nothing to Severian and were unseemly coming from her full-lipped mouth. Severian felt a tug as *Terminus Est* was removed from its scabbard. Then, having been on the receiving end of a powerful shove, the carnifex was led away.

A door opened and closed as Severian was forced into a great emptiness. And as the carnifex looked upward he could see what appeared to be endless flights of stairs that led to precarious galleries, ramps that zigzagged back and forth across the face of the pitted metal wall, and platforms for which there was no obvious purpose, all lit by the beams of dusty sunlight that slanted down from above.

As Severian was escorted ever higher, he passed tiers of cells all filled with miserable human beings. Some, having left all sanity behind, screamed words that no one knew. Others, upon seeing the deathly darkness of his cloak, shrank into the recesses of their filthy cells. In spite of their misery, they were still eager to live out another minute, hour, or day. Steel clashed with steel somewhere, chains rattled, and Severian heard the high, eerie sound of a song, the words filled with longing. And *here,* he decided, was where hell lay, not in the land beyond death.

The Chamber of Truth was equipped to accommodate the needs of a professional torturer, though none was in attendance. So that as Hethor was questioned, it was in a room furnished with a chair of spikes, also called a Confession Chair. In one corner an Iron Maiden stood, her hinged body open to receive the next offender. And that was to say nothing of the bench-mounted skull crusher, the dangling chain whip, the horizontal rack, the stork, the thumbscrew, or the aptly named knee splitter. All of which was frequently sufficient to loosen tongues without the sending for a member of the torturer's guild. All Hethor could do was stall, try to retrain control of his bowels, and hope that something would break his way.

Hethor was seated on a sturdy chair that occupied a platform. It was located below a bright light, which caused him to squint. "What is your *real* name?" the Exsecutor demanded.

"I have many n-n-names," Hethor replied. "I am called the buyer, seller, and transporter of goods useful and otherwise. A merchant am I, sailing the shining seas, always far from home. Andeth, Fosfer, and Umbay. I am known by all and n-n-none of those. For names are as numerous as pebbles on a beach and of no particular importance."

"I grow weary of your witless prattling," Savek said sternly. "Perhaps I will send for a torturer. All we need is your tongue. The rest can be cut away."

There was a momentary commotion as the door was thrown open. Severian stumbled into the room, caught his balance, and looked around. A woman entered behind him.

"M-M-Master," Hethor said pitifully, "is it truly you?"

The woman spoke. "Yes, your master came looking for you, or what you were carrying. The question is which. Tell me Hethor, who do the objects on this table belong to? You? Or your employer?"

"T-T-To me."

"The lout could be lying," Savek observed, "but we will come back to that. Now," Savek said, as he removed two mirrors from a nearby table. "Tell me what these devices are."

Hethor accepted one in each hand. He held them up as if to admire himself. "T-T-They are mirrors, lord, which I planned to sell."

"Our devices tell a different story," Savek countered. "And these are not ordinary mirrors. They have a numinous aura of some kind. Are they haunted?"

"No, lord. Not that I know of," Hethor replied, as he continued to manipulate the mirrors. Once they faced each other he blew so as to fog them.

"Stop that," Savek said, as he took the objects back.

"S-S-Sorry, lord. I know not of what you describe. For me they are but trinkets, purchased beyond the western sea, and brought here by ship." The last being true.

"And this?" Savek demanded, shaking the sail out to its full size.

"A t-t-tablecloth, lord, or a shroud. Depending on what the customer may choose."

"You are a liar."

"If you say so, l-l-lord," Hethor said humbly.

It looked like Severian was about to object when a commotion came from outside. Then the door slammed open and a beast man entered. It uttered a series of urgent grunts, and a scream was heard coming from somewhere behind him. Savek swore and led the rest of the guards out of the chamber. A heartbeat later a roaring *whoosh* sounded.

Hethor left his chair and retrieved his belongings. "Master," he said, staring at the open door, "what was that?"

A tongue of fire shot past the door in answer, and a glowing insect appeared. Its wings were a blur. It had a gauzy appearance, and seemed to shimmer like a mirage. Then, as the head with the hooked beak turned to look at them, it opened its mouth and another gout of fire flooded the entrance to the chamber.

That was when Kevas darted in and fired her laser pistol . . . to no effect.

Another tongue of fire shot out of the creature's mouth and wrapped Kevas in a cocoon of yellow-orange flames. There was nothing melodious about her scream. Death came quickly, but the corpse continued to burn as it hit the floor.

Severian had reclaimed *Terminus Est* by then, and held it ready.

The creature turned away and disappeared onto the platform beyond—and more screams were heard.

Severian turned to Hethor. "Come on. This is our chance."

"Yes, Master," Hethor said obediently, as he followed the carnifex to the door. There was good reason to look around before exiting the chamber, and what he saw surprised him. The platform was empty. But off to the right, and many chains below, the glowing insect hovered in midair. A streamer of fire shot out to set a beast man alight. The soldier howled and rolled on the floor in a futile attempt to extinguish the flames.

There was a great cacophony of noise as inmates shouted all manner of things, a bell began to toll, and hundreds of beast men swarmed out onto the galleries, ramps, and platforms, ready to do battle.

Severian turned to the left and was forced to step over Savek's charred body before he could access the stairs. He ran down them to a long gallery lined with cells. A beast man saw Severian, took him to be an escaped prisoner, and came at him with sword swinging. The carnifex ducked to let the blade pass over his head and took a swing at the creature's left leg and followed it with a downward blow that split its head open.

"It's wearing a key," Severian observed. "Take it. Open those cells."

Hethor hurried to obey, and as he opened door after door, Severian fought a succession of bloody duels. Then, once enough prisoners had been released, they became an army in their own right. They howled as they rushed down ramps, swarmed any jailer they could find, and opened *more* cells.

One by one the beast men fell, and as they did, the escapees took their weapons. All Severian and Hethor had to do was follow the mob down to ground level and find a way out.

They did so, but as Severian entered the tunnel that lead north from Piteous Gate, he turned to find that Hethor had disappeared. Swept away by the crowd perhaps—or determined to continue alone. Not that it mattered. He wanted to find Dorcas and assumed she was somewhere ahead.

Now, as Severian pushed his way through the surging crowd, he saw signs that the pyrausta, the flame-throwing insect, was somewhere in front of him. Two burnt bodies lay sprawled in the street, the faint odor of sulfur hung in the air, and there were screams ahead. In moments, he came across the man named Jonas, who was kneeling next to a dead onager. The animal was badly burned and its throat had been cut.

"It was hurt," Jonas explained. "I had to give it peace."

"You did the right thing," Severian assured him. "Come with me. I can see the north end of the gate from here."

Jonas stood, and with the merychip following along behind, they walked north. Neither man was aware that the object in Severian's sabretache had started to glow, nor did they take notice when the light began to fade, because their eyes were on the road ahead.

New York Times *bestselling author William C. Dietz has published more than forty novels, some of which have been translated into German, French, Russian, Korean, and Japanese. Dietz also wrote the script for the* Legion of the Damned *game (iPhone, iTouch, and iPad), based on the popular series of the same name—and cowrote Sony's* Resistance: Burning Skies *game for the PS Vita.*

Dietz is a member of the Science Fiction and Fantasy Writers of America, the Writer's Guild, and the International Association of Media Tie-In Writers. He and his wife live near Gig Harbor in Washington state, where they enjoy traveling, kayaking, and reading books. For more information about William C. Dietz and his work, visit www.williamcdietz.com.

Michael Andre-Driussi wrote The Wizard Knight Companion: A Lexicon for Gene Wolfe's The Knight and The Wizard, *as well as* Lexicon Urthus: A Dictionary for the Urth Cycle, *both with Gene Wolfe. This story would have been impossible without Michael's advice and guidance.*

Soldier of Mercy

On Gene Wolfe: *He is the single biggest influence on the way that I think today. I first encountered him by accident in the fourth grade when a friend of my father gave me a box of books, which included a hardcover of* The Claw of the Conciliator. *I had to get the first book, of course, and when I reread Wolfe I realized how profound he was—a modern and sophisticated man who can write breathtakingly about everything from spirituality to despair without ever falling victim to banality. He could build on ancient formulas and traditions without destroying them. I wrote him a fan letter in graduate school, and since then he has become a far more trustworthy hero to me than any of his protagonists. This story is of course inspired by his Latro books and their exploration of memory, identity . . . and mercy.*

I opened the golden pyx as deftly as I could, fumbling for a second, thinking of the words that had caught my attention at the Christmas Vigil last week in the dark pew—the monophony of a chanting tenor echoing in my skull. I tried to believe that there was something sublime or transcendent waiting to happen. That old chant of time's passage was stuck in my head, of how very much time it had been since the Earth was new, since the flood, since the two of us had seen each other clearly—time oppressed us both as I tried to remember the proper words. Only this hungry lie drew his gaze toward me, though we were alone in his little silent room.

His lips were dry, irritated from the growth above them. I could almost feel his lust for the unleavened bread in my hand. He was wearing a dark gray dress shirt today, and black slacks, with his red undershirt the only splash of color and vibrancy. St. Jude Thaddeus flashed in gold around his neck as he leaned forward to better see the wafers nestled in the pyx. The fluorescent lights above played shadowy games with his pale skin, hiding the dark blue eyes in deep recesses, but revealing the angry red marks around his scarred forehead, almost like tumors, though they proved flat to the touch.

There was a discernible reflection of that artificial light nested in his eyes when I returned his scrutiny. With the use of his left hand he must have fastened the buttons himself, or the aides would have left him in only the red shirt. It seemed to me that his right one was reaching out toward the pyx now.

"You were here last week," was firmly spoken.

"Yesterday."

He was silent for what seemed a minute at my reply, and I decided it was as good a time as any to get this over with.

"Behold the Lamb—"

"But last week, too," he interjected, gathering steam now that silence was most expected. "I showed you the letter they sent. Questioning my document. I translated it, you know."

"Yeah, yeah, the document. We can talk after, you know." I caught myself mimicking him, unconsciously. "And about other stuff, too. Eleanor has some questions I would like for you to answer."

"Rome was already a republic when that last script was trapped, sealed up in that wall for so unbearably long. I knew it would be there. Before the accident. I found it." He touched the scar near his left temple. "And right after the accident I was sure of what I had found, at last."

I did not think he had been a very religious person before, but things had changed—if not from the time of his accident and that ghastly but apparently harmless skin infection, then later with the stroke, when his gait had become so labored.

"Hey, Grandpa, speaking of Rome: This is the Lamb of God who takes away the sins of the world; happy are those who are called to his supper." My voice sounded reedy to my ears.

"Lord, I am not worthy to receive you, but only say the word and I shall be healed."

I could hear him humming under his breath, the old songs he had enjoyed so much, but in a fractious kind of concatenation only someone who truly knew him could follow. (And the traitor thought: *Did he even know himself anymore?* flashed through my mind.) I could hear the words of his haphazard humming in my head as if he were vocalizing: "and drink of his blood, you will live forever . . . *Agnus Dei, qui tollis peccata mundi, miserere nobis . . . dona nobis pacem.*"

Then those shadowed eyes noticed me again, and they shifted to encompass my existence. "You should read it—I rewrote it all, but I think I lost the first half. I corrected a few of the words, from the Latin. I don't think *Sol Invictus* was the right term, as I did before."

"Look, I don't have time for that now. I know you kept impeccable records about what happened before the accident, maybe after. You always did. Your study had so many, but nothing about that last trip. Have you stored them somewhere? I need to see them. A key for a safe box? A vault? Anything?"

"Your mother used to ask the same way when she was alive."

"Yeah, and she's still alive. But you know why she can't come here." As I said it, I wondered if it was true.

"That key won't help you get what you seek. That's not worth knowing. Only what I have written here. On some paper towels, if you'd help me look." He gestured at the small table in front of him, laid out with clean towels and a large safety cup. His bookshelf, filled with some of his hardcovers, was almost within reach from his wheeled seat. "Roy—it's all you need."

I ignored that. I saw where he was pointing, to the bits of crumpled paper between two volumes. Despite myself I reached out to retrieve and straighten it. "Did you put that there?"

"I think we could say Sol or Mithras, but since it hasn't been published yet, we can change it. I need to summon the spirit, not the letter. That's harder, isn't it?"

I knew what he was talking about; I had seen his scrawled work weeks ago, and further, I knew its source. "I'm sorry, pops." I couldn't tell him that any historian would know in a few seconds. There was no solar cult in Rome until five centuries later; his allusions were getting less consistent.

Yet the imp of the perverse grabbed me, and I glanced down despite myself.

The sun reflected off the waters of Hiberus, and it suffused everything with such an inviting glow that I wanted to bathe in its warmth. The image was stuck in my head as surely as the knowledge that I am a soldier of the Great King. Senator Hadrianus Drusus had taken me to his apartment, and though he believed himself a clever man, I could see that he was trying to position me in a way to make the most of my talents—whatever he believed them to be.

It was a small and mostly tidy place for someone who had identified himself as a senator of the republic. His voice was not fast, yet there was something not entirely languorous in him. "We are not a greedy people, you know. Life is getting better—and we can make it even more so."

"This 'we' you speak of," I interposed, "is it this city, the eagle's hordes? Or is this you and your friends? Or the two of us?" I would not be spoken to as a slave by this man—not anymore.

Cautus had bared his teeth at the bridge, where the scarred girl had left us and Hadrianus had first called to me. Though I could not remember how he had responded to everyone, I knew that Cautus loved me. And for a while after that I had been distracted by the maiden with the sheath of grain, as she whispered in my ear that I was blessed by Asopus. Yet all that was behind me for now, and I had accepted Hadrianus's offer to accompany him to his nearby residence.

Hadrianus aimed a crooked leer at me. "You are a young and handsome man, and we have heard about the way you handled those plebes. I thought, here, this is what we have sought so long. I want to take you to a man named Aelius in the city, where we will see many things."

"It was not because they were plebes—" But I could not finish, for it was fading. For an instant on the road today, the woman with the grain had made me feel good as she brushed against me, but when she had mentioned it would be many and many years before she married the sun, I felt nothing but a bitter cold.

That dread had carried me through the ambush, Cautus mauling along with us, until our inexplicable attackers were routed. We had little of value, and it made no sense, neither to me nor to those others with more context. Hadrianus handed me these scraps to write upon, saying that he was familiar with my process and that I must find time to write. Then he continued.

"Lucius Brutus was a great man. My older brother spoke of him often, revered him, and loved him for all that he embodied. But the Tarquins were great in their way, too, the old ways. Remember them? You might be old enough. I do, my father did. Tarquinius Superbus had real power. That cuckold Lucius Collatinus rode a bad situation to great success like any man with little talent in the right place at the right time. But Lucius Brutus was the one who saw beyond the surface."

I nodded, though I had little idea where this would go.

"You see, Brutus in an instant twisted the oracle's words to his own ends and the ends of Rome, but even he did not foresee that these plebes would be dissatisfied with an all patrician consul."

"I have little to do with that." Cautus was sniffing at something in the corner. He had become used to the apartment now, though I could not remember if he was normally comfortable in such tight surroundings.

"But you will have something to do with it." At that point Cautus had pulled up the screaming woman from the corner altar as if from nowhere, the space between her legs and the gash in her throat a bloody mess.

Hadrianus ignored her completely, and I tried to do the same. Her face was marred with an angry red stain, that much was clear, and I was thankful that soon, all too soon, I would forget it. Yet her wails stirred something inside me.

"You see the plebes as your enemies, though you are from the same city. They see you as oppressors, I think. One can never vanquish an enemy if he does not stand in his place, for a time."

Hadrianus's leer turned into a genuine smile then. "So you shall, then. You will stand in their place." He reached out his hand. "For me."

"You still believe this stuff—that you found it?" I asked. "That you wrote all that?" I pointed to the shelf. Suddenly inspiration struck me. "Do you remember anything? About Rome? About your wife? What's the earliest thing you remember?"

At that question, his eyes shone blue in that little dark room, its cheap tiled floors and unused TV perennially silent, for this man had no use for the trappings of modern times, only for that which was long gone, sealed away in his scarred head.

"I wake." He paused for a second, as if he considered stopping. But he continued, and I had not seen his eyes so blue in many years, or the skin on his forehead look less angry. "I run down the hall to see my grandmother in the kitchen. The light from the window suffuses everything in an interminable glow, the sun blurring the physical limits of the sill or the table and even my grandmother herself. I see the large pot of water on the stove. She places it in a basin and begins to heat another, and another after that. And she turns to me, and the hot water for my bath is ready, heated up with painstaking care, for we had no hot water. Pot by pot, heated and emptied, the purifying wholeness of love, love, love, bathed in that impossible light." He looked down at his legs in that binding chair, averting his increasingly reddened eyes. "When it is time for me to run down another hallway into the dark, she will be there with that love, to wash me clean again."

That oversized white mustache he insists on keeping glistened with moisture, though he had never worn one for the entirety of his youth. It looked oddly out of place on that emaciated frame, with those hollow cheeks.

"But sometimes I remember other things than that," he said, and when he looked up, his eyes were dark once more, hidden in the shadows created by his brow.

"Like the war, on guard duty. We had been fighting, boxing. He was a lot bigger, you know, and strong. But he was afraid, when it was time to relieve me on guard duty, because there are some things that can take away all those advantages. All I had to do was say he did not answer the challenge. I hid behind the ammunitions dump, and tapped him on the shoulder as he walked by. He thought I was going to kill him, Barkis did. Barker, I mean. He had flattened me rather badly, you know. Syngman had just released thirty-four thousand prisoners, they said. Even if it was two-thirds that number, that many enemies behind your lines is a nightmare. Around that time a carrier plane with more than a hundred men on R&R had crashed. It was alive in the air. It's funny what you remember so clearly, from so long ago. It doesn't even seem like you could have been there. I could have killed him, you know; it happened all the time. An accident."

"Yeah, there was an accident. That's what I want to talk to you about. Do you remember Eleanor? She is helping me work on this, and I need to get it resolved. It's wearing on me, Grandpa. I feel like you look. And don't you want to shave? It will make you feel better."

"Why? That's why the time was right, you know. Everything was better. The whole world was at peace. That's what He was waiting for, to instantiate into temporality."

I couldn't help myself. "Sure. In a manger with the stinking beasts. You know the sun cult is like at least a five-hundred-year anachronism in your little notes, right?"

Then he smiled, and paraphrased one of his insidious hymns at me. "A thousand ages are but an instant gone."

"Yeah. Gram's gone, too, Grandpa, and you need to let me know why."

He wouldn't answer me, and I knew that I was wasting my time, that he would just sit there and begin to glare, as he had every week after the initial success. But did he really forget that we had spoken of this over and over?

I asked him a few more questions but was met only with silence. He did not complain when I walked out with his garbage napkins in my hands.

"Eleanor, you have to understand what caused it; the accident had him bleeding in multiple places inside his brain. Even back then some days he wasn't the same. But he was lucid afterwards, it's only lately he's like this."

She was sitting at her home office desk, her mute little Chihuahua sitting placidly, staring up with love from her lap. Or with something. Maybe it was obedience. I wondered if it was mute, or just scared to disturb her.

"Sweetie, if you ever want to see this money, if you want to be able to know what they were really doing there and get those documents released that the company has sealed, we need a competent witness. A witness to what happened to your grandmother and to the state of the study. Tone, you sure your mother won't come forward?"

I looked at the red of her lips as she spoke, and remembered the way she had leaned against me those months ago, pretending to trip ever so slightly in that oldest of fashions, though there was little else I could see that was very old-fashioned about her.

"We can't get that old man in as a reliable witness. Can you imagine when they ask him to identify himself?" As I said it, a picture of the thin twisted man hobbling up there with his thin twisted cane, repeating his name for the record, and the travesty that would follow.

"So does he forget? Is that what his association is?" Eleanor's face was placid, but I remembered her last week in the throes of what should have been passion between us, and felt her claws once again along my back.

"He pretends to forget, I think. I don't know why they were there, both of them. He said it was the last remnants of the followers of some ancient cult, but his scholarship is shoddy, second-rate. He was always full of crap; his life sounded like a circus if you believe his nonsense. Then it got even worse. But the problem was—" Here I paused, trying to take in the way her hands caressed the Chihuahua's head, but still held it contained, so that its movements were restricted. I wondered if it was content.

I repeated myself when she looked up at me. "The problem was his partner really was a genius, whatever it was they were working on. My grandfather had biochemistry experience, but he was a scientific joke. But the partner was something else, a real prodigy. I don't know, stopping cell death, reprogramming the cellular limits of reproduction without inducing unlimited growth, animating dead tissue. It was kind of mystical. Nobody really liked the idea, or messing much with it. They had sampled natural specimens globally—with some anomalous results. They claimed there was some naturally occurring substance in the area that had catalyzed a mutation—one that resembled what they sought to reproduce in the lab. It wasn't in a modern church or anything, but certainly an older part of Rome they were looking in. Even digging. And that's where the argument started."

I knew Eleanor would not be interested in that—she had other concerns here—ones I happened to share. All that he had hinted to me in our correspondence before his trips and in the incoherent babbling when he would almost nap, but in his most lucid moments he had been extremely tight-lipped.

The Chihuahua bit at her fingers, but I could see it had no teeth, and for some reason that fact filled me with dread. I pulled my own fingers into the pockets of my jacket, and the ache in my eyes suddenly made me pull out the napkin there, and toss it toward the small basket at the end of her desk.

The dog looked to the movement excitedly, its tail beating even faster, maybe longing for a chance to search through the trash. I was tired of rifling through Grandfather's trash.

"It might have been futile research, baby, but you need to keep your eyes on getting what should have always been yours. It's justice." Yet she didn't look directly at me.

"Do you think I can get a shower here?" I suddenly felt I needed the hot water to clear my eyes for the drive I would obviously be taking to my own apartment soon.

"Not tonight, it's a mess. You have to go talk to him again, and again, until he tells you something you can use."

I knew she was right, but I wished then that I wasn't doing it for her. And I knew her shower was very far from a mess.

Later, as I cried in my car, I realized I had been using his dirty napkins to wipe the tear streaks away.

Antonius told me that the Crimson Men had called me Lewqys, but that they had left and that I must write again as I had before, though

I did not have much room here. When I looked at Aelius I remembered that I could see through him, that he was not all there, but indeed, though transparent, there was something hidden. The boy Antonius was tow-headed, and the older woman with him was stern despite her painted face.

"My father," Antonius said, "has brought a Dacian here."

They were not slums, but the dwellings were far more humble than the ones Aelius had taken me to when he handed me off to Antonius.

"He has fascinated some of my father's friends with some talk. It is not only justice he speaks of, but something that will last a sight longer." Antonius was speaking to me, but I could tell the woman Aenora had a hold on at least some of his focus.

"And why would a Dacian have anything to do with the Eagle's Republic?" I asked.

"He speaks of man rising with the sun anew, and a paradise that will never, ever end."

Thus it was that as we walked, others joined us, the plebes. Some seemed to be well dressed and fed, others to be sun-browned and weary. The meeting house was of decent and sturdy quality, though I have not time to describe it here. We entered together, but dispersed throughout the seats. Aenora had tied Cautus about thirty yards away to a large tree, something I was at first concerned over but later had reason to rejoice.

Antonius whispered to me as the crowd settled, while Aenora took her place at the front with the others. It was Antonius's father who spoke for them.

"Our consul has agreed that it is the moral responsibility of the republic to at least consider that nonpatricians may hold a yearly office, selected by those they will represent," Antonius's father began. Though he had seemed easy enough to read before, I could not tell what the boy thought of his father. "His peer is still reluctant to accede, but it is in the manner of Lucius Brutus, who fell and kissed the earth so that we would all rise up, that we too shall have a voice, perhaps even seats in the Senate. Our Dacian friend Isokrates has other matters to speak of, ones that I hope you consider. It would be foolish to look at things from only this worldy perspective we have adopted."

This Isokrates was a stout man, bearded and with a mottled and uneven swarthiness, but his voice was resonant and penetrating. At his neck, a golden boar-headed medallion hung suspended with a depiction of the sun.

With a taper lit from a wall sconce, he lit a small censer that had been ignored behind the supposed leaders of the community.

I do not have time to write what he said, nor space, though I knew it was important because the woman of the thread, who called herself Lachisis, came through the rear altar wall in rage. The Golden Man pushed her back.

Worse things happened. Soldiers armed with pila and daggers opened the rear doors to the meeting hall, and trained dogs burst through. In the confusion I saw Antonius's father fall, and, as I moved close to Antonius to protect him, I saw Aenora behind the would-be representative, the bloody claw already disappearing in her robes and the smile on her face already subdued. I vowed to write it down as quickly as possible—as I have, at the risk of cutting out Isokrates's rhetoric.

When Grandfather had first come back, they had run a lot of tests on that skin infection. It was not malignant, and eventually we just assumed it was a discoloration or an innocuous condition. He had been acting strangely then, but when they finally found those bodies over there and a trial was scheduled, his stroke and eccentricities had postponed everything.

Now it was light enough to see what he had written, which I had read before. I skimmed over the rest to the end. There, in the temple of the sun that had never been there, my grandfather always concluded the narrative he had rewritten at least twice already. What made me really irate about all this was that his insanity, so lucid, was based on a complete misreading of the source material.

"A sphere is the most perfect shape," I said to her, and she held that sphere in her hands, though her eyes were the eyes of a lioness.

And Aelius, with the golden hair, the effulgent face so radiant—he stood near her, flickering away into her shadow. "You were right to treat Hadrianus as you did," he said, "though he was my friend."

I nodded, and admitted then what I had feared to admit before, when Aelius had cast aside the fleshly appearance of a Senator and the plebian retaliation and the rise to arms had stopped dead before it could begin. Hadrianus had known they would trust me, and gambled that the consul would listen to him in forcefully putting them down.

"Once I would have fought for him, or fought against him with the outraged. Now I don't want to fight, not anymore. I spared him, though he did not beg for mercy."

"Even you can be redeemed. Us, too." The lion-eyed goddess picked up the iron thunderbolt that had fallen in my wrestling match and held it at her waist. "You no longer remember the screaming woman at his altar, do you? You would know why he hated them, then. Perhaps we have not stopped that."

It was at that point that the great boar burst through the ground itself, as if he had been tunneling since time began, creating some cavern of darkness and death, his skin itself an angry red glare as his weak eyes opened with rage, taking in the goddess with the lion eyes, Aelius, and myself.

It screamed with a rage that seemed to have all the power of the dead behind it, a nacreous and chaotic mess left in its wake that murmured of slimy and desperate disappointment.

The sword at my side had been blunted over time, but I knew that this enemy was one I would have more difficulty sparing.

Aelius only regarded it with sorrow, and with all my speed and all my strength I grabbed its tusks and turned its charge into the marble altar. The tusks stuck in the hard marble, and with a wrench of desperation the bore jerked to the side, shattering its tusks in jagged and grotesque fashion. While it freed itself, I was able to get one hand loose and draw the sword at my belt, and scoured it across the head, hoping that I would not have to actually kill it. I jumped back as it completely extricated itself, turned, and charged again, and I cut it shallowly over and over, until I was sure that it was not a great boar I fought but a man. And when he sank to his knees, I managed to restrain him in my hands, and his resistance ceased. I turned and faced Aelius.

The sun was fierce indeed, blinding me, such that the ruined buildings of the consulate were as nothing.

"Why do you want me to do this?" I asked, but Aelius made no answer. It felt for a second that I was talking only to myself, that there was nothing else in existence. That feeling, too, passed, and it spoke in my head. The angry flesh of he who had been a boar furrowed under my hands, and though I halted my hands from twisting that sturdy neck, he squirmed as if he could escape into the earth, into the embrace of Mother Ge to be reborn again. He melted through the floor of the temple of the sun. But I knew that he wanted nothing so much as to grab the light shining through Aelius and call it his own.

"You have recalled dimly and only in part, but I have heard through you," Aelius said. There were many voices behind him. "Though you could not remember, at each point losing more of yourself, something was gained, too. I have heard, and those things will never be forgotten again. You have been one of my rays, and now there will be rays of mercy. Tomorrow you will come back to me, and we will both go forward, to another and another tomorrow, to the great peace we have begun by stopping this rebellion. We need a more unified Republic for now, and we have taken that first step. As for him, we shall spare him, not once, not twice, but every time, when he supplicates for mercy."

"And when he does not know to ask for it?"

He was silent for a time. "Write tonight, and return tomorrow."

And all I could think was that it was impossible, and that this, too, would fade away, lost forever, though it was so very bright.

I felt that I myself would become one with that golden figure, in casting away my sword. I thought that the distance which had seemed so great, the mist so strong, was nothing but the parting of all the ages of both men and gods, in one immutable moment, the setting and rising of the sun. Were Ge and Sol to wed yet again, or would this ray of hope forever end it? Do you see the guilt on me? I spared the creature of zalmo, so that tomorrow, or even two hundred thousand tomorrows from now, this mercy will be remembered. Let it be, for I have had enough. I wanted to call it enough killing and loss, I am misremembering. It is something—the trumpet sounding across the river, and the light from the sun reflected so powerfully it is blinding, blinding as the first opening of an infant's eyes must be, for one who has never seen before. And for just that instant I felt it: the light—the light of the whole world at peace.

It was nonsense, and he knew it. I did not go to church the next Sunday, but I knew I would have to go see him later, and confront him about the truth—what he had found, why he was lying to himself and to us. I had to have this finished, quickly. I did not call Eleanor, perhaps in fear of her questioning. Eleanor would be happy then, I was sure, when I confronted him. It was late by the time I drove to see him, my eyes burning.

Yet he was still sitting there, his crippled little hand all close to his body, the other playing with his scarred forehead. He looked up and smiled at me as I came in, and then those blue eyes darkened immensely.

"You . . . you didn't bring the communion?"

"There's no time for that nonsense now. I need to know the truth. You know what happened to your wife and your research partner. There was no sun cult in Rome until centuries later. No more scribbling pointless lies."

And then his eyes were dark, and the skin on his brow looked angrily red. His stress caused it to shift, and then I noticed that the St. Jude was off his neck, cradled in his right hand.

"*Toto urbe in pace composito,* eh? You held everything that was worth knowing in your hands, while it was I who had been looking for the answer. You've thrown the answer away. At least I won't be stuck here anymore."

He reached out for me, and though there was no one to shut the door, I heard it slam, and felt his hand reach me, felt the medallion press into my skin. And as we touched, I knew then what he had been trying to tell me—and though it would very long, there was no mercy in it.

Marc Aramini was born in Washington, D.C., to military parents, but he spent most of his childhood in the southwestern United States. He has a degree in biochemistry from Notre Dame and has worked a variety of jobs from teaching to banking and even attaining properties and permits for a family business. He is currently teaching at Mohave Community College in Kingman, Arizona.

The Dreams of the Sea

JODY LYNN NYE

On Gene Wolfe: When one lives in the same town as Gene Wolfe, one can never be the most notable writer around. But knowing Gene and his works, I don't mind at all. Personally, he is a courtly gentleman with a twinkle and a sense of humor, modest, patient, appreciative, who loves hearing a good tale as well as telling one. Professionally, he is a one-man literary tour de force. His fiction is so carefully constructed, his vocabulary so extensive, and his imaginative scope so broad that all one can say (other words being used up by this prolific and talented gentleman) is "Wow." Every time I open one of his works, I gain two things. First, I get a lesson in my chosen craft that will be of use to me the next time I write something. Second, I get a humility lesson, because I realize that I will have to learn a lot more if I ever hope to reach the pinnacle on which he stands. I am proud to call this wonderful man my friend.

I stood at the bow of the ship as the storm came upon us, and laughed with joy. Waves broke over my head and sluiced into the drains cut beneath the rail, leaving it almost dry. The sailors around me ran to haul sheets and bring in the lines. They were in no danger. Nor was the ship, but the habits of a life on Ocean were hard to break.

Each of us possessed, although not fastened around our necks, a necklace that enfolded us in a cloak of air. If we were thrown into the water we would not drown, at least not right away.

Most of these brave sailors could swim. I could not. It was a failing of mine. I never learned. I feared large bodies of water; I had seen my doom in them. Now, though, I had the added pain of finding humor and tragedy in shapes, and those that the sea threw up in our faces were so hilarious that I couldn't restrain myself from laughing. I could not explain my merriment to my fellows. They feared me, as they feared all us witches of the tower from whence I came. I could not blame ordinary folk from withdrawing from us. We asked "why" when no one else would so dare.

I wished that I was on a quest to discover my own "why," but I was not. A larger matter had overwhelmed us. At that moment, the great, blazing ball of the New Sun was concealed behind storm clouds. When it could be seen, it was a matter of great interest and study. As had been long predicted, the sorrowing, sanguine sphere of the Old Sun had vanished in a white fountain of light and heat. Ushas, once known as Urth, basked in the rays of its long promised New Sun. Yet in the van of that one enormous change had come countless small ones. My own situation was one of those changes, or so the oracles had told me. A wave jumped, spraying white foam in an arc, and I laughed.

"Nedell, come down from there," Iria said peevishly, her words glowing pale blue with annoyance. The whip-lean woman fought her way against the wind and put a cloak over my thicker shoulders. At once, I felt a deep, sorrowful longing. Iria saw the look on my face and pulled the cloak away. The cloak had belonged to one of her forlorn lovers. Sensation, too, affected me differently than it had before. Instead, she wrapped a long arm around my shoulders and drew me down from the bow. The sailors immediately ran forward and began hauling down more sheets. They had not dared approach while I stood there.

In between heaves of the deck, Iria guided me over its rough boards and into the cabin. With some difficulty, she grabbed hold of the scornful door and slammed it, then made me sit on the bunk.

Our servant Chettor huddled in a corner of the cabin, holding onto the leg of a table that had been bolted in place under the port. The eleven-year-old boy keened in a silvery green voice that cut through my head. I could almost feel the bones splintering in icy shards. Our brothers in the Matachin Tower could have tortured me no more expertly.

"Quiet!" Iria barked. The deep brown of her tone surprised Chettor into silence. "Help me with her!"

Together, they worked off my soaked gown, exposing my body to the derision of the cold air. I pushed them away and removed my chemise. Chettor took it and spread it over the back of the heavy chest at the foot of the large bunk we all shared. Iria scrubbed at my skin with the rough linen towels from the washbasin, the water of which now slopped across the floor. What difference did a few more bucketfuls make? We were surrounded by Ocean. It could not be long now before we were entirely engulfed.

From our trunk Chettor fetched a dry linen chemise and gown and brought them to Iria's side. Once my skin had been rubbed red, she threw the garments over my head. The cloth soothed me. I ran my fingers over the weave. I marveled at the visions behind my eyes of our sister witch Menida at her loom, the love of her craft glowing from the threads. I refastened my belt and attached the scrip in which I bore the tools of our craft. I barely had it on before the ship began to heave up and down as if it would tear itself apart.

In a calm, mellow tan, Iria asked, "Are you all right now?"

I sighed, a silver whisper that rippled with gray, the result of my fear.

"Yes. I can't help myself."

"I know. I must go out again. They will steer against the storm unless I stop them."

I looked up at her and took her rough, slim hands in my own plump palms. In them, I felt care and worry and understandable impatience, overlaid by the kindness Iria always tried to conceal.

"Go safely, sister."

She smiled, her eyes narrowing into amused slits. "Mother Emoranali said we would all be together until the guide was found. I have no fear of an accident in the meanwhile."

The boards under us pitched nearly vertical. We clung to the bunk and one another. Iria fought loose from our grasp and pulled herself by means of the ropes looped against the wall to the door. She forced it outward against the wind. It slammed behind her, a harsh, dark blue sound.

Chettor put a hand on the cloth over my knee. Through it I could sense his terror. He admired the two of us, so he had been content to follow us aboard ship when asked, but he had never had a deck below his feet in his short life. It was an adjustment for him. For us all.

Iria's high-pitched voice came clear as gold through the sounds of the storm, the creaking of the ship's boards, and the harsh, dark grunts of the seafarers. Her gift was that of direction. Many had natural talents that could help them keep a true course, sensing which way was north by literally following a magnetic gland in their noses. Her sensitivity reached further. It was only because I trusted her with my life that I believed we could succeed in this quest that our Guildmistress had given to us. Chettor crept closer to me. In spite of my own terror, I embraced him as I would have one of my own children and cuddled him close.

"She speaks truth—we won't die?" he asked, his large blue eyes turned up to mine.

"She speaks truth," I said. Somewhere about his person I sensed love, hope, and desperation. "You wear your mother's charm, don't you?"

Chettor plunged his hand into the small purse at his hip and drew forth a mass of colored string tied in complicated knots.

"There, you have your protection," I said, with as much sincerity as I could muster. I heard the brassy tang of a needful lie in my voice, and hoped he did not discern it. I was glad he could not share my sensitivity or know my fears. The world had become too strange for me to cope with it.

Our lives had begun their inevitable change months ago, when we departed from our age-old home within the Citadel in Nessus. The Order of Esoteric and Practical Knowledge, or witches, as we were known by outsiders, had always occupied a courtyard and tower close by that of our brothers the torturers, whose official title was the Order of the Seekers for Truth and Penitence. Where their home was metal and seemed made to withstand a cataclysm, ours had the air of a folly, put up by its architects in a mood of whimsy and left to deteriorate and be patched as needed. In spite of its appearance, I never felt that our home lacked any requirement. We made and made do, as any thrifty housewife without the Citadel's mighty walls, but a sturdy structure was not important to any of us. If we were warm in the steadily lengthening winter and cool enough in the shrinking summer, had enough to eat and drink, and were free of fear of assault from without, what mattered were our studies.

Alongside the armorers and engineers, we stood as a bulwark between the Autarch and his or her enemies. Our activity was scarcely noted most of the time. We detected subtle upsets in the aether, studied, and then reported on them to our Guildmistress. Sometimes a subject would undergo study for days or centuries before any official notice was taken of it. We interacted often with the cacogens who moved freely among our number. To the ordinary citizen of Nessus, they might be fearsome and deadly; to us, they were fellow seekers.

Our studies and interactions were not always welcome among the common folk. The two chief reasons we lived within the Citadel were that the Autarch might require immediate knowledge of our discoveries, and that at times our received and gleaned knowledge was unwelcome or frightening. We as its messengers were often assailed for the content of our revelations, though we were not responsible for the answers.

We couldn't always provide those answers. The wisdom of the Autarch understood that, and was not angry when we could not offer counsel. He (and it was always he, until the last Autarch before the New Sun, Valeria) kept us safe to use us as a resource, a haven against those who did not understand those who could perceive beyond normal human senses. Always it has been human nature to fear what you could not understand, and kill what you feared before it could kill you. The wise among us knew that was the way of the world, just or unjust, and troubled not to protest over it. Why rail against the wind? Save your breath to cool your soup!

With the coming of the New Sun, however, we had to leave our safe home. For thousands of years, we had portents that one day the dying sun would be superseded by another that came in a fountain of white light. Before it came to pass, the psychometricians among us sought a place on the map to which we could retreat. Nessus would be drowned deep, as has been proved true.

On the day of our departure from Nessus, we left in a group protected well by the House Guard. The Autarch Valeria accepted that we were required to go and had given permission. To avoid panic, we let it be known we witches were being exiled from the Citadel. Jeering mobs turned out in force along our road until we reached the Piteous Gate. Then they turned back and left us to find our way to our new home. The Lady Valeria escaped when the floods came, I heard, but I know not where. That matter is in the purview of one or another of my sisters, and I have no need of knowledge of her whereabouts. I am glad of her safety.

Since the coming of the New Sun, the ice caps that bedeck verdant Urth, now called Ushas, at its top and toe have receded from their occupancy of a quarter of the globe, and Ocean has risen to cover much of the land. The first onslaught of tidal waves happened so quickly that millions drowned. Those sensitives among us attuned to our fellow man heard their death cries. Since then, land that the cooling sun left dry among ice fields has been returned to concealment under Ocean. In every splash of the waves, I feel particles of the lost cities and towns, the pride, the dread, the high hopes and aspirations, and the drudging toil that made them.

The day of the coming of the New Sun was one of grand rejoicing among our Order. The blaze of light that filled the sky cast many to the ground with its force, I among them. When I came to my senses, the sky was many times lighter than it had ever been in my lifetime, the stars that we could pick out concealed behind a firmament like a great, pale agate bowl. We all abandoned our dignity to lie on our backs and stare up at the beauty of it. I fell asleep with that wonder in my eyes.

But when I awoke, it was to the call of a voice of deepest maroon. Our Guildmistress stared down into my bewildered eyes. I realized not only that Urth's setting was altered, but we were all changed in some way by the New Sun's rising. Every voice and noise wove a tapestry of color around me. Sounds made me see colors. The feel of objects brought forth the thoughts of those who had made or possessed them. Shapes evoked emotions. Everything had a second chord that I had never perceived before. And music, which I dearly loved, became too painful to enjoy. Any song moved me from tears into despair. A long piece overwhelmed me so much I felt it must kill me. No brew or simple could cure me. No device in our infirmary or library could deaden the sensation.

There was no time to deal with my pain. Immediately, our Order was besieged with questions from the survivors of the flood. From being reviled and feared, we were suddenly a source of answers. In a way, no one seriously expected an ancient legend to come true, certainly not in their lifetimes. Most undoubtedly believed that if such a thing ever came to pass, it would change nothing else—but that could not be further from the truth. The people required guidance. They had no one to whom they could turn.

The Autarch had vanished with Nessus. Rumors spread over the land like the teeming waters that Severian the Lame had returned, rejuvenated, to herald the new light. If so, where was he? Was it true that he was the Conciliator come again? Who could make sense out of our world as it was now?

Unlike the torturers, we witches almost never departed to other cities or villages out in the wide world. We were too vulnerable. Our clients must come to us. Yet this was a time that required sacrifice. For the first instance in our history, our Guildmistress sent many of us to the various centers of population, offering good sense and practical knowledge. We must keep fear from taking hold while we rebuilt, or the return to civilization would be delayed for years, if not centuries.

The rest of us were set to finding the answers. With the aid of the cacogens who still remained, chief among them the Cumaean, now unbelievably ancient, we did our best to seek out the path of the Autarch. Two of our number went off planet in search of Yesod. Others received missions here on Ushas. With my heightened senses, the Guildmistress directed me to the depths of Ocean, to plumb for drowned Nessus and whatever clues remained there. We must bring the Autarch back, to guide us forward under his New Sun.

Dark green shouting brought Chettor and me to our feet. The door of the cabin slammed open. A fresh gust of spray swept in, mirroring the sense of urgency of the barefoot seafarer who followed it.

"Mistress," the young woman panted. "The sea has a face. And a hand."

We hitched our way outward. I felt shipwrights of the ages in the rails that I clutched.

The sea still tossed, its fleering whitecaps taunting us, but the ship seemed to have been set in glass, so motionless it stood. I gasped as I perceived the reason: The bow was clutched in a massive hand as white as death.

Before it, Iria stood, looking as satisfied as any witch could. She beckoned me forward.

Chettor clung to me as I made my way to the side. The hand, larger than a goods wagon, each finger longer than my body, was attached to a salt-white arm. The curling water played around the enormous elbow like a frilled lace sleeve.

The face beside it, upturned, even in its monstrous size, was lovely enough to break my heart. I found deep satisfaction in the shapeliness of her cheekbones and chin. Long tresses of green and purple-brown hair floated upon the surface like sea wrack. As soon as I appeared, the gigantic eyes widened, and the plump lips parted to show white pointed teeth. Her other hand broke water in eager swirls and eddies. Before I could retreat, it seized me. A sorrowful yellow cry from the deck followed me down, until, with a metallic blue *plunk,* the sea closed above my head. Bubbles danced in my eyes.

The icy waters derided me, numbing my limbs. I had only half a breath of air. The pressure, both from within and without, threatened to crush my lungs.

I kicked and struggled to free myself. The creature's grip was too strong to break. The gray sky vanished behind veil upon veil of green-gray seawater. My eyes stung. I squeezed them closed and pleaded with the Incarnate for mercy. I had been a good daughter of the faith. I was not so young that I was unaware of death. I had already borne children and given another generation to the guild, but I had so much more I wanted to learn and do. My hair streamed upward. The air in my lungs ran out of nourishing oxygen. I choked, and inhaled a mouthful of seawater.

Fool! I chided myself.

Before blackness filled my eyes, I had the presence of mind to fumble in my sodden scrip for my necklace. I put it on. An envelope of air surrounded me. I drew a deep gasp, and coughed out brackish water. I fought down my gorge. The supply of oxygen would not last long. We sank rapidly through the silken waters. Now that I did not fear immediate suffocation, I sought knowledge that would aid my escape, if not my quest.

I knew my captor. She was one of the Undines, the brides of Abaia, ruler of the abyss. Such creatures were subjects of our study. They were intelligent but rarely motivated to do anything outside their own interests.

I wriggled in the huge female's grasp and pounded my fists on the edge of her palm to draw her attention. She stopped her descent and bobbed in place, then drew one massive eye down to the level of my head. Cnidaria and anguillas swirled around us like living streamers. I held the bubble formed by my necklace against her nose.

I beseeched her. "Sister, I will die if you take me to the depths."

Her eyes crinkled with merriment. The very lines at the corners radiated amusement. Her voice caused my whole body to resound like the head of a drum.

"You shall not die!"

She brought her tremendous mouth up and pressed her lips to mine, penetrating the necklace's bubble. Suddenly we seemed of a size, though I was still trapped within her hand. Her arms surrounded me, and one leg hooked behind my knees, pressing our bodies together. The kiss was as silken as a lover's, but went deeper than any ever had, suffusing me not with warmth but with coolness. I trembled desperately, feeling as if I would break all my bones. Then suddenly, the shivering ceased.

The Undine poked a long fingernail under the circle of my necklace and flicked. The circlet broke and sank into the depths. I cried out, then realized I could breathe.

I had always liked the taste of salt, but it seemed that when I respired seawater, the flavor was lost to me. I should have been choking my lungs out, but they had turned to an expanded gill that filled my chest, giving me oxygen. Whether it was a permanent gift, it saved my life. But how could she be two sizes at once?

The Undine left me no time to ponder.

"What seek you here in my lover's domain?" she asked.

Her voice boomed with colors of wine and ultramarine, like

horns and harps together. I felt in her skin nothing but gentle curiosity. She truly meant me no harm. I relaxed and summoned my wits.

"The Autarch Severian," I said. "He vanished with the waters from Nessus. Now Ushas floods, and we seek his guidance for the way forward."

"Nessus is here," she said, gesturing downward with her huge hand, a move that made me tremble. Beyond the murky currents I could see faint shapes, gray on gray. "But Severian is not."

"Then I seek his wisdom," I pleaded. "His words. He wrote his memoirs and left them in the library of the Citadel. So much has changed that the knowledge left behind of the old world has scattered, drowned, or dissolved, but wisdom is eternal. We need guidance. Those memoirs would offer a concrete symbol that would give hope to the people who survived."

She shook her head, and the tresses of purple-green hair traced puzzled curves in the water.

"I know not of that. Such things are of little importance to us."

"But you befriended our Autarch!" I said.

"Not I; one of my sisters, Juturna."

"May I speak with her?"

Again, the hair danced in the current.

"You seek dreams. Nothing is eternal. You seek to follow one who has stepped out of your world."

"Then, give me dreams," I said, firmly. "Ideals are always dreams. Kingdoms have been built on less."

She smiled. "For those, you must ask my master."

My heart pounded. My voice rose to a thin, white pipe. "Abaia? Where . . . where must I go?"

"Nowhere and everywhere," the Undine said, her white teeth a threat in her soft mouth.

I felt the sea around us warm slightly. The water became thicker, like honey. Fear built in my heart, until it hammered at my ribs, demanding escape. What little light there had been, fled. This was my darkest fear, drowning in the dark. I struggled to escape. Nothing held me, but there was nowhere to go.

Gradually, I became aware of a voice of the deepest red. As the Undine said, it came from nowhere and everywhere. My body thrummed with it, became part of it.

"A new bride? Ulundra, you honor me!"

I felt rather than saw the dimpling smile.

"My love, all that I have is yours."

I could not see him, so I glared straight ahead of me.

"I am not a toy to be given away!"

The red voice boomed. "You have entered my realm, and all here is at my pleasure! You have become mine, to do with as I choose!"

It was a foolish gesture to protest, when both these enormous presences held my life between them, but I despised a bully.

"If you want me for a bride, then I demand a bride price," I said. "When the Exultant Odaracus wooed me in the court of the Autarch, he gave me gifts. In exchange for that, I gave him fifteen years of devotion and two daughters until he left me for one of his own rank. What do *you* offer me?"

The viscous substance surrounding me suffused with merriment.

"A challenge! Name your price, then, toy."

"My name is Nedell," I declared. It gave him power over me, but if I could fulfill my mission for the Order, I would do it. My life was only one of the myriad I could save. The New Sun had come; I had lived to see it. It was enough. I steeled my quavering heart. "I want Severian's memoirs, to bring back to the people of Ushas. I need to save my world. Give me that, and I am yours forever."

"Forever?" the voice echoed. "Do you even know the meaning of that, Nedell?"

"No," I said simply.

"Then, learn!"

Long ago, when I had crossed into the sixth level of initiation of our Order, I had to learn to blend my thoughts with others. For my elevation, I had to follow the mind of a many-times senior initiate, a cacogen from the star that circled the head of the Ram. She drew me out of myself until I joined with her. Our minds together flicked between the mirrors in the Guildmistress's study and out toward that star, where I saw worlds illuminated with blue light instead of red. At the time it was as much as I could bear. The girl I was then would have quailed against the sight I now beheld. Even my elder self feared, though we both marveled.

The gray-green murk dissolved, leaving a curtain of blackness. Myriad pinpoints pierced that curtain, diamonds against the dark. Their beauty and their number overwhelmed me. I saw the universe as I never hoped to see it. Tears overspilled my eyes and rolled in every direction, freezing on my forehead, nose, and cheeks, some trickling off to hang around me like tiny stars.

"There, you form your own worlds," the red voice murmured. "They, too, will spawn life." I turned my head, and my whole body spun. I flailed to control myself. Ulundra laughed.

I saw her, then. In the void, she swam as easily as she did in the deeps. Her sleek nakedness was more beautiful than any mortal, any work of art I had ever seen. Her hair curled and flowed like the tail of a comet. Her breasts were perfect half-spheres, tipped with blue-green nipples. I had suspected a fish's tail, but her legs were like mine, but ideal in shape, with pillowy thighs and slender calves. Beside her was a male, as naked as she, corded muscles rippling beneath gray-blue skin. His shoulders were as broad as a blacksmith's, his arms a swordsman's, and his manhood longer than I was tall. His hair was pure black with a few silver threads brighter than the suns that surrounded us. His eyes glowed as red as his voice.

"I set you a challenge of my own. Where is your New Sun?"

I tore my eyes from his beauty and looked around me. The flecks of light shone. I saw different colors among them, blue, gold, red, even green. The New Sun was white, but there seemed a preponderance of white.

"There are too many," I said.

"If your world means so much to you that you would give me your life in exchange, can you truly tell me that you do not know it?"

Know it? How could I distinguish it?

I cudgeled myself to remember what I had learned in Mistress Cinitha's astronomy lectures.

Ah, but I might! The old Nedell, who had been maiden, mother, and now encroaching upon crone, could not, but the new Nedell, as new as the New Sun itself, had been given a gift on the day of its birth.

I closed my eyes and concentrated. Where was my sisterhood? They were in my heart, as they had been all of my life.

"Well, toy?"

"Patience!" I snapped, as if Abaia were no more than Chettor.

He chuckled.

Unlike most guilds, we did not often raise apprentices from infancy. Rather, a baffled-looking child was occasionally left at the Mercy Gate outside our tower, or a young man who knew the spots on the dice before they fell too often for chance, or a frightened woman, pursued by an angry mob, rang our alarm bell. Most of the time, the fact that she had reached our tower kept the mob back long enough for us to rescue her. Sometimes it didn't. Our small cemetery had an ossuary of bones of those whom had sought our protection yet not survived to enter the guild. We had plenty of charlatans and wish-they-weres come to the door, but they did not stay, as we could easily discern the falsehood. For the others, they knew from the moment the great door shut behind them that they had come home.

I had the very smell of the herb gardens in my nostrils. Scents as thick as wax and soft as silk caressed me. Gentle breezes brought birdsong and the chirring of insects. Unlike my present misfortune, that is a genuine memory, one I will always treasure, and hope to hold again, once the new gardens are grown and I have returned to the bosom of my family—the Guild of Witches. I sought for that single point of light that meant home. It was faint, so faint, at this distance, but I knew the kindness of the Infirmaress, the patience of the teachers, the love that the Guildmistress had for us all, and the children I loved and had to let go so that they, like I, could fulfill their destinies. It was there, I knew it!

I opened my eyes. A cluster of stars hung before me like a cloud of gnats. Ushas was among them.

"Well, toy, which one?" Abaia taunted me.

From this coign the tiny spots of white light seemed alike, taraxacum seeds dancing in night air. All of them felt like strangers going about their business but one, that faint point just to the right of the topmost light.

"That one," I said.

"Are you certain? Would you stake all their lives as well as your own?"

I quailed in dread.

"Please don't make them suffer more than they have," I begged. There was no floor on which I could drop to my knees, but I crouched low and held my tiny hands out to him. "If I am wrong, let only me pay. I offered you my life. Take it. Let them be."

"Who are you to demand anything at all?" Abaia asked, the magnificent eyebrows lifting high on the broad brow. "Order is at my whim, because chaos reigns when I will it."

I swallowed. "But the Autarchs . . ."

"Are a mere moment in all of history. All but one. I rule for infinity! But you are correct, Nedell." He smiled, showing all his teeth. In that flash of whiteness, I saw an infinity of reflections of myself, and suddenly we were back in the grayness of the deep. Ulundra clapped her hands with delight, as if I were an animal that had just done a trick.

Arms again enfolded me, but they exuded the majestic intelligence of Abaia himself. We spun together. The rags of my clothing fell away, until I was as naked as Ulundra. I felt his body explore mine, seeking its inner secrets. I felt passion as I had not for years as his lips and hands explored my flesh. The lapping of the seawater around us only excited me more greatly. But when he opened up my vulnerability, our minds were shared, as mine had been with the cacogen. I saw stars in the blackness within him, and realized that he was the universe turned inside out. I knew his truth.

When our passion was spent, he returned to titan size and floated lazily beside me.

"You don't fear me."

I considered the question.

"No. I am curious about you."

He extended a huge hand. I kissed the nearest fingertip.

"I could snuff you out between two fingers."

"That would not stop my curiosity," I said. "I have faced my greatest fears and lived. I know yours. You fear being unmade by order. You are chaos. This is a time for you to thrive, but all will settle again, and you will lose the upper hand you have now."

"Be my bride," he said. "Join my women. You shall learn the beauty of chaos."

I bowed my head. "When I have brought back to my Order that which we require."

"I grant you leave," Abaia said. "The coffer that held your Autarch's memories is buried deep, and the other flung into another existence, where not even the cacogens can retrieve it. It belongs to the ages and the void."

"Then we are lost," I said.

"Chaos will reign, as is right."

"I will seek the coffer," I said stubbornly. I fought against the void of despair into which he sought to drag me. I had the strength of my sisters behind me, as well as the training and the weight of my years. We mystes were initiates in many disciplines. "Will you guide me to the archives? That is its most likely location."

He waved the hand. The swirling current it caused flung me outward several leagues and brought me back again.

"Ulundra will take you."

I expected the Undine to be jealous of Abaia's proposal. Instead, she was delighted. She gathered me up in her hand and swam down toward the shadows on the sea floor.

"We have had no new brides for an age," she said. "We will so love having you join us. Come, this way! This is the way to seek your dream."

My heart rent again and again as we flitted among the ruins of the great Citadel. No bodies of human or animal remained, but all the buildings and possessions left by those who fled or drowned cried out the stories of their makers to me.

The farther we descended, the smaller Ulundra became, until we could swim side by side. She guided me into the labyrinth of chambers once occupied by the Autarch, the exultants, and all those who governed us. I passed council chambers where schools of fish were in session, storehouses with polypi clinging to the walls, and a bedchamber that had become home to a massive cloudlike cnidarian.

At last, Ulundra came to a painting of a landscape with a small farmhouse in the foreground, crops and herds in the background.

"This is the door," she said.

A mystery is only a mystery for a time, for it relies upon a sense of wonder and curiosity to maintain its air, and that needs energy. If it is not revealed before the energy runs out, then the mystery becomes a conundrum, a problem, an annoyance, and a pestilence. My guild had little patience with mysteries. Our task was to solve them and reveal their workings to those who inquired of us in a manner that they would understand, if such a thing were possible. If we could not, that mystery was relegated to the collection of things that we studied when we had the time to do so. Our Guildmistress, our mother, would present the problems remaining unsolved to us at our semiannual festivals, laying *guerdons* on the table that represented each, and invited us to take one that excited our curiosity all over again. I had seen such portals before. They were illusions. One only had to find the part that looked too perfect, and push through it.

I found a door within that image that had been rendered so realistically that a crack in the uppermost board was trailing a flake of paint. I touched it, and we found ourselves in a long room lined densely with books.

A metal coffer was the object I sought. We floated up and down the many aisles in between shelves that rose to the ceiling. It had been years since I had been in the archives. It broke my heart to see the knowledge of ages submerged and deteriorating with every eddy. I touched the leather spines, softened with salt water. In most of them I felt only three minds: the author, the bookbinder, and the archivist who had shelved it countless ages ago, never to be opened again.

At the end of the room was another door, not disguised, the one through which I had entered coming from the witches' tower. But on either side of that were two smaller doors. With Ulundra's help, I forced one open.

Within it, I felt the force of many wills so strong it knocked me back. I fought my way through and stepped over the threshold. I looked at the artifacts that lined the shelves, seeing helms, books, swords, folded cloaks, cups, and other items. Here was the collection of personal possessions of the Autarchs. They had all been labeled carefully with metal plates that had only just begun to corrode. I found things that had belonged to Tyron, and M, and, yes, thank the Incarnate, Severian. Such modest leavings! A leather scrip, a shard of sharp metal that must have been a sword blade, a tattered fuligin cloak. I touched them, and was overwhelmed by the hive of personalities. It is why the Cumaean never called Severian one man, but the multitude. At the center was one personality: a man, honest, strong, kind, and just. Severian shared the wisdom of many, all the Autarchs before him, and many others besides. It was a wonder that deserved much consideration. I would consult others when I returned to the Order.

I searched all over the room, but found no coffer that felt of Severian. Instead, on a shelf by itself, I found a small brown book. When I touched it, I found the unmistakable stamp of Severian and his multitude. *The Tales of Urth and Sky* was an ordinary storybook. Hundreds, if not thousands of copies existed, but this one held the essence of Severian: Torturer, Conciliator, Lictor, Autarch, and New Sun. The plain brown book, property of so many since its making from the skins of animals and the gall of trees, was one of the few things that he had treasured. In it I sensed the lessons he had learned over his long lifetime. It held the answers we sought, I knew it!

"Is that it?" Ulundra asked. "I thought it would be more impressive. No jewels? No devices?"

I trembled as I took it off the shelf.

"It is as if I am taking the hand of the Autarch himself," I said.

Very, very gingerly, I opened it.

The Tales of Urth and Sky had a new appendix added to it, though not substantial. It included the story of how Apu-Punchau traveled through all the corridors of time, giving gifts of wisdom to those who needed them. I knew from my gift that it was Severian in all his many guises, and of Thecla, the beautiful, lost mnemosyne, repository of dreams, memories, and wishes, who walked down the ages as if they were only paths in a garden. Her memories became his memories, and so passed into the canon of the world. It was a greater legacy than a simple exultant could have achieved, on or off the face of Urth.

I breathed my excitement. It was not merely what he had written in the extra pages, though it was his own handwriting. I could feel what he knew. He could never forget anything that he learned, and that certainty was imbued throughout the tiny volume.

"Let me see it," Ulundra said. She reached for the book. I held it out to her.

In the water between us, the tiny, aged relic came to pieces in her hands. Ulundra flailed for it, her white hands becoming huge. She succeeded only in scattering the shreds of soggy paper and strands of linen stiffened with glue to the far ends of the archives. My heart sank. It could never be whole again.

I was devastated. My mission was a failure. I had nothing to bring back to my sister witches.

Yet while I watched the ruin of my hope, I had a curious sensation. I felt the presence of the disappeared Autarch. I felt as if I was sharing intelligence with him, feeling his feelings, knowing his knowledge, but not only him—*them*.

I had no artifact to bring home. *I* was the artifact, and I carried the wisdom of ages. He did not forget, and neither would I.

"Can you guide me back to my ship?" I asked Ulundra.

The excitement I felt must have been shining from my eyes. She regarded me sadly. Her warm voice was muted in color.

"You will never return to us, will you?"

I took her hands in mine and patted them. For once, they seemed smaller, almost as small as my daughters' hands.

"When I can. When I have given all that I have to Ushas, I will come back to Ocean. It is not what I feared. I have much to learn, here."

Ulundra leaned over and kissed me.

"Then, come," she said. "It is not far."

"What of us, then?" Iria asked, after I had clambered aboard, and been furnished with dry clothes, food, and drink, and told my tale. "Will this be enough to guide Ushas toward the future?"

"There are no guarantees," I said. "But, I think so. We have all been deprived of that which we once had, and must seek other comforts and knowledge. We do not know what lies ahead, but we could guide with the light of that collective wisdom that had lived within the Autarch's mind. Strength tempered with mercy, the honesty of humility, and never to forget where one has been. Such lessons are not only for the humble."

"Huh," Iria said, planting her chin on one bony palm. "To think that we found such tidings in the sea."

"Tidings in the tides," said Chettor. He looked shy as we laughed.

"Oh, and I forgot to tell you," I said, as Iria and I leaned on the rail, watching the lip of Ushas rise above the face of the New Sun. "I am getting married."

Jody Lynn Nye lists her main career activity as "spoiling cats." When not engaged upon this worthy occupation, she writes fantasy and science fiction books and short stories.

Before breaking away from gainful employment to write full-time, Jody worked as a file clerk, bookkeeper at a small publishing house, freelance journalist and photographer, accounting assistant, and costume maker. For four years, she was on the technical operations staff of a local Chicago television station, ending as technical operations manager.

Since 1987 she has published forty-three books and well more than one hundred short stories. Although she is best known as a collaborator with other notable authors such as Anne McCaffrey (the Ship Who series, the Dinosaur Planet series), Robert Asprin (Dragons and Myth Adventures), John Ringo (Clan of the Claw), and Piers Anthony, Jody has numerous solo books to her credit, mostly fantasy and science fiction with a humorous bent. Her latest book is View from the Imperium *(Baen Books), which she describes as "Jeeves and Wooster in space." During the past twenty-five years or so, Jody has taught numerous writing workshops. She also speaks at schools and libraries. When not writing, she enjoys baking, calligraphy, travel, photography, and, of course, reading.*

Jody lives in the northwest suburbs of Illinois with her husband, Bill Fawcett, and Jeremy, their cat.

The Log

DAVID BRIN

On Gene Wolfe: He is known as one of the great literary stylists of our genre, one I admire with a sense of genuine awe. But unbeknownst to him, Gene also helps me teach writing to others. One aspect of fiction narrative that students often find daunting is "point of view"—establishing a reader's perspective riding on the shoulder of the central character, perhaps only seeing what she sees but not sharing thoughts, or sharing surface thoughts but remaining ignorant of dark, inner knowledge. Or else immersed in the protagonist's roiling, deeper conflicts. Or possibly watching from an aloof, detached distance. I've seldom seen a stylist illustrate the power of these many-leveled techniques as well as Gene does, with apparent ease and grace. Any student who wants to master this core element of narrative should—I strongly recommend—learn how it is done by retyping great passages by Gene Wolfe.

At first, during the early months of exile, I seethed with resentment. Our mother had no business yanking us from Moscow, no matter how painful the city had become. Wasn't it bad enough, with our father declared an Enemy of the Czar? Denounced by People, Coss, and State? How *could* she thereupon haul her daughters along, like huddled gypsies, following the slender rails to a stark and snowy place? To a community of self-banished outcasts, encamped within distant sight of the prison-gulag where Father (according to bribed hints) was held.

My sister, Yelena, and I learned from the oldest schoolmaster—
suffering—how to endure the way that only Russians can. The bare
and diminished winter sun had little strength to warm our adolescent flesh. But *cold* possessed power to penetrate, sinking razor
teeth through every bundled layer that we wore.

There we joined work crews of the semi-free, who trimmed
giant-boled trees and harnessed them behind grunting beasts who
puffed, snorted, and vented steam as they dug into icy dust, hauling
treasure toward the rails.

Each evening, when our shifts came to an end, mother made
sure that Yelena and I smoked our weed and opened books, con-
suming lessons, as if our futures still held promise of reward. Study
was hard, as we struggled to concentrate past a fog of fatigue, and
despite nearby wails of mourning. For it was a rare day that passed
without at least one casualty, one frozen corpse—or several, carried
away from our bivouac of the nominally "free."

What kind of mother—I mused angrily while rubbing Yelena's
feet and inhaling fumes while she read aloud—what kind of mother
would voluntarily drag her offspring to a place like this? When the
czar had made a standing offer to the blood relatives of political
prisoners—to work off guilt-by-association in greater comfort,
close to home?

"Comfort, but also time," she told me, on one of the rare occasions when Mother explained anything at all. "The czar and Cos-
sacks live by a code. If we survive, and pay our fines, then you and
your sister can never again be charged for being related to traitors.
Other crimes, perhaps. But not that."

I thought about it while spending my free hour as I normally
did—earning a couple of added kopeks by working in the stables.
Mucking out the stalls of draft animals and grooming their thick
fur. Yelena liked to hang around the elepents, but they seemed too
dour and moody for me. I much preferred the mammuts—so phleg-
matic and accepting. So I worked on that side of the dank, musty

barn, polishing their gleaming tusks and brushing their immense grinding teeth.

"Yesh . . . yesh, Sasha . . . ve-vehind dat one . . . yesh . . ." crooned the one called Big Bennie, who wrapped his trunk around my left arm and drew me so close that I felt enveloped by his breath, a sweetly foul blend of alfalfa and stomach juices. Reaching in to scrape a back molar, I knew at any moment he could nip off my head with a single crunch, and the overseers would let it go with nary a shrug. But I wasn't afraid. Bennie took his meals in liquid form. And those diamond-hard teeth were not for eating.

I wiped the airtight seals and nictitating membranes covering his beady eyes and finished by rubbing his floppy ears, which would expand and swivel during long stretches on the snow, as he sensed the heft and momentum of great tree-hauling sleds, or detected the speedy passage of pebbles, a thousand meters away. At last, Bennie's trunk reached into a pouch and pulled out a five-kopek coin that glittered next to the freshly waxed sheen of his tusk. I made my appreciation known. At this rate, I might earn liberty in mere years.

A low groaning arose from the opposite end of the vast chamber, beginning deep, at or below the hearing range of mere humans. I grimaced as the mammuts let out trumpetings of desultory complaint. Perfunctory, because nothing would prevent that basso rumble from growing, coalescing as a dozen bull elepents joined in, finding their interlaced rhythms, reiterating reflections off the walls and climbing toward crescendo.

Their evening dirge of longing did not bother me—at least not as much as it did some humans—hence the reason why this plum job was available to a mere kid. And the mammuts' complaints soon tapered away, muffled in grudging respect, leaving the soundscape for elepents to occupy, alone.

Yelena, my sweet sister, barely fourteen, did not have to endure. Rather, she grinned in delight, dancing lightly on her toe-tips, like the ballerina she once dreamt of becoming, turning with arms stretched, as if luxuriating in the sonic waves. Around her, bull elepents wafted their long, armored trunks, waggling the fingerlike tips, modulating what soon became a brass ensemble of trombones, coronets, and growling tubas.

Lingering effects of Learning Weed still wafted in my nostrils, sinuses, and brain, reinforcing knowledge-engrams that had come through conscious reading and unconscious pulsations, just an hour before. I now pictured the barn as a *resonant cavity*, within which *reinforcing waves* added and multiplied, like the photons in a laser beam. A queerly obvious insight, now that I could picture what—only yesterday—had been a bizarre mystery.

Not for the first time I wondered: *What was I beforehand . . . before tonight's lesson? Too stupid to see or hear?*

And what will be stupidly opaque to me, tomorrow, that I'll understand the day after?

Long, prehensile tails whipped the air while each pachyderm flexed his four squat legs, ending in hands that shoved against the straw-covered floor, raising the heavy beasts upon stubby but powerful grip-fingers, rising and falling as they sang. Well, that wasn't much of a feat, given where, in the universe, they stood. Still, the push-ups *looked* impressive. The nearest male weighed several tons, most of it packed within a massive globe of grayish flesh. Hairless, unlike the mammuts. And the elepents' radar ears were fully erect, all turned in unison, facing the same direction.

Toward the gleaming opal of Earth's moon. Sensed, if not seen. The paradise of their desirings, where crystal forests gleamed and matriarchal herds roamed, ready to welcome home a few—just a few—of those bulls who proved themselves worthy.

No wonder Yelena liked elepents.

"You should, too, Sasha!" she once said. "They are much like us. Like you and me. Sad exiles, dreaming of home."

Only, that was the problem. Elepents were *too much* like us. All considered, I preferred the simple, cheerful mammuts.

Mother always fussed, when we dressed to go outside, checking our layers and gloves and mufflers, our boots and *ushanka* head coverings, taking special care over Yelena's buttons. As teenagers do, we hissed and complained, even—especially—when she found something amiss.

"I'm almost a grown-up!" Yelena griped. "If we had stayed home I'd be getting ready for *quinceañera!*"

The czar and his royal cossins had taken a liking to that Spanish custom, encouraging it to be shared all over Earth. A rite of budding womanhood while still innocent. The Coss had a soft spot for traditions like that.

Except that, for the crime of having been sired by a traitor, Yelena's party would have been a sadly truncated affair, in some local resettlement work town close to Moscow, say in Siberia. Near the bright lights, but tormentingly so. Might it be better to delay? To return home strong, no longer innocent, but free?

Was I starting to understand Mother's reasons?

No! I shook my head, taking my sister's hand and heading for our adolescent work team, accepting a silent duty from our mother to watch over her. I would do as I was bid. But I refused to accept. This was wrong. The reasons—though growing plainer to me—weren't good enough.

It would take more than this to forgive her.

I checked Yelena's scarf, gloves, boots, coverall, and headgear once again.

"But we already—"

"Stop fidgeting, Yelena Nikolaevna Bushyeva!" I hissed, using formality to emphasize my seriousness.

She grumbled.

"Mammut-loving *nerdoon*."

"Oh, so? What a blessing, if *only* I farted powerfully and often, like a *nerdoon*! I would need no propulsion."

My response made her giggle, and Yelena settled down till I finished the inspection.

"Come my little friend-of-elepents. If we are late, we'll be demoted to *zolotor* duty." To cleaning outhouses.

Together, we wriggled through the hut's exit, a curtain of ten thousand beaded strands that seemed to caress us, probing, pressing, and grabbing up each stray glop of air as we forged ahead...

... to step onto the surface of an asteroid. The snow-covered work camp that was our home.

The overseer shouted hoarsely. "Put yer backs into it! These logs won't move themselves!"

His words, in fact, were more restrained than normal—with none of his usual Ukrainian profanity, aimed at mostly-Russian work crews—but today's *tone* seemed much more tense, almost frantic. And I realized, while speeding up my pace, that he had reason. A sleek little space coupe hovered nearby, amid the brittle-bright stars. Few in the solar system could afford such a craft, except members of the master race. Perhaps it was even the Coss owner of this giant farm, dropping by for an inspection tour.

Accidents happen when you're in a hurry. So I watched Yelena out the corner of one eye, while we hacked at this morning's fall of freshly harvested crystalwood trees, with spiral branches girdling each massive trunk. The stems—each the size of many men—had to be removed, but one misjudged cut with your laser axe could lop off a person's arm, instead of the intended target. We agile adolescents had to be efficient, removing branches and stacking the broad, photocrystalline leaves, while adults lashed cables round the main bole, so that mammuts—grunting even in this minute gravity—might haul the massive, stripped-down trunks toward a waiting freight train.

Always, there was the pressure of expectation. Above our heads, elepents were on their way. Clutching yet more freshly harvested trees with their five strong limbs and tails. Maneuvering them to fall upon our planetoid lumberyard at a steady pace, whether room had been cleared for them. Then each elepent would jet back across a hundred klicks of sterile vacuum to fetch more, from the far bigger, forested asteroid frederikpohl 6523 . . .

. . . a place far worse than our mere hellhole. The gulag where Mother thought—or fervently believed—her husband had been sent . . .

. . . where a vast thicket of vacuum-bred vegetation spread broad antenna-leaves to suck light from the distant sun, while roots sank deep into carbonaceous rock four billion years old, sucking and refining every element that man or Coss desired.

The overseer had reason to be nervous. He supervised a dozen work crews, all of them hampered by shortages of skilled, experienced personnel. Our own team had recently acquired two new members, the teenage Strugalatsky brothers from Odessa who spent half their time goofing off, either loafing or leaping across the toppled trees, making stupid sci-fi sounds while slashing random branches, instead of taking them off systematically, in the recommended order. Cynics laid wagers over how long the two *dolbobs* might survive, and the bookie odds weren't good. After the seventh or eighth time that I grabbed one of them, chided him and corrected potentially lethal faults in his suit-buttoning, I decided to give up and let nature take its course.

"One of the top ways that the Coss rationalize their harsh rule," old Starper Litow had explained one evening, amid the fuming lesson smoke, *"is that our twenty-first-century Earth had become too tame. Too orderly and charitable. Homo sapiens wasn't improving, except with techniques like brain boosting, which helped everybody, and thus canceled out any overall, genetic advancement. The Coss claim to have done us a favor through conquest, by establishing a new, more strenuous order. To restore human progress where it matters most. In the raw makeup of our natures. By restarting evolution.*

Both natural selection . . . and of course, their own special breeding program."

Litow had touched upon topics that deeply concerned me. I hoped someday to get the elderly exile to elaborate. But curiosity must wait. For now, we had a problem. If the schedule wasn't met, all our lives might be in danger, "selecting" Yelena and me for the dustbin of Cosstory.

A trumpeted warning echoed in our ear-pickups—elepent bulls on final approach irritably admonishing us to clear our landing zone as another treefall approached. They, too, had schedules to keep if they ever wanted to rejoin the matriarchal herds, grazing the crystal savannahs of Luna.

The overseer's voice assumed a note of panic. And so, I took a chance. Yelena was experienced enough to finish stacking leaves onto the sledge all by herself. More important, she seemed focused, not distracted. So I signaled her to—*Work alone for a while.* She nodded with evident pride in my trust, an expression—visible through the pitted faceplate of her vacuum *ushanka*—that warmed me as I bent . . . then vaulted high over the work site, in order to look.

Our team foreman, Oleg Yevtutsov, also looked worried. But he was busy hitching up the team—Big Benjy and Lean Lennie—to chains that other space-suited men and women hurriedly wrapped around the mighty bole. The two mammuts waited patiently, passing time by prying up chunks of asteroid with their tusks and chomping them with diamond-hard grinding molars, releasing volatiles and organics to fuel their massive bodies and spilling fine dust from their mouths. Little marmot-gleaners went after the dust, the truly valuable side-product of that munching.

Other teams were finishing, and several had already set off toward the railhead, dragging tree trunks or sleds loaded with photovoltaic leaves, destined for rooftops and highways all over Earth. The locomotive *Nicholas III* huffed and steamed before cars that would take the treasure in-system. Mother worked down there among the freight dollies, with their piles of freshly hewn and trimmed logs, doing the job she had desperately wrangled for, tallying cargo, tracking every item with meticulous care—before the train could finally speed off, riding twin superconducting tether-rails that stretched several million kilometers from asteroid to asteroid, connecting gulag to outpost to colony to town to resort, almost all the way to Mars.

But my eyes and sensor-percept weren't tuned for sightseeing. At that moment, my sole thought was—*Where are those two idiots!*

Using some of my slender propellant supply, I searched . . . and finally found them near the tree's very tip, where Boris Strugalatsky squatted limply on a broken branch. *Weeping.* Soundlessly, having negligently or deliberately left his transmitter turned off. But the cheap plastic panel of his *ushanka* revealed a mouth that gaped rhythmically, and his blond-fuzzy cheeks glistened.

Landing nearby was tricky. The boys had left a botched mess of branch stubs, jagged-skyward with axe-shattered points, making impact dangerous, even at two percent of an Earth gravity. Only the special cleats that I had clamped below each boot—made from salvaged mammut molars—saved me from a cruel stabbing as I danced atop the shards, then flipped around in front of the young man.

"Boris, you and Arkady had better have a good—"

Then I saw his brother, lying facedown amid the nearby craggy tangle. Knife-like, a crystal branch jabbed through one thigh.

It might still be okay, I thought. *If the fool remembered to wear sealant underwear.*

Tugging on one arm of the prone figure— "Arkady, let's get you out of here before . . ."

My voice trailed off.

I gaped at a second spear-like stub that had pierced the mammut-fur helmet, entering one eye.

But no. I hadn't time for staring or disgust.

"Boris, snap out of it! We've got to get out of here."

At any moment, Oleg might lose patience, or give in to the over-seer and yell "Mush!" at the mammut sledge team. Or else, if the delay kept on, a newly falling tree might smash us from above. Ei-ther way, it was insane to remain.

The surviving Strugalatsky stared at me blearily. So I upped transmit intensity and shouted.

"Did Arkady want the second chance? In this cold and vacuum, it might still be possible. Tell me now!"

Boris stared for several more precious seconds, during which I almost decided to clip him in the jaw, sling him over a shoulder, and jet out of there. Only then he nodded. Dammit. I wished he hadn't.

"*Kakashkiya!* Okay then, help me now or lose him forever!" Gin-gerly, I float-stepped into a somewhat stable open niche where I could apply leverage. "Move carefully!"

The niche was a bare patch between branches, and I noticed, with a fragment of attention, that *lines* had been etched—deeply incised—into the hard tree trunk, not far from Arkady's head. Had he been making these marks, or peering at them, when the accident occurred?

No time to ponder such things! Applying my laser axe, I man-aged to cut loose the lance pinning Arkady's thigh, but had to wait for sluggish Boris to get positioned before carefully doing the same under his brother's head, leaving the shard where it was, for the cyborg-surgeons to deal with. Personally, I found this "second chance" option daunting and unpleasant, as did a majority of Earth's human population. And Boris might still change his mind, before committing his brother to another destiny, a different kind of liv-ing, in some far-off place the Coss seldom spoke of, where nearly all the reclaimed dead were sent.

At least they leave it a matter of personal and family choice. It's never imposed. The Coss are that honorable.

Boris wailed again, this time audibly, when he saw his brother's

ravaged face. So loudly that it almost matched the trumpeting elepent cries and warning shouts from Oleg and the overseer.

I grabbed both idiots—one under each arm—flexed, and leaped.
A split second before the great tree shuddered and shifted, amid low
mammut grunts, sending all remaining branches into a shuddering
wave that would have torn us to shreds.

We weren't out of danger yet! Arcing high, I realized we were
about to get smacked between two sharp-studded maces—the tree
stump beneath us and one falling from above. An upward glance
showed the approaching behemoth—till yesterday a living forest
giant—now guided by a half dozen mighty pachyderms, each one
clutching the great bole with four squat foot-hands, while using his
agile trunk to aim a propellant gun. Dimly, I realized that they
weren't even trying to slow the tree's plummet. Only to keep it oriented with one shorn side aimed down, to take the impact, leaving
most of the valuable branches for harvest.

Calculating trajectories, I could tell we were drifting too slowly,
the two trees would only collide glancingly, at their ends . . . where
we happened to be!

I applied my jets, full blast . . . if "blast" applied to that feeble
thrust. Only when the bottle petered out did I realize—*I should
have jettisoned Arkady. It might have saved our lives, Boris and
me. . . .*

Should I have felt stupid about that? Or noble? During those few
seconds, as the sky became a shimmering mass of gorgeously
deadly crystal, I realized that soon it would hardly matter. *At least
it should be quick,* I thought. *And there won't be anything left for
that awful "second chance."*

I braced . . .

. . . which was good, because a gray blur suddenly burgeoned
from the right and *slammed* into us, knocking the air out of my
lungs and cracking several ribs. Bellowing ululations filled my ears,
and a harsh, vise-like grip seized my left leg, swinging me about like

a whip. I clamped down, uttering no more than a grunt while clutching the Strugalatsky brothers with a ferocity I never knew I had.

Boris had no such compunctions or stoic control. He screamed.

In fact, he showed impressive durability, persistence, and sheer lung power, howling as the falling tree glistened all around us in a million faceted rods, spires, and infinitely fractal twinkles, our rescuer blatting defiance while he dodged and zigged and zagged, evading razor-sharp branches—

—till we jetted into blackness above the lumberyard, flying high to escape the dust cloud and a billion glittering shards.

Yelena took care of thanking the bull elepent, whose name was Tok and who had intervened for her sake, not for a *mammut-lover* like me. In any event, I was busy for a while, rushing Arkady Strugalatsky to the administration dome, where a CryoCare Company intern took over, starting the cool-down process while taking a next-of-kin affidavit from wailing Boris. Whereupon, at last, I slipped away, shivering in relief.

A few pats on the back. A gruff nod of respect from Oleg. Those were adequate acknowledgment for my "heroics," though I knew there'd be a price. Yelena wasn't going to let me forget that one of her gray friends had saved my ass.

Only none of that mattered. Right then, I had just one thought on my mind. To hurry back. To find the tree where the accident occurred and join the crew that was final-trimming it for shipment atop a huge, open-sided rail car. Oleg—impressed with my work ardor—urged me instead to rest, to attend to my battered rib cage and throbbing arms. But all of that could wait. I had to be part of finishing this one.

Along the way, I sent a personal blip.

—*Mother, drop everything and meet me.*—

A dark figure over near the train—slimmer and smaller than

most of the burly railroad workers—straightened and turned. I recognized her shabby winter coat and visored *ushanka*. Apparently, word of the accident hadn't even reached this part of the yard. And why should it, yet, with only one casualty added to today's tally board? On the whole, a better than average day. Well, good. She would only hear the story knowing how it ended. The best way.

—*What is it Sasha?*— she sent back. —*I am very busy.*—

I replied simply. Curtly. She would find this worthwhile. Then I made her wait while I scampered along the great tree trunk, applying axe to stub in half a hundred places, before finally summoning her to come forth, picking her way along the path that I had made.

—*Sasha, this had better be*—

I nodded for her to come forward, guiding with my hand on her arm, the first time that I had touched her in months. With a gesture, I insisted that we both cut off our radio transmitters, then touch helmet visors, to speak by conduction.

"I know what you've been looking for, Natalia Alexyevna Bushyeva. The reason that you chose this place, above all others, for our exile."

Her eyes widened, and then narrowed in practiced denial.

"I don't know what you're talking about. Come, we both have work—"

"Do you think I am a fool?" I answered, with unexpected heat. "Or ignorant? Or that the generation after yours would somehow forget the old stories? What did you take me for? *Do you think that I'm not Russian?*"

She rocked back. And this time, after a moment's indecision, she did me the honor of contemplating my words. Understanding them.

All over both planet Earth and the solar system, humanity was coming to terms with harsh reality. With the way of the Coss, whose conquest swept aside such fragile things as "enlightenment," or democracy, or the liberal way of viewing a gracious, benign universe.

That narrow age had flared so successfully, so brilliantly, it created a mass delusion. That all people might have worth, freedom, and unlimited prospects. That competition might be so open, fair, individual, and courteous that it becomes indistinguishable from joyful cooperation. That anyone's child might become as great as any other.

For a time, it seemed that Hawaii or California might be archetypes for a new, endlessly golden age—a sunny beach of prosperity, progress, and opportunity. How few were those who pointed out the chief lesson of history—that ninety-nine percent of human generations had endured a far more classic, more archetypical human social structure.

First tribal chiefdoms . . . and then feudalism.

Mighty lords, applying total power over helpless vassals. During the Enlightenment Summer, some fools—Americans, especially—naïvely thought the long era of noble oppressors was over and done for good. In fact, they still, insanely, call feudalism an aberration, unstable and untenable, instead of the way that nature conspires with the strong.

And so, rebelling against the Coss time and again, Americans have died like wheat in the field.

But Russians never forgot. Amid the brightest days, even when others called us gloomy and dour, we knew. The tartars, the czars, the commissars and oligarchs . . . they murmured in our sleep, never letting us forget. And when the Coss came in overwhelming strength, reestablishing a feudal order—only with an alien caste on top—we Russians knew our options. There were . . . and are . . . and always will be just two.

To knuckle under, and survive.

Or to fight, but with the grinding, stoical patience of Pyotr Alexeyevich, or of Tolstoy. Or Lenin.

"We know the stories," I told my mother, standing with her under vacuum-bright constellations. "How women used to plod for hundreds, even thousands of kilometers, following muddy roads . . . and then metal railroad tracks . . . slogging into far Siberia. Working to get by, doing laundry till their hands bled, moving from village to village to find the work camps. The gulags. Whereupon, each day when the train whistle blew—"

As if I had commanded it, a throbbing vibration shuddered underfoot and our audios picked up the throaty radio call—a five-minute warning from the *Nicholas III*.

"The women gathered by the village siding where the locomotive stopped for water. They would hurry to the flat cars, loaded high with timber cut by prisoners. And they searched, combing the logs with their eyes and groping in among them with their hands.

"What was it they were looking for, Mother? Can you tell me, honestly, at long last, what you came out here to seek?"

I bent and caught her eyes with mine. Haggard from years of sleepless worry, hers glistened with defiant pride.

"Initials," she said with little breath, then adding softly, "Carved into the raw wood . . . by prisoners."

And then, straightening her back.

"Proof that they survived."

So.

My suspicion was confirmed. Her added reason for all this—the one that had gone unspoken.

No single justification was sufficient for all this, especially dragging her children into the wilderness. Not the full release promised by Coss Law. Not the strength that Yelena and I would attain—if we survived. Nor the practical experience, dealing with a new harsh world.

Only . . . might this one, added to the others, tip the scale?

It did. Just barely. Enough for me to nod. To understand. To accept.

And to know.

The Yankees would never learn. Fooled by their brief, naïve time of childishly unlimited dreams, they believed deep down in happy endings and the triumph of good. They would keep rebelling till the Coss left no Americans alive.

We Russians are different. Our expertise? We persist. Resist! But with measured, cynical care. And each defeat is simply preparation. That truth, I had already known. Only now it filled my soul.

We are the people who know how to outlast the Coss.

And so I took my mother by the hand, leading her to the place that I had found, where Cyrillic letters lay deep-incised along the bared trunk of a crystal tree. And I watched her face bloom with sudden hope, with sunlit joy. And I knew, at last, what lesson this place taught.

To endure.

David Brin is a scientist, inventor, and New York Times *bestselling author. With books translated into twenty-five languages, he has won multiple Hugo, Nebula, and other awards. A film directed by Kevin Costner was based on David's novel* The Postman. *Other works have been optioned by Paramount and Warner Bros. David's science-fictional Uplift saga explores genetic engineering of higher animals, like dolphins, to speak. His new novel from Tor Books is* Existence. *More information is available at his website: www.david brin.com/existence.html.*

As a scientist/futurist, David is seen frequently on television shows such as The ArchiTechs, Universe, *and* Life After People *(the most popular show ever on the History Channel)—with many appearances on PBS, BBC, and NPR. An inventor with many patents, he is in demand to speak about future trends, keynoting for IBM, Google, Procter & Gamble, SAP, Microsoft, Qualcomm, the Mauldin Group, and Casey Research, all the way to think tanks, Homeland Security, and the CIA. See: www.davidbrin.com/speaker.html.*

With degrees from Caltech and the University of California San Diego, Dr. Brin serves on advisory panels ranging from astronomy,

NASA innovative concepts, nanotech, and SETI to national defense and technological ethics. His nonfiction book The Transparent Society *explores the dangers of secrecy and loss of privacy in our modern world. It garnered the prestigious Freedom of Speech Prize from the American Library Association.*

The Sea of Memory

GENE WOLFE

Adele helped George, Mike, Ted, and Sy put up the Putman Shelter. (Not that they needed her help.) Afterward, she left them to stand on a high rock at the edge of the sea and look out over the water. The waves were regular, small, and smooth, the water blue and dark with mystery. A bird flew somewhere overhead, weeping endlessly over an imagined sorrow. Adele looked for it, but never caught sight of it. In her thoughts, it was a gull, white and pearl-gray, lost against the high clouds.

Behind her, Sy climbed onto the rock. She turned to stare at him.

"We've got the sleeping places laid out," Sy told her. "We're going to draw lots for them. Winner gets first pick. You'll want to be there."

"No. I don't care. I'll take whatever's left. I'm not going to sleep there anyway."

"Where are you going to sleep, in that case?"

Adele smiled. "Why do you care?"

"I care, all right? The weather's not always going to be like this. It will rain. Snow in winter."

"How do you know?"

"I know, that's all." Sy was the most patient of the four. "We've only been here a few days. We don't really know what it's going to be like. This could be the best weather we'll see all year."

Adele decided she would sleep in the ship. "Has it really been just a few days?"

Sy hesitated. "I think so."

"It seems so much longer. Forever." The wind from the sea played with her auburn hair, so that it streamed toward Sy like two flags. "No, not forever. But a long time."

"We haven't run out of rations yet. We still have food." It was a weak argument, and Sy's voice showed he knew it.

When was the last time she had eaten? Her meal had been of what?

"Will we? Ever?"

"Of course we will!"

"You're sure of that?"

Without a word, Sy began to climb back down. Adele watched him until he was safely on the beach again, and then turned back to the sea. Soundless waves washed the foot of her rock, and the unseen bird wept overhead.

What was on the other side? The silent water was too wide for her to see across. "I'll sleep on the ship." She was quoting a thought. The ship had to be near here. She tried to remember where.

When she tired of watching the waves, she turned to watch the men erecting the Putman Shelter. She counted them and tried to recall their names. The Putman Shelter was already much larger than she had anticipated. Once she had helped two other women erect a Putman Shelter. It took them seventeen minutes the first time, nine minutes the second. Or was that nine hours? She felt quite sure it had not seemed like nine hours, and it had been fun. They had teamed up to pull the stakes, and she had driven ropes with a big wooden mallet. It had been like Girl Scouts, she thought, and smiled.

There were five men working away now: Ted, Sy, Mike, and two Georges. She wondered where the other George came from. Perhaps he had always been there.

At least, he looked like George.

She was climbing down the rock before she realized she was going to investigate.

"Hello, Adele." It was one of the Georges. "Glad to see you made it."

"I was looking at the sea." Why should she explain?

The George nodded. "Glad you were. It's going to take a great deal of study. That's your field, isn't it? Marine ecology?"

Adele nodded. She recalled lying on the floor in her bedroom with Glenys. Glenys did not understand; thus she strove to explain the game. "Heads marine biology, and tails home economics. Heads interactive world history, and reverse, political science, Queen library science, and lion shield-taming."

Or had it been Susan?

"Hell," the George said, "we don't really understand the ecology of the seas of Earth."

"Or know their names." Adele felt confident. When he said nothing, she added, "There's the Holy Sea. It's around Italy somewhere."

The George laughed. "Come over and have a look at the Shelter. I want to show you the parts I worked on."

She nodded, and his hand found hers.

"This is Entrance Seven. I really didn't have anything to do with it. Ted, Mike, and Sven put it up before I got here, but it's how I got in the first time I came. I was impressed by the stitching. Look here." He ran his index finger along a seam. "Isn't that great?"

Dutifully, Adele nodded.

"And look here."

Adele was looking at a chair. She nodded again. It had gilt arms and a velvet back, a comfortable-looking red velvet seat.

"They used a door eraser. If it gets too cold, there's no door."

She sat as quietly as she could. The George was no longer paying attention to her, so why pay attention to him? There was a different view of the sea from here. The beach gave it perspective. There were no ships, no seagulls, no popcorn bags and beer cans littering the sand. Seashells? She strove to remember.

"Hello," a new voice said. "I'm Steve. Who are you?"

She stared at him. He looked like Sy, she decided. Tall and blond. Blue eyes. But Sy was slender, wasn't he?

Steve cleared his throat. "I guess that wasn't polite, just asking like that. Only I, well, I wanted us to get acquainted right away."

"I'm Adele."

"Happy to meet you." He smiled. "Can we be friends?"

Another question. She decided it would be best to ignore it. Five minutes into every conversation, Glenys wanted to know whether she was still a virgin. It was better to pretend it had not been said.

"I suppose you'll want me to cook." She was a bad cook.

"Why, no. No, I won't, I promise." He looked baffled. "I mean, rations heat themselves when you open the pouch, but if there was cooking that had to be done—I mean, like, suppose there's animals on this planet and we shot an animal or something. If we had arrows, I mean, and we wanted to cook it. I'd do it. I'd be happy to. I'm a good cook."

"I'm Adele." She smiled.

"Yes, I know."

"I don't remember my last name. Isn't that odd? I remember I had one, and that it was the same as my mother's, but I can't remember it."

He smiled in return. "We left our surnames back on Earth."

"I never had a surname, just a last name. I never knew for sure who my father was."

Still smiling, this other Sy (who looked, she thought, less like Sy every moment) sat on the carpet. "Same here," he said. "There was an uncle who lived with us for a while." He laughed. "One time I asked my mother who he was, and she said he was her brother. Only another time she said he was my father's brother."

"Was he nice?"

"Sometimes." The new Sy was no longer smiling. "I think he wanted to molest me, but he never got the nerve."

"Nobody ever molested me."

"Maybe they did and you forgot it."

Adele shook her head.

"We edit things out. It's a door eraser. The memory is a door that lets in things we don't want to remember, so there's no door."

"I need a 'you' eraser." It was too soft, probably, for him to hear. She stood and walked away.

Mike was in a courtyard driving a stake with a power hammer. He stopped as Adele approached him. "Hi, Adele. Okay if I ask you a question?"

She nodded.

"How did we get here? Do you know?"

"On a ship. Across the sea."

Mike smiled, encouraging her. His teeth were large and white and a little too regular. "That's right, across the sea of space. Did our ship have sails?"

She nodded, remembering.

"That's right again. Mylar sails a thousand miles across to catch the star winds. Where did we sleep?"

"On the ship." Did he want her to talk more? She decided he did. "I loved sleeping on the ship. There was this stuffed koala bear, all soft and cuddly. I hugged it in bed and stroked its fur until it fell asleep."

"You fell asleep," Mike said.

Another Mike came up behind Adele. "I remember this conversation," he told her. "It upset you badly. Why don't you go?"

"I will." Adele thought for a moment. "Another place than here. Can I go back to the ship? I'd like that."

"There isn't any other place," the other Mike told her.

"Then I can't go."

"I told you this would upset her," the first Mike said.

"No, I told you that."

This was the time to leave, Adele decided, but she stayed.

The Mikes separated, and one tried to take her arm very gently. The Mike on her left said, "I've figured this out, or I think I have."

"So have I," the other Mike affirmed.

"Like, why are there two of me on this planet." Mike paused, looking thoughtful. At length he said, "There may be more. Hell, there probably are."

"You're going at it wrong," the other Mike told him. "There are not two of you. Nor are there two of me. I am you and you are me. There is only one Mike, and no time."

Adele's indifference drowned in curiosity. "No time for what?"

"No time for anything," the Mike who had tried to hold her left arm said. "Eternity for everything."

His twin said, "Eternity means forever."

"No, it doesn't. Forever means endless years, endless centuries. Time piling up, on and on." Ted had joined them.

"Eternity means no time, timelessness," the Mikes said.

"Without time," Ted scoffed, "everything would happen at once."

"Exactly," the Mikes said in chorus.

Adele paid little attention. She was looking across the sand at the girl standing ever so still upon her rock. She had red hair that seemed almost brown, long, straight hair that the wind blew about her.

"Hi," a new voice said, "what are you guys up to here?"

No one answered him.

"I-I'm Jeff." He was big, and thick at the waist.

"Hello, Jeff." Adele felt sorry for him. She held out her hand. "I'm very pleased to meet you."

He tried to hold it between his own. He had large hands, medium hard. "I was in the probe. Suspended and frozen. All those things they do, I guess. Only I didn't feel any of it. I blacked out."

Adele looked around for the Mikes, but they had gone.

"Me, too," she said.

"And then I was here," Jeff told her. "This shirt? These pants? These are the kind of things I always wore before I got involved in the probe program." He pulled three keys on a ring out of a pocket. "See this key here? It's the key to my old apartment, only where is it? Where's my old apartment?" He held up the key so that she could see it.

"Back in time."

"You mean we slept for hundreds of years. That's right; they said we would. Thousands, actually."

"No, Jeff." Adele shook her head, and it moved ever so slightly.

"We didn't?"

"I don't know. This is hard to explain."

"But you can." Jeff's voice was raspy, and very serious. "I want to hear your explanation."

"I can't prove it to you, but I know." Adele turned to walk nearer the girl who stood looking at the sea.

"I want to hear your explanation," Jeff said. He sounded more serious than ever. "I may not agree, but I won't ridicule you. I've been wrong before."

"All right." Adele stopped, took a deep breath of sea air, and turned to face him. "Do you understand time?"

Jeff shook his head. "Einstein said that time was the fourth dimension, but it's nothing like the other three. A particle physicist I talked to one time said that time was really different things we were lumping together. I think he said five."

"I don't know about that."

"Neither do I, Adele. I don't understand time, and I doubt anybody really does."

"I don't, either." Adele was confident now. "But I know this about it: It's not everywhere. Sy thinks it may snow here, and I think he may be right. But there are places where it doesn't snow."

She saw that Jeff did not understand her. Another deep breath. "Where's your watch, Jeff?"

He stared out to sea, but Adele did not speak again. At last he said, "I think they took it from me before I got into the pod."

"If you had it here . . ." She paused, trying to order her thoughts and so make them clear.

"I don't."

"I think it would still run. It would tick away and the hands would move, but it wouldn't work." She repeated, "There are places where it never snows."

Jeff nodded. "Sure."

"My mother's boyfriend had a yardstick he kept in the garage. Whenever we got a big snow, he got it out and took measurements. Then he would tell us how deep the snow was."

Jeff nodded again.

"In a place where it never snowed, his yardstick would still work. It could measure how tall a child was or push something out from under his pickup, but it couldn't measure snow."

"Without time . . ."

"Everything happens at once. Ted said that, and he was right. Anything you do, you *do*." Adele pointed. "See that girl over there looking at the sea? I stood there looking at the sea, then I went over to where the guys were putting up a Putman Shelter. Only I'm still there, looking at the sea."

Jeff whistled softly.

"When you got on the ship, did they say you might die? That it would take the ship thousands of years to get there, and you might die right there in the pod?"

He nodded. "There were things back on Earth that I wanted to get away from. Forever."

"I understand." Adele tried to take his hand. "Kiss me!"

Jeff tried to put his arms around her. It was like being wrapped in fog. Mist brushed her lips.

When they parted, he gasped and stared, reached for her, and drew his hand back.

"We're dying." Adele's tone was flat, neither sad nor happy. "We're dying one by one in the pods. When we die, we go here."

The girl on the rock turned to face them. "I know the name!" Her voice might have been a distant trumpet. "It's the Sea of Memory!"